A CAST OF STONES

THE STAFF & THE SWORD

A CAST OF STONES

PATRICK W. CARR

BETHANYHOUSE
a division of Baker Publishing Group
Minneapolis, Minnesota

Published by Bethany House Publishers
11400 Hampshire Avenue South
Bloomington, Minnesota 55438
www.bethanyhouse.com

Bethany House Publishers is a division of
Baker Publishing Group, Grand Rapids, Michigan

Printed in the United States of America

Library of Congress Cataloging-in-Publication Data
Carr, Patrick W.
    A cast of stones / Patrick W. Carr.
        p. cm. — (The staff and the sword ; book one)
    ISBN 978-0-7642-1043-3 (pbk.)
    1. Christian fiction. 2. Fantasy fiction. I. Title.
PS3603.A774326C37 2013
813'.6—dc23   2012035224

This is a work of fiction. Names, characters, incidents, and dialogues are products of the author's imagination and are not to be construed as real. Any resemblance to actual events or persons, living or dead, is entirely coincidental.

Cover design by Lookout Design, Inc.

Author represented by The Steve Laube Agency

14 15 16 17 18 19 20   9 8 7 6 5 4 3

To the three women in my life who made this possible:

Carolyn Carr,
for loving me and raising me;
Ramona Dabbs,
who never failed in her encouragement
and believed in me even when I didn't;
and ever and always,
Mary Carr,
who brings love and passion to my life
and demonstrates every day
that she really is God's gift to me.

1

ERROL

SMELLS OF EARTH and dung drifted slowly past the fog in Errol's brain. His skin prickled with cold. Water and ooze soaked his threadbare garments and he shivered. Cruk had thrown him out of the tavern. Again. Hanks of brown hair dripping muck hung across his vision. The ringing of Liam's hammer just across the street paused, then started again with light tapping blows, as if in laughter.

Cruk smiled down at him without malice. "Next time I'll carry you out back and throw you in the midden."

Dizzy from his flight and a little wobbly from drink, Errol picked himself up in stages. He closed his eyes against the glare of the morning sun, sluiced the worst of the mud from his clothes, and rubbed an aching hip. His tongue wandered the crevices of his mouth as he struggled to make it obey his commands. The effort made him reel.

"You didn't have to kick me so hard."

Tall, broad-shouldered, and ridiculously strong from long days working in the quarry, Cruk towered over him from his vantage point on the porch. As always, his face put Errol in mind of a sack of potatoes.

Cruk barked once in amusement. "I didn't, you little runt. If you don't believe me, then come back here and I'll have another go at it. If Pater Antil catches you drunk at this hour, you'll end up back in the stocks."

Errol darted a glance over his shoulder at the rectory where Callowford's priest lived, but the curtains still covered the windows and no one stirred. Still, Cruk's warning made his shoulders twitch with remembered pain. "Do you have any work I can do?" He backed away from the look on the big man's face. "Away from Cilla and the inn, I mean. I'm hungry."

"Then stop spending what you earn on ale." He pointed to Liam, who watched the exchange with a smile on his face. "Why can't you be more like him?" A heartbeat later, the harsh planes of Cruk's face softened and his shoulders dropped a fraction as he exhaled in resignation or pity. "Wait here."

He disappeared into Cilla's tavern, returned with half a loaf of bread, and tossed it into Errol's waiting hands. "Come 'round this evening. You can help clean up after dinner. Mind, you stay away from Cilla and her ale."

Errol bobbed his head in gratitude as he stuffed the bread inside his shirt. He cleared his throat to ask for a small advance on his wages, but the thunder of hooves forestalled him. A man clothed in black robes and riding a dappled horse down the street of their village made for the tavern as though his salvation depended on it. A red armband emblazoned with a scroll and pen marked him as a nuntius, a church messenger—crows, they were called. Errol's hand flexed, and he made the sign to ward off evil without thinking.

"Stop being superstitious, boy," Cruk said. "They bear messages. Sometimes they take confessions of the dying." He paused. "That's not our usual messenger." His voice ground the words, and his shoulders tensed as if he were about to throw someone else into the mud. "Anders rides a bay." The horseman neared. "And this rider"—his voice caught—"is of the first order."

The horse skidded to a stop, threw its head in protest against the bit, and gave a little hop with its front hooves, splashing fresh mud on Errol in the process.

"Forgive my hindrance, my lord." Errol's mouth twisted around the words, and he wrung excess water from the front of his shirt for the second time that day. "I was just leaving." He straightened and put out one dripping hand to lean against the horse's shoulder to restore his balance. When he could focus again, he paused to survey the messenger's face. The blunt nose and lack of cheekbones—so different from his own sharper features—proclaimed the nuntius's ancestry as Lugarian, perhaps. Errol stifled a long-familiar stab of disappointment.

The nuntius peered down at him, his face wreathed with disgust. He twitched the reins, and the horse backed away, leaving Errol without his support. He teetered and struggled not to fall. Twisting, he spotted Liam, all eight perfect spans of him, standing a few feet away, his face the picture of innocent expectation. A ray of sunlight reflected off his hair.

Errol tottered away. He didn't like standing near Liam. They were the same age, and proximity invited comparison.

The church messenger's face registered his shock and disapproval. "By Deas in heaven, man, are you drunk? It's not even noon."

Cruk laughed. "It's not even ten, my lord. Errol is a man of some talent."

The messenger's lips pursed, giving his face a fish-like cast. Urging his horse around the puddle until it stood at the hitching rail, he dismounted and retrieved a thick leather purse from his saddle.

"I'm told there's a man who lives near here, a priest named Martin Arwitten. I have letters for him that must be delivered today."

Cruk's face paled at the mention of the hermit. He took a step toward the messenger with a hand raised, as if trying to ward off a blow. "The king . . . ?"

The stranger shook his head in denial. "Rodran lives."

Errol slogged out of the mud puddle to tug the churchman's sleeve. "I can deliver your letters, my lord. I know exactly where Pater Martin's cabin is."

The nuntius backed away, inspecting his clothes. "Deliver? Hardly. I only need a guide." He turned his attention back to Cruk. "A sober guide." He pointed to Liam. "He can take me."

Liam smiled, his teeth flashing under his blue eyes, and shook his head. "I'm sorry, my lord, I owe Knorl another six hours today." He bowed and returned to his forge.

The nuntius huffed.

Errol drew himself up, brought his eyes up to the level of the churchman's chin. "I may have had a drink or two this morning, my lord." He did his best to ignore Cruk's snort. "But no one knows the gorge as well as I. You can't take a horse through there." He gave the dappled mare a pointed glance and let his gaze linger on the legs. "Not if you want to ride her again."

Cruk gave a grudging nod over the churchman's shoulder. "He's got the right of that. If the letters have to be delivered today, the gorge is the only way. Horses don't go through there, and no one knows the area better than Errol."

The nuntius drew up, squared his thin shoulders. "Very well, he can guide me on foot."

"If you wish," Errol said. "It's a four-hour hike." He looked at the churchman, noted the man's delicate boots, and revised his estimate. "Possibly six. If we hurry, we can be there and back by dark."

"Dark?" The messenger's eyes goggled. "I have to be at Benefice Gustin's by nightfall."

Cruk shook his head. "Not going to happen. Pater Martin lives on the ridge. It's surrounded by the roughest terrain, and any man fool enough to rush through it gets a broken leg for his efforts, or worse."

Warmth blossomed in Errol's chest as Cruk pointed his direction. "You'll have to give your letters to him."

The nuntius barked a laugh. "A drunkard? You want me to give the most important messages in half a century to a drunkard? Look at him; he's barely a man. Only Deas knows what's keeping him on his feet." He waved a hand in dismissal. "How would I know he delivered them?"

Cruk shifted his massive shoulders. "You're willing to pay, aren't you?"

The nuntius drew up. "This is a matter of great urgency on behalf of the church. A loyal subject should—"

"Even a loyal subject needs to eat." Errol kept his expression respectful, barely.

The messenger rounded on him and stopped, staring, his mouth working. Errol watched the man's gaze start at his head and slide down his frame until it ended at his worn shoes. The man's eyes narrowed in calculation.

"How will I know you've delivered the message?"

Cruk's amusement resonated from the tavern porch. Liam echoed it from the forge. "You'll have no need to worry on that account," Cruk said. "Pater Martin doesn't stock ale. If you're willing to pay to have your message delivered, then you can count on Errol to be back here before dark to spend his hard-earned wages."

Errol tried to sketch a reassuring bow and nearly fell back into the mud puddle for his efforts. He straightened, arms out, swaying from side to side until he achieved a more or less vertical posture. "Will you return to Callowford, my lord?"

The nuntius nodded. "Yes, tomorrow morning." He drew himself up. "I am needed back at Erinon."

Errol ducked his head in a show of deference to flatter the man's ego. Who knew what a desperate church messenger might be willing to pay? A silver crown? Two? "If you like, I can bring receipt of your message in Martin's own hand."

The messenger's countenance lifted. "You seem possessed of

wits, sodden though they are. Yes, I think that would do well." He proffered the thick leather packet.

Errol accepted the burden and waited, regarding the nuntius with a pronounced lift of his eyebrows.

The man flushed and threw back the right side of his coat. "Oh yes, your pay." With practiced skill he dug into the purse at his belt with one hand. "Far be it from me to question your veracity, but I offer half your pay now . . ." He extended a coin, holding it at the edge between his thumb and forefinger.

Errol reached for the coin, but the nuntius dropped it before their hands could touch. A gold half crown came to rest on the leather packet. Errol struggled to keep his eyes from bugging.

"And a receipt in Pater Martin's own hand will earn you another half crown," the nuntius added.

Greed tightened Errol's throat. "Yes, my lord, and a receipt. You are most generous, my lord, for a message across the gorge."

"Generous?" Cruk's laugh cut the air. "Indeed. You have my thanks as well. You've just guaranteed this tavern a most enthusiastic customer for the next week. It's doubtful whether the lad will know up from down this time tomorrow." He looked at Errol. "Wait a few moments before you depart. Pater Martin asked after bread and wine last week, and Anders should be here soon."

The messenger's head snapped up. "No need. I ran into your messenger at Berea. He asked me to deliver this to you." He reached into his pack and brought forth a skin of wine and a thick packet of flat bread. "Your hermit priest still celebrates the sacrament, yes?"

Errol nodded. "Every day, from what I am told, and why would he not?"

The messenger's face closed, keeping its secrets. "Why not indeed?" He forced a laugh and mounted his horse, favoring Errol with a last look. "I'll see you tomorrow upon my return."

Two hours later and a league and a half from Callowford, Errol paused at the edge of the gorge that marked the beginning of the Sprata Mountains. Water flowed through the cut that lay like a wound on the land. A hint of red against the deep green of a fern's pinnules caught his attention, and he left the path. On hands and knees he burrowed through the thick undergrowth toward the shrub. There. A stalk of crimsonweed grew from the node of the fern, meshing with the plant it would eventually kill. He smiled. Adele or Radere would pay him a silver mark for the herb, enough for two tankards of ale. Errol broke the stalk, careful not to damage the fern, and stowed the plant in the sack containing the letters and the bread and wine that hung from his back.

With two leagues to go, he stopped under a shelf of limestone and adjusted his load. Beneath the outcropping, the ponderous weight of the rock rose over him like a primitive sanctuary carved by the elements. He smiled. Only bandits worshiped there. Few enjoyed their liturgy of violence. His feet slipped in the dusty earth as he trudged the path that sloped toward the chasm on his right, threatening to pitch him over the edge.

He grabbed a walking stick as long as he was tall from beneath a nearby oak. Years of experience with the gorge and the Cripples had taught him to balance his passage with a stout length of heavy wood. Now no one could navigate the way as quickly.

The air, cooled and calmed by the towers of rock on either side, doused the last of the morning's indisposition from his body. Head clear, he eyed the river running below, impatient with runoff from the melting snows of the Sprata Mountains. He passed the Hollows and quickened his pace, thumping his stick into the ground. That collection of shallow caves blackened by unnumbered campfires had long been a favorite hiding place for outlaws in the winter. He doubted any of them still lingered this late into spring, and Errol would present little enticement as a target for robbery. But the unfamiliar weight of the half crown in his pocket troubled him, and he rushed for the heat and light of the sun up ahead.

When he looked back to gauge his progress, a laurel branch bent and waved next to the trail some hundred paces behind. His heart lurched. No wind penetrated so deep into the gorge. He fought to keep his pace steady, weighing his options. If he ran now he'd alert his pursuer, but he could gain some time by shortcutting across the Cripples. The network of scars lacing his back itched, reminding him of past carelessness on those jagged stones. Crossing would take time, time he might not have, and he would have to ford the river that lay beyond. Keeping the sack dry would slow him down.

If the bandits came after him in numbers, they could catch him in the water. At the very least, the letters for Pater Martin would be lost along with his half crown. If the bandits knew how to swim.

If they just didn't shoot him outright.

Nothing moved on the trail behind, but he found little comfort in the fact. Prickles ran up and down his arms like ants. Unseen eyes swept across him, watching, tracking.

His head pounded, and the sour taste of bile and fear spilled across his tongue. *Think.* He needed to think. Maybe he could throw them off by taking the high trail. It might gain him the precious minutes he needed to cross the water; once in the trackless woods beyond the gorge, they'd never find him.

Errol quickened his steps, made for an outcropping to his left. Rocks scraped his hands as he hauled himself up the pocked face to the other trail. He grabbed his stick and ran in a low crouch along the dusty path. A prayer, half remembered from childhood, sprang to his lips, but the image of Pater Antil holding his whipping rod rose with it, and the plea died away.

Bent almost double, he bolted along the upper trail, darting from bush to tree. If the bandits spied him, they'd shoot arrows at his exposed position until they killed him or he surrendered.

And if he surrendered, they'd probably kill him anyway.

Fifty paces behind him, a heron broke cover with a glottal cry and flew out over the water.

Errol forced his legs into a run, rushing for the point ahead where the two paths rejoined, where the Cripples began. Twigs snapped in an accelerating rhythm behind him. A quick glance still showed nothing. He quickened his pace as the path turned downhill and widened.

The Cripples stretched before him—a hundred paces of slick, pitted rock glistened in the sun, eager to catch the reckless or unwary. He paused, searching for the best route. Even with care, the treacherous footing could turn or break an ankle. His stomach flipped at the thought of rushing through that maze. Behind him, a shadow ghosted among the trees.

A rustle of leaves broke his concentration. He floundered, his stick weaving frantic circles in the air. A man dressed in black regarded him from beyond the stretch of mossy rock, a short bow held in one hand. Not a twitch, not a blink of emotion disturbed the pale mask of a face under hair so light it looked almost silver. He reached back over his shoulder and an arrow of blackest hue appeared in his hand. Errol wrenched his gaze away, jumped for the ledge just ahead.

His feet slipped. Errol curled as he fell and gasped as new cuts joined old scars. The impact jarred his teeth, and he growled curses against the pain.

Sprawled across the stone, he angled away from his pursuer so the rock, his pitiful excuse for protection, shielded him as much as possible. He took a deep breath, darted a look back, and then smiled at his good fortune. The man in black was actually trying to follow him. It would be impossible to get off a decent shot standing on the treacherous stone.

Errol slithered around on his belly, reached for his staff when a whine like an animal's scream sounded behind him. An arrow arced overhead, then disappeared among the rocks and water beyond.

He grinned at his pursuer. "I've never heard an arrow make that sound before. You'll find the footing difficult for decent shooting. Why not go back and save yourself the trouble?"

The man in black stopped, considered him in silence, and slowly dropped to his knees. Then he nocked another arrow.

With a shock of realization, Errol leapt for the first shelf of stone, half missed, and slammed into it with his chest. His feet thrashed and slipped across the moss-covered rocks as he tried to thrust the rest of his body up the ledge. Fear filled him, wailed through his blood and bones. He scrabbled at the ledge with his hands and feet. *Move.* He had to move!

The scream of the arrow grew until it filled his hearing. He screwed his eyes shut and pushed against the stones. His feet slipped, and he slid toward the scream. He squeezed his eyes shut, waited a fraction of a heartbeat that stretched to agony.

Behind him the bandit cursed.

A line of fire cut his shoulder before the arrow struck inches from his face. The impact cut the scream and a splinter of stone gashed his cheek. He put his arms under his belly and wiggled the rest of the way onto the outcropping, rolled behind a piece of jutting limestone, and ran to the far edge.

No bandit crossed the Cripples. A sprained ankle meant capture and the gallows. And they didn't use short bows. Errol's mouth went dry. Bandits were a murderous bunch, but they always tried to talk their victims into giving up. It rarely worked, but they always tried. Every now and then they even let one of the few who surrendered live to entice others to do the same.

The man in black hadn't tried to talk him into surrendering. Errol's feet came to the edge of the shelf as his thoughts brought him to an inescapable conclusion: The man hunting him was no bandit.

Errol twitched the sack strapped to his shoulders, and a picture of the nuntius flashed through his mind. Letters, he'd said, the most important in half a century. Important enough to kill for? Errol's heart hammered against his ribs. He looked over the next section of moss-slicked rock. If his hunter gained the shelf before Errol made it to the second outcropping, his aim, already too good by half, would find its mark.

Terror curled its way through his chest. The stranger moved across the Cripples with inhuman skill. Errol shuddered, considered surrender—giving up the letters, the half crown, everything. He shook his head, discarded the idea. The man wanted him dead.

Errol vaulted into the air, ignored the yammering from the part of his mind where he kept his common sense, and forced himself to keep his eyes open. He landed, tried to roll, slipped sideways, and crashed headfirst.

Spots swam in his vision, and he fought to keep darkness at bay. He crabbed sideways toward the next ledge. His ankle throbbed in time with his heart as he hobbled onto the ledge. A crunch of footsteps from behind warned him, and he threw himself flat. An arrow whined in disappointment overhead, pulling the breath from his lungs as it went.

This wasn't working. The next ledge lay less than half the distance across the Cripples, and already the man in black had managed to bleed and hobble him. At this rate he'd be lame in minutes.

Then he'd be dead.

The Cripples spanned the river in a wide arch before ending at a broad, shallow ford. To the right lay a sheer forty-foot drop into a pool fed by runoff that extended all the way to the far bank of the gorge. Water from winter melt spilled over the falls, splashing and churning in a series of whirlpools. Only an idiot would dare those icy depths—or someone desperate to live. The water's chill would leech the warmth from his body in minutes. If his hunter trapped him, forced him to stay in the pool, he would die.

Errol ducked behind a plinth of rock and ran for the far edge of the ledge, his mind racing. If he tried to make the security of each shelf in succession, the mossy pits would slow him, leaving him helpless. If he dared the chill waters of the pool, he'd be lucky to make the far side fifty paces away. Even if he survived, the letter to Pater Martin would be ruined, and with it his chances of keeping his gold.

He should have known not to get involved with the nuntius. "Stupid churchman."

A glance behind told him all he needed to know. The assassin on his trail moved from the first ledge and stepped with goatlike skill across the rocks. The man didn't even have the decency to slip every now and then.

Errol moved from the security of the second shelf in a crouch, hoping to stay hidden long enough to make the ledge above the pool. The mossy coating seemed to writhe under his feet, conspiring to pitch him headlong onto the rocks. He balanced his weight, his hands groping for a staff he no longer held, and shuffled by inches toward his goal.

The space between his shoulder blades itched, and he tensed against the expected impact of an arrow—as if by tightening the muscles in his back he could keep it from killing him. With ten feet to go, he looked back to see the man in black climb onto the ledge he'd just left. In seconds, the man would nock another arrow. In seconds more, Errol would die.

Throwing himself into a flailing run, he made for the pool. A patch of green betrayed him, and he fell. He spun as the ground rushed up to meet him. When he rose, he found himself looking his would-be killer in the eyes. The man nodded. Then he reached back over his shoulder.

With a yell, Errol scrambled to his feet, took two steps and jumped to his right, soaring over the icy water that waited for him so far below. An arrow ripped through the air where he'd been, screaming as it passed his ear and flew out of sight to the far side of the pool.

Errol fell, amazed at the long, long time it took to meet the water.

The impact hit him like a blow to his stomach, forced the air from his lungs. Cold pierced him and light faded. Needles of pain stabbed him everywhere as he struggled to stay submerged, frog-kicking in desperation toward the far end of the pool. He opened his eyes to the sting of the water, but saw only blurred ocher outlines.

He reached and pulled for the far side of the pool, his strokes frantic with cold. Fire burned through his lungs with the need to surface. The man in black surely stood at the edge of the pool by now, bow drawn and waiting.

Errol swam until spots danced in his vision, his body begging for air. With a pair of strokes he surfaced like a fish breaking water, darted a glance behind before sucking air into his tortured lungs and diving again, away from the figure in black.

The sounds of his efforts and splashing filled his ears. He forced his trembling arms forward, jerked them back to his sides. Only the current against his face told him he advanced. Violent chills rippled the water as his body fought to stay warm. His shaking limbs lurched in a parody of his usual stroke. Bolts of pain shot through his calves and thighs. His legs refused to move. They hung from his torso, dragged him down. He reached out, struck mud. One shaking hand at a time, he pulled himself forward.

At last he broke the surface. His hands clawed forward until they brushed against rough bark. They clutched the thin trunk, locking around it as if it were his last hope. Water drained from his ears, and he listened for his attacker. Nothing.

Errol's body convulsed with cold as he clutched the sapling, straining to move, turn his head, anything. His muscles refused to obey. His hands clenched the tree, refused to let go.

Above and behind him the wail of an arrow began. He willed himself to let go, roll over, but spasms pinned him to the spot, left him helpless. The arrow's scream grew, its pitch rising until its keening filled his hearing.

Errol sobbed, tried once more to move, and failed.

He clenched his eyes against the blow.

2

SACRAMENT

THE IMPACT slammed him against the ground. He clung to the tree, waiting for a tearing pain that never came. He slid sideways, tried to roll and couldn't. When he slipped the sack's straps from his shoulders, he discovered the reason he still breathed. The assassin's arrow had lodged itself squarely in the center. Looking back and up at the ledge over the pool, he saw nothing. The man in black was gone.

He grasped the arrow with both hands and worked it up and down until the thick leather released it. With it tucked under one arm, he hurried away from the pool making for Pater Martin's cabin.

As he climbed higher into the ridge he assessed himself. His head hurt where he'd banged it against the rocks, and his cheek still oozed blood. Cuts and scrapes covered his midsection and . . .

He gave up. The exercise was pointless. If he needed help, it would be found at the priest's cabin. Pater Martin or his servant would know what to do. With one last glance behind, Errol forced himself to a shambling run through the woods.

Hours later, the sting of sweat marking each injury, Errol entered the clearing where Martin resided and paused. Humidity clung to him like a heavy cloak.

Martin sat beneath the giant oak that sheltered his cottage, his bulk sprawled across a crude ladder-backed chair. Errol looked away and coughed as he entered the shade of the tree from the priest's left. Martin sat nearly naked, his cassock nowhere in sight. He wore a plain linen under tunic hitched up in the moist air until it barely covered his thighs. At Errol's cough, the priest looked up from the book he held in one huge hand and gave a raucous laugh. Errol blushed and kept his eyes on his feet.

Martin loomed larger than life. Errol had never known the man before his hair silvered, but his eyebrows, dark as ebony, showed the color those loose curls would have been in his youth. A strong nose thrust forward aggressively from wide, high cheekbones over a mouth that was thin and full by turns depending on the state of its owner's thoughts. The deep dimple in his chin, rather than lending the face any expected charm, solidified the impression of dogged determination that Errol always felt whenever he came to visit Martin's secluded cottage. Yet for all the power that emanated from Martin's eyes, face, or bulk, he always greeted Errol with warmth.

"Come now, Errol." Martin called to him across the grassy space. "My under tunic satisfies the demands of modesty, and we are created in the image of Deas, after all." He slapped his paunch and looked Errol up and down in mock jealousy. "However, I seem to have been gifted with substantially more image than you." He pointed to the bulky sack slung from Errol's shoulder with a hand that would have looked more at home dangling from a blacksmith's wrist. "You have the sacraments?"

Errol stepped from the shade to stand before Martin. "Yes, Pater, and letters as well, but I'm afraid it's all ruined." Errol's voice sounded strange to his ears, as if he had forgotten its timbre during his struggle in the gorge.

Martin's smile transformed to a scowl as he took in Errol's

appearance. The old priest's gaze trickled from Errol's crown, paused at his scraped hands, and finished at his bleeding feet.

"Come, boy. Let's go inside. Only a fool could fail to see you have a story to tell. And I would not have it said I kept an injured man on his feet." He levered his bulk from the chair, placed a hand on Errol's shoulder, and guided him into the small cabin.

Errol sat at a small table at Martin's bidding. He tucked the attacker's arrow and his soggy leather pack under the broad oak bench while the priest went to a cupboard and rummaged through an assortment of bottles and earthenware containers. "This will take a few moments, lad, to prepare. Suppose you tell me what brings you here." His voice became stern. "Leave nothing out."

Errol told of his encounter with the nuntius and the man's offer.

Martin turned at the mention of the price, his face wreathed with disbelief. "One of the crows offered to pay you a gold crown? Surely not. Churchmen hate parting with money. It's against their religion. I should know."

Errol dug the coin from his pocket and placed it on the table. "Here's the half of it."

Martin's eyebrows made fair to climb up his forehead, and he moved across the cabin to pick up the coin and examine it.

"I'll have to give it back," Errol said. "I'm sure the message is ruined."

Martin eyed Errol's battered legs. "Boy, if any man's ever earned a crown for delivering a message, you have. Keep the coin, and demand the rest. I'll vouch for you to the churchman, if needed." He retreated to the cupboard and returned with a thick salve that smelled heavily of lemongrass, lamb's ear, and soulsease.

Cupping Errol's face in a beefy hand, he smeared the salve over the cut on his cheek. "Take your shirt off, lad."

When Errol did so, Martin whistled. "I think the churchman may owe you another crown. You know the gorge better than any man alive. How did you come to this state?"

Errol winced. The salve felt cool and hot at the same time, and it stung. "A man tracked me from the overhang where bandits hide. I tried to shake him by crossing the Cripples, but he was nearly as fast across the rocks as me. Every time I made for a ledge, he tried to put an arrow in me."

Martin scowled, his brows knitting together over the deep brown of his eyes. "It's rare to find a bandit possessed of such determination."

Errol shook his head, and strands of brown hair fluttered in front of his eyes. "I don't think he was a bandit, Pater. Bandits don't cross the Cripples, at least not to chase down the likes of me." He reached under the table, grabbed the short black arrow, and laid it in front of the priest. "And I've never seen a bandit or anyone else shoot one of these."

The priest reached out to run one considering finger along the arrow, starting at the point, moving down the shaft to end at the midnight fletching. "Tell me, boy. How fares everyone in the village?"

Errol shrugged. "Fine. Cruk threw me out of the inn again."

Martin nodded without seeming to hear him. "Hmm. And Liam? Is he well?"

"Yes, Pater."

The cabin grew still. At last Martin turned from the arrow and began daubing salve into the cuts on Errol's legs and feet. Martin's gaze met his. "You should rest."

Nothing else was said, but Errol knew what he had seen in Martin's eyes at the sight of the arrow—recognition.

Errol descended into a slumber filled with dreams of stone and water. A face, pale and racked with pain, floated across his vision. He thrust himself from the memory, forced himself to wake.

He stirred to the sound of voices. His dream faded as the plain surroundings of Martin's cabin came into focus. Shadows stretched and lengthened outside. It would be dark soon.

At the table, Martin and his servant, Luis, regarded the contents of Errol's pack. Martin hefted the skin of wine. "At least the wine survived the boy's adventure." He nudged a folded package of waxed paper. "What think you, Luis? Can the bread be salvaged?"

Luis nodded and by way of answer took that portion of the sacrament over to the fireplace. Unfolding the paper, he laid the thin wafers with care on a metal grill and rested it on the hearth. Then he added pieces of kindling to the bed of coals until a small fire blazed. Resting his hands just above the bread, he tested the warmth. Satisfied, he turned and gave Martin a small nod, holding up one finger. "I think it will dry soon. What of the boy?"

Seeing Martin turn to face his pallet, Errol closed his eyes. A momentary pang of guilt coursed through him, but he dismissed it with a mental shrug. If he could learn the identity of his attacker by feigning sleep, then so be it.

"He sleeps," Martin said. "If I'd had to cross the gorge with someone shooting arrows at me, I'd sleep for a month."

Luis snorted. "Yes, as would I, but we're no longer young. Errol lies at the dawn of his prime."

"Prime? The boy hasn't had much chance at a prime. Look at him. He's a handsbreadth shorter than Liam and thin as a wafer. A young man his age should not be so lean." Martin paused in his assessment. "Yet as he has come of age there is something about his visage, the high cheekbones and the dimples that appear when he smiles, that almost reminds me of someone."

A silence ensued, and Errol longed to open his eyes, to question Martin about the resemblance, but he could feel the two men gazing at him and wanted to hear more of what they might say, so he concentrated on keeping his breathing regular.

"He smiles rarely enough," Luis said.

"The boy has no reason." After a brief pause, Martin continued, "It's time for us to return."

Errol opened his eyes the barest fraction. Acceptance marked Luis's face. Martin's wore regret.

Luis lifted his shoulders a fraction, dropped them. "It's been five years, Martin. I'm surprised the king lasted this long."

The priest beat one hand on his thigh. "We're not ready, Luis.

Why did I delay in coming here? I waited nearly a year after you cast for the village, telling myself there was no rush."

Luis shook his head. "Not this again, Martin. All three of us had things to do before we left. We're ready enough. I can complete my work in Erinon."

Three? No one else lived in the cabin.

Martin turned toward him, and Errol quickly closed his eyes.

"You're right, of course, but he's not ready yet. Things will be more difficult now."

Luis laughed. It sounded harsh in the confines of the small cabin. "You still have a gift for understatement. More difficult? They're impossible, and you know it. Even the few friends you have left in the Judica won't believe you."

Martin's voice grew cold. "They will have to believe. Once the lots are cast, they won't have any choice."

"It is not beyond doubt, my friend. They're not perfect yet. We may be surprised in the end."

"Is there a problem?" Martin's voice sounded worried.

Luis chuckled. "No. I'm just tired. I've held the vision of the soteregia in my head for a very long time." He sighed. "The secondus would have been better suited for this task."

"I didn't fancy sharing a cabin with Sarin Valon for five years," Martin said.

Luis shrugged. "He is brilliant, the most gifted reader we've had in generations."

Martin shrugged. "Perhaps, but there was something in me that balked at using him."

Luis sighed. "We have more immediate concerns, anyway." He lifted the short black arrow. "What do we do about this?"

Errol held his breath, strained to hear past the surge of his heart.

Martin sighed. "We've been found. I don't know how, but the good captain will handle it."

Errol started at that, then disguised the movement by rolling over on his pallet.

Luis laughed again. "After half a decade? Don't you think he might be a little rusty?"

"Don't underestimate him, Luis. He left a captaincy behind."

Luis moved to stand before a heavy trestle table. He picked up a knife and began peeling a potato. A moment later he spoke, slow, almost conversational. "Who do you think sent him?"

Martin pulled at his jaw muscles. "It's been five years. It could be anyone."

"We'll have to close the windows and take turns keeping watch."

"I know. I hate closing the windows. It makes the cabin stuffy." Martin reached under a cabinet on the far side of the cabin and pulled out a crossbow.

Errol waited for the conversation to resume. When it didn't, he opened his eyes and sat up to stretch aching muscles. The price for his frolic at the Cripples would be days in paying. Everything hurt.

Martin, seeing him awake, smiled in welcome. "You see, your trip wasn't wasted. Luis says the bread will be dry soon. We will be able to celebrate the sacraments tonight."

A yawn worked its way up his throat, and Errol clenched his teeth around it, grimacing. "What about your letters, Pater?"

Martin sighed, then pursed his lips. "A total loss, I'm afraid. Of course, that means I will have to go to the village and meet your messenger on his return from Gustin's."

"But you never come to the village."

Martin nodded. "Things change, lad, and any news that can separate a churchman from a gold crown is important enough for me to break my solitude—for a while anyway." He gestured toward the door of the cabin. "You'll have to spend the night here, I'm afraid. There's not enough time for you to make it back to the village before dark."

Errol's stomach tightened at Martin's words. *Stay?* He couldn't stay. He needed to get back to the inn. He had agreed to clean up after dinner, and there were other . . . more pressing concerns.

"I can make it back across the Cripples before dark, Pater."

He shrugged to emphasize his point. "Once I'm across, I can find my way along the path in the dark easily enough. I've done it at least a dozen times."

Martin and Luis looked at him with placid gazes, not blinking, until Errol squirmed. He felt as if he'd suddenly turned into glass and they could look through him and read his secret fear.

"No," Martin said. "You'll sleep here." He picked up the arrow and waved it in the air in front of Errol's face. "The man who fired this at you might still be searching for you. You'll stay with us tonight."

He shook his head in disagreement. "There's no reason for him to be looking for me, Pater. I am certain he was trying to make sure you didn't get your message. You didn't, although he might not know that. Either way, he knows he's either failed or succeeded and he won't be hanging around the gorge anymore."

Martin waved Errol's argument away and exchanged an inscrutable look with Luis. Again, Errol sensed undercurrents in the cabin that eluded his understanding, and the assassin's arrow lay at the center of it.

"Are you willing to bet your life on that, Errol?" Luis asked. The words were softly spoken, but a hint of steel lay beneath them.

Errol gave a twitch of his shoulders. "Nobody's cared about my life for a long time. The assassin's no different. I'll leave my pack here. If he's there, he'll see I'm empty-handed and leave me alone."

Martin turned to face him squarely. "No. You'll stay here tonight. I won't chance you getting killed. We'll lock the cabin. Luis and I will take turns keeping watch." His shoulders bunched and then eased under his linen. "In the morning, we'll all go back together. We'll go north to Berea and take the bridge across the Sprata."

Errol drew breath to protest. He wasn't about to stay in this small, ale-less cabin.

Martin drew himself up and his eyes glowered. "Don't make me invoke the authority of the church."

Errol laughed. "The church? It holds no authority over me.

What has the church ever done for me? Nothing. Pater Antil has put me in the stocks more times than I can count. If he ever puts anyone else in them, they'll have to ask my permission first."

Outside, the pace of the shadows increased. He had to leave soon if he wanted to make it back to the village before he got the sweats. Tremors would follow soon after. The mere thought of them made him want to dry the palms of his hands.

Martin stepped forward, pulling his vision from the waning sunlight. "If you stay, I'll make sure Antil never punishes you again." His voice dipped. "That I promise, Errol."

The earnestness in the priest's voice tempted him, but staying in the cabin meant cramps and pain until he could get to an ale barrel. He rolled his shoulders against the memory of the lash. It would almost be worth it to be free from Antil's punishments. Almost, but not quite. He turned toward the door. His hand had just closed on the latch when Martin's voice stopped him.

"I can help you with the shakes as well, if you'll let me."

He turned to see Martin and Luis staring at him, their eyes heavy-lidded with pity—a look he'd seen from friends and strangers a thousand times. Now it made him angry. "What would a priest know about the shakes?"

Martin laughed and shook his head. "Boy, I haven't lived in this cabin my whole life. Do you know how many postulates come to the church just to break the shackles that chain them to their wineskins?"

Errol shook his head. "No, and I don't care. I'll stay if you promise to get me through tonight."

That earned him another nod but no comment.

Martin turned toward his servant. "Luis, I think it would be best if we ate early. Can you prepare a quick supper?"

Luis nodded. "We've got some soup left and a bit of the rabbits we roasted last night." At a nod from Martin, he turned toward the cupboard.

"Errol, our bowls are in that cupboard. Would you get them, please?"

Floorboards complained as he crossed the cabin. When he opened the cupboard doors, Errol gasped, the bowls forgotten. Inside the cupboard, posed in miniature, stood a collection of animal figurines, each one sculpted in astonishing detail. He reached in, withdrew the figure of a dog, his fingers registering the fur painstakingly carved into the stone. He touched the nose, noting, almost in surprise, that it was neither wet nor cold. Replacing that figure he brought forth a bear that stood on its hind legs, its head tilted to one side, and its mouth open in a roar. He could almost hear the creature's deep-throated defiance.

A touch on his arm startled him, and he turned to find Martin there.

"Do you like them?"

He nodded, returned the carving to its place on the shelf. "They make everything else I've ever seen look clumsy. Who carved them?"

Martin gestured loosely toward Luis. "Your cook for the evening. He's not nearly as good with food as he is with stone, but we won't go hungry."

That earned a snort from his servant. "Humph, just because I don't drown everything in pepper the way you do."

The two men proceeded to argue over food. Errol closed the cupboard door. Beneath it was a large drawer, two hands high with heavy iron pulls. He leaned down and, straining, pulled it open a few inches.

The knife in Luis's hand stilled, and a small noise of protest escaped his throat. Martin's hand on his servant's arm kept him from speaking, but a flash of concern bordering on fear blazed in both men's eyes. Curious about what could spark such a response, Errol pulled the drawer open the rest of the way. It squeaked as the wooden runners protested at the revelation of its contents.

Martin appeared at his side. "You've discovered Luis's greatest work."

Errol stood, his eyes darting back and forth between the two men. What work of Luis's could be so precious that he would object to Errol just looking at it? Martin stood with a half smile and a look of encouragement for Luis written large across his broad features. Errol knew that look. He had seen fathers in the village bestow that look upon sons who had just accomplished something difficult and important.

Errol hadn't received such a look since Warrel died. Unwilling to touch the memories that lay behind that train of thought, he leaned forward to gaze into the drawer that Martin and Luis regarded as if it held rare jewels. At first, he suspected the two men of making sport of him, but when he glanced their way he found them as before—Martin with a look of pride and a frown of concern pinching Luis's features.

The drawer lay open at his feet. Squatting, he examined the contents, tried to understand. Dozens of gleaming white spheres lay nestled on a thick blanket of blackest wool. Every orb reflected the muted light within the cabin, creating the illusion they glowed from within.

And they were all identical. Try as he might, Errol could find no difference between them. Each sphere, half a handsbreadth across, was bereft of feature, color, or imperfection. He blinked and rubbed his eyes. The effect of those identical objects reminded him of the times he'd suffered from split vision after a night of too much ale. Curious now, he reached to take one of the spheres in hand. He could almost feel the smooth roundness against his fingertips, cool against his skin.

"Don't touch!" The command, louder after the prolonged silence in the cabin, startled him, and he jerked his hand back from the drawer as if burned.

Martin squeezed Errol's shoulder with a chuckle. "You'll have to forgive Luis. He's probably afraid you'll break one."

Luis shook his head in denial. "Such dissembling ill becomes you, old friend." Turning to Errol, he continued. "The lots are carved from durastone. They're nearly indestructible. You probably couldn't break one if you tried, but the dirt on your hand would mar the stone's balance."

Errol checked his hands. The palms bore telltale nicks and scratches, but the winter runoff from the Sprata had scrubbed them clean. Not a speck of dirt or blood showed on his skin. His confusion must have shown on his face.

"These lots are as perfect as I can make them, Errol. The balance and shape is so wrought that if you were to place one on a perfectly flat, clean floor and nudge it, it would roll for hundreds of paces before it stopped. The slightest bit of dirt or grease from your hands would change its balance."

Luis came forward, reached into a small cranny within the same cupboard, and produced a pair of gloves made from the same midnight wool whereon the stones rested.

He held the gloves by a loop attached to the wrist opening and offered them to Errol. "Here. Make sure you don't touch the fingers or the palms of the glove. Use the loops to pull them on."

Errol did so, and at a nod from Luis and Martin, he selected one of the white spheres and examined it. He'd heard of lots but had never seen one. The stone was indeed as perfectly round as Luis claimed. More, its whiteness was uniform beyond imagining. If he had not felt his hands turning the stone he wouldn't have known it had changed position.

He shrugged. "It's perfect. But what's it for?"

Martin and Luis exchanged a glance that filled the space of a dozen heartbeats. In the intervening silence, Errol found his gaze drawn back to the pristine sphere nestled in his palm. What purpose or power had Luis crafted into the stone? He held it to the light, turning it in idle curiosity. And then he stopped. *Letters.* He blinked and looked up at Martin and Luis. Had he imagined them, or had he seen letters reflected in the stone's glistening surface?

Slowly now, so that he wouldn't miss them, he held the stone against the flickering lamplight, searching for whatever lay written there. Twice the letters flickered against his vision and were lost and he had to try again. On the third time he held the image.

Writing wrapped itself against the surface of the sphere, small and the merest shade of white different than the background. Errol looked toward Luis. "There's writing here. What's it say?" Having never learned to read, he held it toward Martin's servant without thinking. "See? There are letters right there."

Luis just stared at him.

Curious to see what images or writing might show on the other stones, Errol moved to exchange the orb he held and draw another.

Luis came around the table, his movements, slow, deliberate. "Tell me, Errol, do you remember your testing day?"

Errol shook his head. "No." He reached for another stone.

Martin's hand covered his. "Let's wait for another time, Errol. Luis gets nervous when people handle his best work too much. Besides, I think you should eat. You've had a long day."

Errol shrugged his disappointment and snaked first one hand and then the other out of the black wool gloves and, holding them by their loops, replaced them in their nook.

But when he turned, Luis's expression bore little resemblance to nervousness. He stood, eyeing Errol in shock as though he'd become a puzzle to solve. After meeting Errol's gaze for a split second, he jerked away, turned his attention back to their meal. The knife resumed its work, though less rhythmically.

Their dinner bore testimony that Luis's skill extended to more than stonework. The rabbit stew, mixed with vegetables and delicately seasoned, might have been the best meal Errol had ever eaten. Martin took one taste and then, without looking, thrust out a hand, grabbed a spice jar, and proceeded to lace his stew with a generous amount of black pepper.

That earned him a glare from Luis. "Well, at least you tried it first. Why I ever agreed to cook for a fat priest from Ostliche is beyond me."

Martin grunted without raising his gaze from his bowl. "You didn't agree. You undertook the culinary duties by proclamation, exclaiming you'd rather go hungry than eat anything I might prepare."

Luis harrumphed and turned his attention back to his own meal.

Errol ate, gulped desperate bites of stew, hoping the meal would somehow mollify his body's demand for ale. Outside, the last purple rays faded from the sky and unrelieved darkness covered Martin's cabin. As if on cue, Errol's hands began shaking. His spoon rattled against the side of his bowl as he tried to take another bite. Martin and Luis turned toward the source of the noise and lifted their gazes to Errol's face. Embarrassed, he dropped the spoon and clenched his hands under the table. Perhaps they wouldn't notice the sheen of sweat that covered him. He felt the blood draining from his face, knew he would be sick if he didn't get ale soon.

He dropped his gaze to his hands. "Pater Martin, do you have any ale? I-I'm thirsty."

"I'm sorry, Errol. I don't." The priest's voice was soft. "And if this is what ale has done to you, my son, wouldn't it be better to forsake it?"

Errol laughed. Ale hadn't done this. Outside, the last of the purple disappeared into darkness. In the five years he'd served as Martin's messenger, he'd never attempted a crossing of the Sprata at night. But with luck it might be done. It would certainly take longer than the four hours it had taken to bring him here, but in five, possibly six hours he could be back at the inn and Cilla would still have time to sneak him a few tankards out the back window. In five or six hours he'd be fine . . . or dead from a fall.

He clenched his trembling hands, regretting his decision to stay. His stomach lurched, demanding ale. The meal sat on that demand, like dead weight. Then it moved.

His chair clattered, bounced on the floor behind him as Errol bolted for the door. Wrenching the handle, he jumped from the porch to land in the garden, his stomach emptying even as he moved. Cramps forced him to his knees, where he heaved again and again, the spasms forcing blood into his head until his face swelled and burned. Still they went on. He fell to his side.

Later, unsure how much later, his body at last noted his dry heaves, believed his stomach no longer held food. His throat burned, and he longed for something to drink, even water to wash away the bile. Crossing the Sprata was beyond him now. He doubted he could even drag himself back into the cabin. He tried to relax as much as his knotted stomach would allow. As his breathing slowed, images came to him, pictures of himself before he'd disappeared in the ale barrel.

No. He thrust himself from the ground, away from the stink of his meal, and staggered, hunched and aching, toward the cabin. As he set foot on the threshold, hands came to him, supporting his weight, and brought him back into the light and warmth. He found himself looking up into Luis's eyes, their deep brown dry but sympathetic.

"Come," he said, "Martin is ready to celebrate the sacrament."

Errol's memories swam before his eyes, superimposed themselves in a mismatched tapestry against the interior of the cabin. "What could I possibly have to celebrate?"

"Ah, Errol, there is always something to be thankful for."

His response died on his tongue as he saw Martin standing behind a narrow table. While he'd been throwing up in the garden, the priest had donned a chasuble and stole. They were wrinkled, but he wore them with dignity. The interior of the cabin reflected light from a trio of large candles on the table, and the rough furnishings took on an austere grace. Luis deposited Errol on the couch and then offered a dented hand bowl to Martin to rinse his hands.

The priest dried them on a towel Luis had draped over his arm and then took a stoneware pitcher and poured a cupful of water into an earthen goblet. Facing Errol, he intoned the familiar rite.

"May Deas be with you."

"And with all who gather in his name," Luis responded.

Errol had heard the rite hundreds of times, sometimes from inside the church but more often from a distance. Too many times he'd been forced to listen to Antil recite the liturgy from the confines of the stocks. The memory galled him, and he clamped his mouth shut to lock the response behind his teeth.

Martin looked his way, but the old man's eyes held no recrimination that Errol could see. Softly—not looking out over the heads of the gathered communicants, as a priest usually did, but directly into Errol's eyes—Martin continued.

"Lift up your praises," he encouraged.

"Do not be afraid; lift them up to Deas, and Eleison, and unknowable Aurae," Luis replied, speaking as though the response were his own.

"Let us give thanks to the Father Deas," Martin said. Errol would have said the words were the priest's own had he not heard them hundreds of times before.

"It is right for us so to do," Luis responded.

"It is right and our bounden duty, in all times, in all places, to give thanks unto thee, O Deas, Father, everlasting."

Almost, the spell of Martin's sincerity held Errol, but memories of loss and Antil's cruelty festered in his gut. His stomach roiled. He curled over, his folded arms pressing into his midsection, trying to ease new cramps. A metallic taste filled his mouth. A spasm put him on the wooden planks of the floor, and he retched, his stomach trying to rid itself of what was no longer there. Above him, Martin intoned the measured cadences of the sacrament.

"For by Deas, through Eleison, and with the unity of unknowable Aurae, the heavens were cast and the world found purchase in the firmament. All glory be unto thee, Deas, Eleison, unknowable Aurae, world without end."

Errol pictured Antil's likely reaction at seeing him so indisposed at the altar and gave a bitter laugh. The priest would fall over from rage. The image of him, red-faced and gasping, only made him laugh harder, his breath wheezing past the cramps that kept him on the floor.

"Lift your voices," Martin said, but something in the priest's voice broke. "Eleison, our champion, has triumphed." The last words were delivered just above a whisper. Errol curled tighter around the pain in his stomach. He knew from experience what would happen next. No priest would suffer their office to be so disrespected. He didn't care—the lash or the stocks, what did it matter? Soon or late he would get back to Cilla and she would give him ale.

He heard footsteps coming toward him. He hoped Martin wouldn't kick him in the stomach. Antil had done that once.

A hand slid between his head and the floor, lifted him gently from the boards, and Martin's voice, so very close now, rested on his ears. "The body of Eleison, interposed to keep us safe so long as the world lasts."

Errol pried his eyes open. Martin held a wafer between his thumb and forefinger, offering, waiting for Errol to open his mouth and accept it. He shook his head. If he ate that, if he ate anything, he would throw up again. "I can't."

Martin nodded his understanding. The priest pulled his hand back, broke the smallest piece from the bread he could, scarcely more than a crumb, and offered it again. Errol opened his mouth, accepted it, and cheeked it with his tongue. Martin stood, retreated a step, and nodded to Luis, who came forward with the cup.

Tears glistened in the servant's eyes. "Errol, this is the offering of Eleison, the champion of our world."

Errol stared at the cup, his eyes just above the rim. Lamplight glittered off the surface of the red liquid. His need spoke for him and he reached out, put his shaking hands over Luis's and tilted the crude chalice until the wine flowed over his tongue.

Too soon, barely a swallow later, Luis lowered the cup from his lips and stood, but the mouthful Errol received flowed to his stomach and his cramps eased a portion. He let his head rest on the floor. In his state he was just conscious enough to feel gratitude for the lack of punishment.

"May Deas be with you." Martin's voice filled the cabin again, washing over him.

"And with all who gather in his name," Luis responded.

Errol opened his eyes, confused. What did Martin think he was doing? Hadn't they just done this? Too tired, too cramped to be curious he closed his eyes and let the priest's voice fill his thoughts. Besides, what did he care if Martin wished to recite his liturgy again?

Moments later, he felt himself lifted again, another crumb of wafer placed on his tongue. Luis crouched to offer the cup as before. Once more a mouthful of wine slid down to his stomach and his pain eased another fraction.

Errol lost track of how often Martin and Luis repeated the rite. Sometime before dawn, he slept.

3

CRIMSONWEED

ASOLITARY SHAFT of sunlight falling across his left eye woke him early the next morning. He sat up to the sounds of packing and turned to see Martin stuffing bread and cheese into a pack, his face serious. On the other side of the cabin, Luis emptied the cabinet of the strange spherical carvings. He wore the black wool gloves, each movement slow and methodical as he placed the balls one at a time into a heavily padded crate. The urge to lift the orbs and see their lettering came over him again, but neither Martin nor Luis looked as if they would tolerate any interruption. Martin's attention to the food seemed only slightly less intense than Luis's to his carvings. The two men didn't look at each other or speak, but tension crackled between them.

He stood, the floor creaking beneath his weight. Surprisingly, he craved food rather than ale. He probed his abdomen with the fingers of his right hand. How long would it be before his stomach remembered itself and renewed its demands for Cilla's brew?

Seeing him upright, Martin beckoned, holding out a piece of bread. "Here, lad, I don't think you're ready for cheese yet, but this should sit easy enough on your stomach."

Errol accepted it as the memory of last night's sacrament ghosted through his mind. "Why are you packing?"

The priest laid several apples into the bag and regarded him, his brown eyes thoughtful. "I don't think Luis and I will be coming back here, Errol. The message you delivered from the church yesterday was almost certainly intended to call me back to Erinon."

Martin's reasoning escaped him. "But you didn't read the message, Pater. How do you know what was in it?"

Martin chuckled. "Errol, how many times have you journeyed forth across the Sprata to make deliveries since we came here?"

He shrugged, his thin shoulders bunching up around his ears before falling. "More times than I can count, Pater."

Martin nodded at him. "And in all those times, how many messages from the church have you been commissioned to deliver?"

"None."

The priest held up a finger to show he'd made his point. "Exactly. In truth, I've been waiting for and dreading this message for the past five years."

Errol shook his head. He could still see the remnants of the message laid out on Martin's table. Tracks of ink like streams that fed the Sprata during the spring floods stained the parchment. Not one word of the letter retained its legibility. "But how do you know what was in it?"

Martin's eyebrows rose and he nodded in approval. "A fair question. Come." He walked over to the still-damp parchment and pointed. "Look at the lower left corner and tell me what you see."

Errol bent at the waist, his eyes searching. There, at the bottom, the parchment still held an imprint of a seal: three tongues of flame surmounting a rectangular block. He'd never seen its like before.

Martin's voice became serious. "That's the symbol of the arch-benefice's office at Erinon. I've been expecting his summons."

"For what?"

The priest's face became grave. "To help select a new king."

"Why would we need a new king?" Errol asked.

"Because Rodran has no heir."

"Oh." He shrugged. People died all the time. What was the need to select a new king to him? Nothing, really, but he would miss Martin, especially after last night. The priest was the only clergyman who'd ever been kind to him. "When are you coming back?"

Martin shook his head. "I'm not. I'll be needed in Erinon." He looked around the cabin before returning his gaze to Errol. "We'll let the people in Callowford and Berea know that whoever wants the cabin may have it. We won't need it anymore."

Errol pushed away the thought of his life without Martin or Luis. People constantly left or died. That was the way of things. Unbidden, a craving for ale came over him, and he thought of leaving Martin and Luis to undertake the trek north to Berea by themselves so he could cross the gorge and get back to Cilla's inn and the ale barrels it held.

"What about you, Errol?" Luis asked. "Have you ever thought of leaving Callowford? The kingdom of Illustra is far larger than you can imagine from here. Someday you might even see Erinon. Would you like that?"

The tension between Luis and Martin seemed to heighten at this, but Errol could see no reason for it.

"I will not travel far from Cilla and her inn."

Martin nodded and turned away, but not before Errol saw the look of relief in his eyes.

Errol's craving for ale strengthened a notch. "I was thinking I could go back across the gorge and meet you in Callowford," Errol said. "That way, if the messenger comes back before you do, I can tell him to wait."

Martin gave a self-assured laugh. "He'll wait, Errol. He has to. The archbenefice has little patience for incompetence." He gave Errol a look that seemed to plumb his soul. "Have you forgotten the man who tried to kill you?"

In truth, Errol had forgotten. But surely the man was gone by now. With the message ruined, he had nothing the man, or anyone else for that matter, wanted.

"Come, Errol, you carry the food. Luis will need me to carry his tools. He won't trust his lots to anyone, I'm afraid. They're practically like children to him."

Luis smiled as he slowly hoisted the crate to his back, snaking his arms through a pair of ropes so that it rode just below his shoulders. "The stones require as much work as children, and sometimes they're no better behaved than the meanest brats." He glanced at Martin. "Someday you may learn that for yourself." Without a backward glance he strode out of the cabin and into the early morning sunshine. Martin and Errol followed. Outside, Errol looked back once. The cabin door hung ajar and it was dark inside. Already, the life had gone out of it.

They picked up the path leading west toward the village of Berea, skirting the Sprata for most of the way. Two hours out, Martin called a halt, sweating and panting as they climbed another of the interminable hills that lay between them and their destination.

"How much farther?" Sweat plastered his gray hair to his forehead, and he dabbed the sides and back of his neck with a wet cloth. Dark splotches of effort marked the rough fabric of his cassock where it stretched over his bulk. Sunlight reflected off the itch vines to his left, giving his face a greenish cast. His chest heaved.

Luis wiped his brows, the tanned skin of his bald head gleaming wetly in the light. "It's another hour to Berea, then, once we cross the bridge over the Sprata, two more to catch Falls Road and then another three hours back east to Callowford." He gulped for breath between sentences.

Errol smiled. Aside from the occasional craving for ale, he felt better than he had in a long time. His sweat cleansed him, and after crossing the Sprata yesterday, this hike was insufficient to tire him. "It would have been a lot quicker to cut across the gorge. Even allowing for a trip across the Cripples, it would have cut this trip in half." He made no effort to keep the overly cheerful tone from his voice.

Luis smiled, but Martin shot him a look of irritation as he brought the cloth forward to mop his face. "Speed is the least of our considerations. There is news I need before I meet with the church's representative, and the priest of Berea is the closest source."

Luis's mouth drew to one side, and he gave a slight shake of his head. "You don't even know if they've bothered telling the local priests what's happening, Martin. Berea is so far off the beaten path they might not hear about it for a year or more."

Martin nodded, as if conceding the point, but said nothing that would indicate he'd changed his mind. The priest sighed and levered his bulk off the rock he'd used as a seat and continued along the path. His steps faltered. He stumbled over nothing, then righted himself. "Luis, I think that messenger was sent just in time. My isolation in the cabin for the past five years has taken its toll."

Luis, gray and sweating, nodded his agreement. "I seem to be feeling the effects as well. My legs feel like lead."

Errol watched the two men struggle up the trail, suspicion and panic growing in his mind. He stood transfixed, looking on in horror as first Martin and then Luis fell panting to the dust. He ran to the priest, kneeling to pour water for him. The old man's skin felt cool and clammy to the touch. He poured again. Martin drained the cup before nodding weakly toward Luis.

Errol raced over to Martin's servant, offered water as his mind reeled. What was wrong with them? The walk, like any other in the Sprata foothills, tested a man's endurance, but the pace had been easy and both men had seemed fine only a few moments ago. But they were old. They'd never mentioned any infirmities to Errol, but who knew what ailments the men brought with them to Callowford?

Luis drained the cup, his tanned skin blanched to the color of dust. He struggled to a half-sitting, half-lying position on the trail and took the waterskin from Errol. "See to Martin."

The priest lay sprawled across the dirt and rock of the trail, his eyes closed and his breath coming in shallow gasps. Errol put his hands on his chest, rocking him back and forth. "Pater Martin? Tell me what's wrong."

The priest's eyes fluttered open, and he rolled his head toward Luis. "Poison," he whispered.

A blow like the strike of a smith's hammer hit Errol in the chest. Pulling his pack from his shoulders he flung it open and dumped the contents on the ground, hoping against hope. He searched, throwing each item to the side. "Where is it? I just picked some." There. Smashed under the spare waterskin lay a damp clump of crimsonweed. He grasped the plant by the roots and in a single motion stripped the foliage with his spare hand. Discarding the stalk, he grabbed half the pulpy leaves that lay on the ground and rolled them between his hands until they massed into a wet lumpy ball and a sharp tang filled the air.

Opening Martin's mouth, he forced half of the wad into the back of his throat and then poured water across the old man's lips until he was forced to swallow. He waited, his heart hammering, just long enough for the priest to catch his breath before rushing over to Luis to repeat the process. Martin's servant seemed to be in better shape, if barely. His eyes were open and aware. His breathing was less labored.

When Errol placed the first wad of crushed crimsonweed between his lips, Luis roused himself. "What's wrong with us?" he gasped around the medicine.

"Martin says you've been poisoned."

Luis blinked and gave a sparse nod, then chewed twice, juice rolling down one cheek, and swallowed thickly. Errol tilted the waterskin, letting him drink.

Luis struggled, taking a deep breath. "You know Adele?" he asked.

Errol stilled, caught off guard by the question. He did know Adele. The herbwoman lived outside of Berea, seeing only those she trusted. Errol was one of those. He brought her the plants she needed that grew along the Sprata. If he was clever and managed to procure the roots and mushrooms that grew in the cracks and caves of the river, she paid him enough to keep him in ale for a couple of days. She and her sister, Radere, who lived outside Callowford, did a fair trade with the villagers and farmers for a couple of leagues around.

The church barely tolerated the two women. More than once, needing some excuse to give Errol a beating, Antil had caught him coming from Radere's hut and put him in the stocks. Not Radere, just Errol.

"Boy." Luis's breathing slowed as the crimsonweed took effect. "Do you know Adele?" At a nod from Errol, he continued. "Then hurry."

He left each man a waterskin and raced away without a backward glance, his feet churning the dust on the trail. As he ran, his thoughts swam sluggishly in his mind and his peripheral vision blurred until the trees and plants at the side of the trail blended into an unbroken swath of green.

Luis and Martin were dying. The image of Martin, gray-skinned and sweating, flashed across his mind and he held it. Casting about for any sign that might help Adele decipher the poison, he called up the image of the two men over and over again. They had stopped to rest. At the time Errol had paid no attention, but now it seemed strange that they should tire so quickly—and on the easiest part of the trail at that. Then they had fallen.

Errol cudgeled his memory as he ran, trying to recall any detail, no matter how insignificant, that might help. But aside from their gray, clammy skin and the sudden onset of fatigue, he could think of nothing.

Sudden pains shot through his calves, and he grimaced, struggling against unaccustomed weariness. He shouldn't be tired. He'd run this trail and others as difficult a thousand times. The days when the pathways around the Sprata could challenge him were long past. Sweat blurred his vision. When he raised a hand to wipe it away, the chill of his skin surprised him. With a shock he stared at the back of his hand. His mind recoiled at the pallor of his flesh.

The poison was in him too. He stumbled, stubbed his foot against a rock. *Keep moving.* Adele would know what to do. He ran on, forcing his legs to obey his will.

The twists and the turns of the trail conspired against him. The rocky pinnacles, so often his friends when he needed to flee his thoughts or memories, now hindered his path. Sweat poured from him. When it ran from his forehead, down his face and into his mouth as he sucked in great gasps of air, it gagged him with the taste of sulfur, its saltiness hidden by the unfamiliar odor.

His vision swam. The terrain distorted, became strange and unfamiliar. Where was he? *Adele.* He was trying to reach the old healer, but was this even the right path? He couldn't be sure. It looked strange.

He ran ten paces past the fork that led to her cabin before he stopped and reversed course. By the time he reached Adele's hut, dark spots filled his vision. He wanted ale. Weaving on his feet, he stepped under the worn, dirty thatch of her roof and up onto the gray stone threshold. His legs, surprised by the sudden lack of motion, stopped, then buckled, dumping him. His head fell against the rough oak planks of her door, sounding the first knock. He lay on the stone like a village girl's discarded rag doll, beating his fist against the door like a pendulum.

"Adele. Please be home."

The door opened and he flopped inside, lying on the packed earth of her floor. The smell of woodsmoke filled the hovel. Adele knelt beside him with a groan and lifted his head.

"Thorns and thistles, boy, you look awful." He pried his lids open. Her eyebrows, thick and iron-gray like the wild strands of hair that peeked from under her head cloth, knit in accusation. "What did you do, drink some bad ale?" Her hands stroked his sweat-stained hair back from his face.

He looked into her eyes, old and gray like the rest of her. "Poison. Pater Martin and Luis are on the trail."

Her glance sharpened, and her voice became curt. "Tell me, quickly!"

Errol cast back, trying to remember everything. The room spun, and it felt good to lie on the cool floor. A scent of earth ghosted through his nose, beckoning him to sleep. Yes, that was it. He'd sleep a little and then he'd tell Adele. He blinked, working to open his eyelids again. What was he going to tell her? The thought died. It could wait, he needed to sleep.

Cold water splashed across his face, and his head rocked to one side, his cheek stinging. He opened his eyes to see Adele's face over him, contorted with anger, her hand raised to strike him again. "Wake up, boy. I don't care for folks dying in my home." Her voice rasped across his ears.

Errol nodded, or tried to. His head didn't seem to want to move. "Poison," he said.

"I know that, boy. Now, tell me the manifestations."

Breathing, speaking, took a concentrated effort. "They got tired, so tired, and then they fell. By the time I got to them their skin was gray."

The herbwoman grimaced. Errol wondered how long it would take him to die. "I need more, boy. Any number of poisons could do that; yellowthorn, hemsting plant, bracken root. All of them attack the muscles and the skin."

Errol sighed. Slow waves of dizziness pulled him downward. Then he remembered. "Sulfur," he breathed, hoping Adele could hear. "Sweat . . . smelled . . . like sulfur."

Adele's mouth pinched, and she tugged at a stray lock of hair, thinking, as Errol had seen her do countless times before. "Sulfur? Are you sure, boy?"

Errol tried to nod. Had his head moved? "Yes. Strong smell. Sulfur."

She went to all fours and sniffed his skin, like a dog going to scent. "Phew, boy. You smell like an alchemist's shop."

His awareness blurred. Moments later, she was gone but he heard voices coming from behind her hut. One of them he knew as Adele's, her speech soft now, yet surprised as well. He didn't recognize the other voice, couldn't have recognized it. It thrummed with authority, and the air breathed tones that encompassed and surpassed human hearing with the barest pauses. If the wind could have conspired to whisper its will through the stones and trees, he imagined it would have sounded like that.

Adele's astonishment drifted to him. "Him as well?"

The response dipped, lulling him. He closed his eyes and drifted. . . .

And woke to a presence in the hut that was not Adele's. An impossible wind, like the exhalation of earth, moved along him, registered his feeble movements with eddies that fanned out over his skin, tracing its way down his torso to his stomach.

Struggling, he opened his eyes, but there was nothing to see. His awareness of Adele's hut, the earthen floor, even himself faded to wispy insubstantiality. The rush of air filled Adele's hut as she mixed powders from earthenware pots, her ear cocked—listening, nodding.

Errol floated or slept, but when he opened his eyes he was alone with Adele. She knelt, lifted his head, and poured a draught that tasted like liquid earth down his throat. He coughed once, twice. A spasm shook him, and a sudden chill spread from his stomach outward until he shivered. His head cleared.

The herbwoman smiled, showing crooked teeth. "Nice to see you among the living, boy. You nearly killed yourself, running here with that poison working through your veins." The squint in her eyes warred with her smile. Adele considered him as though he'd become a stranger.

He rose, wondering if his legs and feet would obey him. "What about Martin and Luis?"

The healer's face clouded. "It was a miracle you survived, boy. It takes a young heart to survive moritweed poisoning. They are surely dead."

4

TIDINGS

ERROL HUNCHED OVER, tried to protect himself from the blow of Adele's words. Her simple, emotionless pronouncement of death struck him. *Not again, not again.*

A light hand touched him, the back of Adele's fingers tracing the curve of his jaw. "I'm sorry, Errol. Moritweed works slow, it does, but still too quick to save your friends." She turned toward the door, her movements as birdlike as her appearance. "I'll go get Nurl. Killing is mayor's business."

Memories surged from somewhere deep inside him, and he reeled. *No.* He grabbed Adele's arm as she passed him. "Crimsonweed," he said. "I gave them crimsonweed before I left."

Adele's face met his, shock and anger written on it. "You gave two old men crimsonweed, boy? What were you trying to do? Make sure they didn't survive?"

Errol ducked under her gaze. "You're telling me they're dead anyway. When Martin said they'd been poisoned I knew I had to do something."

"But why crimsonweed, boy?"

"It was all I had."

48

The woman snorted, a wisp of iron-gray hair floating at the gesture. "Well, I'll give you this much. If the weed didn't kill them right off, it might have bought you enough time to take them the cure. Here." She stumped back to her shelves and their containers. Soft grunts and wheezes whispered through the hut as she jerked several containers from their place. A handful of scents blended and filled the room before she gave a crisp nod and placed the powder in a bag and cinched it. She grabbed a waterskin from the shelf.

She gave both to Errol. "Fill the waterskin from the barrel. Mix a handful of powder with water and get it down their throats." She shook her head. "Though I don't know how you'll do that with crimsonweed in their systems. They'll look dead, even if they aren't."

The old woman frowned, then fetched one last jar, poured a handful of dirty white powder into a square of cloth, and returned to thrust it at him. "Mix that in as well. It'll counteract the weed. Off with you now."

She wasn't coming?

"Don't give me that look, boy. You know how the church feels about herbwomen. Martin is better than most, but he's still a churchman." She motioned her chin at the door. "Now go. I'll leave it to you to tell Nurl if they've died."

The door clattered shut behind him as he left.

Errol flung himself down the trail, fighting against the nausea that sapped the energy from his legs. An hour later he found Martin and Luis as he'd left them. Martin lay as if dead, the skin of his face slack and gray beneath his white hair. Errol put his head to the priest's chest, struggled to hear the telltale beat that would indicate Martin lived. The sounds of the forest, though muted, prevented him, so he covered his exposed ear with his hand and waited.

Twice he thought he'd heard the pulse of the old man's heart, only to discover with a pang that it was his own beat he heard, thrumming through his eardrum with the effort of his return.

He sat back on his haunches, fought back tears. He couldn't hear the priest's heart. Errol put the back of his hand to the priest's neck, just below the jaw. Martin was still warm.

His fingers fumbled the string of Adele's pouch before he ripped it open. He took a handful of both powders and poured them from his shaking hand into the neck of the waterskin. Clenching the neck, he shook it, then held the opening to Martin's mouth and poured.

"C'mon, Martin," he breathed. "Just take a little."

Most of it—maybe all of it—spilled on the ground. He tried again with the same result. With a sob, he rose and repeated the gesture with Luis, with no better results. Not knowing what else to do, he shuttled back and forth, poured medicine into their unresponsive mouths, and waited for Martin and his servant to grow cold.

Then it happened.

Luis coughed. The gurgle was so weak Errol wasn't sure whether he'd heard it or hoped it into existence. He left Martin's side with another useless trail of wet running down the priest's shirt and ran to Luis. Did he imagine it, or did he look less gray than a moment before? He knelt, placed the mouth of the waterskin between the man's lips. There. Luis's mouth clenched ever so slightly. Errol tilted and poured. Luis coughed louder this time, and his arms twitched feebly at his side.

Errol left him and ran back across the path to Martin. "Please, Pater. Luis is waking up. Just take a sip." He shook the priest and begged as he poured, but Martin's mouth remained slack and unresponsive and the pallor of his skin refused to change from its gray hue.

Errol flopped on the dust and pebbles of the trail. He'd failed Martin. For certain, the crimsonweed had slowed down the priest's body and delayed the killing stroke of the moritweed, but he'd given too much. One of the poisons was killing Martin. It didn't matter which and Errol had no way to get Adele's potion into him.

Without it, Martin would die.

Now nothing remained for Errol except to tend Luis and wait.

Martin's servant lay on his side, his arms pushing at the ground, trying to lever himself up. Errol pulled him to a sitting position. His eyes fluttered open and pawed without strength at Errol's arm. "Water."

Errol lifted the skin with the potion in it to Luis's mouth and watched as he drank. After two swallows he pushed it away.

"Ugh. What is that?" he whispered.

Errol lifted the skin back to Luis's lips. "Drink some more. Someone poisoned you, us, with moritweed. Adele made the cure."

Luis drank again, then raised trembling hands to force the skin away, his eyes burning into Errol's. "What about Martin?"

Errol shook his head. "I can't get the potion into him."

Luis clutched at his arms. "Try again."

His frustration and fatigue boiled over. "I've been trying! Don't you think I've been trying? I gave him too much. He's going to die."

Luis closed his eyes, and Errol watched as he drew several breaths, his chest expanding a little more each time as strength returned.

"Martin is tougher than you think. He's not dead. Try again."

Errol crossed the dusty path and sat in front of Martin where he lay shaded by an outcropping of gray limestone. He could detect no sign of life from the priest. His chest did not rise or fall, and Errol could feel no pulse within the priest's neck. Errol desperately did not want to sit and watch the priest die. A thirst, an aching need for ale, overcame him, and he half rose to begin the walk to Berea and its inn. He still had the half crown he'd received for delivering the churchman's message. Its weight, cold and heavy like lead, still filled his pocket. He could keep it. Martin had said so. Surely the nuntius would not require its return after all he'd been through. It would buy enough ale to last him a week.

He let the thought of a week's worth of ale roll over him. He could almost smell the malty light liquid. A seven-day would be his, no washing dishes, no gathering plants for the herbwomen, no shoveling out Braen's stables. Just one crisp tankard of ale after another. And then sleep. Sweet, dreamless sleep after that.

"Errol," Luis called to him, breaking his reverie into pieces. "Try again."

With a slump of his shoulders, Errol lifted the potion to Martin's mouth one more time. Nothing changed.

Or maybe it did. Had he seen a bubble between Martin's lips? He lowered the skin, poured a bit of the watery elixir over his hand and then held his palm to Martin's mouth. *There.* For a moment he thought he felt a hint of breath across his skin. His hands shook as he poured a tiny amount into the priest, hardly more than enough to wet his lips. It disappeared. He poured again, a little more this time. It too disappeared, and now he could see the priest's throat tighten and loosen the smallest bit as he swallowed.

Errol whipped around to face Luis. "He's alive!" He levered the skin again, the tremble gone from his hands.

Minutes and uncountable sips of potion later, Martin's hand twitched, then rose to rest on Errol's. His lips and tongue worked as if they labored to remember their purpose. At last he spoke, his speech a mere burble of sound. "Enough." As though a dam broke with that word, his face turned a shade less gray, and color began to return.

Errol felt a hand on his shoulder, turned to find Luis on shaky legs behind him. He looked up into brown eyes that crinkled at the edges and a gaze that returned his with warmth. "Thank you, Errol. Help me get Martin up and moving."

They each took an arm and pulled. Errol grunted under the priest's weight. They tottered back and forth before Martin gestured toward an outcropping of rock. The priest seated himself and eyed Luis and then Errol before he rubbed one hand down his forehead and across his heavy jaw. "I think it would be good if someone told me what happened." His gaze rested on Luis, who shook his head and nodded toward Errol.

The priest's brown eyes locked with his, and Errol felt the tug of the man's ecclesiastical authority. He ducked his head and answered as briefly as he could. "Moritweed."

The word's effect on Martin and Luis was immediate. The two men stared at each other for a long moment, their eyes unreadable. Luis started to speak, but Martin forestalled him with one raised hand and turned toward Errol.

"How do you know it was moritweed, Errol?"

"Adele told me."

Martin's eyes tightened at the mention of the herbwoman's name, but he nodded, chewing on the corner of his lower lip. "And why did you go to Adele?"

Luis cleared his throat and grimaced, looking embarrassed. "I sent him."

Martin nodded. "Well, we'll leave that discussion for another time." He paused, eyeing Errol as if trying to choose which question to ask next. "Errol, moritweed is rare, especially in this part of the world. How do you think Adele knew we'd been poisoned by it?"

For a moment, Errol thought Pater Martin accused Adele, but that didn't make sense. She had no reason to poison the priest or his servant, and no one had a reason to want Errol dead. Besides, the old woman didn't have access to the priest or his servant. No, Martin sought something else. With a flash of insight, he knew. Martin knew about the presence Adele talked to, the one that spoke like a rush of wind. But Errol could not speak of it.

"I don't know, Pater." He shrugged and tried to look away. "By the time I got to her hut, the moritweed had done its work on me. I passed out on her floor."

Martin pursed his lips, as if digesting Errol's evasion. "We'll come back to that later. Maybe you could tell Luis and me how we managed to survive. Moritweed is slow acting, but once it starts to take effect, it's nearly impossible to stop. Luis and I should be dead."

Errol's throat tightened, locking away his answer, but Martin refused to be denied. His eyes bored into Errol like an awl going through leather. Errol scuffed the dirt of the trail with one worn shoe. "I gave you and Luis crimsonweed, Pater."

Martin's eyebrows climbed in surprise until lines of strain showed on his forehead beneath the white of his hair.

Luis laughed.

"I don't see the cause for amusement, Luis," the priest admonished. "The boy could have killed us."

Luis shook his head. His smile under the broad prow of his nose showed even, white teeth against olive skin. "Let it go, Martin. We were dead anyway. The boy saved our lives. I'll warrant nobody's ever thought of slowing the effects of moritweed with crimsonweed before. The healers in Erinon would be most interested, I believe."

Martin grunted. "I don't think it will become normal medical practice. However, you have my thanks, Errol." He turned to Luis. "Throw away the bread."

Luis nodded. "Ah, of course." He fished through his pack until he found the waxed paper that held the communal bread. Stepping to the side of the trail, he dug a shallow hole with his boot, dropped the bread into it, and covered it. He gave the barest lift of his shoulders. "No sense killing the birds."

"How do you know the poison's in the bread, Pater?" Errol asked. He made a mental list of everything they had eaten the night before. Any one of them might have been poisoned.

Martin took a deep breath. He ran a hand through his thick shock of silver hair, then steepled his fingers underneath his chin. His gaze found a spot somewhere over Errol's left shoulder. "Where do you think the poison was, Errol?"

He thought back. They had eaten a rabbit stew for dinner. It might have been in there. Or someone might have slipped something into the rain barrel Martin and Luis used for drinking water. But either one of those would have required someone to get to Martin's cabin, poison the food or water, and then slip away unseen. That seemed unlikely. Few people outside Errol's village knew Martin and Luis lived in the rocky hills above the Sprata River. Even fewer knew how to find him. There were a lot of people in his village Errol didn't care for, but there weren't any he would put the title of *murderer* to.

That left the bread and wine Errol delivered the night before. He met Martin's gaze. "I can see the poison had to be in the sacraments, Pater, but why the bread and not the wine?"

The priest nodded his approval as if he'd followed the weave of Errol's thoughts. "Good question. If our would-be assassin had poisoned the wine, Luis and I would have had to make the run to Berea instead of you."

Errol's confusion must have showed on his face.

Martin smiled. "After the first sacrament, Luis and I didn't drink the wine. If the poison had been in there, you would have been in worse shape than we. Much worse."

An image of himself curled on the cabin floor clutching his stomach came to him, along with innumerable sips of wine as Martin repeated the rite again and again for his benefit.

"But Luis and I each ate a complete wafer of bread. You had the smallest crumb each time."

Errol nodded at Martin's logic, then frowned. "Who would go to the trouble to poison you, Pater?"

The priest grew thoughtful but didn't answer. When Errol sought an answer from Luis, the man turned away, shouldering his crate of stones and eyeing the trail to Berea.

Martin levered himself off the boulder and stepped onto the path. "I think it best we continue our journey. It will take a small miracle to get us to Berea before nightfall. Oren may have news."

Dusk turned the sky crimson as they crested the last ridge and began the descent into the village. Thatched, whitewashed houses covered the rolling hills like scattered sheep, guarding the hedges that lined the fields. Larger dwellings lined the north-south lane that passed through the hamlet and gathered around the brownstone church that lay on the outskirts.

As they crossed the field and set their feet on the road, Martin set one hand on Errol's shoulder, giving him a gentle squeeze as he imparted directions. "Luis and I need to speak with Pater Oren. Why don't you go to the inn and get us rooms for the night. Tell the innkeeper I'll be along presently to pay for it." His voice dropped until he almost whispered. "And keep an ear out. I don't know who tried to poison us, or where they might be now, but you will be able to hear much that Luis and I would not." He gave a chuckle. "You'd be amazed how fast a priest's arrival stills the more interesting conversations in a tavern."

Errol set his feet toward the inn, leaving Martin and Luis to continue on toward the church. He stopped some few paces short of the Sheep's Crook, eyeing the dark interior. Cilla's inn boasted a larger common room, but the owner of Berea's establishment took enough pride in his inn to cover it with a slate roof. The dark canopy stood in stark contrast to the wheat-colored thatch covering the few houses that bordered it.

A din of voices spilled out of the open doorway of the tavern, carried on the same breeze that held smells of mutton, ale, smoke, and people. Errol stepped onto the boards of the porch and entered, searching the crowd for unfamiliar faces, merchants or travelers who might carry word of events at Erinon.

Then he saw them. Two men at the bar, dressed in the fashion of traders, spoke to each other in quiet tones and held about themselves a space the locals respected. Errol spotted an open table next to the pair and sidled over to it, ignoring the sniffs of protest and the way the villagers drew back from him as he passed.

He helped himself to the chair nearest the fire, facing the men. Soon or late Braen, the portly keeper, would notice him. But the man knew him too well. Errol rubbed a spot on his backside in memory of the last time he'd been in this tavern, and Braen, a burly Soede far removed from home, had made plain what he thought of customers who drank more ale than they paid for.

Errol leaned to one side, fished his precious half crown out of his pocket, and placed it on the table in front of him.

Braen squeezed through the narrow opening that separated the bar from the rest of the common room and lumbered toward him, his eyebrows—so blond they nearly disappeared against his ruddy skin—pulled together. Errol covered his coin with one hand.

Braen reached across the table to grab Errol by the arm. "No ale for you."

For a moment, Errol thought he would be hurtled out of an inn for the second time in as many days. Quickly, he showed the innkeeper his half crown. "I can pay this time."

Far from being mollified, the sight of the coin seemed to make Braen angrier. "Have you taken to thieving, boy?" He gave Errol a shake that rattled his teeth and lifted him from his seat.

Errol was halfway to the door, his feet skimming the ground and his free arm flailing, before he managed to make himself heard over Braen's growls. "It's mine. I got it for delivering a message to Pater Martin. He and Luis are over at the church talking to Pater Oren."

The innkeeper stopped but didn't let go of his arm. "Boy, if I decide to go over to the rectory and your story isn't true, you'll regret it."

Errol yanked his arm. It didn't come free. Braen's hand was a flesh-covered vise. "It's true. Have you ever known me to steal? What village would ever let me stay if they thought I was a thief?"

The big man's brows unknotted until they'd almost resumed their normal position. He let go of Errol's arm and wiped his hand on the smock tied around his ample waist. "You still owe me for two tankards you filched the last time you were here."

Errol nodded, happy to feel his full weight on his feet again. His arm throbbed. "I'll pay for them." He met Braen's eyes. "Can I have a drink now?" He looked with longing at the foamy tankards that offered comfort to the inn's other customers.

Braen signaled his daughter, Anya, who stood behind the bar. Then, without a word, he left with Errol's coin clutched in one fist, as if he doubted its authenticity. The sight of the tankard made Errol's mouth water, and he grabbed it from Anya's hands before she could place it on the table. She smiled, her blue eyes gleaming beneath flaxen hair. She resembled her father the way a beautiful sculpture resembled the slab of marble from which it would be carved. "How are things in Callowford?" she asked with a lift of pale, delicate eyebrows.

Errol shrugged. Since he made a habit, and a meager living, of running plants to the herbwomen of the region, he doubled as a source of news to both villages. "A messenger from Erinon came through yesterday, looking for Martin."

Anya's eyes widened a fraction at the mention of the seat of the kingdom. "Erinon? Really? What do they want with our hermit?"

"I don't know, but their man was willing to pay me a crown to deliver his message." He looked into the welcoming foam of his ale. For a brief moment he thought of Martin and Luis, who celebrated the sacrament over and over again to help him through the previous evening. A flash of guilt fired through him. He didn't really need the ale in front of him, not yet anyway.

But he wanted it.

An image of Martin and Luis, gray and unconscious on the trail, blossomed in front of him. Unbidden, older memories came to him. With a savage thrust, he pushed them away and raised his tankard for a long pull. When he lowered it after a long moment, half its contents were gone. "I think you can go ahead and bring me another, Anya."

A cloud passed over her eyes, and she grew still. "Going to make fast work of yourself tonight?"

Errol heard the familiar accusation in her voice and chose to ignore it, as usual. He took another pull, lifted his shoulders, let them fall. "It was a rough trip from Martin's cabin. Thirsty work."

She turned her back on him and moved off to answer the call of a pair of sheepherders on the far side of the room.

Errol gave his attention—mellow now that the ale had begun

to work its intended magic—to the two merchants sitting at the bar. They both wore the finery of their houses, long waistcoats over thick breeches, but while one man could have been from anywhere along the Sprata range, the other had the dark skin and hair of a Basqu.

Curiosity wormed its way through Errol's ale-muddled thoughts, and his ears perked. He had seen someone from that far southern region only a few times in his life. What would a merchant from the arid plains want in Berea?

"I'm telling you," the Basqu said, "something's not right in Erinon. The messengers coming from the citadel are thick as the swallows coming to Basquon's shores in winter." He spoke with the clipped speech common to his province. His face, dark even after the months of winter, pinched around his words.

The other man snorted, his jowls shaking with the effort. "The church is always in a lather about something. Why should this time be any different?"

The Basqu leaned in, lowered his voice. Errol strained to hear. "They say someone's been poisoning readers. They may not have enough come the succession to choose the new king."

The other man rolled his eyes. "By heaven's dome! They? Who is 'they'?"

The Basqu refused to be put off. "Men from my village who've overheard the church's messengers talking where they think no one can hear."

The other man waved one hand in dismissal. "You know how villagers are, Paolo. They grab a morsel and make it a meal to help themselves feel important. Who can tell what they really heard? All these stories of strange things are just fancies. Tomorrow they'll be talking about something else."

"I've seen things myself," the Basqu said. "Things that look like men but act like beasts hide in the swamps near Madera and the neighboring townsfolk too afraid to go near the place."

"People are always fearful—especially villagers. They rarely see past the ends of their noses."

The merchant from Basquon flushed and ground his teeth. "That's not all. Spring looks fine here, but down south the plants have a yellowish cast to them, blighted, and the winds across the Forbidden Strait bring a foul smell."

For the first time the other merchant looked alarmed. His eyes widened and his face paled, but he quickly schooled his features. "Yellow? It's probably just a trick of the light. Everything looks strange under a cloud of dust."

The first speaker shook his head. "It's not just Basquon, you know. Two weeks gone I ran into Jarl Pencivik."

"The ice merchant from Soeden?"

The first man nodded. "The very same. I bumped into him two weeks ago at Longhollow. He says spring is coming late up north."

The features of the second merchant relaxed at this, though Errol failed to see why. He took another long pull from the first tankard, set it down after it emptied, and started on the next one. The merchants' voices faded into the background, swallowed by ale-induced lassitude.

⚜

Hands on his shoulders, gentle but firm, pulled him up from the table and back into his chair.

Martin's voice came from his left. "Let's go, boy."

Errol looked around. Customers still sat at most of the tables in the inn. He blinked in confusion. When did he ever leave a tavern before it closed? A tankard still sat in front of him. Tilting it, he noticed it still held ale. It wasn't like him to be wasteful. He hoisted it, opened his mouth in preparation—and watched as those hands left his shoulders to cover his tankard, forcing it back to the table.

Luis's face came into view. "I think I'd prefer my guide to Callowford be functional in the morning."

Errol blew his lips like a horse. "Guide? You don't need a guide. Just follow the road."

Luis's face clouded, but he didn't say anything more.

Martin pulled the tankard from his hands and moved it beyond his grasp at the far edge of the table. "Berea's priest has sent word for the nuntius to await our arrival tomorrow morning and has given the three of us lodging for the night. Come, Errol, you can sleep better in a bed than on the floor of a tavern."

Martin hauled him bodily out of the chair and guided him into the night.

5

THE ROAD FROM BEREA

ERROL WOKE the next morning, his face pressed against the unfamiliar softness of bedding and his legs and feet warmed by a thick wool blanket. Martin had been right. He rose, pushing aside the unaccustomed covering. A draft raised gooseflesh on his skin, and he looked with longing back at the blanket, gave brief consideration to begging Berea's priest for it. With a sigh, he dismissed the thought. The people of Berea and Callowford knew him too well, even Pater Oren de Voral. Possessions given to him were bartered for ale sooner rather than later, and people had long ago given up on trying to change him.

Errol opened the door of the acolyte's cell they'd let him use and stepped out into the hallway. He made his way past the sanctuary, with its high-ceilinged austerity, toward the rectory. The smell of food—eggs, salted pork, and tea—drifted to him from ahead. His stomach growled. Maybe, just maybe, his unexpected good fortune would last and he would be able to capitalize on Martin's company to finagle a free meal to go with last night's lodging. Being in the company of the priest had its benefits.

He walked into the kitchen, where the cook—he didn't know her name—and her assistant, dished up steaming platters of food.

She eyed him up and down and then smiled, her ancient blue eyes twinkling. "You look as if you've a few meals to make up for." She held out a platter of eggs to him. "You must be Errol. Pater Martin and Pater Oren are in the dining room with Luis. Take this in and tell them the ham will be coming soon."

She pointed to a heavy wooden door at the far end of the kitchen. Errol held the platter in front of him, breathed through his nose, and floated on the savory smell of scrambled eggs. He kept his mouth closed, but it watered every step of the way. He backed his way through the door and into a simple dining room with a large maple trestle table surrounded by eight chairs. Only three of them were filled.

Martin sat at the head of the table with Luis on his left and Oren on his right. Errol thought it odd Berea's priest would defer to Martin but didn't comment. The strangeness of the place and the fact that he might not be allowed to stay for breakfast served to stitch his mouth closed. He put the platter of eggs on the table within easy reach of all three men and stepped back, waiting.

Martin motioned him to the chair next to Luis. "Tell me, Oren, why does Mara still put up with you? She's the finest cook in the foothills. And don't tell me it's because you pay her so well. She could walk out your door, ask for twice the pay, and get it before lunch."

Oren de Voral laughed, his mouth stretching beneath his red nose. His thin old man's shoulders moved up and down, and the wisps of his remaining hair waved with his mirth. "To tell you the truth, Martin, I don't know. I've asked her that same question any number of times, and every time I do, she just tilts her head and looks at me with those eyes the color of belle flowers and says she wants to stay here."

Luis dropped his gaze to his plate, a ghost of a smile playing on his lips. He scooped eggs on Errol's plate and passed the platter. "Eat well, Errol," he murmured. "The surprises of the day will be easier to face on a full stomach."

It was lightly said, but something in Luis's tone set Errol on his guard. Surprises? He didn't want any more surprises. Deas should have used them all up by now. He shoveled eggs into his mouth as though he could keep the unexpected at bay with food.

He looked up to find the priest of Berea staring at him.

Pater Oren started and sought Luis's gaze. He cleared his throat. "Tremus, are you sure that you wish to do this thing?" Oren asked, his attention darting back to Errol. "After all, there are certain, ah, hazards to taking postulates that are, um, more mature than usual."

Errol kept his eyes on his food, but his ears tingled. *Tremus?* Why did Oren call Luis Tremus?

"Pater Oren, please call me Luis. It is my name after all. I haven't been tremus for five years."

Oren nodded and bobbed his head as if he'd been rebuked. Errol frowned. The men spoke in arcs, hinting, relying on the other men's familiarity for understanding. And it was obvious that the other men at the table understood. Errol sat, fidgeting and trying to puzzle out the conversation's meaning.

Martin grabbed his cup, downing his tea in a gulp. "Luis is right, Oren. The conclave has probably long since named a new tremus. As for his decision—" Martin snorted—"I wish you luck in swaying him. I did everything but order him against this course." He waved one hand toward the window. "You might as well preach to the stones."

Luis stiffened. "This matter is for the conclave. I may no longer be tremus, but I am still a reader. This decision is under my jurisdiction." He slumped back in his chair as if defeated. "Besides, you know I don't have any choice, Oren. There are special considerations here, and if what you tell us of the news coming from Erinon is true, we'll need every resource we can muster."

The door behind Martin opened, and Mara bustled through, laid a platter of ham on the table, and smiled at Pater Oren before she left. The men at the table fell silent. Errol cleared his throat, afraid to speak but wanting to find some way to keep the men talking. He suspected the conversation involved him, but exactly how eluded him.

He coughed and ducked his head when all three men turned to look at him with various expressions. Oren wore a look of surprise and Martin that of mild expectation. Luis looked like a man braced for bad news who attempted to hide it. His expression so surprised Errol that he nearly forgot what he was going to say. He stared, his gaze locked with Luis's.

Martin smiled. "Yes, Errol? Was there something you wanted to say?"

Errol flushed as he turned to Martin, felt his ears grow warm and pink. "In the tavern last night I overheard two merchants talking, and one of them said that someone was killing the readers in Erinon." He stopped, waiting for a reaction, but the faces of all three men grew blank, held to strict impassivity from within.

Errol, following instinct or impulse, looked away from Martin toward Luis. "What's a reader?"

Luis opened his mouth to speak, then closed it as Martin and Oren voiced inarticulate sounds of protest at the same time.

"I concede your right in this, Tremus," Oren said. "But take care. Once done, it cannot be undone."

Luis's face clouded at the interruption, and his dark eyebrows gathered like a storm. He faced Errol once more, smoothing his features before beginning again.

"Errol, the church has many parts, some more . . . visible than others. The structure of the church mirrors our theology. As Deas is the head, so the *clergy*—the archbenefice, benefices, and priests—are head of the church. But there is another part of the church, much smaller, called the *conclave* that consists of a group of men referred to as readers—though that description belies the complexity of their task. The purpose of the conclave is to provide information and guidance to the church and the king." Luis drank and then inhaled like a man preparing to dive into a pool. "The head of the conclave is titled primus. Only the archbenefice and the king outrank him."

Errol cut his gaze to Martin and Oren. They sat in their chairs like statues of flesh, lifelike, yet not moving, bound by Luis's will and apparent authority, but resisting it in silence.

Before Luis could continue, Cruk entered—wearing a sword, of all things—and the tension in the room broke to exhales of relief and disappointment. For an insane moment Errol thought the man would cross the room, grab him by the back of his shirt, and throw him into the street.

He looked back to Luis, but Martin's servant, or the man Errol used to think of as his servant, no longer seemed inclined to speak. The moment of Luis's revelation had passed. Errol wavered between disappointment and relief. He couldn't escape the feeling Luis wanted something from him, something important. Instinctively, he resisted.

Martin levered his bulk away from the table, grabbing a last slice of ham in the process. "We thank you for your hospitality, Pater Oren," he said in formal tones with a bow. Then he smiled. "You still set the best table in the Sprata foothills."

Oren rose, bending from the waist in acceptance of the compliment, and bade them farewell. Martin trailed Cruk out of the room, followed by Errol, who preceded Luis. As he passed Pater Oren, he caught a glimpse of the old priest reaching out to grab Luis by one arm.

On the street in front of the church, four horses stood saddled, snorting plumes of mist into the cool morning air and stomping their forefeet on the earth. Cruk lifted his leg, slipped his foot into the stirrup of a large bay gelding with practiced ease, and swung himself into the saddle. Errol watched as Martin sketched a rough imitation of Cruk. The horse in front of Errol, a piebald that looked ready for pasture, tossed its head in expectation.

He backed away, his hands raised. "I don't think so."

Cruk grunted, towering over him. "Mount up, boy. You're coming with us, and we don't have time to walk the horses so you can keep up."

Errol craned his neck to meet his gaze. "Why do I have to go with you?"

"That was my decision." Luis stepped from the church and mounted, his skill nearly matching Cruk's. "There are still things we need to discuss." At a look from Martin he paused, then added, "At the proper time."

Errol wished he could find some way to leave Martin and the rest of the company to their journey. The inn would be opening in a couple of hours, and he still had plenty of coin. It would be better if he stayed behind. The look on Cruk's face, however, convinced him they meant him to ride back to Callowford in their company, lack of riding experience or not. "I don't know how to ride."

Cruk's eyes narrowed. "You'll have to learn on the way. I'll teach you. First lesson, don't ever annoy your teacher. Second lesson, put your foot in the stirrup and mount up. Horses think in groups—most of them, anyway. Relax and let your horse follow ours."

Errol circled around the part of his horse with the teeth, trying to remember how Cruk had mounted. Holding the reins and gripping the saddle with his right hand, he placed his foot in the stirrup and lifted himself. Halfway up his foot slipped out to leave him sprawled across the horse's back, his head next to the neck and his feet wiggling in the air next to the hindquarters. The horse shied, sidestepped to the right, and snorted.

Cruk rode forward, leaned over, and grabbed the horse by the bridle. He spoke in soothing tones. "Easy, Horace. The boy will stop his thrashing in a moment."

Martin's and Luis's laughter didn't help matters.

Once Errol righted himself into some semblance of horsemanship, they set off at an easy canter. That is, the other horses set off at a canter, while Errol's horse settled into a teeth-shattering trot. After a hundred paces he could feel Horace's backbone through the saddle. The other riders pulled ahead without a backward glance, leaving him to his four-footed torture.

Half a mile out from Berea, they rounded a sharp turn in the dirt track that served as the road to Callowford. Errol reined in, ignored Horace's snort of protest, and slipped from the saddle to rub his backside. Cruk, Martin, and Luis disappeared down the long tunnel of foliage. Stillness fell as the sound of hooves diminished and then faded altogether.

Errol clutched the reins in one hand and walked bowlegged around to the horse's head. "Do you think you could stop trotting," Errol pleaded, "just for a while?" He might have imagined it, but he thought he saw Horace smile.

He sighed. "I didn't think so." Errol looked at the saddle, felt a throb in his backside. "Come on." He tugged the reins. "We'll walk for a bit."

They trudged along for a couple minutes. Errol stopped every few seconds to massage the ache out of his inner thighs. He winced. The pain, unsatisfied with his posterior, seemed intent on spreading down his legs and up his back. He fished the change out of his pocket and counted: three silver crowns and four pennies. The way he felt right then, regardless of any further damage Horace inflicted, his money wouldn't buy more than two days' worth of ale at Cilla's inn.

"Stupid churchman," he said. The horse ignored him. "I should have let him take his own message across the Sprata and stuck to gathering herbs for Adele."

"Quite," a voice behind him agreed.

Errol whirled. Astride a dappled stallion, a man regarded him, his face wreathed with a cruel smile. His hands rested on the front of his saddle with apparent unconcern. He was dressed in black.

Errol's first thought was that the assassin who'd tracked him across the Cripples had found him again, but one look at the man's face dispelled the notion. That man had had white hair and light blue eyes, while the man before him possessed hair and eyes so dark they were almost black. The eyes crinkled in a friendly smile as he drew his bow and nocked an arrow.

Maybe it was the fact the man had spoken to him. Perhaps, he was just tired of not understanding anything that happened. Possibly, it was because he was horse-sore and didn't want to run yet, but he spoke to the killer in front of him.

"Why?"

Another smile graced the face that held those dark, dark eyes. The bow and its arrow, fitted and ready, rested against the neck of the horse. "Because I'm being paid."

Errol's mouth went dry, and he worked his tongue to find the moisture to speak. "What happened to the other one?" He bent down to grab a rock that lay at his feet, the ghost of a plan forming in his mind.

A cloud passed over the man's features, and the smile slipped, replaced by something cold. Then the smile came back. "You saw him?" He nodded. "An irritation. I'm not surprised Merodach let you escape. But no matter." The bow came up, and two fingers and a thumb pulled the string with practiced ease. "The day wears on. I have a lot to do."

The arrow slid back, ready to fire. Errol jumped behind Horace, using the gelding as a shield.

"I don't kill horses unless I have to." A note of compassion came into the assassin's voice as he said this. His mount stepped forward, closing the distance in response to some unseen command from its rider.

Errol darted a glance back up the trail in the hope Cruk would come thundering around the far bend in the road, like a hero from the stories. But no one appeared. Why would they? Heroes appeared for important people, not drunks. "Easy, Horace." He needed to be quick. Errol gathered his courage, feinted left as if to run into the forest, then darted a step from Horace's protection before jumping back.

The arrow whistled just past his ear, and his hair lifted at its passage. Errol sprang toward the protection of the trees on the right and flung his rock at the assassin's horse. From the corner of his eye he saw the stone strike the stallion on the chest. The horse barely moved. A brief whistle, and then a line of fire and agony traced a path across his back.

All pain from his ride forgotten, Errol threw himself into the trees, darted in and among the boles trying to put as many barriers between him and the assassin's arrows as possible. The man wouldn't be able to catch him if he brought his mount in—the undergrowth would slow him. How good would he be on foot?

The forests around Berea and Callowford were Errol's home, every gully and path known to him. Before the coming of the nuntius, before he'd met the first man in black, he would have wagered every tankard of ale he would ever drink that none could catch him on foot. Now he felt sure the man would overtake him, and then smile pleasantly as he put an arrow through Errol's eye.

Not a sound came to his ears over the noise of his flight, and he fought the urge to look back. He didn't want death to take him unaware and for some odd reason he couldn't identify, he didn't want to die with an arrow through his head. Better the heart. He held no illusion that he possessed features anyone would call comely, but the thought of his face marred by an arrow bothered him. Would he have time to shield his head with his arms, force the assassin to take him through the chest?

With a mental thrust, he pushed the thought away and concentrated on escape. His legs began to tire. He slowed, ducked behind the bole of a giant oak as big across as he was tall. He edged forward to peek out from behind the tree, unsure whether he wanted to see his pursuer or not. If he didn't see him, it might mean the man lay in wait for him, arrow ready to fire. Of course, it might also mean the assassin had given up. If he did see him, given the thick growth of the forest, it would mean he could die any second.

There! Fifty paces away a shadow moved, and sunlight gleamed where it hadn't before. Errol turned and ran, keeping the tree between him and his pursuer. He felt the sticky wetness of sweat and blood running down his back. Spots swam in his vision, pinpoints of darkness that painted the forest. Worry gnawed at him. What if he passed out from blood loss? Worse, what if the assassin's arrow carried poison? The road. He needed to get back to the road. Soon or late Martin or Luis would notice his absence and send Cruk back to check on him.

He hoped.

He circled back in an arc, fought the clumsiness and fatigue of his legs. Deadfalls he could have leapt minutes ago, he now clambered over. Behind him, he saw a shadow in pursuit, a shadow that glided through the trees without effort and flowed over every obstacle, bow clenched in one hand.

Errol cut more sharply to his right. It was the road or death—though even with the road it would probably still be death. He made for the dusty track in a straight line, ignoring the branches that whipped across his face in the hope Cruk would be there.

He burst from the forest, felt the ruts of wagon tracks through his thin soles. The lane was empty. With a growl, he forced his protesting legs to move again, mustered a trot down the road toward Callowford. He'd never make it. His village was still a league and a half distant.

He would be dead in minutes.

A bone-deep weariness settled into him, and his legs refused to rise any more. His feet scuffed the dirt track of the road for a few more steps before they stopped altogether. He shuffled around to face his killer, feeling as though he'd spent the entire morning in the ale barrel. The man in black stepped lightly from the forest, no more than a score of paces away.

Too tired to move, Errol sat down on the road and waited.

Again the assassin fit an arrow to his bow, wore his victor's smile. "Not a bad chase, boy. It will be interesting to see if I can take the rest before they reach the village." In one smooth motion, he drew the bowstring to his cheek.

Errol tensed.

Hooves.

He heard hooves. A horse rounded the bend behind the assassin. Cruk.

6

Divisions in the Watch

The assassin took one quick glance behind at the horse bearing down on him, cursed, and fired. Errol threw himself flat. He felt, rather than heard, the arrow pass just over him. He rolled, flung himself toward the ditch, toward the trees, anywhere that would buy him time. He came to his feet next to a sapling too thin to offer any protection and stared.

He'd expected any number of things: that Cruk might have left thinking Errol not worth the risk, that the assassin would fire at him again, or that Cruk and the man in black would be locked in a struggle to the death. What he had not expected was that the assassin would be walking toward Cruk, now dismounted, smiling as if he'd found his long-lost brother.

Cruk didn't bother to return the smile. If anything he looked put out, as if he were going to have to clear Cilla's inn of every drunkard for fifty leagues around.

The assassin pulled his sword, the weapon sliding from the scabbard with a long, metallic hiss. "So, Captain, this is where you've been hiding the past five years?" He looked around at the road, the trees, as though he smelled something foul. "Here?"

Cruk's sword appeared in his hand as if by magic, and he shrugged. "It suits me." He pointed the tip at the assassin. It looked more like a gesture than a threat and he stood rooted to his spot next to his horse. "Is this what the watch has come to, Dirk? Are we nothing more than assassins now?"

The smile slipped a fraction. Dirk stopped. "You don't know, do you." He shrugged. "Well, it is a remote place you've chosen to hide in." He waved his sword in invitation. "Come, I must finish you and the boy before I take care of the priest and the reader."

Cruk advanced, weapon drawn. When he stood a dozen paces away, the man in black dropped his sword, picked up the discarded bow and fired so fast, Errol thought he'd imagined it.

The arrow hissed through the narrow space between the two men. Cruk dodged right.

His reflexes saved him. Instead of taking him in the throat, the arrow lodged in his shoulder with a wet crunch of mail and meat. Cruk cursed and closed the distance, but the assassin held his sword at the ready.

Cruk growled. "You never could win a fight without tricks."

The assassin smiled, showing his teeth. "Fighting nice is for people who want to die."

They circled each other, the arrow still sticking from Cruk's shoulder. Dirk feinted, laughed as Cruk moved to parry, and tapped the arrow that still stuck from Cruk's shoulder.

"Hurts?"

Cruk grimaced. With a look of hatred he took two steps back and yanked the arrow free. A steady stream of blood followed, tracking down his left shoulder.

Dirk smirked and retreated as Cruk tried to close again. "I think I'll just wait for blood loss to weaken you and then kill you at my leisure. Although, it doesn't look as if the last five years have made you any quicker."

"Come and see, Lieutenant Puppy."

The man in black snarled.

Now Cruk wore a grimace that Errol recognized as the closest thing to a smile he possessed. "I see you remember your training name. You were so happy to join the watch . . . just . . . like . . . a . . . little . . . puppy."

With a scream, Dirk closed, aimed a slash at Cruk's head that whined in the air. Cruk parried and circled to his right. After that, the blows came too fast for Errol to follow. He kept track of the fight by the slashes and cuts that blossomed on the two men. Cruk had a gash across his right forearm. The assassin had shallow cuts along his cheeks.

Dirk lunged, thrusting for the chest. Cruk circled the blade with his own, then whipped his wrist so quickly that the steel of his sword flexed and put another, deeper, slash across the assassin's face.

"I'm afraid you won't be so pretty anymore, puppy."

The assassin cursed and pressed, putting everything into his attack. Whether that was the moment Cruk had been waiting for or not, Errol didn't know. But in the next instant, Cruk pulled his opponent close with his free hand and head-butted him on the nose. When Dirk stumbled backward, Cruk took him through the throat with his sword.

Blood fountained from the wound as the assassin slid backward and collapsed to the ground.

"You never could keep your pride out of a fight, Dirk." Cruk returned to his horse and beckoned toward Errol. "Come here, boy."

Errol walked toward Cruk as if the man had become a stranger, approached with his head down. The drawn sword made him nervous. He'd never seen Cruk use one before, but it was obvious that he held a more-than-passing acquaintance with the weapon.

As Errol came within arm's reach, Cruk tossed the assassin's bow and quiver to him. "Can you shoot?"

He nodded. "I know how it's done, but I'm not a very good shot," he confessed.

Cruk sighed, squeezed his eyes closed. "Don't you do anything well besides drink?"

Almost, he smiled at Cruk's words. They sounded familiar—like the man who threw him out of the inn, rather than the one who killed trained assassins. "I never really needed to learn. Nobody's ever tried to kill me before. Now it's happened twice in two days."

Cruk nodded. "I suppose that's true enough. Well, it's done now. Your would-be assassin is dead."

"What about Merodach?"

Cruk's head snapped up. "Where did you hear that name?"

Errol crept back, away from the look of violence in the other man's eyes. He pointed to the dead assassin lying in the road. "It's what he called the man who came after me in the gorge."

Wiping his face with one hand, Cruk sighed. "Two of them. They sent two of them, and both from the watch. What in blazes has happened at Erinon?"

He turned to Errol. "Why did you fall behind?"

Errol found something on the ground to look at as he answered. "I couldn't get Horace into a run, and that trot of his hurt my backside so much I got off and decided to walk for a while."

Cruk rolled his eyes. "Boy, you could've gotten both of us killed. Did you try digging your heels into his flanks?"

"No." At the look of disgust from Cruk, he flushed. "I told you I'd never ridden before. I don't know how to make a horse run."

"It's called a canter or a gallop. No matter. We've got to get out of here. It's not safe. Nowhere is safe, but some places are better than others." He nodded back toward Berea. "Horace is back there, just around the bend. Get him and bring him back here." He grimaced. "And don't walk him, ride him." He pressed his right hand against the wound in his shoulder. "By Deas, Eleison, and Aurae, all three, I hate it when people put holes in me."

Errol found Horace as Cruk said, his reins thrown around a sapling just off the road. The horse regarded him without interest as he approached and then turned to rip another mouthful of grass from the base of the tree. The horse followed without protest or interest when he tugged the reins. Thankfully, the gelding didn't move when Errol swung himself into the saddle, but Errol's backside gave a twinge, and he clenched against the ache. Turning Horace's head toward Cruk, Errol dug his heels into the horse's flanks.

Horace responded with a canter that lasted all of five strides before slipping back into that same painful trot.

"You just don't have a whole lot of ambition, do you?"

The horse twitched one ear and slowed to a walk.

Errol dug his heels into the horse's flanks again. "C'mon, Horace."

The horse rewarded his effort with a lazy canter that lasted four more strides before he subsided back into a trot and then to a walk. By then, they'd rejoined Cruk.

Cruk sat on a log next to the road, his shirt off to reveal a vest of lightweight mail underneath. Errol watched as he struggled to remove it without moving his right arm. After a moment, he gave up.

"Come here, boy."

Errol approached, stood in silent expectation while Cruk stared at him as if wondering whether he could be of use or not.

"I need you to look at my shoulder."

"Why?"

"Because I don't know if Dirk put anything on his arrows."

The stinging sensation in his back reminded him of his own encounter with the assassin's bow. He reached behind with one hand, brushed his fingers across the slash Dirk had given him. The wound felt clean and the bleeding seemed to have stopped. The flesh around it felt warm, as he would expect, but not hot.

He looked at Cruk. "He didn't."

"How do you know that?"

Errol shrugged. "One of his arrows grazed me across the lower back."

Cruk's eyes widened a fraction. "Show me."

Errol lifted his shirt, felt Cruk probe the wound with his thick fingers, and winced.

He heard a low whistle. "That's quite a collection of scars back there. You don't fight, boy. How did you come by them all?"

Cruk's scrutiny made him uncomfortable, and he stepped away, letting his shirt fall back into place. He didn't answer. Everyone in the village knew what Antil did to him. How many times had he passed out from drink to wake in the stocks with Antil behind him, holding his whipping rod? Cruk's brows drew together, and his face clouded.

The big man shrugged his broad shoulders and turned away, toward his horse, and remounted. "At any rate, you're right. The arrows don't appear to have been poisoned." He spat in the direction of the assassin's body. "Not that I would've put it past Dirk to have forgotten that restriction as well."

He eyed Errol, his face grim. "Something's going on in Erinon, boy. Members of the watch are not assassins. At least, they didn't used to be."

Errol pointed to the middle of the road at the assassin's body, the blood from his throat pooling in a thickening puddle on the hard-packed earth. "Shouldn't we hide him?"

Cruk shook his head. "Leave it. If Merodach is following us, it will give him something to think about, maybe slow him down. Besides, the puppy already cost me more effort than I wanted to use on him." He turned his horse with the barest twitch of the reins. "Come, I told Martin and Luis to make for Callowford. They'll need to know what happened here. Keep your eyes open and yell if you see anything—I mean *anything*—that doesn't look right."

⚜

They met Martin and Luis at Cilla's, nestled in a table in the back corner, past the large fireplace that formed the center of the common room. Cruk waited until they motioned the pair of them over. The big man paused, scanned the empty room. Apparently satisfied, he led the way over to the table, then took a chair and placed it so that he could watch the front entrance as well as the door to the kitchen. A loaded crossbow rested on the floor at his feet.

Errol sat, squirmed around in his seat, and tried to catch Cilla's attention, waving two fingers for a pair of tankards.

Martin's eyes lingered on Cruk's bloodstained shirt. "You need a healer." He turned to Errol. "Boy, go find Radere."

"No," Cruk said. "The boy needs the herbwoman himself, but we can send Cilla. Once we meet the nuntius, we'll need to get a room, one easily defended."

Martin's brows lowered over his brown eyes. "Why?"

"Merodach is here. He's the one who tried to kill Errol yesterday, and he may not be alone."

Luis started. "Surely you're mistaken. Merodach is a captain in the watch. They aren't assassins."

"Weren't," Cruk corrected with a grimace. "Dirk trailed us from Berea. That's how I got this new decoration in my arm. From what the boy says, he and Merodach were both trying to kill you."

Martin shook his head. "That doesn't make any sense. Why kill us when they could just leave us here, ignorant in the middle of nowhere?"

Luis steepled his fingers under his chin, his eyes thoughtful. "Impossible to say. But there could be any number of reasons. Church politics are rough enough even during normal times. What must they be like now, with a throne at stake?"

Cruk glanced at the door and then leaned forward, lowering his voice. "Have you read something, then, Tremus?"

Luis waved his hand in dismissal, but at the title or the suggestion, Errol couldn't tell. "I haven't finished the lots yet."

Cruk blushed at this.

"I'm not blaming you, Cruk. You've done your part as quickly as you could have. Durastone is difficult to find and harder to quarry. I didn't have the man power or the tools to craft the lots as quickly as I would have liked."

Martin shook his head. "We know who it is, Luis. You've

already drawn his lot twice in wood. I've sent word. He'll be coming to Green Isle with us."

Luis shook his head. "I will not trust this to wood, and a draw from a partial cast means nothing, even if it does—"

"Nonsense," Martin interrupted. "Wood or stone makes little difference. You know it as well as I do—the hand of Deas has been on the boy since the day of his birth. He's the one."

Luis rubbed his temples and sighed. "Granted, the boy appears special and Antil thinks very highly of him, but we can't be sure until every lot has been crafted."

Errol started. Antil thought highly of him? That ruled out Errol. The priest despised him.

Errol kept his eyes on the table, his mind racing. The conversation flowed away from his understanding like water parting around a boulder. For years, only one person in Callowford commanded such tones of respect: Liam. Errol contemplated life in the village without Liam and found the idea pleasant.

Martin smiled, his eyes shining. "Ah, Luis, you leave too little room for the will of Deas. If he had not wanted us to find him, he would not have sent us here."

"That was a complete cast," Luis said.

Martin opened his mouth to reply, but Cruk raised one hand a few inches from the table in warning and they sat back. A sudden flood of light from the front door lightened the room, casting a new set of shadows to go with those from the fire.

"There's a church messenger at the door," Cruk said. "It's the same one who gave the boy the message."

Errol twisted in his seat, saw the familiar hooked nose, and nodded.

"Finally," Martin said. "Maybe now we will get some answers. Bring him over, Cruk, and let's see what tidings he carries."

Cruk retrieved the man, placed a chair for him across from Martin, and resumed his scan of the room.

"How are you called, nuntius?" Martin asked.

The man before Errol, so proud two days ago, ducked his

head, unwilling to meet Martin's gaze. "My name is Seamus Quentin, Pater."

Martin nodded. "What is your rank?"

Seamus ducked his head again, but his words belied his posture. "I am a nuntius of the first cohort. Now that the messages have been delivered, I really must be back in Erinon. The church thinks highly of my services."

"I'm sure they do, Seamus." Martin's voice sounded amused. "I wouldn't ask you to delay your return needlessly. I think, perhaps, you remember Errol?" He pointed across the table.

Cilla had chosen that moment to place two tankards in front of Errol. Out of reflex he'd immediately hoisted one, but he lowered the tankard at the mention of his name, saw the look of disdain on the church messenger's face.

"Yes," Seamus said and turned back to face Martin. Sweat beaded on his upper lip. "You must understand, Pater. I would not have entrusted the messages to him had not my mission been urgent."

Martin made placating gestures with his hand. "No one is questioning your judgment, nuntius. But there was a problem. Through no fault of the boy, the messages were ruined before I could read them."

The messenger's face blanched. "Ruined? They will think I've failed."

Martin shook his head. "Nuntius, just tell me the contents of the message. You know it." Martin's voiced dipped into a soothing tone. "Simply tell it to me and your charge is complete."

The messenger looked anything but soothed. His mouth worked as though his mind couldn't decide which language he was supposed to speak. Errol passed him his spare tankard. The nuntius grabbed it, lifted it to his face, and drank deeply.

"There were two messages, Pater," he sputtered. "Yes, I can relate the church's message, but I was not permitted to see the other one."

Martin leaned back in his chair with a frown. "Who entrusted this message to you?"

Seamus squirmed. "I don't know. After I memorized the recitation of the first message, I found the second one in my pack—with instructions not to open it." The messenger's chin lifted a fraction. "It's not the place of a nuntius to question those who use our services."

"Interesting," Luis said with a smirk. "Even readers can't account for the machinations of the church."

"Leave it," Martin said, though his eyes belied his casual tone. "Seamus, I'm sure you are in a hurry to return to Erinon, and I would not delay you any longer. Please, recite the missive from the church in Erinon."

As if Martin's words unlocked a page of the messenger's memory, Seamus's eyes grew blank and he straightened in his chair.

"From our most holy church to all servants of Deas, Eleison, and unknowable Aurae within the boundaries of the kingdom. Greetings to you from the Archbenefice of Erinon, seat of the church and home of the one true king. By order of Bertrand Cannon, Archbenefice in the blessed isle, you are commanded to make all haste to Erinon to attend the Grand Judica, the purpose of which to determine the means of succession upon the death of our most beloved servant, King Rodran. The Grand Judica will convene on the first moon of the eighth month."

Seamus's eyes refocused, and he relaxed where he sat.

"That's it?" Luis asked. "There's nothing more?"

The messenger looked at Martin and bowed from the neck. "I swear by my office that I have delivered the message."

"Seamus," Martin said, "I would ask you questions, if I may. There is much in your message that needs clarification, and there are other matters that are not mentioned."

The messenger fidgeted in his seat before he nodded. "I will answer as best I can, but as you know, I have no memory of the contents of the recitation, Your Excellency."

Errol had barely followed the conversation to this point, but now he could not fathom why the nuntius would address Pater Martin with such a title.

"Very well," Martin said. "The message seems to indicate that Rodran is still alive."

Seamus looked surprised at this. "Oh yes. The king lives."

Martin frowned. "Is he sick?"

"No, Excellency." He shrugged. "At least, he wasn't sick when I left Green Isle four weeks ago."

Martin leaned forward, his eyes boring into the messenger's. "Seamus, did you know that the archbenefice has called for a Grand Judica?"

Seamus nodded. "It was rumored, though no one would confirm or deny it."

Luis put his hand on Martin's arm, leaned over, and whispered. Martin nodded. Turning to the messenger, he spoke in slow, careful tones. "Seamus, rumors have come to us from several sources that say the readers at Erinon are being killed. What do you know of this?"

The church messenger stilled, and for a moment his eyes took on the cast of someone who wished greatly to be elsewhere. "It's true, Excellency, though we are forbidden to speak of it."

"How many? Who?" Luis looked ready to jump across the table and take the information by force.

Seamus bit his lip, glanced at Luis before he answered. "Nearly a score when I left the isle." His mouth hung open for an instant longer, and then he closed it and sat still.

"Come, Seamus," Martin said. "You are a nuntius of the first order. Few are positioned to hear as much as you. Tell us the rest."

"I am a nuntius. We do not trade in rumor."

"Then, for a moment, I want you to be a man," Martin said. "We have been attacked by assassins, Seamus. I left a church at relative peace five years ago to come to this region." He grimaced. "Now things are not as we left them. Whatever you can tell me will be helpful."

The messenger hung his head. "That's just it, Pater. The rumors are so thick at Erinon that it is impossible to sort them."

"Try."

The nuntius sighed. "Very well. The king lives. The king has died and the church is hiding his death. The readers are all dead. No, only some of the readers are dead and the rest are in hiding. The barrier is weakening. The Morgols are coming from the steppes." Seamus took a breath, looked around the table and then found Martin's gaze. "It goes on and on, each rumor contradicting the one before it."

Martin leaned back. "Thank you, Seamus. Nuntius of the first order, you have delivered your message," he intoned. "You may return."

Their messenger popped out of his seat like a prisoner unexpectedly paroled. "Thank you, Excellency." Without another word, he turned and left the inn.

Cruk's gaze followed the nuntius from the room. "I don't recall messengers being so nervous."

"You are overly suspicious, my friend," Luis said. "Troubled times make for troubled people."

Errol drained his tankard. His mind swirled with all that had been revealed since being charged with the nuntius's letter packet. But a church crow was no concern of his. The cool drink slid down his throat and began the job of warming him and wiping away his concern. Soon, he felt sure, Martin and the rest of them would leave Callowford and he could go back to gathering plants for Radere and Adele in exchange for ale. Who knew? Cruk might leave as well, leaving Cilla to make all the decisions. Errol found that he enjoyed that prospect. He smiled into his tankard.

Martin turned to Cruk, his voice low and businesslike. "Cruk, can we be ready to leave for Erinon in the morning?"

The big man nodded. "I think so. The boy and I need a few moments with the herbwoman, and then I can see about getting supplies."

Martin's faced pinched at the mention of the herbwoman, but

Cruk either didn't notice or chose not to respond. "How many horses should I get?" he asked. Errol tried to ignore the way Cruk glanced in his direction.

Martin glanced at Luis, who gave a sharp, stubborn nod. "Five. I'll have to talk to Knorl. It's time for Liam to challenge for the watch."

"Will he release the boy from his apprenticeship?"

Martin shrugged. "I'll buy out his service, if I have to."

Errol's flagon jerked in his grasp. Five? Though he paid more attention to his ale than the conversation, he'd heard enough to realize that they intended on taking Liam with them.

But Liam would bring the traveling party to four. Five meant . . . they planned on Errol going as well.

He cleared his throat. "Um, five? Who all is going with you, Pater?"

Martin never answered. Luis leaned across the table. His dark brown eyes glinted under the shade of his black eyebrows. "Don't play the fool, Errol. We touched on this in Berea. You will be going with us."

"Why do I have to go? Why would you even want me to go? I can't ride. I don't know anything about fighting." He waved toward Cruk, who sat in his chair like a giant sack of grain. "Ask him. The only things I know how to do are gather herbs and drink."

Cruk grunted and grimaced his imitation of a smile. "The boy's got the right of it. He is pretty useless."

Errol nodded with satisfaction. "See?"

By way of answer, Luis rose from the table. "Wait here a moment." He looked around the empty common room. "Cruk, could you lock the door for a bit? This won't take long." Then he ascended the stairs.

Cruk moved to the door, leaving Errol momentarily alone with Martin. "What's he doing, Pater?"

If Errol hadn't known better, he would have thought the look Martin gave him held pity in it. He shivered and edged closer to the fire. The bottom of his tankard stared back at him, but Cilla was nowhere in sight.

Luis stumped back down the stairs at the same time Cruk returned to the table. The reader resumed his seat. With one hand he placed the black gloves that Errol had seen in the cabin on the table. With the other he pulled an object wrapped in black wool from his pocket.

"Put the gloves on," Luis directed. "And remember to use the strap."

After Errol had done so, the reader placed one of the large white balls from the cabin into his waiting hands. Then he placed a folded piece of parchment on the table in front of him.

Luis leaned close, catching his attention. "Do you remember in the cabin how you looked at one of these and saw writing on it?"

Errol nodded.

"It might surprise you to know that very few people can do that. It calls for an extra special gift."

Cruk snorted. "Him? You can't be serious."

Luis held the big man's gaze for a long moment before turning away. "Errol, I want you to look at the lot in your hand and tell me what's written on it."

He glanced at the three faces looking at him: Cruk, disbelieving, Martin, with that strange look that resembled pity, and Luis, quietly expectant.

Holding the lot so that it caught the light, he turned it slowly, searching, marveling again at how a person could craft something so perfect. His mind wandered, meandered paths of random memories until he forgot Luis's instructions.

Then, for the briefest instant, he thought he saw something different in the stone, a subtle alteration in the way it reflected the light. He stopped, rotated the stone the barest amount. *There. Letters.*

"There's writing here."

Cruk gave a low whistle. "By the three, I would never have believed it. What does it say, boy?"

Errol shrugged. "I don't know. I never learned how to read."

Luis pushed a piece of parchment and a charcoal stick across the table. "Take the glove off your right hand and copy the letters as best you can, one at a time."

Errol gripped the stick in his fist with one hand even as he held the stone in the other and wrote each letter in thick, clumsy strokes. It proved harder than he'd expected. Twice he got one of the letters backward and had to scratch it out and rewrite it. At last, he laid down the stick and surrendered the stone to Luis.

Cruk thrust his face over Errol's shoulder to read the heavy scrawl. "Goff," Cruk said. "It says Goff."

Errol knew him, the eccentric thatcher who roofed the houses in Callowford and Berea. He talked to himself a lot.

Luis unfolded the parchment in front of him and turned it over. The same name lay written in a neat hand.

Cruk whistled again. "Him? The boy?"

Errol caught Luis's gaze, and there was something of sadness in it.

Luis straightened in his chair and raised his hands. "In front of these two witnesses I, Luis Montari, declare that Errol Stone of the village of Callowford possesses the gift of sight. More, I adjure you, Errol Stone, to present yourself to the primus at the conclave of readers in Erinon." He lowered his hands. Errol felt a sudden chill, as if someone had uncovered him in his sleep.

Martin's sharp intake of breath drew his attention and he turned to find the priest glaring at his friend, his face white. Luis held that gaze for a heartbeat, two, before he looked away. "It cannot be undone."

Then Martin spoke, his voice low. "I'm sorry, Errol. You belong to the church now."

7

BOUND FOR ERINON

ERROL SAT on a three-legged stool in Radere's cottage. The herbwoman of Callowford lived much as her sister, although her floor was made of rough-hewn pine boards instead of packed dirt and she kept her herbs in glass jars instead of earthen containers. Radere looked like her sister, Adele, too, except her eyes were hazel instead of green. Both women possessed a calm, no-nonsense approach to their art.

His focus on the similarities and differences between the two sisters slipped, and he flinched as Radere vigorously rubbed into his wound a salve that burned and felt cool at the same time. Cruk had left moments before, bent on his mission to ensure they left the village as close to daybreak as possible. Daybreak. What had he gotten himself into? Why did people insist on starting journeys before the sun got warm? It couldn't be healthy.

When he and Cruk had made their way to the healer's cottage, he'd assumed Radere would see to him first. After all, he'd been the one to risk life and limb on a regular basis to provide her with the herbs and plants she needed for her practice. He'd even hinted as much a couple of times, but the woman had turned to Cruk as if he were the only one in the cabin and ignored Errol completely. Only after the big man's departure did she acknowledge him.

Radere got to the point without preamble. "What happened to drive you to Adele?"

"We were poisoned," Errol said. "Martin says it was in the bread. I ran to Adele's for help." He paused. "There was . . . someone in Adele's cabin . . . some . . . thing . . ."

The herbwoman nodded as if in understanding and the pinched look around her eyes relaxed. "Don't speak of it, boy, not ever."

"What was it?"

She didn't answer but slapped a different salve into the wound. This one stung briefly, and then the entire area around the wound went numb. He rolled his shoulders. Better. She stepped around him, peered first into one eye and then the other before she rattled through one of her myriad cabinets to retrieve needle, thread, and a long strip of linen.

She caught his chin in one hand. "Suppose you tell me why I'm acting the field doctor when there hasn't been a war around here since Prince Jaclin graced us with his presence." Old bitterness tinged her voice.

Errol started to shrug, thought better of it. "We were attacked on the way here from Berea. Ever since that messenger from the church showed up, I can't seem to go more than a few hours without someone trying to put an arrow in me. Cruk says they're people that used to be in something called the watch."

Radere's hands jerked in surprise, but she didn't speak. She knotted his stitches, then motioned for him to raise his arms and began wrapping the cloth around him, binding his wound. "What else?" she prompted.

"When we got back to Callowford, Pater Martin spoke to the nuntius who gave me the messages." He paused. "Do you know what a nuntius is?"

She gave a curt nod, her lips pressing together in a line. "A church messenger. They know a dozen languages and have a gift for memorization." She sniffed. "Not overly bright, most of them. The church uses them to carry sensitive messages. Their minds are—" she hummed as she searched for the word she wanted—"split. They have a very high opinion of themselves."

Errol laughed. "Yes. That sounds like him. Anyway he said the king was still alive, but the church wanted Pater Martin back for some kind of big meeting. I can't remember the name."

Radere twisted the cloth, reversed the direction of the bandage. "Judica," she said, her voice clipped and short.

The herbwoman had never cared for churchmen, an implacable resentment she never bothered to explain. He couldn't blame her. "That wasn't the strangest thing, though," he said. He savored his secret in the silence and waited for Radere to ask.

"Spit it out, boy," she commanded after a moment.

"Luis had me look at this stone ball, and . . ." He stopped at the look on Radere's face. "Are you all right?"

She grabbed him with one hand, her small, bony fingers digging into the meat of his shoulder. "You can't read, boy. I know you can't."

All anticipation of sharing his secret fled. He shook his head, spoke in tones that barely escaped his lips. "I, uh, didn't have to. When I told them I could see writing on the stone, Luis gave me a piece of parchment and had me copy the letters." He grimaced. "Writing is a lot harder than it looks."

Radere shook him, her face angry now. "Were there witnesses there, boy? There have to be at least two witnesses."

A knot of fear bloomed in his stomach, like the feeling he wouldn't be able to get to an ale barrel in time. He nodded. "Pater Martin and Cruk. Luis said I had the gift of sight."

Tears sprang to Radere's eyes. "Oh, my boy, my poor boy. You should never have looked at the stone." She shook her head. "But you didn't know. Of course not. There was no way for you to know. The church owns you now."

Errol jumped from his stool. "Owns me? I won't go! Luis said I have to present myself to somebody called the primus. But I don't have to, do I?"

Radere paled, then thumbed his lids to peer into his eyes again. She spewed choice words for Luis into the stillness. "He put a compulsion on you, boy. You'll find yourself going whether you wish to or not. Luis will take you to Erinon to train you in his craft."

Errol scrubbed away tears. "Isn't there anything I can do?"

Radere nodded, became calm and businesslike once more. "Yes. Go to Erinon and become a reader. The hand of Deas is on you. You're a good boy, Errol, and if you can ever manage to pull your head out of the ale barrel, you'll be a good man. The kingdom needs good men." She turned away, moving to her jars. "I'm going to give you some supplies you may need for your trip."

Whether she spoke to him after, he couldn't remember.

He left her hut and crept from shadow to shadow around the front of Cilla's until he reached the back and then slipped into the cellar where they kept the ale barrels. Sometime later, he passed out.

⌭

Water splashed his face, and he thrashed, convinced Cruk had thrown him into a puddle while he slept.

More water. "Wake up, boy." Strong hands lifted him, set him on his feet.

He blinked against the light that streamed through the doorway. The blur gradually resolved into the figure of Cruk.

"By the three, boy, couldn't you leave the ale barrel alone for one night?"

Errol glared, or tried to. His eyes didn't want to cooperate. Two versions of Cruk held him at arm's length, faces wrinkled with disgust. "Just charge it to the church. They own me now, don't they?" He tried to straighten. The floor seemed to ripple under his feet. "As a reader of the church, I order you to let me sleep until I'm sober enough to travel." He favored the ale barrels with a smile. "Which will be a while."

Cruk growled. "If you think I'm going to wait for Merodach to find us just because you're feeling sorry for yourself, you're in for a sad disappointment."

Errol belched and waved one hand, pretending to brush away a fly. "Just take care of him like you did Dirk."

Cruk laughed a sharp sound that cracked on Errol's ears, his lumpy face contorted into a parody of amusement. "You need to learn to pay attention, whelp, if you want to stay alive. Comparing Dirk to a captain of the watch is like comparing a puppy to a wolf. On my best day I might have been a match for Merodach, but my best days are long gone." He shoved Errol toward the door. "Now, move. We're leaving even if I have to tie you onto your horse."

Errol stumbled into the sunshine and blinked away sudden tears in the glare. He followed Cruk's shadow to the front of the inn. Horace waited for him, saddled and listless in the early morning air. His ugly head dangled from his neck. Errol rubbed one dirty sleeve across his eyes to clear his vision. Martin and Luis sat mounted on horses.

Liam waited off to one side—on a pearl-white stallion, of course. He sat his mount as though he'd been born in the saddle, which, Errol reflected, was just possible. The bundle tied to the back of his saddle confirmed Errol's earlier suspicions; the epitome of human perfection would be coming with them.

"Good morning, Errol," Liam said. He held out one arm, palm up. "Isn't it a glorious morning?"

Errol didn't feel well enough to pretend to be polite. He grunted in reply, struggled into the saddle, and moved Horace as far away from Liam as possible.

Martin frowned. "We're going to be together for quite a while, boy. Long journeys go better if everyone's polite."

Errol couldn't keep himself from gaping. "You've declared me something called a reader and you're forcing me to travel to Erinon, and you want to lecture me on manners?" He turned away.

Cruk mounted a large roan gelding leading a packhorse and clucked twice as he tapped his heels to the horse's flanks. His mount set off at a brisk walk, with Martin, Liam, and Luis following.

Horace brought up the rear.

They rode west out of the village past Radere's cottage. The herbwoman stood on the granite stoop out front and watched them approach. When Luis came into view, she called out, "Reader, a word if you're willing."

Luis pulled his horse aside, but when Errol moved to follow, Radere shook her head. "Not you, boy."

Puzzled and hurt, he rode on. What could the herbwoman have to say that she wouldn't want him to hear? When Luis caught up and passed him minutes later, Errol urged Horace into that maddening trot and sidled up to the reader. "What did Radere want?"

Luis gave him a sidelong glance before answering. "She told me to watch after you."

There must have been more than that. Radere didn't waste her time on the obvious, and it was a given Luis was interested enough in Errol to look after him. "That's not all, is it."

Luis grunted, looking troubled. "No. But if you want to know the rest of it, you'll have to circle back and ask her yourself. Not that she'll tell you. If she'd wanted you to hear, you'd have heard. Silly, superstitious woman."

That last annoyed Errol. Radere had always been kind to him. "I don't think she's silly or superstitious," he said. "She patched up Cruk and me last night, and Adele knew enough to save us from poisoning."

After that they traveled in silence until a league from Callowford a circle of vultures caught Cruk's attention. "Wait here." He returned a few minutes later, his face grim and troubled.

Errol longed for a drink.

"We have a problem," Cruk said. "Or maybe not."

At a look from Martin, he pointed. "What's left of the nuntius is in a gully a hundred paces that way. He was killed with a borale."

Martin rubbed his heavy jaw with one oversized hand. "Merodach's work."

Cruk nodded. "Or someone who wants us to think it is."

"I can cast for it," Luis said. "But it will take time."

The priest shook his head. "No. We've only just started. At this point I'd rather have distance over clear knowledge. Let's move on."

They cantered for close to an hour, then trotted for two more before slowing to a walk. Luis pulled the reins to slow his chestnut mare until their knees almost touched. "It would be best if you didn't mention Adele, Errol. There are all kinds of ignorance in the world. There are educated men in Erinon who wouldn't see the herbwomen in a favorable light, even if one did happen to save our lives." The reader waved one hand in dismissal of the topic. "Since we're going to have a lot of time on the road, I think it best if we begin your education now. I'm going to teach you how to read."

Unbidden, Errol's conversation with Radere from the night before rose in his mind. The church owned him now. Did the compulsion driving him to Erinon include forcing him to learn how to read? He wasn't sure he wanted to know the answer. If he tried to resist and found that he couldn't, what would Luis think? What would Luis do? He'd known Martin and Luis for five years, ever since they'd come to the village just after . . . He shut the thought away.

He wanted ale. He needed ale. "Have you got anything to drink?"

"Water?"

Errol wrinkled his face in disgust. "I want a drink, not a bath."

Luis gave him a look of compassion mixed with disappointment. Errol shrugged. He was used to that look. He'd seen it on any number of faces since he was fourteen. It bounced off the shell he'd built to keep people at arm's length. He'd long since passed the point where pity could rouse any guilt or anger in him. He just wanted a drink to wash away the memory.

"We brought ale." Luis gave the admission with a sigh. "I was hoping you might make it to noon before you soaked your mind. It's hard to teach a man with soggy wits."

Errol saw a bargaining point and reached for it. He really wanted a drink. "If you let me have a drink now, I promise to be an apt pupil for the rest of the day."

With a grimace and a shake of his head, Luis handed him a skin. Errol lifted it to his mouth and drank.

Cruk's voice intruded on his bliss. "By heaven, is the boy into the ale already?"

Errol lowered the skin, saw the big man red-faced and glaring at Luis.

Luis gave a shrug. "I have to teach him how to read. We struck a bargain. Ale now, reading for the rest of the day."

Cruk growled his disgust. "If we're attacked, it's going to be hard enough to fight without worrying whether the little sot there is sober enough to stay on his horse and ride to safety."

"I'm not giving him that much," Luis said.

Quickly, Errol raised the skin and took another deep pull.

Luis pulled the skin away from him in mid-drink. Errol surrendered it, but the cool amber liquid had done the trick. Memory still lurked, but the ale tamped it down enough for him to function.

"Now," Luis said, "the first thing you need to know is the alphabet."

True to his word Errol applied himself to Luis's tutelage as they rode. From time to time Martin, Cruk, or even Liam would drift back to the two of them and check on his progress. Martin gave a nod of approval each time, and Liam would praise his efforts, but Cruk usually just grunted.

For some reason Errol couldn't identify, Liam's encouragement annoyed him. He searched the young man's words to find some hidden insult but could find none. Liam's presence broke Errol's concentration, and he made a series of foolish mistakes. Seeing the other man smile irked him.

"This isn't as easy as it looks, you know."

Liam nodded in agreement, his blond hair ruffling in the breeze. "As well I know. There were times when I thought learning to read and write were the most difficult things I ever attempted."

Luis snorted. "Liam is being modest. Antil says he's never seen as quick a pupil."

Errol sighed. It had always been this way. He glanced over at the blond-haired god next to Luis, riding as though he were part of the horse. Liam excelled at everything he put his hand to. Roughly the same age as Errol, his shoulders bulked large under his shirt, while Errol's garment hung on him like a sack. Where Errol was dark, Liam was light. He could outride any horseman in Sorland province, could read and speak in three languages, and was skilled enough with a sword to make Cruk sweat. And on top of all that, every village girl or woman looked on him as though something higher than man had deigned to walk among them.

If Liam had been cocksure or arrogant, it might have been bearable. Then Errol would have been able to take comfort in the other man's overweening pride. But no. Even in temperament, Liam proved to be more than human. In spite of his perfection, he remained genuinely modest and kind. His support to Errol during his reading lessons carried the same heartfelt well-wishes that he gave to everyone.

Errol wanted to be like him so much it hurt.

Late in the day's ride, Luis decided Errol's education would progress more rapidly with more teachers. Martin and Liam agreed to work with him. Cruk refused.

"What's it like?" Errol asked Liam during his lesson.

Liam's brows lifted a fraction and he smiled. "What is that, Errol?"

"Being perfect at everything."

He shook his head. "I'm not perfect. No one is."

Errol exhaled. "You know what I mean."

"We're all the same," Liam said. "I just concentrate and try really hard at everything. Anyone can do it if they just try hard enough."

Errol stared. Did Liam really believe that?

"Now," Liam said, "recite the vowels and consonants."

He really did.

They rode west, the miles lost as Errol worked his lessons. When he stopped to take notice of his surroundings, rolling hills thick with new grass formed a rim around them on three sides. Cruk guided them to a river, the Stones he called it, and led them through the shallow water for a mile or better before he led them up onto a rocky bank next to a thick copse of fir trees.

"I think we'll stop here," he said as he slid to the ground. "If Merodach is tracking us, he'll have a hard time of it."

Luis took charge of the cooking. "Here." He handed a pot to Errol. "Fill this with water from the stream. It's going to be beans and cheese tonight."

Errol wrinkled his nose. He hated beans and doubted whether even Luis's skills would be able to make them palatable. But he fetched the water.

Cruk and Liam took charge of the horses, unsaddled them before wiping them down with a square of wool cloth. Unbidden, Liam took out a heavy brush and curried each of the mounts in turn. Horace nickered and shook his head as the brush smoothed his coat.

After dinner, Errol took the dishes to the stream, scrubbed them with sand, and rinsed them. When he returned to camp, he found Cruk waiting for him. The big man held two wooden swords. Errol found his grin unsettling.

"We still have an hour or so of light left, boy." Cruk beckoned toward a stretch of mostly flat ground next to their camp. "It's time to teach you how to defend yourself."

"Why?"

The grin faded from Cruk's face, replaced by the same look of deadly seriousness he'd worn when he fought Dirk. "Because if Merodach comes at us, I'm going to be too busy to keep you from getting skewered by the men he'll have with him." Errol caught the sword, held it with both hands toward the middle.

"It's not like you have any choice in the matter. Hold it by the pommel, boy. It's not a stick."

Errol knew Cruk well enough to know he spoke the simple truth. If he refused to fight, Cruk would just beat him until he complied. With a sigh, he gripped the sword in his right hand. It was really just a handle attached to four thin wooden laths, bound at intervals by leather strips. He held it out in front of him, as he'd seen others do, but the sensation of imbalance caused him to stumble.

Cruk's shoulders slumped. "You can't be serious. You really don't know how to hold a sword?"

"When have I ever needed to fight?" Errol shot back. "What honor or glory is anyone going to get from beating the village drunk?"

Cruk's shrug conceded the point. "Glory or not, they'll kill you if given the chance. We'll start at the beginning, then, the very beginning." He turned so that he presented his right side, sword arm forward. "Stand like this."

"Why?"

That earned him a growl in response. "If you're going to ask that every time I tell you to do something, this is going to take a lot longer. Liam didn't ask so many questions."

Errol's face heated. "I'm not Liam."

"You should probably tell him why, Cruk," Martin called.

Errol turned to see the priest seated on a fallen oak, flanked by Luis and Liam. He turned back to Cruk. "Do they have to watch? Isn't it bad enough I have to do this? Do I have to have an audience?"

Cruk smiled. "Do you think you'll get to choose how and when you're attacked?"

And then he struck. The blow came so quickly that Errol wasn't even sure he saw it coming. He had a faint impression of a blur coming toward his ribs, then a loud *clack!* sounded as Cruk's sword landed. His breath exploded from his mouth, and he dropped his sword to hold his side.

A blow landed on his head, making him see stars.

"What did you do that for?" he yelled. "I wasn't even holding my sword."

"Lesson one," Cruk said, lifting him to his feet. "Don't ever drop your sword. You'll die."

The laughter from the edge of the clearing didn't help. He didn't want to learn how to fight. He just wanted a drink. Why couldn't everyone leave him alone?

Cruk waved his weapon. "Pick up your sword."

Errol did so.

"Now, try again. Stand like this." He nodded. "That's better. Now what do you do if someone attacks you?"

"Run."

Cruk shook his head. "Yes, if you want to get cut down from behind. You parry, boy."

He must have noted Errol's confused look. "A parry is when you block your opponent's strike with your sword. Here—aim a blow at me."

Errol struck toward Cruk's midsection. He would have aimed for the neck, but the idea of deliberately trying to cut someone's head off repulsed him. Cruk waited until the last instant before he parried. The shock of contact vibrated up Errol's arm, and he dropped his sword. That earned him a quick rap on each shoulder.

"I told you, never drop your weapon, boy. Every time you let that sword out of your hand, I'm going to beat you until you pick it up." He gave Errol a grimace of a smile, smacking him in the ribs.

"Now, there are three basic parry positions. They look like this." Errol watched as Cruk's sword moved smoothly from one position to another designed to protect against attacks to the head and body.

"Now," the big man said, "you do it."

He mimicked the moves, then looked up to see Cruk rubbing his temples and shaking his head, disgust written on his face. "When you get attacked, try not to make too much noise as you get killed. You might distract me."

"It wasn't that bad," Martin said from his seat on the log. "Remember, Cruk, he's never held a sword before. Be patient."

Cruk turned toward the priest. "We don't have time to be patient. Merodach is out there. He'll kill us all without pausing for breath."

Errol remembered the cold blue eyes that stared at him as he fled across the Cripples. "Does he like killing so much, then?"

That brought Cruk up short. He straightened, lowered the point of his practice sword until it almost touched the ground. "Like? Merodach doesn't like, dislike, love, or hate anything. He does what he's ordered to do. The man is as close to stone as you can get and still breathe. He's the perfect captain of the watch." His sword rose back to the ready position. "Again, boy."

Errol raised his sword to block the blow that came slowly toward his head.

Cruk grunted. "Now the outside."

The attack came toward his sword arm. Errol parried.

"Now the inside."

He moved his sword across his body, deflecting the strike.

"That was better," Luis said.

Cruk rounded on him. "Better? If I were moving any slower I'd be stopped." He gestured at Liam with his weapon. "Come here."

Liam rose from his seat. As he approached, Cruk tossed the sword. Liam caught it deftly in one hand. "Work him through the parries until he can't lift his arm." He glanced toward Errol. "And remember, if you take it easy on him, you might as well cut his throat yourself." He turned toward Martin and Luis. "I'm going to scout around before it gets dark."

Liam stepped into Cruk's place, gave Errol an encouraging smile. "Actually, you're not doing so badly. That's just the way Cruk teaches. I hated him when he started training me. Just concentrate."

Errol waited until Cruk left the clearing, then lowered his sword with relief. "Why don't we stop for a drink?"

Pain bloomed in his right side.

"I'm sorry, Errol. Don't ever lower your weapon until your opponent is either dead or unconscious," Liam said, his dark blue eyes earnest. "Now, parry."

Errol forced his arm up to block.

Liam grinned. "Good. Now try to go faster."

An hour went by, and the sky darkened. Errol stood drenched in sweat. Liam looked like he might have gone for a walk. "How can you keep at this for so long?"

Liam shrugged his massive shoulders. "I've worked for Knorl in the smithy since I was fourteen. Lifting a sword gets easy after you've stroked a hammer for a few years. When we get back I could ask Knorl to let you help out." The smile ran from his face, and it became pensive. "You'd have to give up drinking. A smithy's dangerous enough without ale in the mix."

Errol felt Martin's gaze on him. He lifted his sword instead of answering.

Liam nodded. "Try to go faster."

By the time they finished, Errol had lost count of how often Liam uttered that refrain.

And when he woke the next morning and tried to roll over in his blanket, he groaned. Every part of his body felt as though it had been beaten with a sword. He thought back and realized most of them had. Even those places that miraculously escaped chastisement ached. He gave serious thought to running away and letting Cruk and the rest of them continue to Erinon without him. He discarded the idea when he shifted his legs. Running was out of the question. He doubted if he could even manage a crawl. If he could have moved, he would have dragged himself across the ground to where Cruk lay, grabbed those evil practice swords, and thrown them in the river. At that moment all he wanted was sleep.

A boot thumped him on his backside. "Get up, boy. We've got company."

Errol opened his eyes to chaos.

8

WINDRIDGE

BLANKETS, cooking utensils, and every other loose object, including Errol, was thrown onto the back of the nearest horse as they scrambled to get away from the telltale signs of their camp. Cruk threw water on the remains of their campfire, then kicked apart the ashes. "There's no way to keep them from knowing we were here, but it might keep them from knowing when we left."

Errol tossed away the empty skin of ale he'd filched during the night. He mounted, then bit his lips against a sob as his groin muscles screamed in protest. Horace followed Cruk, Martin, and Luis from the clearing. Errol scrubbed the sleep from his eyes as he ducked a low-hanging branch. They were nearly a mile out from camp, cutting back and forth among the pines, when a thought struck him.

"Where's Liam?"

Cruk frowned at him. "Keep your voice down, boy. Sound travels too well when the air is still." He twitched the reins, and they moved off to the left to ride through a stand of cedars. "I sent him to lay down a false trail. Luis says we need time."

Errol shook his head in confusion. Why didn't they just run? "Time? Time for what?"

Luis dismounted and pulled a knife and two blocks of wood from his pack. "Time for this. Come here, Errol. It's time to begin your real education."

Martin dismounted and held his hands over the knife and wood. The priest intoned a prayer that sounded as though he'd done it many times before. Even before he finished, Luis began whittling chunks from a block of pine he held in his hands. He turned the blank in precise increments, chips of the soft wood flying. Martin drifted away to speak with Cruk. Errol gaped as the block smoothed and its contours melted until it no longer resembled an obelisk, but a sphere.

As he worked, Luis swayed over his work, his brows knitted in concentration, his voice crooning. "A reader's work is to fashion lots, Errol. These lots represent the choices before us, in this case to turn south and make for Escadrill, or take the road north and ride for Windridge."

Errol stood transfixed as the grain seemed to flow under Luis's hands. "But how does it work?"

A smile split his face, though his eyes never wavered from his craft. "Readers must know the choices that they spin. Otherwise the result is mere random chance. Some are born with the ability to imbue the lot with some essence of what we know. Much of our craft lies in our ability to ask the right question." His hands stilled, pausing long enough to look Errol in the eye. "I want you to go to my saddle. In the left bag you'll find several pieces of rubbing cloth. Bring them here." He put the wooden sphere on his lap and started carving the next block of pine.

When Errol returned, carrying the various grits of cloth, Luis favored him with a smile. "I don't suppose you've ever been to Escadrill or Windridge?" he asked.

Errol shook his head. "I've never been anywhere except for Callowford and Berea."

Luis nodded. "That's too bad. This would go more quickly if you could assist."

A thrill coursed through him. "Me? I don't know anything about making lots. How could I help?"

Laughter answered him. "Casting lots is at once more difficult and easier than you realize. Only a reader can cast a lot, and we've already established that you have the talent."

With a flash of resentment, Errol thought of the compulsion that had been laid upon him, but Luis's knife and hands wove a spell that captivated him, and he pushed his irritation to the back of his mind.

"As for the rest of it, it's a simple matter of concentrating on each choice as you fashion the lot that matches it." The reader frowned at the wood as he turned it. "Pine's not the best. The grain is too loose. Walnut would have been better and maple best of all." He sighed. "But we don't have time, and softwoods are the quickest."

He set the second sphere in his lap, retrieved the first and then took up the roughest cloth and attacked the lot with brisk strokes. A mist of sawdust floated up to Errol's nose, and he sneezed.

"Sorry," Luis said. "That's one of the hazards of the craft, I'm afraid."

Ten minutes later, his brow damp with effort, Luis held two identical spheres to Errol for his inspection.

Errol reached out to take them, then stopped. "Shouldn't we be wearing gloves or something?"

Luis nodded in approval. "Good. That's very good, but we only have two choices here and we don't have time for such exactitude. Now, take the lots and close your eyes."

Errol did so, held one in each hand.

"Can you tell any difference between them?"

He hefted the lots, felt their weight and grain against the ridges of his skin. Unsure, he swapped hands. The difference between the two spheres resting in his palms was so slight he might have been imagining it. He changed his grip, held them with his fingertips and rolled them back and forth, searched for any variance in the grain. He opened his eyes.

"They feel identical."

Luis dipped his head as if Errol had just paid him a compliment. "Thank you. We're lucky that I've been to both of those cities often enough that I can hold a picture of them in my head as I work." He stood. "Wait here." The reader walked with purposeful strides over to his horse and pulled a plain burlap sack from one of the saddlebags. With a smile, he returned.

Luis opened the sack and extended it to him. "Put them in here, gently. We don't want them to get chipped."

Errol reached to the bottom of the bag before he released the wooden balls. After he'd withdrawn his hand, Luis took the bag and rolled it along the ground. Soft clacking sounds came from inside.

"Why are you doing that?"

Luis nodded in seeming approval. "When drawing a lot, it's important to make sure the process is as random as possible. I'm trying to guarantee that you can't determine which ball is which when you draw."

Errol recoiled in surprise. "Me? You want me to draw? I don't know anything about being a reader yet."

Soft laughter rippled across Errol's hearing. "It doesn't matter who draws them, Errol. The craft is in the wisdom to ask the correct question and our ability to concentrate with single-minded intensity on each answer as we fashion the lots.

"Martin," Luis called. "We're ready." He lifted the bag from the ground and extended it toward Errol with an air of formality as he opened it. The smell of pine floated on the air.

Martin raised his hand in supplication. "Choose, Errol Stone," he intoned. "Choose and let the will of Deas be known."

Errol's pulse quickened as he put his hand in the bag, felt the smoothed grain of Luis's handiwork brush the ridges of his skin, and pulled out a lot. He held it out for inspection, but Luis shook his head.

"You know enough of reading to recognize the difference

between a W and an E." His eyes brightened above his smile. "Tell me, Errol. Which way do we go?"

Errol turned the wood against the light just as he had done with the stone orb in Martin's cabin days ago. The process felt almost familiar to him now, but his heartbeat sounded in his ears nonetheless. And then he saw it.

"It's a W."

Luis leaned forward, cupped Errol's hand, and turned the wooden lot before he nodded in confirmation. "Place the lot back in the bag. We'll have to draw again."

Again? "Why?"

The reader rolled the bag along the ground again as he answered. "The lots are less than perfect, which introduces error into the cast, but even were they sculpted from the hardest substance available to us, durastone, we would draw again to confirm the choice." The olive skin of his face crinkled around his brown eyes as he smiled. "The conclave has striven for centuries to create the perfect lot, but it seems that skill is still beyond us." He extended the bag again. "Draw."

Errol drew and held the wood to the morning light. "It says W."

Luis nodded. "Very well. It's not what I expected, but we're going to Windridge." He turned toward the horses.

A thought struck Errol, rooting him to the patch of earth where he stood. "What if I had picked the other one?"

Luis smiled with a light of mischief in his eyes. "Every reader asks that. As a matter of fact, there are very few occasions when we don't ask that."

"Then how do you know we're supposed to go to Windridge? You said yourself it was a surprise."

Luis stepped back to him with the bag open. "Put it back in."

Errol did so and watched as Luis shook the bag, less gently than before. The clatter of wood against wood sounded again in the clearing.

The reader held the bag out to him again. "Draw and choose, Errol."

Errol repeated the process, but as his hand entered the bag a sense of pointlessness swept over him. As he pulled out one of the lots and cupped it against the light of the morning, he knew what he would find before he looked. "It's a W," he said.

Luis nodded, took the ball from him, dropped it into the bag, shook it, and commanded him once more, "Draw."

He put his hand in, grabbed a ball. At the last instant, he let go and dove for the other one. Smiling triumphantly, he held it against the light. There, in plain view was the W he had seen before. Shocked, he looked to Luis for an explanation.

"Would I always draw the same lot if I continue?" he asked.

"With wood you might draw the same lot seven out of ten times. With stone, even more often," Luis said. "I commend you. When I first took my orders as a reader I spent a night and a day with the same lots trying everything I could think of to change the outcome. For a week afterward, I wouldn't go near the conclave where the other readers worked. I was convinced they'd seduced me into some sorcery."

He took the lots and threw them into the thick underbrush. "Come. We need to be leaving. Windridge awaits."

They mounted their horses and set off to the north. Liam's absence weighed on Errol. Though the two of them were hardly friends, he didn't want anyone else to drop out of his life. That train of thought awoke a craving for ale inside him. "How is Liam going to find us?"

Cruk smirked. "He'll find us. I'm going to leave him a trail."

"Won't Merodach be able to follow it?"

The big man shook his head. "Not much chance of that. Liam knows what to look for, and he is a better tracker than he is a horseman."

Errol rolled his eyes. "Is there anything Liam doesn't do better than anyone else?" he muttered under his breath.

He hadn't spoken quietly enough. Martin gazed at him until he squirmed.

Cruk only laughed. "No, boy, there isn't. With a couple more years training, there won't be a man in the kingdom he can't best with a sword, Merodach included." He paused, pulling at his jaw muscles. "He may be close to it already. If he drew on me, it's not a sure bet I would win."

Errol digested that before he spoke. Surely, there was something Liam didn't do well. "What if they catch him?"

Cruk snorted. "Not likely. Whoever is tracking us is going to be at least a day behind by the time he gets done with them, maybe two." He twitched the reins, and they cut back to the west following the remains of an old track.

Errol pushed away a stab of jealousy. Liam's perfection grated on him. "Why don't we just ride in a straight line, then?"

"It's nice to see you can think if you want to." Cruk gave him a nod of approval. "The chances of Liam getting caught are slim, but just in case he does, I don't want to make it easy for them to find us."

"Who's them?" Errol asked. "Merodach?"

Cruk shrugged, his massive shoulders rolling underneath his tunic. "It could be Merodach. It could be bandits. At this point it doesn't matter. I'll rest a lot easier when we're safely inside Windridge."

They continued riding in switchbacks for the rest of the morning, and Errol found his mind wandering. Horace followed after the other horses without encouragement, which left Errol time to think about his ultimate destination. Luis's pronouncement that Errol possessed the talent to be a reader forced his life into an unfamiliar route—like water diverted by a change in the riverbed. Radere's admonishment still hung in his ears, but how did one learn to be a reader? Would he have to learn to carve as well as read? How did anyone learn what questions to ask? In spite of Luis's demonstration back in the clearing, Errol had nothing on which to base his expectations.

It had something to do with those stones Luis carried. The man hovered over them as though they held the power of life and death. They went wherever the reader went. The intricate carvings of animals, exquisite in their detail, had been left at the cabin without thought, while those stone balls had been carefully, almost lovingly, packed into padded crates that Luis and Martin kept tied to the back of their horses.

Errol made up his mind. Compulsion or not, when they got to Windridge, he would corner Luis and demand answers.

A little after noon, Cruk led them west toward a line of hills just visible through the infrequent gaps in the trees. An hour later their horses stepped onto the road that ran north toward Windridge. Without a word Cruk nudged his mount into a canter. Errol groaned. Sure enough, Horace slowed after half a dozen strides and lapsed into that torturous trot.

Sore and frustrated, Errol dug his heels into Horace's flanks. Holding the reins with one hand, he reached back and smacked his horse on the rump. His hand stung, but his mount responded with an unexpected burst of speed and galloped until they caught up with the others.

Cruk smirked at him before he returned to his methodical scan of the terrain ahead. "I was wondering when you'd get frustrated enough to teach that bag of bones you meant business."

Errol didn't know whether to smile at Cruk's backhanded compliment. His hand still stung. "I don't like hitting things."

The smirk slid off Cruk's face. "Fair enough, boy, but we're not in Callowford anymore. Martin, Luis, and I have been out of Erinon for five years, and the truth is we don't have a clue about what's going on there. We know people are trying to kill us. Not me. Not Martin and Luis. Us. That includes you. If you get into a scrape and hesitate because you don't want to hurt someone, you'll die."

Errol found himself both repulsed and fascinated by Cruk's businesslike attitude. "How many people have you killed?"

The big man shrugged. "About twenty years ago the nomads swept off the steppes and flooded through the Ladoga Pass in waves. They overran the garrison at Tampere as if it wasn't there and were on the doorstep of Soeden before we could sail enough men through the Noric Sea to slow them down. I joined the Reine garrison. They sailed us up the Perik River. Our job was to find a way to slow them down. We got to the battle line a day after we landed. I didn't have time to count kills."

Cruk hung his head for a moment and then shifted his gaze to the horizon. "After the war, I challenged to join the watch. I hadn't killed a man since."

Errol frowned. *Twenty years?* "Until Dirk found us."

Cruk nodded. "Until Dirk. Church politics has always been messy, boy, but it was never like this. By the three, members of the watch aren't even supposed to leave the city unless the king does, and Rodran's too old to travel. He's been too old to travel for years."

They rode north in silence after that, the mountains to their left and the forest to their right. Late that afternoon they caught up to a merchant caravan, its wagons and horses stretched along the road in a sinuous column.

Cruk looked toward Martin. "It might not be a bad idea to ride along with them, Pater, if we can spare the time."

Martin nodded. "As long as we make Windridge by nightfall. Morin may offer to guest us in the abbey. A dangerous offer, but better the enemy you can see than the one you can't."

Luis snorted a catarrhal sound that reverberated in his throat. "He hates you. What would make you think he would want you as a guest?"

Martin sighed. "Morin's always been well connected. He's bound to know more than what we've learned about what's happened at Erinon. I'm hoping he won't be able to resist the opportunity to prove it."

Luis looked unconvinced. "Just try to keep your temper in check. Your last meeting with the abbot was hardly the essence of polite discourse, don't forget. It's a sure bet he hasn't."

Though most church matters put Errol to sleep, he found his curiosity piqued in spite of himself. "What happened?"

Luis smiled, showing his white, even teeth in a huge grin.

"Our esteemed priest, the man who used to be one of the most influential clergymen in the kingdom, hit Abbott Morin."

Martin blushed.

Cruk laughed.

Errol stared. "You struck an abbot?"

The priest turned his head, clearing his throat. "Yes, well, theological discussions can get pretty heated at times, and Morin has always been insufferable."

"What were you talking about?" Errol asked. The idea that Martin would actually hit another clergyman both astonished and amused him. He looked at Martin in a new light.

Martin's eyes lost focus as he stared ahead. "Morin's men captured an herbwoman in the act of talking with a spirit, or said they did at any rate. She said she was speaking with Aurae, but the abbot insisted on digging up the centuries-old proscription against consorting with spirits." He turned his head and spat. "The fool. As if anyone, even a backwoods herbwoman, could confuse a spirit with one of the malus."

Errol tore his gaze from Martin's remembered anger and turned to look at Luis and Cruk. Both men wore expressions of understanding—Luis, sad and resigned, Cruk, as angry as Martin.

"What is a malus?"

Martin gave him a long steady look before answering. "When men say 'by the three,' they're referring to, invoking, Deas, Eleison, and unknowable Aurae. There are some among the herbwomen or herbmen who claim to speak with Aurae, to know what is unknowable. The notion that Deas would send Aurae to communicate to them directly is ridiculous. But even so, they are good people and gifted healers."

"A malus—" he sighed—"is something very evil, a spirit aligned against Deas, so different from Aurae. Not that Morin really cared." Martin waved toward the hills on his left. "He dragged the old woman in from somewhere in the hills. She confessed, of course—soon or late, they all do."

Errol's stomach fell. *Radere. Adele.* "What happened?" The

words hung in the air before dying, leaving an oppressive silence behind them.

Martin didn't answer, and Errol didn't ask again.

Luis pulled his horse over to Errol's until the two of them rode knee to knee. "Not all adversaries carry a bow," he murmured. "Once we enter Windridge, say little."

An hour later they crested the last hill. Errol gaped at Windridge spread out before them. A stone wall ten feet high surrounded an area large enough to hold the villages of Berea and Callowford a dozen times over. A road running north and south through massive beamed gates teemed with carts, horses, and wagons that jostled for position along the rutted track. Houses and shops, some of them three stories high, competed for space like saplings fighting for light.

He stared, a sense of something wrong nagging at him. The city didn't look right. More than just the size, something looked out of place. At last he realized what it was. There were no thatched roofs. Even the houses and shops were covered in the bluish slate that sheltered only the churches in the Sprata foot-hills. Hundreds of chimneys thrust into the air, and tendrils of smoke mingled and writhed until their tenuous existence frayed on the breeze.

"What do you think, Errol?" Martin asked. The gray-haired priest smiled at him and his eyes twinkled.

Errol eyed the commotion that still lay silent in the distance and shook his head in disbelief. "I've heard people talk about cities before, but I always thought they were exaggerating. Why do they live here?"

"Money, mostly," Martin shrugged. "Cities spring up wherever trade routes cross, and Windridge holds an envious position." He pointed toward the river. "The river gives them access to the villages and provinces to the west while the road lets them trade as far south as Basquon and as far north as Soeden."

They regarded the city as the caravan they'd accompanied pulled away to join the press to enter the eastern gate. Errol looked at the other members of their party, but no one made any motion to move forward.

"What are we waiting for?"

Martin gave him a glance that might have held a measure of disappointment. "Liam hasn't joined us." He turned his disfavor to Cruk, who jerked his head in a nod of acknowledgment.

"The boy will be here," Cruk grunted. He looked Martin in the eye. "He has to be—does he not?"

Martin's eyes tightened at this, but Luis looked uncomfortable.

As though the mention of his name held the power to summon him, a thunder of hooves sounded from behind and Errol twisted in his saddle to see Liam, bent low over the neck of his horse. His blond hair flew and his smile was visible even from a distance.

"Humph. You see," Cruk said. "Deas's chosen."

Martin cut the air with one hand. "Let no one, no one, hear you utter those words." He looked back at the city. "Especially here."

Liam thundered up, sawed the reins to bring his lathered horse to a stop. He leaned down, patted his stallion heavily on the left shoulder. The horse tossed his head and pranced.

Errol looked down at his mount and, with a shrug, gave his horse like treatment. Horace breathed deeply and leaned down to pull a tuft of grass loose, chewing without interest. Errol rolled his eyes in disgust. "That's showing them, Horace."

"You're late," Cruk said to Liam.

The smile slipped a fraction from Liam's face. "I wanted to make sure they took the bait. A couple of times they looked ready to turn around and begin searching to the north."

Cruk gave a grudging nod. "How many?"

"Hard to tell." Liam shrugged. "I doubled back as often as I could to lay down more than one set of tracks, but if they look closely they'll know it was only one horse."

Cruk nodded approval. "If they think to dismount and take a close look."

Martin turned his horse toward the city. "Come, I want to meet with Morin tonight." He turned toward Errol, gave his clothes a quick glance. "And I think it's time that we began dressing Errol in something more suitable to his future."

They rode through the gates of the city without a challenge from the soldiers at the entrance, who they seemed more interested in extracting a bribe from the caravan just ahead of them. Then they entered into noise. All around them people of a thousand varieties teemed and pressed in on them from every side, in endless whirlpools of humanity. Men, women, and children laughed, cried, and yelled to each other across the streets.

Errol had never heard the like, yet in all the variety, none of them looked like him. He tried to look everywhere at once. A hundred voices fought for his attention as shopkeepers competed with street merchants. A woman old enough to be his mother strutted through the crowd and proclaimed her wares. She sauntered up to Liam on his horse, her heavily painted eyes sultry.

"Are you in town for long, milord?" Her fingers traced a slow line down his leg.

Liam gaped, his mouth working fishlike in his attempt to respond.

"Don't you like women, milord?" the woman asked. Her silk dress accentuated every breath.

Liam jerked his eyes forward and struck his heels against his horse's flanks. Laughter trailed behind him.

"What about you, boy?" the woman asked.

Errol shook his head, still smiling at Liam's discomfort. For once, Horace cooperated with his commands and trotted briskly to catch up to Liam and the others.

"That . . . that woman," Liam spluttered.

Using his hand as a shield, Errol hid his smirk. "Yes, she certainly seemed to favor you."

Liam's color deepened from pink to crimson. "She needs to see a priest."

Errol laughed. "I don't think she's interested in priests."

Sometime later they stopped in front of the largest building Errol had ever seen. The sign out front, painted in garish yellows and reds, proclaimed their destination as the Dancing Man. Errol didn't know about the dancing part, but there were easily two-score rooms divided among its three floors, and travelers packed the courtyard in front of the stable.

They walked into the common room, lit by a bank of large windows that faced the street, and spotted the proprietor directing serving maids with curt gestures and commands. Martin, Luis, and Liam worked their way toward him through the press, leaving Errol and Cruk near the entrance.

Errol took advantage of the opportunity to examine city dwellers in more detail. At a table next to one of the large windows, a woman not much older than Errol fanned herself with quick motions of pink silk stretched across thin strips of wood. As he watched, she looked at the man across the table from her with a smile, snapped the fan closed, and used it to trace a slow circle around her left ear. The man smiled, rose, and extended his arm, which she took.

Cruk snorted. "Well, that was quite a conversation."

Not one word had been spoken between the two. "What was that about?" Errol asked. "They didn't say a word."

The right side of Cruk's mouth stretched into his approximation of a grin. "Oh, she said plenty. She just didn't say it in words. A woman of noble birth can use one of those fans to speak volumes."

"What did she say?"

Cruk shrugged. "At first, when she fanned herself, she was telling her suitor she was unattached. Then, when she snapped it closed and traced the circle over her left ear, she told him she would like to go for a walk with him where they could speak more privately."

Errol frowned. The exchange didn't make any sense to him. "If they wanted to talk to each other, why didn't they just do it here?"

Cruk rolled his eyes. "It wouldn't be proper. An unmarried woman talking with a man without a chaperone present would be scandalous." He snorted. "At least, that's what they think.

Some of the things I've seen some of these highborn ladies say with those fans when they thought no one else could see would make a soldier blush."

Intrigued, Errol started to ask what was said, but Cruk waved him to silence as Martin and the rest returned.

"It's done," the priest announced. "I've arranged for baths and fresh clothes." He paused. "And rooms as well, if we need them. I don't think Morin will go so far as to break protocol by refusing hospitality to a priest, but it's hard to say. We don't like each other much."

An hour later, cleaned and clothed, they moved through the less crowded part of the city away from the main gates. Errol twitched in his clothes, trying to figure out what bothered him. Made of soft cotton and wool, they fit him comfortably enough, but he felt stifled. Realization struck him. He couldn't feel the air. The clothes were new. His threadbare clothes from Callowford had long ceased to serve as an impediment to the most inconsequential breeze.

As they rounded a corner, he lifted his hand to undo the top two buttons of his coat, and froze. There, rising in majesty above a large square, towered a building beyond imagination. It loomed over them as they approached. Each of the stone foundation blocks spanned twice Errol's height. Enormous stained-glass windows depicted men in robes in various poses. Six mounted men would easily have fit through the main doors.

A man cowled in gray, with the hood pulled up, stood beside the door, a silent sentinel observing the square in front of the church. When they were still fifty paces away the head turned toward them and a pale hand lifted from the sleeve, pointed their way, and beckoned them toward the dark space of the entrance.

Gooseflesh covered Errol's skin. Martin took a deep breath and let it out slowly, puffing his cheeks. "It seems we are expected."

9

THE CATHEDRAL OF WINDRIDGE

THE BROAD DOORS drew shut behind them, the light narrowing in a gap that shrank until it disappeared. Darkness descended, lifted only when Errol's eyes adjusted to the dim lamplight. They stood in an entryway that could have held the entire sanctuary of the church in Callowford. To one side stood a bank of candles, some lit, most cold, a few with weak whispers of smoke rising upward to be lost in the gloom.

"I am Brother Fenn," the man in the cowl said. His voice sounded dry, dusty—as if he'd forsaken water when he'd taken the rest of his vows. "If you will follow me, Abbot Morin is waiting for you." He bobbed his head and moved to enter the sanctuary.

Errol trailed the rest of them down the right-hand aisle, conscious of the vaulted stone ceiling that soared above them like the gorge at dusk. Despite the squared edges and mortar, the sanctuary's stone struck him as less reliable, as though it might fall and bury them at any moment. He reached out, gave one of the granite blocks a tentative touch, brushing his fingers across the gray surface. It was cold, cold like the pooled waters below the Cripples, but dry also. Like Brother Fenn.

They passed through an archway at the back of the sanctuary, then took a series of turns that brought them to a complex of rooms behind the church proper, rooms that appeared to hold the offices and living quarters of the abbot and those who served him.

Fenn stopped before a closed set of double doors, bowed Errol and the rest to a halt, and knocked on the thick wood. The door opened a crack, and their guide leaned forward and whispered, his conversation punctuated by slow bobs of his head.

The door swung open to reveal a dining room, and Fenn stepped back, extended a pale, hairless arm, and waved them through.

Errol moved from the gloom of the corridor into brightly lit opulence. A long, burnished table rested on a heavily embroidered rug. Brass sconces mounted on the walls at even intervals illuminated the space with candles that burned without smoking, and everywhere Errol looked, signs of wealth dominated. Someone had set the table with porcelain and crystal. Silver serving dishes steamed with food.

"Please, gentlemen. Let us not stand on ceremony. Seat yourselves."

Errol jerked in surprise. The speaker sat motionless at the far end of the table, one hand draped around a goblet. He nodded toward the chairs. "Please, my guests, I insist." Black eyes glittered above a tight-lipped smile.

At a nod from Martin, they took their seats. Without preamble, Martin reached forward to lift a decanter from the middle of the table and fill his glass with its dark red liquid. Two men—men who very much reminded Errol of Cruk—stepped in behind Liam as he passed through the entrance, blocking their escape.

With his foot, Errol nudged Cruk, who sat opposite him, and jerked his head toward them.

Without the slightest suggestion of haste, Cruk turned to inspect the pair. Errol saw flashes of recognition register in his eyes, though the pair showed no such surprise.

Cruk grimaced, his beard ruffling. "Members of the watch."

"Exactly," Morin said from the head of the table. "I see the three of you know each other." He gave a mirthless laugh. "Well, of course you would. You were all in the king's elite together." He gave a wave toward the seats next to Cruk and Errol. "Jarel, Koran, join us."

The two men separated and moved around the table to take places next to Errol and Cruk. The burly blond sat beside Errol, while the other guard, dark and squat, took the seat next to Cruk.

"Well," Morin said with a fleshy smile, "isn't this festive?" Everything about the abbot of Windridge spoke of indulgence, from the loose flesh of his face to the languid gestures he made with his soft pale hands. Only his eyes were different. They glittered, hard as agates and nearly as cold.

Martin sighed. His wineglass sat untouched, the ruby liquid stilled. "What do you want, Morin?"

"I?" Their host wore a look of injured hospitality. "I only want to treat a traveling priest with the honor and grace he deserves." His look grew intent. "Most of your party is known to me. You and I, of course, have a long history." He turned to Luis. "And I recognize the former tremus from my visits to Green Isle. How are you, reader?"

Luis bowed politely from where he sat on Martin's right.

"Do try the duck eggs," Morin pointed. "Delicious."

The abbot raised his hand palm up toward Cruk. "I've never had the pleasure of our meeting, Captain, but Jarel and Koran have told me all about you." Morin looked away, dismissing Cruk as though the man presented no danger.

Errol started when he noticed the abbot's dark gaze locked on him. Morin held the stare for the space of a dozen heartbeats before moving on to Liam, who sat on Errol's left. The abbot addressed Martin. "I don't think I've seen the lads before." He smiled. "And a study in contrasts at that." He pointed toward Liam. "That one moves as though he could be a member of the watch. He only lacks a few years and a couple of scars."

"Tell me, boy," the abbot addressed Liam. "How did you come to be in such august company?"

Liam cocked his head to the side. "Haven't you answered your own question, good abbot? I'm bound for the watch."

The abbot laughed as if Liam had made a jest. "Well then, perhaps I should let you spar with Jarel and Koran."

Cruk smiled, but Liam became thoughtful. "What is their rank?"

Morin smirked. "They are both sergeants."

Liam nodded. "There's no need. They would lose."

Jarel's face clouded and Koran started to rise, but Morin waved him down. "You're brash for one so young."

Liam shook his head, his expression neutral. "I don't favor bragging, good abbot, but I am nearly a match for Captain Cruk. I don't think a sergeant would be as skilled."

Morin's smile slipped, and Koran no longer appeared eager to draw his sword. The abbot turned his attention to Errol. He smiled, but his eyes held mockery in their depths. "You always took your vow to help the least of the kingdom so seriously, Martin."

It took Errol a moment to realize he'd been insulted. He hardly cared. His mouth watered after the wine, but no one except Morin drank. Was it safe?

Luis's eyes narrowed. "Have a care, Morin. The boy is on his way to Erinon to become a reader. You may find your path crossing his again someday."

Their host snorted and wine slopped over the edge of his glass. "A reader? At his age? How old is he, sixteen? Seventeen?"

Errol fumed. "I'm nearly nineteen."

Morin smiled at the interjection. "Dear me, I thought the age of testing was fourteen."

Luis leaned back in his chair. "The conclave will welcome him as any other."

Morin shrugged. "As you say. What of the other lad? Is he a reader as well?"

"Just a youth," Martin said before anyone else could speak. "Cruk has been training him at arms. He has the talent to become a member of the watch, as you've already noted."

The abbot smiled. His dark eyes glittered in triumph. "My apologies, gentlemen. I'm sure I've kept you from your meal with all my talk. Please, eat." At a look from Errol, he laughed a thin wheeze that left Errol checking the distance to the door. "I assure you the food and drink is quite safe."

No one moved.

Morin sighed. "Very well. Koran, bring me the decanter that sits in front of our esteemed priest. The man next to Errol rose without a sound and fetched the wine to the abbot, who poured.

"Your health," he toasted and drank. He smacked his lips and leered at Errol.

Martin nodded and slowly, with abbreviated motions, they sampled the food and wine. Errol topped his glass, drained it in two gulps, and filled it again. The liquid warmed him as it descended into his stomach, where it spread its comfort outward. Only then did he try the food.

Cruk took a sip of wine, or pretended to. The level in his glass didn't change. He turned to the large blond, the one called Koran. "How did you end up here? You and the rest of the watch are supposed to be in Erinon, guarding the king."

Koran looked up the table toward Morin, who smirked and nodded.

"The Judica met," Koran shrugged. At a startled look from Martin, he shook his head and amended. "The lesser Judica, I mean. The king still lives, so far as I know. But the benefices met and decided to strip two-thirds of the watch from the king and distribute it among the clergy."

Cruk's eyes widened. It was the first time Errol had ever seen him surprised. "Deas in heaven, man, why?"

Koran shrugged, looked at his wine. "After Benefices Guillame and Worthan were assassinated, the decision was made to offer the rest protection. They want the benefices in full number when the Grand Judica is called to select the new king. Jarel and I were allotted to Benefice Weir." Koran shrugged. "He sent us here."

"The conclave will select the new king," Luis said.

Morin smirked. "The conclave will do as they are told."

"What about Dirk and Merodach?" Errol asked. The words tumbled out of his mouth before he thought to stop them. Every head at the table turned in his direction.

"Well." Morin smiled. "The boy seems to have some interesting names on his tongue. Tell me, young reader, how did you come to hear of those men?"

In silence, Errol sought Martin's help, but the priest busied himself with a roast chicken as though nothing untoward had occurred.

Errol stumbled over his words. "Cruk must have mentioned them when he was trying to teach me how to handle a sword." He felt the blood draining from his face under the abbot's stare.

"Really?" Morin leaned forward with interest. "That's quite unusual. It's rare that a reader would ever have need for or desire training in weapons." He gave a lift of his dark eyebrows toward Luis. "If memory serves, readers take an oath of peace."

Luis's eyes narrowed, but he made no other sign that Morin's comments had any effect on him. He shrugged before he addressed his reply to the wineglass he held. "We live on the edge of strange times, times not seen since the first king purchased the boundary with his life. Who can say what may happen." He waved one hand toward Errol. "Besides, as you say, the boy is not a reader yet. Who knows? Perhaps he will be a member of the watch one day."

What Errol said next might have been due to the howls of laughter this comment produced—from Koran and Jarel, but mostly from Cruk. Perhaps the wine loosened his tongue, or it might simply have been his frustration at everyone calling him "boy" instead of giving him the simplest courtesy of using his name.

Blood rushed to his face and his pulse roared in his ears. "I may not be able to handle a sword, but I managed to escape from Merodach when he held a bow and those Deas-forsaken screaming arrows and I had nothing! Can any of you boast as much?"

Silence engulfed the room. Martin closed his eyes, whether in thought or prayer Errol didn't know. Cruk edged away from Jarel under the guise of reaching for his glass. Both men, as well as Liam and Koran, looked ready to draw swords. Luis looked at Errol in horror.

Morin alone showed no reaction, merely reached out to pluck a grape while he studied Errol. "That sounds like quite a tale. Merodach is perhaps the best of the watch, which of course means he is the best, period. How did such a thing come to pass?" He spared a thin smile for Martin. "You might as well tell the boy to cooperate. The best you can do is delay until I tell Benefice Weir. Having him call you in front of the Judica would be uncomfortable, would it not?"

Martin pursed his lips, waited. Then he turned to Errol and spoke without rancor. "The abbot is quite correct, Errol. There's nothing to be gained by refusing to answer. We are both servants of the church, after all." Morin smirked at this. "Go ahead," Martin continued. "Tell the abbot all about your encounter with Merodach."

Martin's eyes held his, and Errol had the sense the priest tried desperately to tell him something, but what?

Slowly, in halting tones, with frequent checks for assurance from Martin, Errol related the tale of his trip across the gorge and the Cripples. He saw Koran and Jarel give grudging nods as he described the arrows his would-be killer used. As he came to the end of the story, he lifted his shirt to show the crescent scar Merodach left on his shoulder.

Morin nodded in acknowledgment and even clapped his hands as though Errol were a bard or a fool. "Well done, boy. But is it true?"

Errol nodded.

"Jarel?" Morin asked.

The squat man shook his head, his brows furrowed. "It sounds true enough." He pointed at Errol's shoulder. "And the boy wears a wound that certainly looks like it came from a borale. Captain Merodach always did prefer the black arrows, but it just doesn't make sense." Jarel met Errol's eyes. "How many times did you say he shot at you, boy?"

Errol glared at the absence of his name, but kept his tongue, counting. "Five, including the last that struck my pack."

Koran turned to Morin. "That's just it. Merodach wouldn't have missed once, much less four times. Watching him use that bow was more like watching someone practice sorcery."

Jarel nodded agreement. Even Cruk looked thoughtful.

Errol felt his face heat. Did no one believe him?

"He was trying to shoot from the worst footing," he protested. Even as he said this, he knew it wasn't completely true. There had been at least one shot where the assassin stood on the firm ground offered by dry stone.

And he had still missed.

Morin sprawled back in his chair, his hands draped in casual disdain over the arm. "Nobody's seen or heard from you in five years, Martin. And now you come through Windridge with the tremus, a captain of the watch, and a pair of oddly mismatched youths in tow. The skinny one's speech marks him from the hill country east of here. Tell me, Martin, did you and Luis find what you were looking for amongst the huts and pigsties in the hinterlands?"

Martin took a sip of wine, gave no sign he'd heard the question.

Morin's smile slipped a fraction, tightening on his face. "What was the name of that village you disappeared to?"

"No place important," Martin answered. He gazed at the furnishings that surrounded them. "And not nearly so grand as Windridge."

The abbot's smile disappeared and his eyes glittered. "And does the local priest allow those cursed herbwomen to practice their deceit in this village?"

Errol watched Martin lean forward, his eyes hard over his broad nose. "The herbwomen are many things. They are simple. They are uneducated and many times they are ignorant of what they are dealing with, but I have yet to meet one who was evil."

Morin leaned forward, his unfocused eyes bulged and spittle dripped from his lower lip. "Pah. Evil is whatever the church says, whatever I say, is evil."

Errol's stomach churned with fear at the arrogance in the abbot's statement.

Martin looked as if he might throw up. He leaned back, his face twisted with disgust. "Tell me, Abbot, did the execution of one old herbwoman get you anything? Did it advance the church or the kingdom? Or did it simply take away healing for peasants?"

Morin's mouth opened to emit peal after peal of shrill laughter. "You think I killed her? I wouldn't dream of it. She is far, far too useful to waste in such a manner.

"Ah, I see I have surprised you at last, good priest." He rose, knocked his chair over. He ignored it. "Come, I will show you the folly of your misperceptions. Koran, Jarel, let us escort our guests to the cells. I would not have it said the abbot of Windridge is stingy with his knowledge. Come, good priest. The herbwoman awaits."

They left through the small door located behind Morin's seat and entered a small gloom-shrouded hallway that smelled of must. Errol's eyes strained to adjust to the dim lighting after the brightness of the dining room. He put one hand on Cruk's belt to serve as a guide.

They turned down a corridor that held a single door on the far end. As they approached it, the musty smell grew stronger. Morin pulled a large iron key from somewhere beneath his robe and placed it in the lock.

"Only I have the key," he said. "Such treasure as the herb-woman offers must be protected." He gave Martin an evil leer. "Words do not suffice. Come and see, good priest."

Martin peered through the small opening at the top of the door and shook his head. "You threw her down here to rot?"

Morin flared, the whites showing around his eyes. "We are locked in a battle for control of our world. Sacrifices must be made."

Martin snorted. "I notice the people who say such things usually expect someone else to make the sacrifice."

With a snarl, Morin turned the key in the lock and threw open the door. The stench of unwashed bodies drifted up the stairwell. Errol threw an arm across his nose. He knew that smell. Many times it had covered him during the worst of his binges.

The abbot led the way down a circular granite staircase. After ten steps, the door above them clanged shut, cutting off the light from the corridor. Morin grabbed a torch, one of the few that burned, and smiled in triumph.

Errol couldn't make out Martin's expression in the dark but saw the priest give one curt nod toward the abbot. Cruk continued in front of him as before, but something in the set of the big man's shoulders looked tight, as if he expected an attack any second.

For another minute they descended in unrelieved darkness except for the bob of Morin's torch. At last the stairwell opened out into a cavernous guardroom, a circular affair with pikes and swords mounted along the walls. At a large table in the center, two men, unkempt and rough-looking in spattered uniforms, rose from a game of dice to stand at attention before the abbot.

The far end of the room contained the only other door, bound with iron straps and blackened with age.

The worst of the smell came from there.

"Is this necessary, Morin?" Martin asked. "You have the poor woman in your power. Your authority in the province is absolute. There is no need to parade her to prove it. If I had the authority to order her released, you know I would have done it by now."

Morin smiled, his dark eyes glittering in reflected torchlight. "My good priest, you have no idea why I've brought you here. Far be it from me to allow you to remain in your ignorance. When we go to the cells beyond, follow my instructions to the letter if you would obtain enlightenment." With a jerk, he pointed at the guards. "Unlock the door."

They entered a niche carved into the dark granite under the city. Four vaults—fewer than Errol had expected—filled the space, separated from each other by black iron bars. A man stood in front of the nearest, dressed in red livery. Officer's stripes decorated his sleeves. He stared straight ahead, impassive. Errol edged around the back, moving from behind Cruk to stand next to Liam, straining to see in the dim light.

Black cloth draped the first cell, and no sound came from behind the veil.

"What game are you playing at, Morin?" Martin asked as he pointed at the first cell and its heavy shroud.

Morin's voice floated out of the darkness. "Doubtless, you wish to see your precious herbwoman." He paused. "She is in the next cell." The abbot stepped through the knot of people to approach her prison.

Errol stepped to the bars along with the others. His eyes searched, but failed to see anyone. The cell was sparsely furnished. Besides a straw pallet that lay crumpled in the corner farthest from the first cell, only a waste bucket and a pile of rags broke the unrelieved emptiness of the space.

Morin's laughter whispered in Errol's ears. "She is somewhat shy." He turned to address the lump of rags. "Come, Odene, we have guests."

The rags stirred without rising.

Steel crept into the abbot's voice, and he gestured toward the officer on guard. "I'm sure you don't want me to call on the services of Captain Balina again."

The rags unfolded themselves from the edge of the pallet, and a woman, made small by age and neglect, tottered toward the bars.

She kept herself as far away from the first cell as she could.

"You see, Martin," Morin said. "She is well. I gave her mercy she did not deserve. The church could have demanded her life, yet as a gesture of grace I have allowed her to live and render such service to me as she is capable."

Martin's hands and eyes filled with an emotion he could not contain. "*Mercy* you call it? To be locked in this lightless hole to render service? What service could she possibly render to you?"

"Ah, well. I do not expect you to understand." He gestured toward the herbwoman, his face hard. "Speak with Odene. I insist." The guards behind him tensed at the hard note in his voice.

Cruk's hand drifted toward his sword. Martin's hand on his arm stopped him. "What is it you hope to accomplish, Morin?"

The abbot smiled but did not answer. "Talk to her. I find her insights . . . informative." His eyes darted toward Liam.

Martin's eyes narrowed. "Errol, speak with her."

Morin smiled in triumph.

Errol stepped toward the herbwoman. Her head rested against the bars in front of him, her eyes milky with blindness.

One shriveled hand stretched through, touched him on the face. It was warm. A voice too soft to carry past the bars greeted him. Old eyes gazed at him in wonder. "You've been touched by Aurae. Thank the creator! I did not know any other of the solis yet lived." She paused. "Deas's hand is on you."

The singsong cadence of her voice caressed his ear. "Solis?"

She smiled. The teeth that remained were broken, testimony to the abbot's hospitality, no doubt. "Our name for ourselves." She dropped her head as if he held no interest for her. "Is the abbot still in the room?"

Errol strained to hear her, and it took him a moment to understand her question. He breathed his answer through the bars. "Yes."

"Beware. There is a malus here. The abbot thinks to make it serve him. He is under its influence, though he knows it not." The hand withdrew. "I had better move on."

Errol locked his emotions away where they would not show on his face before he faced the others. He saw dismissal on Morin's face.

Martin drew himself up. "I see no need to continue this, Morin. Take us out of here."

"What you see is no concern of mine," Morin said. He pointed at Liam. "Let us see what kind of reaction the herbwoman has to him."

Liam stood like a rock, showing none of the nervousness that plagued Errol.

"I insist," Morin said. Behind him the guards and Captain Balina drew steel.

The herbwoman crept toward the bars. Errol saw her start in surprise, then cover the motion with a cough. He watched her repeat every gesture she'd made with him, beginning with the touch on the face. Minutes later, she withdrew her hand from Luis and retreated back to her pallet.

Errol turned to see the abbot's face etched with disappointment.

Martin's palpable relief filled the cell. "If you are quite finished, Abbot, I think we should be going."

The abbot's eyes narrowed. "Do you not wish to know why I have the herbwoman imprisoned?"

"I assumed it was to satisfy your need for vengeance."

Morin sneered at the jibe. "Did I not say she rendered service? The herbwoman can sense the presence of a malus."

Martin shook his head. "Morin, they cannot. Do you, a servant of the church, now believe their claim to know Aurae? If so, then the herbwoman is innocent."

Morin laughed. "Innocent? I don't care if she's innocent. She's useful." He leaned forward, the torch he held casting ghoulish shadows across his face. "Even the most depraved spiritist can be a source of valuable information, Martin. If one had access to someone enslaved by a malus, their knowledge would be there for the taking."

"You're mad, Morin. Even if you could find one—which is impossible—would you befoul yourself with the knowledge of the fallen?"

Morin laughed. His cackle bounced from the stone walls until it filled every niche of the prison. With a snap of his fingers, he signaled Captain Balina, who stepped forward and removed the thick covering from the first cell. With a cry like a wounded animal, the herbwoman retreated to the far corner of her cell and curled into a ball.

Behind the bars facing Morin stood a woman in her twenties. Lithe and raven-haired, she leaned against the rough stone that made the right wall of her imprisonment. The barest of smiles curved her full red lips, and her eyes, dark brown against the flawless chestnut of her skin, shone with amusement.

Her eyes swept over Martin and Luis, and she stalked toward the pair in a sinuous strut. At the bars, she challenged them with a gaze that smoldered underneath her lashes. "Hello, priest." Her voice, breathy and low, carried suggestions in those two words that made Errol's ears burn.

"Morin, what have you done?" Martin asked. He tore his eyes from the woman to look at the abbot. "She is undoubtedly a wanton, but a malus?"

The abbot looked at her, his mouth open in naked hunger. He took a step toward the cell as if unaware but then shook himself. "She is not what she appears. She came into Windridge with a caravan from Basquon. She's from Merakh. Though she may appear calm and rational now, Karma is quite insane."

"She came across the strait?" Cruk asked.

The abbot nodded. "Strange, is it not? We've had almost no contact with them in hundreds of years, and now their caravans appear in every city."

"Granted, it is strange, but strange things happen somewhere every day." Martin waved one hand at the woman. "What makes you think she is possessed?"

"If you do not trust me, trust the reaction of the herbwoman. She cannot stand the sight of her."

Martin glanced at the curled figure in the far cell, his brows knit over his eyes. "What other proof can you offer?" he asked.

"Friend Montari, step forward where Karma can see you."

Luis stepped from behind Martin to enter the pool of light cast by Morin's torch. A light flared in the woman's eyes at the sight of the reader, a thirst and hunger that showed in the widening of her eyes and the quickness of her breath. A presence of danger filled the cell. Errol counted the number of steps and guards between him and the door.

"Hello, reader." The woman inhaled deeply with her shoulders back, the suggestion obvious. "I am honored to be in your presence. I assure you that what the abbot says is untrue." Her eyes shone. "Come, take my hand, and I will show you the truth."

Errol turned, watched Luis, eyes unreadable, take one faltering step toward the bars. As the reader moved, he caught a glimpse of Captain Balina, his face still hard but etched now with the jealousy of one betrayed.

The abbot turned toward Martin. "You wanted proof? There, you have it."

Martin shook his head in denial. "Explain."

The abbot grabbed Luis by the arm, shook him as evidence. "I never told her he was a reader; we never mentioned it in conversation!"

Errol cast back, tried to remember every word spoken since they'd entered the cell, saw the others doing the same. His sense of foreboding grew. No one had said anything about Luis being a reader. No one had said anything about Luis at all.

He edged away from the woman's cell, bumped into Liam, and stumbled—throwing the two of them off balance and into the shadows.

The motion caught the Merakhi woman's attention. Her eyes widened until the whites shone all around.

Violence erupted in the cell. With a scream of fury and terror, the woman threw herself against the bars arms out, straining to reach them. Cry after cry filled the prison, echoed from the stone, compounded until the screams filled his ears, his mind. And still it went on.

Again and again, Karma threw herself against the iron, oblivious to the cuts and blood that blossomed on her face. Her arms strained through the bars, and clawed hands stretched toward Errol and Liam. Her insane gaze darted back and forth between them.

Everyone turned to stare at the spot Liam and Errol occupied, the spot the malus tried to reach with all the strength the woman possessed. Morin stood transfixed, but his black eyes glittered with triumph.

A hand knotted the front of Liam's tunic. "Come!" Martin hauled him to the door. Cruk clenched Errol's arm, pulled him after them. As they passed in front of the cell, the screams intensified into shrieks.

"The kingdom of Illustra is doomed! Even now your barrier is weakening. Rodran will have no successor. The three will not save you. You are not the soteregia! There is no savior and king!"

10

DARK FLIGHT

HANDS—HE WAS UNSURE of whose or how many—half carried, half dragged him from the prison. Martin, flanked by Cruk, crashed into the abbot, pulled the torch from his hands on his way back up the stairwell. The sounds of labored breathing and muffled screams followed them.

Questions assaulted Errol in the darkness—hit him again and again with the impact of blows. Stunned into immobility, he stopped on the stairs, and the distance between him and his companions grew until he heard the abbot and his men racing from behind to catch up. His thoughts fled from him like minnows darting in the shallows. With a shake of his head, he forced his feet back into motion, made them slap their way up the stone, back to the light.

Luis held the answers. The answers lay with the spherical stone lots the reader rarely let out of his sight. Suspicion grew in Errol's mind, and a thrill of fear rushed through him as he found himself torn between warring emotions. His curiosity gnawed at him like a live thing. Why had Martin and Luis come to Callowford? What would make a priest and a reader leave their calling behind and live like hermits in a cabin, tucked away in a backwater village?

The questions only led him to other questions. Inevitably, he came back to the same conclusion: Luis, the man who'd laid the compulsion of the church upon him, held the answer.

They burst like a flood into the hallway next to the cathedral. Errol blinked in the light, searched for Luis. He found him, his face turned toward Martin's, whispering as the priest leaned sideways to hear. The reader's gestures, quick, jerky, spoke of his agitation. Martin nodded, curt and short, whether in agreement or acknowledgment, Errol couldn't tell.

For a moment his curiosity faded and the other emotion within Errol gained ascendancy. *Drink.* He needed a drink. He wanted nothing more than to run away and find an alehouse. Events threatened to run away from him, and they were accelerating. He didn't know how to slow them down, but he knew how to dull their impact on his nerves and emotions. He licked his lips, thirsty.

They retraced their steps back to the abbot's dining room. Errol grabbed the half-full bottle of wine still on the table. No one noticed. He took a pull from the bottle. The wine cleared the dust from his throat before it settled in his belly, where it spread warmth and peace outward.

"Idiot." Cruk grabbed the bottle and threw it with a back-handed flip against the wall, where it shattered, spraying red wine like blood, over the wood. "Listen, boy, we may have to fight our way out of here yet. Since you can't handle a sword, you need to pretend you can. Draw your blade."

Every man in the room held steel. Why would they fight?

Morin came through the doors flanked by the two members of the watch. They stood, tensed and coiled, eyes darting, swords forward. Martin turned, and for a long moment that Errol measured with the rise and fall of his lungs, the two groups measured each other. A kaleidoscope of emotions chased across the abbot's face before his countenance froze, masking his thoughts.

"You'll forgive me, I hope," Morin said. At a gesture, his men sheathed their swords. His gaze passed over Errol before coming to rest on Liam. "The malus has never reacted that way to anyone's presence."

Martin exhaled; the sound loud in the stillness of the dining room. "Yes, as you say, she is quite insane." He inclined his head for a brief instant. "Peace be with you, Abbot."

Moments later they rode back across the square. Errol's blood rushed with the need to dig his heels into Horace's flanks and gallop away. His neck itched with the sense of being watched. The slow clop of hooves grated, and he made to turn and look back at the cathedral.

"Don't," Cruk snapped. He stared ahead, and for a moment Errol was unsure who the former member of the watch addressed, but the man continued, "Give the impression that we think we're out of danger."

The group rode on. Martin contrived to have Liam surrounded. Luis rode at the front, guiding them back to the inn, where the lots remained hidden. Cruk and Errol flanked Liam on either side, and Martin brought up the rear. Liam said nothing, but Errol could see his eyes flick left and right, and he looked as often at his friends surrounding him as he did the streets ahead.

Unable to resist any longer, Errol twisted in his saddle to listen for the sound of footsteps, hoofbeats, anything that would warn they'd been followed. But nothing came. The noises of the city washed over them without lull or interruption, just as they had on the ride to the cathedral. Errol gave a mental shrug. Maybe their fears were unfounded. Perhaps Morin thought the Merakhi's outburst was nothing more than the demon-driven insanity of a possessed woman. Or if the abbot did believe the malus saw truly, he saw no need to act upon the information.

Maybe.

Errol snorted at his own reasoning. Too much of what he'd seen at the cathedral bothered him: the herbwoman, imprisoned and used as a tool; the possessed Merakhi, seductive, savage, and insane; and Morin, hungry and calculating at the Merakhi's revelation.

The memory brought Errol up short. "Pater Martin."

The priest, lost in thought, started, then turned toward him. A crease showed between his eyebrows. "Yes, Errol?"

"The herbwoman told me the abbot was already under the malus's influence."

"She spoke to you?" He turned to Liam. "Did she speak to you as well?"

Liam nodded. "She said the hand of Deas was upon me."

Martin looked unsatisfied. "Nothing else?"

Liam shook his head, but the look he gave Errol held doubt.

Errol licked his lips, unsure how to proceed. "I saw something else, Pater. When Karma spoke to Luis, Captain Balina wore the same look Knorl, the smith, gets whenever someone starts making eyes at that pretty wife of his."

The priest's face grew serious. "Are you sure about this, boy?"

Errol nodded.

Martin looked back at Cruk. "You heard?"

Cruk nodded. "It doesn't change anything. Not unless you were planning on trusting the abbot's word and staying the night at the Dancing Man."

"No. That would be unwise," Martin said. He chuckled at his understatement. "I want to be out of the city before nightfall. I don't care if we have to camp out in the open without a fire." His eyes cut toward Liam. "I don't want to be anywhere Morin or his men can put their hands on us."

They rounded a corner. The sign depicting a man perched on the toes of one foot with both arms lifted rose before them. At last. They rode around back to the stable, where a stable hand came to take charge of their mounts.

"Water and food," Cruk said. "Leave the saddles on. We'll be leaving within the hour." He tossed the man a silver mark. "We'll need a bag of oats too." He pointed to Horace. "Put it behind the saddle of that one."

The man nodded and showed a gap-toothed smile. "Miss Hallye will be disappointed you didn't stay for dinner, Pater. She says you look like the sort of man who appreciates good food."

Martin's face stretched into a smile, and he patted his stomach. "Your Miss Hallye is a shrewd judge of character. Unfortunately, business calls us unexpectedly away." He turned to address the rest of them. "We should retrieve our things with haste. I suspect our safety depends upon a certain measure of alacrity."

Luis sped toward the inn, halted, then turned and beckoned Errol after him. "I need your help carrying the lots to the horses."

Errol felt complimented and shocked at the same time. Luis never brought those lots into the light of day, and he absolutely never, ever, let anyone besides Martin and himself carry them.

"Me?" Errol asked. "What if I drop them?"

"Don't. I've spent the better part of four years making them as perfect as craft and talent can."

Errol followed him up the wooden staircase to the rooms they had rented but wouldn't be using. Under the bed, in two ordinary-looking crates, lay the stones so precious to the reader.

"Why didn't you leave them with the innkeeper to guard?" Errol asked.

Luis shrugged around the crate cradled to his chest. "There was no need. No one can read the lots except for the one who made them."

"Or another reader," Errol said.

Luis gave him a long look. "Yes, of course." He made for the door. "We should get down to the stable."

They descended the stairs, each with a padded crate on his back, and found Cruk seated at a table, a fresh tankard of ale sweating in front of him. Martin and Liam sat on either side. None of them appeared to be in a hurry.

"Have a seat," Cruk said. He gestured with his head toward two chairs across from him. One was empty, the other piled with dark cloaks.

Errol sat down, sandwiched between Luis and Liam.

Cruk took a pull from his tankard as he looked out of the left corner of his eyes. "The inn's being watched. Don't look out the window! Morin's got at least two men out there I can see, which means there's at least another four that I can't see."

"He didn't waste any time," Liam said. In the depths of his eyes, Errol saw something in them he'd never seen before; he saw doubt.

Martin leaned toward Cruk. "Could we ride through them to the city gates?"

Cruk shook his head before Martin finished. He glanced at Liam. "Not with any guarantee of keeping everyone safe. A couple of bowmen on the rooftops and they could pick us off at their leisure."

"Can we sneak our way out?" Luis asked.

"If Morin has any sense, probably not." He sighed, his massive chest lifted with the effort. "Still, it's the only thing I can think to try." He gave an inquiring glance at Martin, who nodded.

"We'll have to wait for dark and make our way out the back," Cruk continued. "We'll leave one at a time. I'll go out first on some pretext and try to draw as many away from the rear as I can. The rest of you follow." He looked toward Martin. "How do you want to order everyone?"

"I'll follow you. Liam will come behind me. Then Errol and Luis can come."

"I think I'd like to precede Errol out, just to make sure the way is clear," Luis said.

He offered nothing further, but Errol sensed the reader would not negotiate on this point.

Martin must have caught the hint of iron in Luis's voice as well. After a momentary silence, he nodded and turned back to Cruk. "How do we get the horses?"

"I'll have the hands take them to the west gate. They'll hold them there until we arrive." He looked at Luis, his face as close to apologetic as Errol had ever seen it. He pointed at the crates.

"You'll need to send those ahead with the horses, Tremus. I'm sorry."

Luis's face blanched until it reached the color of boiled fish, but he jerked a nod. "Morin must not get his hands on the lots. Where will we go from here?"

Cruk's lumpy face hardened until it looked like flint. He signaled two men by the door who took the crates out to the stable. Then he reached into his tunic, withdrew a map, and smoothed it out on the table in front of them. One thick forefinger pointed at a large dot. "This is Windridge." The finger traced a path west. "And here's Haven Mirk. It's two days hard ride from here, but there's grass and water to be found on the way for the horses. If we get separated, we'll meet up there." He lifted his head, and his stare found Errol. "Whatever you do, make sure you're not followed."

Errol nodded and tried to swallow past a sudden tightness in his throat.

Apparently satisfied, Cruk turned his attention to the rest of their party. "It'll be dark in two hours. Let's not give Morin's men any suspicions. We'll stay here and eat, as if we planned on staying the night, before setting out."

Martin gave a grim chuckle. "It looks like I'll have the opportunity to sample Miss Hallye's fare after all."

Dinner arrived an hour later. The smells drifted across the edges of Errol's thoughts. The meal probably lived up to the stable hand's boast, but worry quenched his hunger, and the few bites he raised to his mouth tasted like ashes. When the serving girl arrived moments later with a pitcher of ale, he perked up.

Cruk's hand grabbed his wrist, stopped his hand just short of the pewter handle. "No ale for you."

Errol tried to pull his hand back. "One drink's not going to hurt."

Cruk snorted. "You don't know how to have one drink." To make his point, he set the pitcher beyond Errol's reach.

A thread of panic wormed its way into his stomach. "I-I need a drink. If I don't have something to drink, I'll get s-sick." The words stuck in his throat, and the sympathetic looks from Martin, Luis, and most of all, Liam made his face heat.

"The boy's right," Martin said. "But just one tankard."

Errol didn't even look up. He wanted nothing more at that moment than to crawl away where no one could see him. If he could have willed himself to die, he would have. The sound of his tankard being filled brought tears to his eyes, and he squeezed them shut and lowered his head even farther, trying to hide them.

Luis took one of Errol's hands and placed it on the cool metal of the tankard. He held it close to his chest, cradling it but not drinking. He couldn't, not this time, not in front of them. Rising, he fled the table, making for the kitchen.

"Let him go, Cruk."

The words struck him in the back as he left, and he took one sobbing pull of his drink. The Dancing Man served the best ale he'd ever tasted.

He hated it with all his might.

Later—he didn't know how much later—he still sat in one corner of the kitchen, the staff eyeing him, the now-empty mug still clutched to his chest. The door swung open and Cruk came through. He nodded in Errol's direction.

"It's time."

Cruk opened the door that led from the kitchen to the back alley. A whiff of decomposing vegetables drifted from the compost pile and in through the door. Then Cruk was gone. Errol listened between the pulses of his heart for any sound that might indicate an ambush or an attack, but the alley behind the inn stayed silent.

Moments later, Martin entered, a turkey leg in one hand and a tankard in the other. He swayed as he came in, ale slopping over the side of his mug. But as the door closed, cutting off the view to the front of the inn, he straightened, set the mug aside, and approached the corner where Errol sat.

"Luis is very possibly my oldest friend. He is noble and good and stubborn in ways I still don't understand. He sees in you something rare and precious." Martin's eyes clouded. "I know him. If he thinks it's necessary, he'll die to get you to Erinon. Don't let him."

Errol shook his head. If possible, Martin's and Luis's regard hurt worse than their pity. He couldn't make the mental jump, couldn't see himself in the way Martin described. He was a drunk-ard. Why would Luis sacrifice himself for him?

He looked up to see the door swinging shut and Martin gone.

Liam came into the kitchen. Even his footfalls sounded self-assured. Errol stood, unwilling to have Liam look so far down to speak to him. Liam stuck out a hand. "If you want, I'll stay back. We can try to make it to the west gate together."

Errol shook his head. No. Liam was too important to risk. He didn't know exactly how or why, but the abbot's naked hunger betrayed Liam's importance. Morin might try anything. "Martin knows what needs to be done." He jerked his head toward the door. "You should go."

Liam nodded and left without looking back. Hollowness settled into Errol's stomach, and for a moment he considered refilling his tankard. Then Luis entered. Sweat shone on his bald head, but his brown eyes were calm.

Errol swallowed before forcing himself to speak. "Only an idiot would leave the back of an inn unwatched."

Luis pursed his lips and nodded.

"Morin's not an idiot, is he?"

A shake of the head.

Errol took a deep breath, savored the feel of air coming into his lungs. "What makes Cruk and Martin think we can get away?" He forced himself to hold Luis's gaze—as if by sheer will he could force the truth from him.

"The goal is for Liam to get away." A rueful grin stretched his mouth to one side. "I've never been much of a fighter." He held his arms out, accentuating his slight build. "I'm not made for combat. You and I have that in common."

Errol nodded at the simple truth in his words.

"Cruk is a better fighter than you know," Luis went on. "He'll be doing everything he can to clear the way to the gate. He'll die if he needs to. So will Martin, and that fat priest is no stranger to the sword."

Errol frowned as he tried to imagine Martin with a sword. The picture refused to hold. It contradicted the image of the man whose pity compelled him to offer bread and wine to Errol over and over again. Despite the priest's build and the thickness of his hands, Errol couldn't see Martin as anything other than peaceful.

Luis took him by the hand and hauled him to his feet. "Come. We should be leaving. We don't want the others to get too far ahead of us. Here." He held out a cloak, black, like the one he wore.

He shrugged himself into the cloth, pulling the hood up.

Luis stepped to the door, paused and turned back. "I'll lead. Keep twenty paces behind. If anything happens to me, run. Get to Erinon however you can and find the first of the conclave, Enoch Sten." The reader's gaze became intense, as if by his stare he could force Errol's obedience. "Tell him everything about your test for the sight. Leave out nothing, not even the smallest detail." Without another word, he left Errol to stare at the space where he'd been.

Tightening the hood of his cloak, Errol crept out the back of the inn, spotted the dim figure of the reader some twenty paces away, and made to follow. A breath of wind wormed its way under the warmth of the thick cloth to chill him, and he pulled it close.

They stuck to the shadows until they cleared the immediate surroundings of the inn. After that, the reader moved toward the busier main streets, always heading west toward the gate and freedom. Errol checked behind often for signs of pursuit. There were none.

A man bumped him as Luis turned a corner, and for a moment Errol lost sight of his friend. A muffled shout sounded, quickly cut off. Errol's feet raced the sudden pounding of his heart to catch up. He ran to the cobblestoned intersection and spied the reader a scant ten paces ahead, going west.

His breath shuddered with relief, and he forced his feet to match the pace of his guide. He could just discern the outline of the city gate in the gloom, perhaps half a mile away. His steps quickened in anticipation. They were almost there.

At the next street, Luis turned left, away from the approach. Errol followed, the gate disappearing from view behind a row of two-story shops. He felt a pang at its passing. What had Luis seen to make him take the detour?

They walked on. The reader backtracked now to narrower, less-traveled streets. Many times, it was just the two of them. A sense of unease filled Errol. Why weren't they making for the gate? He swiveled, checked every visible alley and street for the cause, and couldn't find it.

Enough. He would ask the reader. Errol quickened his pace, but Luis sped up as well, keeping his distance. His feet hastened until his shoes slapped the pitted cobblestones, and still Luis stayed ahead of him. He turned a corner and a beam of light from a dilapidated shop fell on his guide. The gleam revealed a strand of long glossy black that had escaped the confines of the hood.

Errol stopped. It wasn't Luis. Footsteps followed him. Without thought, he broke into a run. The rasp of metal clearing scabbard came from behind. He flew past the alley. As he flashed by, a figure leapt toward him with a snarl, nails clutching for his face, tearing skin.

Blinded by panic he ran. Steps pounded behind him. The gray stone buildings blurred, interrupted only by the darkness of alleyways opening between them, alleys that might lead back to the west gate and safety, or to a dead end.

He couldn't chance it. Not knowing what else to do, he ran on, hoped the street would merge with a larger, more populated, one. He glanced back and saw the Merakhi woman, Karma, chasing after him, running with the graceful strides of one accustomed to traveling by foot. Behind her another figure ran, sword drawn.

Water. Instinct guided him toward the sound of rushing water, and he followed it until it roared in his ears. Errol entered an intersection and stopped in the midst of a broad street with the comforting rush of a river coming from his right. He'd done it; he'd put himself in the middle of the largest street in the city, the one that led to the bridge over the river—the Keralwash, if he remembered Luis's mention correctly.

And the street was deserted.

Almost.

A figure stood at the far end, cloaked in black and beckoning him.

The river raged in the height of the spring rains, pounding around the pillars that supported the bridge. He ran toward the figure, his breath rasping through his throat with a plea for help. Halfway across, he stopped. In the lamplight, beneath silver hair, he recognized a pair of light-blue eyes, eyes he had seen at another river.

It couldn't be. How? "No," he breathed. "It's not possible."

Merodach ran forward, his bow in one hand and a black arrow nocked. "Come with me, boy, if you want to live."

Errol reversed, took two strides, and stopped. A dozen paces away Karma waited. Savage glee twisted her face, turned her mouth into a rictus of hate. Behind her, his eyes burning, stood Captain Balina.

"Come, boy. If you make me chase you, I can promise your end will be uncomfortable." The possessed Merakhi's voice rasped; it no longer held the seductive tones he'd heard in the prison. Her eyes glowed as if lit from within.

Merodach called to him from behind. "Boy, I could have killed you any time I wanted. If you want to live, stay out of her reach. Look at her, boy. She's possessed by the malus, and the guard is under her spell."

Errol, trying to look in two directions at once, backed away from Merodach and the Merakhi until the stone rail of the bridge pressed against his back, stopping him. Below, the floodwaters of the Keralwash thundered.

The woman took another slow step toward him, her smile stretching the cuts and bruises on her face. "I don't care who kills you, boy, but do you really want to die by the borale?" She laughed. "Do you relish feeling it rip and tear its way out of your flesh, leaving you to die from blood loss, screaming in pain?" She nodded back toward Balina. "The captain has a sword, freshly sharpened. He can make your end quick and painless."

"Don't believe her, boy," Merodach said. He pitched his voice to carry over the flood below. "A malus never kills quickly. They feed on pain. Come with me. I can take you to safety." He took a step.

Errol tried in vain to watch everyone. The pounding of his heart merged with the floodwaters. He cast the briefest of looks down, fought to keep from sobbing. The roiling depths were too far away for him to survive a jump.

He was going to die. All that remained was to choose between the arrow, the sword, and the water.

Without turning his back to Merodach or the malus-possessed woman, he climbed the railing.

The three of them inched forward.

"Come, boy," the woman crooned. "There's no need for such a death." Her voice grew mocking. "Don't you want to be buried in your faith? Don't you want the priest to bless your grave?"

"Errol, don't." Merodach's voice cut across the woman's.

For a moment, something in the assassin's voice penetrated the fear that clouded his thinking. Could he be telling the truth? If he'd wanted Errol dead, he could have simply fired. It would be impossible to miss at such short range—but shooting at Errol would leave Merodach open to counterattack by the Karma and her guard.

He didn't want to die. Errol took a tentative step toward the assassin, tried at once to ignore the arrow aimed at him and brace for the impact that would kill him.

An animal-like snarl erupted from behind him. Merodach raised the bow, drew . . .

Errol launched himself into space, heard the whine of the arrow merge with a cry of rage and pain. The water rushed up to meet him.

11

The Keralwash

ERROL FELL. accelerating through the mist off the river until the wind roared in his ears. He closed his eyes and pulled his arms up to protect his chin and face.

When the impact came, it pounded against his feet as though he'd landed on stone instead of water. His knees buckled, twisted to the side with a tearing pain. He drew breath to scream. The blow of the water against his ribs forced the air from his lungs. Deeper into the water he moved, slowing, but without air in his lungs to buoy him, still sinking.

At last he stopped, somewhere above the riverbed but far below the surface. Deep beneath the pain that painted his thoughts red, he knew the river must be sweeping him downstream. But he felt nothing of such motion. He kicked, ignoring the pain in his knees and tried to surface, but it was dark and the river's currents tumbled him. Which way was up?

His lungs protested, and his muscles ached with the need for air. Errol put both hands over his head, cupped them, and brought them down to his side, pulling for what he hoped was the surface. Again. He felt sleepy now, and though his knees still ached, they didn't seem to hurt so much. Spots swam in his vision, then merged into a soft light, comforting him.

As consciousness faded, his hands bumped something hard and rough.

⊰⧫⊱

Noise. At first Errol didn't recognize the sound. He opened his eyes, exchanged one blackness for another. Clinging to a piece of wood as big around as his waist, he bobbed in the flood like a twig. And the roar grew.

With a sense of resignation, he placed the sound, knew where he'd heard it before. *Falls.* Somewhere ahead of him the river dropped, spilling over a precipice high enough to carry the sound back to him. He searched for some glint of light, but the darkness was complete. Laughter bubbled up in him at his plight. For all he knew he might be right next to the riverbank, with safety no more than a few kicks away.

He would never know. Without warning, he rose in the water, then plunged as the river pitched him through a series of rapids. Air exploded from him before he realized he'd smashed into a boulder. He reached out, groped for some handhold, but the current tore him away, washing him toward the falls. Twice more it threw him against rocks jutting from the riverbed. Each time he was too slow to grab on and climb to safety.

The noise of the falls intensified at the same time the water calmed. He floated faster now, picking up speed. And then he fell again. At the last second, he thought to push the log away to avoid being crushed by it.

⊰⧫⊱

Time passed in disconnected segments. Sensations mixed, and he moved from chills to fever. Hands, sometimes gentle, moved him, held his arms as chills thrashed him, or beat his chest. It hurt to breathe. Errol no longer battled the river, but his lungs protested at each breath. Fits of coughing took him, ripped through his chest with tearing pains severe enough to make him vomit.

In the brief interludes between bouts of coughing and unconsciousness, someone spooned broth into him. Most of it dripped down his chin. Why couldn't they just let him rest? In stages too slow to be measured, he became able to discern that three people managed his care: two women and a man. The women's hands were gentle, one pair soft with age and warm and the other pair cool and firm. The man's hands held him when his fever shook him. Then they would restrain him until the fit passed. Once, calluses like bark ran across his bare skin before the hands stripped him of sweat-soaked garments.

Errol woke to sunlight, so weak he couldn't lift his head from his pillow. He tried his arm instead and discovered he possessed just enough strength to lift it from his side before it collapsed on his stomach. A hand, one of the warm soft ones, took his.

"Here now," a woman's voice said. "You just lie still. The soup will be ready in a moment."

He made to speak, wet his lips in preparation. "Wh-ere . . ." His voice croaked with disuse. His keeper placed a waterskin between his teeth, allowing him two swallows before taking it away.

"Where . . . am I?" The sound of his voice barely reached his own ears. He tried to pull enough breath to make himself heard and succeeded in producing a fit of coughing that brought spots of exhaustion to his eyes.

A hand stroked his forehead for a moment before it withdrew. "If you promise not to do that again, I'll tell you everything I think you want to know."

He nodded. The hand belonged to a middle-aged woman, her long brown hair tied back, accentuating the deep blue of her eyes. Full lips parted in a smile. A network of fine wrinkles ran to her temples.

"I'm Anomar Reven. My husband, Rale, found you washed up

on the riverbank like a piece of driftwood." She brushed back a stray lock of hair, tinged with gray. "He thought you were dead, so he threw you over his horse and brought you back here." The voice turned wry. "Rale figured to bury you. Said he didn't want you rotting on the bank and drawing vultures to his favorite fishing spot. The ride back to the farm may have bounced some of the water out of your lungs. I don't know, but you coughed once as we took you off Chester's back, so we knew you still had some life in you. Right now you're flat on your back in our home, which is about five miles outside the village of Rivenwash."

Without fighting or drawing too much, Errol inhaled until he held enough air to phrase a question. "Windridge?"

The woman's eyes widened. "Is that where you fell into the river?"

Errol tried to nod but was unsure if he succeeded.

When the woman began again, an edge of uncertainty had crept into her tone. "Curse me, boy. I don't know how you survived. That's more than thirty miles upstream. You've had the worst case of pneumonia I've ever seen, and I've seen more than a few. Rale says you're touched." She gave a short laugh. "Touched or not, you've been on the edge of crossing over for the past two weeks."

He let his surprise show.

"Oh yes. For a fortnight now, Rale and my daughter, Myrrha, have helped me tend you. Your fever broke again this morning. It might keep this time, but it'll be some while yet before you can get out of bed, much less travel."

Travel. How long would he be able to stay in one place before the compulsion overtook him and forced him to Erinon? At the thought, he felt a tug deep within his chest. Or was he just imagining it?

⊰✦⊱

Under Anomar's watchful eye Errol regained his strength. Four days after he first woke, he left his bed and tottered past the fireplace of the cabin, its two bedrooms, and through the door into unexpected sunshine. He leaned, trembling against the rough oak frame of the house and lifted his head to the late afternoon light.

The sound of displaced air to his left caught his attention. There, silhouetted on a low rise, Rale moved, spinning a staff that blurred and hummed. The farmer slipped from one stance to another, flowing as though in a dance, the staff in constant motion. To Errol, it looked at once more beautiful and deadly than anything Cruk had ever shown him with the sword.

Anomar stirred behind him, arms crossed and wearing a grin made all of pride. "Rale says he hasn't got much use for a sword, but I'd wager he's one of the most dangerous men alive, even so." She sighed, shifted to lean against the other side of the door from Errol. "I do love to watch him move." Her smile turned dreamy.

Errol nodded and continued to watch her husband in his private dance. "Do you think he'd teach me?"

Anomar breathed a soft laugh that he felt as a featherlight touch on his neck. "Are you sure you want him to? Rale doesn't do anything by half measures, he doesn't. The young men from the village come out sometimes to learn the staff from him. Most of them tire of the bruises after a week or two."

To Errol, Rale sounded a lot like Cruk. Maybe collecting bruises was the only way to learn how to fight. "He sounds like someone I know."

Her eyebrows lifted. "And who would that be?"

He lifted his shoulders. "A man from my village named Cruk. He used to be in the watch. He was teaching me how to use a sword."

"The watch?" Anomar's eyes widened, then narrowed. "Boy, I haven't asked for explanations. I usually don't when I tend someone who's closer to dying than living, but if you're bringing danger on my house, I better know about it."

She gave him a look made of sparks and tinder, ready to blaze into anger in an instant. He took a step back, stumbled from sudden weakness, and lurched. Anomar grabbed him, threw his arm around her shoulders, and hauled him inside, where she deposited him in a chair.

"I think you need some real food." Her gaze bored into him. "I'm going to get Rale." She paused. "And Myrrha as well. After you eat, I think we need to hear how you came to be drifting down to us on the river."

Minutes later, Errol got his first good look at the man who'd saved his life. Rale topped him by several inches. Gray eyes glinted over a broad nose that had been broken at least once. He moved with a step light enough to belong to a man twenty years younger, despite brown hair shot with gray.

Errol related his story, starting with the message from the nuntius. Anomar, but more often, Rale, stopped him and bade him go back and explain some part. At the mention of Merodach's name, Rale's eyebrows moved up his forehead.

Errol stopped. "You've heard of him?"

Rale nodded, laughed without humor. "We're closer to the island city here. News comes to us that probably never makes it to your village. Merodach is one of the captains of the watch. It's the highest rank they have and there are only ten. Men who talk of such things say he is the best of them." His lean body edged forward in the chair, his eyes intense under his dark brows. "You say he missed you not once but four times?"

Errol nodded.

"What does it mean?" Anomar asked.

Rale shrugged. "I don't know. Maybe the reputation of the watch is overstated." His eyes narrowed. "Boy, you're caught up in something bigger than you can understand. Rodran is the last of his line. One of the thirty-three benefices may come out of the Grand Judica as not only the next king, but the founder of the next dynasty."

"Won't they decide the next king by lot?" Errol asked.

Rale shrugged. "If they were all immune to the temptation power offers they would. The rumors coming out of Erinon tell me someone is trying very hard to prevent the conclave from choosing the next king."

He looked at Errol and took a deep breath, as if hesitant to give voice to his thoughts. "Any of them might want you dead."

Errol started. Him? They didn't want him; they wanted Liam. "Me?"

Rale thumped him on the head with one blunt finger. "Think, boy. Three times now you've escaped people who wanted you dead. Three."

Errol shook his head in denial. "But those were just coincidence. Merodach was just trying to keep me from delivering a message to Pater Martin."

"Then why did he shoot at you after you'd come out of the water?" Anomar asked. "He had to have known the message was ruined by then."

Errol ignored the question. "Dirk was following our whole group. I just happened to be trailing the others."

Rale gave a grudging nod. "It could be coincidence, but that word always sends a chill down my back, boy. The church has power and resources you can't imagine. Why did the Merakhi chase you?"

"I . . . I don't know." Why had she been there? It was Liam the abbot had wanted.

Rale snorted. "That's the problem, boy. There's too much you don't know, but you need to find out. Someone is hunting you." He paused. "Humph. And maybe more than just one someone. If you don't find out why, you're going to wind up dead."

"And just how is he supposed to do that, Da?" Myrrha asked, her voice tight and angry. "All he's known is his village."

Errol looked over to see Anomar's daughter gazing at him with liquid brown eyes—eyes like a fawn. He broke the gaze and raised another spoonful of soup to his lips. Myrrha made him nervous. He wasn't stupid. Hanging around the inns of Callowford and Berea had afforded him a certain education when it came to men and women, and he recognized the look Myrrha bestowed on him. He'd seen it hundreds of times whenever a woman set her eyes on a man.

He'd just never seen the look directed at him.

Rale's gaze ran over him, his mouth pursed in a way that reminded Errol of a farmer looking at a scrawny calf. "So your friend Cruk has been teaching you the sword?"

Errol nodded.

That brought a snort. "Fool thing to do, trying to teach someone as small as you how to use a sword." The man shook his head in disgust. "That's the thing about most men of the watch—they can't seem to understand that not everyone's built like a legend. The sword's no good for you, boy. You haven't got the reach for it. What you really need is a good bow." He gave a wolfish grin. "Actually, what you need is a less troubled destiny, but don't we all.

"I don't have a spare bow to give you, but I can teach you the staff if you're willing to learn. It's not as pretty as a sword, but for you it's probably better." He nodded. "Yes. And it attracts less attention."

Errol nodded his assent. "I'd like to learn. I don't really like swords."

Rale stood. "Good. We've got another two hours of daylight. Let's go."

Anomar put a hand on Errol's shoulder before he'd half risen out of his seat. "Are you crazy, Rale? The boy's barely out of the grave."

Her husband smiled, the expression lightening the countenance of his heavy features. "Is he in any danger?"

"Well, no."

"Fine," Rale said. "I'll try not to hurt him too much. He doesn't have time to be coddled, Anomar. If what the boy says is true about the compulsion, he may leave us at any time."

Rale's wife gave a thin-lipped nod at this.

"Have some bandages and some of that soothe-hurt tea ready." He turned to Errol. "Let's go, boy."

Errol swallowed. *Bandages?*

He followed Rale across the yard to a low-ceilinged barn. Rale bade him wait while he went inside. When he returned he carried two staffs, each somewhat longer than Errol was tall. Rale tossed one of the staffs to him. The wood slapped into his palm, the grain smooth against his skin.

"Your staff is made of ash," Rale said. "It's light and springy. Until you put some muscle on that frame of yours, you'll want to stay away from the weight of oak." He brandished his own staff, and Errol noted the honey-colored striations in the wood.

Rale moved into a stance similar to a swordsman. "Now, the first thing you need to know is what most swordsmen won't expect." Without warning his staff moved, and before Errol could step back out of the way, the wood cracked across his leg midway between his ankle and his knee. The blow wasn't hard enough to break his leg, but even so it dropped him to his knees.

"Even with your limited training in the sword, you didn't expect me to strike at your legs," Rale said. His voice cadenced as though he'd said these words many times before. "Swordsmen are taught, and rightly so, not to strike for the lower legs. For them it means death, but for a man with the longer reach of a staff, the legs are just another target. And one of the better ones, since a swordsman won't expect a blow to be aimed there."

The pain ebbed enough to allow him to stand.

Rale nodded his approval. "Now, hold your staff like this. . . ."

An hour later, Errol sat at the table shoveling chunks of mutton and potatoes into his mouth. Rale reminded him of Cruk. Both men seemed to think the quickest way to teach someone to fight was to beat them until they couldn't defend themselves. Maybe they were right. After one session with this strange farmer, Errol knew one thing for sure—he preferred the staff to the sword. The length of wood fit him in a way that a sword never would. Perhaps the sword's lethality repelled him, or maybe the span of the ash in his hand felt more comfortable because of his less-than-average height. But speculations aside, he enjoyed the staff more.

"You've got a knack for it, boy," Rale said around a mouthful of stew. "Some people are born swordsmen; some are made for the staff. There are a lucky few who can master both." He pointed his spoon at Errol. "You have balance. I don't know where you got it, but it's the best I've ever seen, and I've seen more than a few. You're a staff man."

Errol felt a stare upon him and glanced over to see Myrrha looking at him, eyes bright and shining. He ducked his head, his face red, and tried to concentrate on his food.

Anomar must have seen the look as well. "Myrrha, run to the spring and fetch us some water for the dishes." The look Anomar gave Errol after Myrrha left the cottage bore no resemblance to her daughter's. Anomar rose and disappeared from Errol's vision for a moment before returning with a pitcher of dark, foamy liquid.

Ale.

As his mouth watered, Errol counted back. How long had he gone without a drink? Three weeks? Four? He stared at the pitcher, his hand moving toward it of its own volition. When his fingers were close enough to feel the cooled air surrounding the thick stoneware, he stopped.

Anomar's laugh drifted across his hearing, sounded at once friendly and far away. "Go ahead, lad. Our ale is a little darker than most, but I've never had a complaint."

He pulled his hand back, aware now that sweat beaded on his forehead and that Rale watched him, his eyes dark, intense. Errol licked his lips. Did he want a drink? He hadn't gone more than two days in a row without a drink since he was . . . since Warrel . . . the quarry . . . stone.

Memory crushed him, blinding him to the cottage, to Rale, to Anomar. His arms covered his chest. He rocked back and forth, heard whimpering noises in a voice he recognized as his own. *Stone.* He reached out a hand without seeing, groping for the pitcher of ale.

He couldn't find it. Images assaulted him. He couldn't see past them.

"Boy!" Anomar's voice sounded in his ear, close enough for him to feel the breath of her words. A hand came to rest against his cheek.

"Leave us, Anomar," Rale's voice ordered. "This is beyond your healing."

Footsteps.

Motion.

His chair scraped the floor. A pop of sound and his head whipped to one side, and an instant later his cheek stung. His eyes snapped open to see Rale in front of him, arm raised for another blow.

"Can you see me, boy?"

Errol managed a nod.

"Good."

He felt himself lifted from the chair. Rale threw him over one shoulder like a sack of grain and carried him out to the yard, where the farmer dumped him on the ground.

Pictures of his past drifted across his vision. He couldn't seem to stop them. Blood everywhere. And silence. Not even a breath of sound. Errol opened his eyes, but the memories followed him.

An ash staff rested on his ribs.

"Come, boy," Rale said, soft but commanding. "Fight it."

As though Rale's voice had the power to command him, he groped for the staff like a drowning man grasping for a rope. His fingers closed on the wood, gripping it tighter and tighter until his knuckles cracked and ached with the effort.

That was as far as he could go.

Tears wet his cheeks. Warrel . . . blood . . . so much blood.

Hands gripped him, strong, implacable. "Fight, boy!"

Errol stood, stared as Rale's staff whistled through the air, coming for his legs.

He ground his staff, felt the impact of wood against wood. His palms stung with the vibration.

"No!" The word's echo still hung in the air as he lifted the butt end of his staff and struck, trying with all his might to smash through Rale's defense. Wood struck wood. Errol twirled, reversed his grip and struck again.

And again Rale parried.

He thrust now, hands at the lower end, trying to put the end of the staff into the farmer's midsection, face, throat, anything.

Errol screamed with every attack.

Nothing landed.

He didn't know how long it went on, but when at last he found himself on the ground with his vision clear, his voice was raw from screams and blisters were forming on his hands.

Rale pried the wood from his grasp and sat by him in the dirt of the yard.

"How long have you been in the ale barrel, boy?"

Errol drew a racking breath into his lungs. "About five years, I think. I'm not sure exactly how old I was when Warrel died."

A nod. "I've seen it before, though not in any so young. It's usually a man who's lost a wife or son. Men mostly—women seem to be stronger somehow. I saw a lot of it in the last war, with soldiers that lost their company. I think they felt guilty for living—all of them desperate to escape the pain of their loss. Most of them chose the ale barrel. A few opted for the healer's concoctions. Some chose the sharp end of the dagger."

Rale fell silent but made no move to rise.

They stayed that way, sitting side by side in the dirt until dusk crept over them and the fields and trees beyond the cottage and barn blurred, becoming indistinct.

"Who was Warrel?" Rale asked.

Who indeed?

"Warrel Dymon, the man who raised me." He sucked in air, squinted against that last bloody memory. In a voice like a child's he made one last plea. "Do I have to tell it?"

He sensed rather than saw Rale's nod. "If you ever want to be free of the ale, yes. I've known a few who could manage the drink and something of a normal life, but there was no mistaking how broken they were."

"I think I was fourteen," Errol said. "Warrel worked in the quarry at Callowford, my village. It's just a village, nothing like Windridge." He stared into the deepening gloom, saw the village street in front of him. "I was playing. There weren't many chores for me, since it was just the two of us. I spent a lot of time in the smithy, watching Knorl make horseshoes. I liked the way the water boiled and steamed when he put the hot metal into it.

"Cantor came riding up the quarry road like he had demons chasing him, screaming my name the whole way. When he found me, he didn't say anything, just lifted me with one arm and put me on the saddle behind him. We pounded back up the road. He wouldn't answer any of my questions." Errol shrugged at the memory. "Maybe he didn't hear.

"When we got to the quarry, a couple of men grabbed me and ran me down into the pit at the bottom. Warrel was there, lying under a block of . . . stone."

He didn't think he could go on. The memories were—

Rale's hand found his shoulder. "I'm sorry, boy. It would have been better if he could have said good-bye."

Errol barked a laugh that tore at his throat. "Better? No, I don't think it was." He shook his head. "Warrel wasn't dead, not yet. The fool. He knew better than to walk under a piece of hanging stone, no matter how strong the ropes were. But he hurried, or maybe he just forgot. He never said. They tell me he heard the creak of tackle at the last second and dove away. It was almost enough. The stone came down on his legs, just below his hips."

He drew a breath, forced himself to go on. "Durastone is heavy." Now that the moment held him, he wanted to tell it all, every detail. "The slab crushed his legs, forcing the blood into his body. He lost consciousness. The men didn't dare move him. The moment they moved the stone, Warrel would bleed to death in an instant. Instead, one of them opened a vein, let enough blood out for him to regain consciousness. He sent for me.

"By the time I got there, he was already fading from the shock and pain." Errol's head bowed under the weight of the memory, and tears splashed on the dirt, making mud. "I ran to him, begging him not to die, calling him Da over and over again. 'Don't go, Da. Don't go.'" The recollection overwhelmed him. He started to laugh.

"My head was on his shoulder. I knew what was coming. Quarry men are careful, but even careful men make mistakes, and more than one man died before Warrel." He fell silent. The image had him now.

"And then?" Rale's voice croaked in the darkness.

"Then he told me I wasn't his son. Not 'I love you' or 'I'm proud of you'—just that. Then the pain wrenched his face into something unrecognizable, wiped away whatever he might have said next. He waved at the men around us, and they hoisted the stone off his legs. Warrel was gone from the hips down. He bled out in less than a second.

"I walked back to the village. Warrel had some gold saved, and I spent it all on ale. It helped keep the memories away. When I didn't show any sign of sobering up, Pater Antil took Warrel's name from me. He changed my last name to Stone so everyone would know I was an orphan. He started trying to beat me sober about then."

Errol stopped, finished and hollow. His tears made faint splashing sounds.

They sat in silence. Errol felt the memory spreading, taking Rale and his farm back to Callowford, back to Warrel's end.

And his own.

12

COMPULSION

ON A CLOUDY MORNING some days later, Errol woke with the nagging feeling he'd lost something. The sensation persisted throughout the day, relieved only by the repeated amazement he experienced at being able to think clearly for more than an hour at a time. Now that the twin effects of sickness and ale no longer plagued him, he found he could see and think with a clarity he'd never experienced before.

True, without the ale's dulling effects his emotions, raw and powerful, lurked just beneath the surface, easy prey for memories that came upon him unaware, and unbidden tears tracked his cheeks more than once when memories of Warrel took him by surprise. But the pain faded a little each day, and every day that he refused Anomar's offer of ale, he felt his resolve and strength grow.

Rale often beckoned him to the yard in front of the cottage with a sideways tilt of his head, and the two of them would dance with the staff. At those times, moving the two spans of wood, he imagined himself whole, or almost, just another young man trying to please his master so that he could spare himself unnecessary bruises.

Errol drank in Rale's advice—"Don't keep your hands so close together on the staff. You struggle against the weight of the wood, and it slows your strike. Every weapon is fought with the whole body, not just the arms, and half the battle is fought from the neck up"—and strove to master every nuance of technique, balance, and strategy the man showed him.

One day, after parrying a blow, all the hours of training and advice clicked together. He pivoted, moving faster than thought, spun his staff, and struck.

A soft *thwack* sounded, followed by a grunt from Rale, who stepped back to rub his shin. "Bones, boy. That was quick."

Rale smiled and Errol's heart soared at the farmer's approval. "Let's see how you handle this, lad."

Errol retreated before an array of blows so fast and numerous they should have come from two men. Each thrust and strike of Rale's onslaught came closer and closer to landing until at last the oak staff found the meaty part of Errol's thigh and he backed away, wincing.

That earned him another nod. "Not bad, boy. Not bad at all. Most men wouldn't have lasted half the time you did. The only thing you need now is the one thing I can't give you."

Errol's heart leapt and sank with Rale's words. "What can't you give me?"

Rale came forward and tapped him on the chest and then gripped his arms. "Muscle. You're fast, boy. One of the fastest I've ever seen, and your balance is perfect, but if you want to move that length of wood fast enough to knock the lightning from the sky, you'll need to thicken up."

Rale laughed. "I wouldn't worry too much on that account, though. If you can manage to stay out of the ale barrel, you'll be fine. As long as you get enough to eat and work the staff, your body will do the rest. It'll make up for the years you lost. You may not end up like this Liam you told us about, but you'll have nothing to be ashamed of, and no man will take you for granted in a fight."

Looking down at his arm, sinewy but thin, Errol imagined how it could look and found the idea appealing.

"Now, boy," Rale said, pulling his attention forward, "let's see if you can touch me again. Attack."

An hour later, sweating and panting so that the air whistled in his throat, Errol held up one hand for a halt. The moment their staffs came to rest, the feeling of displacement returned, as though he'd lost something. It was ridiculous. He didn't own anything. There was nothing to lose, nothing. Perhaps the church's compulsion to go to Erinon acted upon him at last.

Two days later he felt the sensation again and told his host of it. Rale paused in the midst of feeding the cows to lean on his pitchfork and consider him. "It's yourself you've lost, boy."

Errol made as if to look for something. Then he patted himself. "I'm right here. That's a relief."

Rale smirked in a way to show Errol he didn't think the joke very funny. "Keep your sense of humor, boy. You'll need it, such as it is. What I meant was you've lost your sense of self." He threw another forkful of hay over the fence. "I've seen it happen to other men who've crawled out of the barrel. For the last five years your aim has been to keep yourself drunk enough to keep from remembering Warrel's death. Now, without that, you'll have to find some other purpose."

At the mention of Warrel, Errol's mouth watered and an image of a foaming tankard of nut-brown ale rose in his mind. Waving one hand, as though he could shoo the picture away, he made himself relive Warrel's last moments. He wanted to throw up.

"Come, Errol," Rale said. "We've time for a bit of staff work. It will give you something to distract you, at least for a while."

Errol looked at the pile of hay and the pitchfork lying discarded next to it. "What about the cows?"

Rale laughed. For a moment his face lost some of it hardness. "You've never worked a farm, I see. The work is never over, just delayed. The cows will be fine."

They sparred for nearly an hour. Errol wore an assortment of bruises that made him look as if he'd been born with spots. Rale sported exactly one mark, a slight purpling above the ankle. He sat on the ground, rubbing it and gave Errol a considering look. "You're getting better. I have to work harder to get through your defenses and you can get through mine one time in ten. Most of the lads I've trained can't touch me until I've worked with them for a couple of months or better. And then, they can only do it once."

Errol ducked his head in acknowledgment of the compliment that eased the ache in his muscles. "Will it work for me to use the staff?"

Rale's brows furrowed. "For what?"

He shrugged. "To replace the ale."

"I don't think so, boy. The ale was never your problem. The hole that Warrel's last words and death created was the problem. You tried to fill it with ale. That didn't work so well, did it?"

Errol rubbed one cheek, remembering the feel of Cilla's wood floor that had sufficed for his bed. "No. Not so much."

Dark gray eyes considered him. "I've known men that gave themselves to the sword, or the bow, or the staff when they sobered up. I'm not sure they were much better off."

Errol felt a shock of surprise.

Rale held up a hand. "Don't misunderstand me. The staff is as close to making music as I can come with these hands, but it's not enough. You need something to fill that hole inside you, lad."

"What?"

Rale smiled. "Deas will tell you when the time's right."

Talk of Deas reminded Errol of Antil. He didn't pursue the subject.

On a cool morning nearly a week later, Errol awoke outside the door of the cottage with the rising sun at his back. He stood in his smallclothes and gave a shiver against the chill of the early morning air. He had no memory of leaving his bed, traversing the floor of the cottage, or opening the door. Yet here he stood, his skin pebbling against the breeze and his face set to the west in expectation.

Myrrha's laughter, deep and throaty for a girl whose age did not exceed his own, took him by surprise. His head snapped to the left to see her carrying a basket of eggs across the yard and eyeing him broadly. She darted glances left and right before she spoke. "You could do with a few more weeks of food and work with the staff before strutting in your smallclothes, but you're not half bad to look upon." She finished with an exaggerated wink and a slow head-to-toe gaze that made Errol's face flame into crimson. Her laughter followed his hasty retreat into the cottage.

During breakfast, he told Anomar about his experience, careful to omit her daughter's comments. To his surprise, she nodded as though she'd expected no less.

"You've been here more than four weeks. If the reader did lay the compulsion on you, then you can expect something to happen." Her eyes turned serious, almost sad. "I've only heard of the compulsion twice in my life, but it's never been denied. It will grow stronger with each passing day, moving from your dreams into your waking hours." She laid bread and cheese on his plate. "You'll be leaving soon, I think. Best to build up your strength before you go."

Errol spent the next few days working with Rale on the farm and trying to eat the mountain of food Anomar piled in front of him. His hips and legs complained with a persistent ache that no amount of exercise with the staff could relieve.

One afternoon, when a warm southerly wind ruffled his hair and carried the scent of honeysuckle, Rale stepped back to consider him. He wore a thoughtful frown and then walked to where Errol stood. "You're growing."

Errol felt a flush of warmth as though the other man had just paid him a sought-after compliment. After Warrel died, the other boys in the village and almost all those that passed through with the caravans had been taller than he. "Really?" The smile stretched across his face.

Rale nodded, without smiling. "Aye. You'll have to be careful. Your strike distance will be different, and if you're like most lads, you'll be awkward until you get used to the change." He tapped Errol's chest with a thick forefinger. "Be careful. Clumsy fighters don't win very often."

Errol's grin subsided, but Rale's tone couldn't erase it completely. "I will be, but I'm still glad to be growing."

Rale smirked in response. "Aye. No one can blame you for that."

❧

At noon the next day, Errol let the axe slip from his fingers in the middle of splitting wood and walked west. He made it nearly half a mile before unseen hands shook him and brought him back to self-awareness.

Errol blinked against sweat he only just noticed, jerked in surprise to find Rale in front of him. "Where am I going?"

Rale looked back in the direction of the farmhouse. "West. You'll have to leave tomorrow. The church's call is getting too strong. Better you leave at a time of your own choosing than to have the compulsion take you unawares." His face became as hard as stone. "Churchmen. You could put blisters on your feet or walk until you dropped dead from lack of food and never know what killed you. Come. I'll take you back to the cabin. Anomar and Myrrha will want to fuss over you one last night before you leave. I'll go into the village and get some supplies you'll need for your journey."

Errol accepted the man's decision without argument. Rale was much like Cruk in this respect as well—if he said something was so, then it was a very good chance it was so.

❧

The sun's last rays streamed through the kitchen window, casting long shadows that striped the light in the cabin as Rale came through the door. He slammed it closed behind him in haste and checked the window, holding one hand up for silence.

He faced Errol, his eyes hard, angry. "You're leaving, boy."

Errol nodded. "I know."

Rale shook his head. "No. I mean you're leaving tonight, as soon as it gets full dark."

Myrrha stood. "Why, Da?"

"There are men in the village, looking for a lad that fits Errol's description."

Errol's heart skipped a beat, and he stood. "My friends. Can you take me to them?"

Rale's growl warned him. "I think I know the difference between friends and enemies, boy. These are guards from the cathedral at Windridge. They have a writ from the abbot accusing you of the death of their captain. I listened for a bit. They're not giving any details on your crime."

Errol's insides tried to escape in any number of directions without him, and he sat in stunned amazement. "But, but surely I can wait 'til morning, can't I?"

Rale's expression said plainly he could not. "They've got a reader with them. I only caught a glimpse because he was surrounded by guards, but he was carving pine lots like he had demons chasing him."

Anomar gave a sharp intake of breath. "A reader so far away from the capital? How can that be?"

Her husband shrugged off the question. "Strange times. And two of the guards wore the black of the watch." His face twisted and he shook his head. "As I recall, they're not supposed to leave the king. The abbot is using them like hounds with the reader to guide them. They know Errol's near the village."

Errol shook his head in mute denial. *No.* It couldn't be. How could they even know he was alive, much less somewhere near the village? "That's impossible."

Rale snorted without humor. "Boy, they've got a reader with them, and something about him has his guards more than a little scared. I haven't seen men snap to orders like that since the war." He gave him a look of exasperation. "How much did Luis tell you about what readers can do?"

"He didn't talk about how much—mostly it was just him telling me how." At Rale's look, his voice strengthened. "We didn't have much time. We were too busy running from Merodach and whoever else we thought was trying to kill us. That put a damper on our conversation. He carved a pair of lots out of wood to choose which way to run." He still felt a sense of wonderment. "It kept coming up *Windridge*." He lifted his shoulders. "You know what happened after that."

Anomar stepped behind him, laid her hands on his shoulders. Her touch felt warm through Errol's shirt, but he sensed worry in the tightness in her fingers.

Rale sighed. "Think, boy. Think. If all you had to do to know anything, anything at all, was to carve a few round balls out of wood or stone, do you know how much power that would give you?"

Errol's mind reeled. It couldn't be true. "Luis never said anything about that."

Rale squinted as if he had a headache. "Readers are dangerous, boy—not because they're evil, but because there's so little that can be hidden from them."

"But they're churchmen," Errol said. "Don't they help people?"

Rale pulled in a breath, let it out slowly. "Boy, a man is either born with the ability to be a reader or not. It's like having blue eyes or a natural ability with the sword. Readers work for the church because King Magnus wanted to cement the provinces under the crown. He instituted the test and gave the church permission to compel anyone with the ability to Erinon."

Errol's heart seemed to be trying to break free of his chest. "But how could they know I'm alive, or that I'm here?"

A string of curses, the sounds of Rale's frustration, battered his ears. "All they have to do is find someone that knows you. It's not perfect, but with enough throws it'll do the trick. Try to understand this. They find someone who can describe you; what you look like, how you act, the fact that you like to drink—or used to. Then they carve two lots. One lot says *Alive* and the other, *Dead*. A couple dozen draws later, they have their answer."

"Why a couple dozen?" Errol asked. "When Luis had me draw to choose cities, I did it less than ten times, and only that much because he wanted to prove that casting lots really worked."

Rale nodded impatiently. "Yes, because he knew the cities himself. You wouldn't have drawn the other city more than two times out of ten. But if a reader doesn't know someone directly, he can still use the knowledge from someone else. After that, it's just a matter of drawing the lots often enough to get a clear answer." He lifted a hand, pulled at his jaw muscles. "After they determined you were alive, finding you was easy. They wouldn't need to know you then, just the villages in the area."

This pronouncement hit Errol's thoughts like a whirlwind. That something so simple could hold so much power, that he held so much power, astonished him. A thought struck him like a blow to the stomach. "But they're already in your village. They'll be drawing lots to see which family I'm with."

Anomar's hands tightened on his shoulders.

At the same time, Rale nodded. "That's right, boy. And darkness won't slow them down. These people want you, and they're not of a mind to wait."

His stomach seemed to be trying to drop through his legs onto the floor. He stood, but Rale waved him down at the same time he lifted his gaze to Anomar. "Pack him as much food as he can carry. I'll saddle Midnight." He turned back to Errol, untied a pouch at his belt, and shook loose a pair of heavy iron tubes on the table.

Errol lifted one. It was closed on one end. "What are these?"

"Knobblocks." Rale's tone was grim. "I picked them up after I saw the abbot's men in the village. I've never cared much for them myself, but I fear you're going to find them useful. Look inside."

He turned the tube so the light from the lamp shone down into it. Twin barbs stuck out from either side. "What are they for?"

"They go over the end of your staff. The barbs keep the weights from slipping off." He sighed. "With those on, you can kill or cripple a man with a single blow. But be careful of them—until you get used to their weight, they'll slow you down. Work with them each day until you're as fast with them as without."

"But I'm not ready! I can't fight!" Errol shook his head in denial. "I can barely touch you one time in ten."

Anomar turned from the bag she was loading with cheese, bread, and dried meat. "He touched you? More than once?"

Rale nodded, and a rueful grin pulled his mouth to one side. "Maybe I'm slowing down a bit." He gave Errol a wink.

His wife shook her head. "Not likely. I've watched you every day for the last ten years." She favored Errol with a gaze made all of respect. "You must have a talent for the staff, Errol. No one touches Rale unless he lets them."

The thought struck him again how much Rale reminded him of Cruk. He knew fighting at least as well as Cruk, and he knew other things as well. "Who are you, Rale? You're not really just a farmer."

Those somber eyes measured him, nodding. "If you can stay out of the ale barrel, I think you just might live. You're learning to think." He rose. "But we don't have time for the tale." Rale crossed the cottage, took the bag of food from Anomar, gave her a kiss on the cheek, and turned toward the door. "It's time for you to leave, Errol. I'll guide you to the river. Follow it southwest until you hit Longhollow. Travel at night. Rest during the day and work the staff as much as you can. When you get to Longhollow, sign with one of the merchant trains as a guard. They don't pay much, but you'll be almost invisible, and it'll get you to Erinon." He shrugged. "After that, get to the conclave. Try to find your friends."

Errol saw Rale's eyes squint as he said this last and knew what the warrior-farmer purposely had not said.

If they still lived.

He cupped the heavy knobblocks in one hand, his imagination conjuring images of blood and pain. Those two pieces of iron communicated Rale's concern. The man didn't expect him to survive. He followed Rale to the door of the cottage, where Myrrha stood with tears brimming that threatened to spill down her cheeks.

Her lower lip trembled before she took it between her teeth. She put her arms around his neck and managed a quivering smile that looked ready to flee at any moment. "I would have liked to see you in your smallclothes once you'd spent time with the knob-blocks." She tried to laugh, but the sound broke into splinters. Myrrha leaned forward so quickly Errol had no time to dodge. She caught him in a fierce embrace and kissed him on the lips.

Errol stood dumbfounded, tasting salt as she turned and ran to her room. Anomar studied him with a mix of emotions on her face he couldn't hope to untangle, but there didn't seem to be any anger present.

Rale opened the door, and Errol followed him into the night. A crescent moon glowed softly above the eastern horizon, casting tenuous shadows limned in silver. The farmer's voice came as a murmur from his left. "You'll have about two and a half weeks of moon to travel by before you lose her light altogether. Stick to the riverbanks, so you can see. Hide among the trees during the day. Midnight will graze along the way."

A hand, hard and callused, gripped his arm. "Trust no one you meet along the river. Someone powerful wants you dead, boy."

The pressure on his arm eased and they proceeded to the barn, where Rale saddled the black gelding and tied the bag of food onto its back.

"I'll lead you to the river. I know the path even in the dark. After that, ride and keep your ears open."

Errol nodded, then blushed at his foolishness for doing so when Rale couldn't see. They left the barn, Midnight's hooves making a soft padding sound on the dirt that changed to a swish as they circled around and entered the tall grass. The river lay a mile to the north, though the distance stretched in the dark and quiet.

The moon had just started to rise off the horizon when Rale led him through a copse of cedar trees, fragrant in the stillness, and the river came into view. Scant moonlight blocked by clouds sparkled off the water, dancing, uncaring of dangers or fears.

Rale's voice sounded close. "Mount up. One last piece of advice on the staff—don't hesitate to kill if you have to. Deas knows your enemies won't."

Errol's throat closed on his words. Rale and Anomar's cottage was the closest thing to home he'd had since Warrel died. And though he wouldn't have said so aloud, especially where Anomar could hear him, Myrrha intrigued him, and the idea of her wanting to see him in his smallclothes, even as a jest, flattered him. Leaving them all behind felt like having pricklehog quills pulled out of his flesh.

He thrust out his hand, waved it from side to side until it bumped into Rale. The big man took Errol's hand in his own, gripped it hard.

"Boy, if you live, I'd enjoy hearing the story of how you managed it." His voice, rough as always, held a note of warmth, and Errol laughed in spite of himself.

"I don't know how good I am at fighting, but I'm really good at running away. I don't want to die."

A chuckle rumbled in response. "You're an honest lad, Errol Stone. Mind, you don't tell anyone you're a reader. The church isn't universally loved, and there's more than a few that put the blame on the readers misusing their power. Best if you just pretend to be an orphan out to see the world as a caravan guard."

Errol laughed. "That shouldn't be too hard. That's pretty much what I am."

He waited for a moment for Rale to say something more, but the air stilled, and he sensed his teacher had already begun his journey back to the cottage. He twitched the reins to direct Midnight's head west and resolved to ride until the sky brightened.

13

THE ROAD TO LONGHOLLOW

THE WEIGHT of solitude descended upon Errol as he rode. The noise of tree frogs and the occasional animal cry served only to accentuate his isolation. Each step of Midnight's hooves took him farther away from the warmth and security of Rale and Anomar's hospitality. He would have stayed with them if he could have—if the church's compulsion and the abbot's search hadn't driven him from cover like a hunted animal.

Hours slipped by, marked by the steady plodding of Midnight's steps and the moon's glint on the river that flowed on his left. In the dark, he imagined that he didn't really move at all, merely pretended to in a scene that never changed. Only the moon betrayed the passage of time, rising higher from her unveiling in the east until it reached its zenith and began its descent to the west. When it stood a handsbreadth above the horizon, the sky in the east began to change from black to gray and then, finally, to a ruddy crimson.

A large stand of cedar and pine presented itself to his right, and Errol made for it. He dismounted and unsaddled Midnight, using thick handfuls of grass to rub the big gelding down before he staked the leads so his mount could graze in the clearing. The horse confirmed his suspicions about Rale. Though Midnight was past his prime, it was clear what he had once been—no farmer needed a destrier like that.

He ate from the provisions Anomar had packed for him. She kept a well-stocked larder and, it seemed, possessed a strong maternal instinct. The food she'd provided was the best she had to offer, but as he sat alone, without Rale, Anomar, or Myrrha to share it with him, his meal tasted like dirt.

His body craved sleep, and the sun's rising only accentuated his fatigue, but he brushed the crumbs from his trousers and hefted his staff. Rolling his head to loosen the muscles in his neck, he stifled a yawn, pulled the knobblocks from his pocket, and fit them over the ends, tapping the butt of the staff against a nearby tree until he felt the ash bottom against the iron. Curious, he hefted the newly weighted staff in one hand. The iron pieces weren't that heavy, really. How much difference could they make?

When he took the first swing, he got his answer. The knobblocks' weight, multiplied by the distance along the staff from his hands, made the ash feel as heavy as iron. Errol went through the forms against a small sapling. Every move he made crept at half speed. Before five minutes passed, sweat poured down his back. The more he tried to move the wood at its accustomed pace, the slower it seemed to go.

Twenty minutes in, he stopped, gasping, his shoulders refusing even to lift the weighted staff, much less swing it with any threat or authority. He plopped on the ground, hung his head, panting like a dog. "Rale wasn't kidding. At this rate it'll take me forever to muscle up enough to use the staff with these things on it."

He ate a little more of the bread and cheese and then, using his saddle as a pillow, he slept.

✦

A shaft of sunlight from just above the western horizon woke him. Midnight grazed, still tied to the tree, but some sound or absence of movement put Errol on his guard. He grabbed the staff and yanked the knobblocks off in haste, searched the trees, peering through the shadows, his heart yammering in his chest, urging him to flee.

What had set him on edge? Nothing moved. Even the breeze had died. Silence ruled, as though the woods in which he hid were nothing more than a painting.

He froze. *That's it.* There was no sound.

He turned in slow circles, searching the shadows between the trees. Then Midnight threw his head and gave a soft whinny. The horse looked directly over Errol's shoulder.

At something behind him.

He whirled, spinning the staff.

The wood parried a thrust aimed at his gut. He jumped, seeking distance between himself and the man whose sword moved back in line, pointing again at his midsection.

A predatory smile revealed crooked teeth beneath a sharply hooked nose. "They told me you had a demon's own luck." The man stepped forward, light and sure on his feet. "But they also told me you didn't know how to handle a sword. Do you think that stick is going to save you?"

Errol took a step back, his mind churning, trying to keep pace with his heart. *They?* Who were they?

"How did you find me?"

The man shrugged, blinking. "Once we found the farmhouse, one of us was bound to. That stupid farmer wouldn't talk. Tough as a boot he was. The captain knocked him unconscious." The man shook his head. "Too hasty, that. No man can talk when he's out cold."

Errol shook his head. He couldn't believe Rale would go down without a fight. "I don't think so. He fought you, didn't he."

Another shrug and a blink began the man's answer. He circled to Errol's left. "Aye, he fought. Put down three men before the captain rapped him on the head." The swordsman nodded toward Errol's stomach. "I like gut wounds. People scream more, and they take longer to die."

He flicked his sword, and Errol twitched the staff. His arms shook so that the staff wiggled in his hands like a live thing. Bile rose in his throat. The man's sword weaved leisurely figure eights, and Errol moved to the man's left, desperate to keep himself out of reach. "Rale didn't tell you where to find me. Who did?"

For the third time the man gave a shrug and a blink before he answered. A plan formed in Errol's mind.

"That farmwife told us." He punctuated the revelation with coarse laughter. "She would have told us anything when we put our hands on her daughter."

Errol's throat tightened and he fought to breathe. *Myrrha.*

A grimace tightened the man's face. "Captain told us not to harm her. Said we couldn't afford to leave that kind of trail. Too cautious, Captain is." He circled back to Errol's right, dark eyes becoming intense.

Now. It has to be now. "What's your captain's name?" He waited the merest fraction of a second, saw muscles tense as a prelude to a shrug and a blink. The eyelids started down.

Errol struck.

He stepped and swung the staff, forced the ash to move faster than he had ever pushed the wood before.

The man finished his blink, eyes growing wide in surprise, and tried to parry. The staff slipped under the blade. The man hadn't expected a low-line attack. The crack of wood against bone sounded in the clearing. Using the momentum of the rebound, Errol shifted his hands, brought the staff around as his opponent tried to shift his weight.

The wood whistled, crying in the air as he brought the staff around its circle to strike the man's head. Blood erupted. Crimson drops blossomed in the air even as the man's eyes struggled to focus. With a snarl he hobbled forward, head shaking, his sword still pointed at Errol's gut. But it trembled now.

Errol gritted his teeth, changed his grip to slide his hands closer to the end of the staff, and thrust. A groan, deep and tearing, sounded from the man as the wood crushed into his solar plexus.

The sword fell. The man followed a second later, dropping to his knees.

Swinging with all the terror and fury his heart couldn't hold, Errol hit him across the head. He watched, brandishing the staff in readiness as the man fell face forward.

His chest heaving, he watched the still form on the ground in front of him, ready to strike again at any movement greater than a drawn breath. Finally, he picked up the sword and went to his saddlebags. There was no rope, but there was a long strip of burlap Anomar had used to wrap the food. It would have to do. Cutting it into three pieces, he tied the man's feet and ankles and used the final piece to gag him. It probably wouldn't hold for long. He'd never learned how to make a decent knot, but by the time the man freed himself, Errol would be gone.

He searched the woods until he found his assailant's horse, took the food and money from the saddlebags, and put the flat of the blade against its rump so hard, it took off with a scream.

Dusk settled over the landscape, painting the shadows in soothing shades of purple, but Errol's heart continued to beat against his ribs as if he still fought. He scrubbed away tears as he saddled Midnight and made for the river.

He needed to get stronger. That the man had still come after him after that blow to his leg frightened him. With knobblocks the strike would have broken the bone and the fight would have been over before it started. As he reached the riverbank and turned to follow the water southeast, he resolved to spend every possible minute working with the weighted staff.

Darkness wrapped him like a blanket. Only the moon's washed-out glimmer shining off the water relieved the night. By feel he lifted the staff, fished the knobblocks out of his pocket, and fitted them to the ends of the wood. Careful to avoid hitting Midnight, he moved through the basic staff movements Rale had taught him. The moves felt clumsy on horseback, but he pressed on. When his arms tired and the weapon threatened to strike the horse, he rested and ate. As his strength returned, he forced himself through the forms again.

At last the sky pinked, and with a sigh of relief, he guided Midnight into the forest away from the river. The cedars and pines still dominated but were interspersed now with hardwoods. He dismounted at the forest's edge, took the reins in one hand, and searched for a secluded clearing.

He rubbed Midnight's nose. "I need to sleep, and I bet you're tired of the bit and saddle." Gloom lived beneath the branches of the trees. That was fine by him. Whoever pursued him would find it difficult to see him among the shadows. He unsaddled Midnight, his shoulders trembling with the effort. But after he staked the leading rein to the ground, he took the staff and cudgeled his muscles through the forms for defense and attack for another hour, after which he collapsed to the ground, sweating and out of breath, and slept.

Every day and night he followed the same routine. Gradually the ache in his shoulders began to subside and his lungs no longer labored as hard during his workouts. Midnight became so used to the swish of the ash staff that he seldom more than cocked an ear when Errol practiced the forms. But the incessant workouts took their toll. A voice in the back of his head told him he pushed himself too hard, needed to take more time for rest and food.

One morning as the sun peaked over the horizon, he slipped from the saddle, took a step forward to remove the bridle from his mount, and collapsed. He pushed against the ground, tried to rise. The movement caught the attention of Midnight, who pushed against him with his fuzzy nose, whickering.

"I'm fine, boy," Errol said. The earth pulled at him, weighed him down. His eyelids took on a weight of their own. "I just need . . . to . . . sleep."

He woke to the sightlessness of dark and the sound of crickets and tree frogs. The moon shone from well above the treetops, looking small and isolated as it tracked across the sky. He shielded his eyes from the moonlight and waited for the darkness to fade. Midnight grazed off to his right, still saddled. A long growl accompanied by a twisting cramp came from his midsection. He fumbled with the saddlebags in the dark until he located a wedge of cheese and a chunk of heavy bread to eat on the ride. The moon glowed on his right as he led Midnight northeast, back toward the river.

He froze.

A flicker of torchlight winked in and out of sight through the gaps in the trees. The light split, became two. The pinpoints separated over and over again, until eight of them bobbed up and down like corks in a river.

He stood transfixed as they headed downstream. If not for their lights, he would never have known they were there. What errand or mission constrained them to travel at night? Perhaps he could journey with them to Longhollow. They must surely be traveling more quickly than he, but could he trust them?

The lights stopped, and in the stillness, as though they were whispers of wind, he heard voices calling to one another. Then they came toward the woods, horses' hooves crunching through twigs and pinecones.

Coming toward him. Searching.

He pulled his eyes from the hypnotic bounce of their torches and led Midnight away, deeper into the forest. What followed became the strangest game of seeker-and-lost he'd ever played. Casting glances behind, he discerned their strategy. Somehow they must have known where he'd camped. There was no other way to explain the precision with which they'd been able to locate not only the woods he slept in, but his campsite as well. Now, they fanned out in an arc to scoop him up like a minnow caught in a pool.

How had they known where he was?

He cursed himself for a fool. They had a reader with them.

With a shake of his head he thrust the thought away. There would be time for speculation later. His only chance lay in flight.

Silence rested on the wood. No tree frogs, nightingales, or owls broke the quiet. The slightest noise could be heard a hundred paces away. Errol scooted his feet forward along the ground, trying to push aside any sticks whose sudden crack might give away his presence. As much as Midnight meant to him, there was no chance the horse would miss every twig in the dark. He led the horse, pushing aside the branches with his shins.

Behind him the arc of riders advanced, but the constant interruption of trees kept Errol from knowing whether they gained or fell farther behind. Sweat beaded on his brow. The silence took on life, pressed against him, and an insane desire to make some kind of noise to dispel it pestered him. He clenched his jaws and continued leading Midnight with his shuffling gait, trying to move faster.

He conjured Rale's face, tried to recall everything the farmer ever said about the terrain between his farm and Longhollow. There wasn't much. Stick to the river, he'd said. Sleep in the woods each night.

But how big were the woods? If Errol didn't cover enough distance to conceal himself by dawn, he'd be caught. If he could find a way out of the dense growth before his pursuers caught up to him, Midnight might be able to carry him to safety. Did the trees even have an end? He might be looking for something that didn't even exist or, if it did, would take him days of travel to find.

The torchlight seemed farther away now, mere pinpoints among the boles. He decided to risk a little noise for the sake of speed. He picked up his feet, increased his pace to a quick jog. A large crunch sounded beneath his boot as a stick snapped in two. He stopped, held his breath, and strained his ears for any sound that he'd betrayed his whereabouts. Errol cursed himself for a fool. He'd been building a lead on those who chased him.

The forest remained silent. He resumed his stiff-gaited shuffle and moved ahead. His eyes strained to make use of the splintered moonlight that penetrated the canopy of foliage overhead.

The torches fell farther behind, but always they came on, never completely lost to sight.

Time passed, and Errol found he could see through the gloom with less difficulty. Shapes held more definition as the moon ascended. Hints of shadows across his path showed him where the sticks were. He thought back. It had taken Luis twenty minutes to cast a pair of lots. Even if it could be done in half the time, he could escape as long as he kept moving.

Fatigue dulled his brain. His feet had been working through thick grass for ten paces before he realized he'd left the forest. Tiny specs of light, mere pinpricks, still moved in the forest. They would not catch him now. Errol hugged Midnight's neck, then gave the big destrier an apple before he mounted and set off in a fast trot.

Two days later he entered Longhollow, stepped into mud and chaos.

14

THE CARAVAN MASTER

THE CITY of Longhollow seemed more a massive collection of caravans interspersed with buildings than a city. It squatted atop a low bluff overlooking the river. A palisade of sharpened logs served as a barely definable boundary between the exterior and the interior. The few buildings, some of which leaned over the street on tilted supports, were made of unpainted wood rather than stone.

Porters sweated and cursed their loads into position, then cursed some more when instructed to remove what had just been moved. Dozens of trader emblems flapped in the breeze, each caravan fighting to get their goods and begin their journey to profitability. Stock that didn't come in by the four roads that converged on the city came floating in by barge or boat on the river.

Errol fought to keep his hands from twitching the reins and fleeing back to the quietude of the forest and the river farther west. The color and cacophony of the press assaulted his senses. He looked down, convinced by the smell that Midnight must be stepping through sewage.

A voice intruded on his disgust. "Move, boy. This isn't getting any lighter."

Errol turned to see a young man about his own age with a huge sack of grain thrown over each shoulder.

"Sorry." Errol moved Midnight aside.

The man took a step, slipped, and dropped his burden with a curse. "Look what you made me do."

Errol dismounted. "I'm sorry. Here, we can load the sacks on my horse." He picked one up with difficulty and plopped it on the saddle.

The young man looked at him, suspicion written across a freckled face under dark red hair. "Your first time here?"

Errol nodded. "I came to sign on as a guard."

That earned him a laugh. "Well, at least your horse looks the part. I'll wager he's not used to carrying sacks of grain." He hefted the second bag onto Midnight. "I'm Etann." He caught Errol's look of disgust and grinned at him. "Not many people stay here for long. Not even the harlots or blacksmiths. Soon or late the noise and the smell drive everyone away."

They walked toward the southern edge of the town. The noise never lessened.

Etann's hand on his shoulder brought him to a stop next to a stable that looked as if it had been hastily built the day before. "Thanks for the help." He shouldered his grain.

The chaos of the town was just as daunting as at first glimpse. "Can you tell me how I should go about becoming a caravan guard?"

Etann gestured with his chin toward a heavy man in robes that matched the standard under which a dozen porters labored. "That's the merchant master. With the smaller caravans, it's the merchant himself; with the larger it's usually his factor, the man responsible for the hundreds of small decisions that make the merchant train profitable." Etann smirked, his green eyes twinkling. "One of those small decisions includes who guards the goods." He lumbered away.

How did one address a merchant or his factor? For that matter, how was he to know the difference?

Not knowing what else to do, Errol led Midnight to the merchant master and opted for the general honorific. "Excuse me, sir?"

The man rotated to face him, his bulk making the yellow and black horizontal stripes of his robes wave and distort around his middle. He looked like a giant bee. Errol hoped his smile would be misinterpreted.

It hadn't. The merchant curled his lip. "What do you want, boy?"

He leaned on his staff and tried to fix a confident grin on his face. Maybe the factor would think him experienced. "I'm looking for work as a caravan guard."

The man laughed so hard Errol could feel the puffs of his mirth. Then the man's face hardened, though the redness of his laughter remained. "Get out of my way, boy. I have all the guards I need, and I don't have time for jokes."

He moved to turn away, but Errol stepped around and forced the man to face him again. "Do you know of any caravans that *are* looking for guards?"

The man glared at him for a split second before the look melted away to be replaced by a smile as ingratiating as it was false. He tapped a sausage-like finger against his chin. "I think I heard Naaman Ru say he needed a new guard or two. He's got a couple that like to drink too much." The merchant master leaned toward him, draping a thick arm around his shoulders. His voice dropped to a conspiratorial whisper. "You can't have that, you know. What if the train gets attacked while the men are drunk?" He clucked. "That would never do."

"Where do I find him?" Errol itched to shake the man's arm off. He didn't trust the fat bee any farther than he could haul him, but he couldn't afford to let an opportunity, any opportunity, to get to Erinon undetected pass him by.

A striped arm pointed across the chaos. "Ru's at the far end of the camp. Look for purple and black diamonds." The grin returned, looking almost savage. "He has some strange ideas about how he picks his guards, but that should be no trouble for you. I can see you're an experienced fighting man."

Errol nodded, certain the man must be making sport of him and doubting any such merchant existed. Not one of the flags that fluttered weakly in the breeze bore a diamond pattern, purple or otherwise.

Fifteen minutes later, still walking with Midnight trailing behind in the direction he'd been sent, he began to hope there was no such man. The buildings and camps on this side of the town reeked of petty and not so petty crime. Men stared at his horse and belongings with hungry looks, and more than one fingered belt daggers as they did so. Errol paused just long enough to put the knobblocks on his staff. The looks continued, but the faces appeared more wary. *Good.* Right then he only wanted to get back to the better side of Longhollow. If he had to ride alone to Erinon, so be it.

Then he saw it. Purple and black diamonds on a yellow background waved over the teeming masses. He took a breath, like a diver about to plunge into water, and elbowed his way through the press toward the man whose tunic matched the flag in every detail. As he narrowed the distance, the smell of newly tanned hides assaulted him, and he fought to keep from gagging.

Guards of every description lounged about the site. A man with a puckered scar running down the side of his face stalked among the wagons kicking any guard who appeared to be sleeping. Many of those struck made a brief show of attentiveness before returning to their half-lidded somnolence. Errol almost turned back, convinced he should try his luck elsewhere, but the man in purple and black noticed him and beckoned to him with a smile.

He led his horse toward the caravan master, a man whose dark hair and coloring marked him as a Basqu. Unlike the other caravan masters he'd seen, this one wore a sword. Errol stopped short of the weapon's reach. "A man in yellow and black stripes told me you might be looking for a new guard."

A smile blossomed beneath the caravan master's mustache. "Ah, that would have been Orbeck. I'm Naaman Ru." At Errol's nod he continued. "I already have a full complement of guards, but I'm always looking to improve the quality of my protection." Ru's gaze wandered away from Errol's eyes and stopped at his hip. "Where's your sword?"

Errol hefted the staff, tapped it against the ground twice. "I use this."

This earned him a lift of Ru's brows, and the man caressed the hilt of the blade strapped to his side. "I find it easier to kill someone if I have something sharp."

"If I have to kill someone, I can do it just as well with my staff." He shrugged, trying to appear confident. "A crushed windpipe may not be as clean as a thrust to the heart, but it accomplishes the same thing." He gripped the staff, hoping his face didn't betray the sudden racing in his veins. What had he gotten himself into?

Ru seemed to enjoy his answer. The man's eyes lit with pleasure. "Well spoken. What's your name?"

Errol licked his lips. "Call me Stone." He bit his cheek, frustrated by the slip, but he doubted anyone outside of Callowford would know his last name. In fact most of the people in his village didn't seem to be aware that he even had a full name, but Rale's admonishment against giving away information needlessly still rung in his ears.

"So, another orphan looks to make his way in the world. I had a man named Wood for a while and another named Tanner. All right, Stone," Ru said. "If you want to become one of my guards, all you have to do is prove that you're better than the least of them."

Naaman smiled, enjoying Errol's confusion. "Here in Ru's caravan the guards fight to establish their position." He pointed to the man with the puckered scar on his cheek. "See him? He's the first. There are fifteen in all." Ru lifted his shoulders. "All you have to do is beat the fifteenth and you're hired."

He pivoted on one heel. "Rokha! Rokha, where are you?"

A woman, tall, lithe, yet muscled through the shoulders, stepped between a pair of wagons. "What do you want? I'm not supposed to be on duty for another two hours." The voice wore the same traces of Basqu accent that Ru's did.

But the woman's eyes and dark glossy hair marked her as Merakhi.

Ru sketched a mocking bow toward Errol. "We have a candidate. Who's fifteenth this week?"

She pointed. "Him? What's wrong with you? He probably doesn't even shave yet."

Ru lifted his arms in an exaggerated shrug. "Who am I to turn away a lad seeking adventure and employment?"

The woman snorted, then turned her dark-eyed gaze to Errol once more. "More like he's on the run for dealing falsely with some lord's daughter." She looked him over the way horse traders examined a prospective buy. "Yes. Skinny little girls like skinny, pretty-faced boys." She shot an inscrutable look at the caravan master that Ru missed. "We don't want this one."

Errol stepped forward. Rokha threatened to scuttle his chance to join Ru's caravan. "Who's fifteenth? I mean to join up with a caravan headed to the capital, if not this one, then some other."

The woman's eyes hardened, and Errol's skin pebbled with remembered insanity. "Loman Eck." She spat, then smiled at Ru's sudden consternation. "You still want to let the boy fight? You know the constable is just itching for some excuse to take you in."

The merchant licked his lips, disappointment plain on his face, as if he'd been promised a sumptuous meal and then deprived of it. He chewed on his lower lip. With a smile, he straightened. "Rokha, fetch Loman. Make sure he understands not to kill the boy. I make it your duty to prevent it."

Rokha shot the caravan master a look of pure disgust. "Have you told him the rules?" Rokha asked. At a shake from Ru, she turned to Errol. "The contestants fight until one surrenders or is disabled." She stepped toward Errol, and her voice became soft, dangerous. "Eck prefers the latter. He fights with *punja* sticks."

Errol's incomprehension must have showed. She took him by the elbow, guided him away from Ru. "Punja sticks have a heavy knob on the end. Eck is as stupid and mean as they come. He's hard to put down, and he likes hitting his opponents on the head before they have a chance to surrender. The last man to lose to Eck still can't remember his own name. Go find a different caravan."

He met Rokha's eyes even as the blood dropped from his head to his stomach. "I need to get to Erinon, and traveling as a caravan guard is the best way. Thanks for looking out for me. Go get Eck."

She snarled, baring her teeth. "Fool boy. I don't care what Eck does to you, but if he kills you, that fat constable will keep us here while he investigates your death. Lost time means lost money." Her voice dropped. "Who are you running from, boy?"

Errol turned away from her question, ready to appeal to Ru. Warring emotions chased across the caravan master's face. Rokha's words had struck a chord with him, stoking some caution or fear.

Something needed to be done. "Here." He handed her Midnight's reins. "I need to warm up." He took his staff, checked the knobblocks at each end, and took a few steps to put him out of striking distance of Ru and the woman.

Despite the urgency pounding in his chest, he started with the most basic moves: spin, block, thrust. As his shoulders loosened he glided through the more complex forms. Thoughts of Eck and fighting drained away as he lost himself in the poetry of his staff. He moved faster until the ends of the staff buzzed and blurred through the air.

Ru's voice broke the spell. "Stay here, Rokha. I'll get Loman Eck myself."

Errol grounded the staff. Rokha stepped close. "You flow like water, boy. I sure hope you know how to fight." Her expression opened, became almost sympathetic. "Eck is a drunk, but drunk or sober he fights dirty. If you let him get close to you, you're finished. Don't ever turn your back on him—even when you think it's finished."

Between the wagons stepped Ru and a big ugly man carrying a pair of sticks with heavy wooden knobs on the end. Errol judged the sticks—punja, Rokha had called them—to be about the length of a sword, maybe a bit longer.

Eck took a pull from something in a bottle and wiped his mouth, leaving a dirty smear across his face. "You brought me here to fight this?" he spat. A long scar down his cheek puckered with his disgust. "Did you tell him to write his death letter?"

Ru pulled a handkerchief from a sleeve, hid a smile from Eck behind it. "You know the rules, Eck. No killing blows. Rokha is here to make sure you both survive."

Eck leered at Errol before turning back to Ru. "Of course, but you know accidents have a way of happening."

Rokha tied Midnight to the nearest wagon and returned, filling the space between Errol and Loman Eck. "Ru has already told you the most important rule. No killing blows. Other than that, you fight until someone gives up or is rendered unable to fight." She turned to Errol. "That means until you get knocked unconscious."

She turned to Eck. "You got that?"

He waved a punja stick with a flip of one thick wrist. "Of course." He grinned, gaps showing where teeth had once been. "I'll try to be more careful this time." Eck's gaze grew intense.

Rokha stepped back. Errol slid his hands along the grain of his staff and removed one of the knobblocks. Eck nodded, waiting. When Errol reversed the staff to take off its mate, Eck rushed him.

Surprised, he flailed, trying to block the blow aimed at his head. He was too slow. The weight of the punja knocked the staff aside, and Errol's vision dimmed as the weapon glanced off his head.

Eck tried to finish him with a blow from the other stick. He ducked. The wind of its passing ruffled his hair. He struck for Eck's ankles with the staff. The weight was all wrong. The remaining knobblock changed the balance. His stroke went high.

Eck grunted as Errol's staff struck him in the calf. "You'll pay for that, you little whelp. By the time I'm done, you won't have a whole bone left in your body."

Errol retreated, tried to open space so he could remove the other knobblock. Eck pressed his advantage, swinging blows so quickly that Errol could only defend. The weighted knobs struck his staff so that his hands stung. He fought to hold on.

Blood trickled down his scalp and into his right eye. Eck grinned and circled to that side. Errol tried to back away, but Ru's wagons prevented him. He was running out of room. In seconds Eck would have him pinned and he'd have to surrender.

Or get beaten to death.

Rokha's voice cut through the din of fighting. "Call it quits, boy, before he kills you."

Errol couldn't spare the attention to speak, gave a brief shake of his head instead. Having no time to remove the other knobblock, he searched for the new balance point of his staff instead. The wood clacked against another wild blow. Errol scrubbed blood from his forehead with his sleeve.

Eck's breathing became labored and his attacks became more frantic. He pressed, swinging the punja sticks as if he meant to break the wood of the staff. Errol parried, slid his hands a couple of inches closer to the knobblock. *Better.* Eck swung again.

Errol moved to parry, felt the back end of the staff catch on the wagon behind him.

Time slowed. Realization dawned in Eck's eyes. Errol wouldn't be able to avoid the blow coming at his side.

He thrust, pushed the end of the staff at Eck's midsection as the punja stick struck him in the side.

Both men collapsed. Air exploded from Eck's mouth.

Errol fought for breath, circled to his right. He couldn't breathe. The harder he fought to draw air, the less of it came. Dark spots appeared in his vision. Dimly, he saw Eck rising, murder in his eyes.

He slid his hands on the staff, searched by feel.

Loman Eck limped toward him, face purple with pain and

rage. One of his sticks lay discarded behind him. He gripped the other like an axe.

Errol's fingers brushed the metallic cylinder on the end of his staff.

The punja stick lifted, rising higher.

He twisted, felt the staff weight come loose.

Air, blessed air, flowed into his lungs.

Eck brought the stick down toward Errol's head. He watched it accelerate, heard displaced air as it came for him.

His hands were in the wrong position.

Errol jerked his head to the left, saw Eck shift his swing. He threw himself to the right, rolling. Eck's foot lashed out, catching him in the hip, thrusting him away.

His hands found the slight indentations in the wood where use had polished the grain. He took a deep breath as Eck picked up his other punja stick, inhaled again and noticed a circle of onlookers.

He spun the staff as Eck approached, exulted in its restored balance. Loman Eck stopped, wary. His advantage of surprise was gone. Blood still dripped from Errol's scalp, but the wound merely trickled now. He could see.

Eck looked about, his gaze darting first at the crowd, then at Errol. With a roar he charged, swinging the sticks as before, but now Errol stood ready. He flowed with the attack instead of against it. The end of his staff parried Eck's blow cleanly. The wood flexed, rebounding, and he pushed it, bending from the knees as his hands spun the ash into Eck's unprotected ankle.

The crack resounded in the stillness. He heard someone in the crowd gasp, but the sound floated past him. He lost himself in the dance.

Even as Eck tumbled, Errol spun, striking hands, head, and knee.

The punja sticks fell from Eck's unfeeling grasp as he landed facedown in the dirt.

Errol grounded his staff, panting.

Rokha regarded him, one dark eyebrow raised in consideration. Then she moved to Eck, put a booted foot on his shoulder, and shoved. After a moment, she nodded and turned to Ru, who stood gaping at Errol.

"I think Eck is done. He's breathing, but I don't think that left hand of his is going to hold a stick anytime soon." She gave Errol an amused glance, a smirk on her full lips, before turning to the caravan master. "You're going to need a new fifteenth."

Ru nodded but didn't respond.

Rokha leaned close to whisper in Errol's ear. "He didn't expect you to win. I don't know what kind of trouble you're in, but if you bring it to us, I'll make sure you suffer for it."

Errol pulled a breath against the pain in his side, picked up his staff, and walked over to the caravan master with as much confidence as he could muster.

He stuck out his hand. "Master Ru, I don't drink, but I like to eat. As you can see, I have my own horse. I understand you're headed to Erinon, and—"

Rokha's voice cut the air. "Watch out, boy!"

15

CONGER'S TALE

ERROL THREW HIMSELF forward into Ru, sent them both sprawling in the dirt and horse droppings. A muted *thwack* sounded behind him, and he rolled off the caravan master to see Eck kneeling on the ground clutching his head. A punja stick lay beside him.

Ru hauled himself off the ground with as much dignity as he could muster. He brushed here and there at his clothes, now smeared with manure, huffing with indignation. "That's it, Loman. You're done."

Eck shook off the pain with a shake of his head and stood. He pointed his swollen left hand at Errol. "You mean you're going to ditch me for this, this boy? One decent blow would snap him in half."

"A blow that you were unable to deliver, Eck," Rokha said. Her fingers twitched on the hilt of her sword as if she considered thumping him on the head again with the flat of the blade. She pointed at Errol with her free hand. "And that despite the fact you took him by surprise while he was removing the knobblocks from his staff."

Eck sneered. "Luck. How many people tried to attack the caravan while I guarded it? None." He pointed at Errol again. "Do you think that a boy with his stick is going to scare bandits off?"

The caravan master appeared to consider this idea. Rokha stepped forward. "He lost. You laid out the rules, and the boy beat him. As judge, I pronounced Eck unable to continue. The boy knocked him out."

Ru tried to shrug away his assistant's logic.

Rokha bored in. "Look at the crowd. How many people saw the ending of the match besides your own guards?" She stopped speaking as he took in the throng of people clustered around his standard, gathered by the excitement of the fight. "How long will it take the story to spread that the word of Naaman Ru is worthless? The other caravan masters and their factors will eat you alive. You'll be lucky to ever make a profit again." She shook her head. "I told you not to let the boy fight."

Ru's eyes widened. He straightened, pointing a finger at Eck. "You're finished, Loman. The boy will take your place as fifteenth." He snapped his fingers. "Get your gear and take off."

Fury burned in the former guard's eyes, and he took a threatening step toward Errol. "You haven't seen the last of me, boy. I'm going to be the worst enemy you've ever had."

Errol raised his staff, slid his hands to the ready position. "You might be surprised how much I wish that were true."

Eck's eyes widened at the unexpected response. Then he whirled and stomped off, clutching his weapons to his chest as he left.

Errol watched him leave, his head throbbing. He probed his scalp with his fingers, trying to estimate the damage. He winced. Radere or Adele could have tended the wound with casual indifference, but there probably wasn't an herbwoman within fifty leagues of Longhollow. "Rokha, is there a healer nearby?"

She laughed. The sound caressed his ears with its warmth. "Not likely, boy, but part of being a guard is knowing how to doctor most things. Caravan people take care of their own. Follow me."

Rokha led him between the wagons. As they approached a

wagon topped with a large arched covering, the man with the puckered scar Ru had pointed out as the first strode up, looking unhappy. "What's your name, boy?"

Errol nodded. "Stone."

The man snorted. "That's an orphan name. Well, whatever your reason for being here, there are things you need to know. The most important thing is I'm the first. My name is Gram Skorik. When I tell you to do something, do it or you'll end up fighting me, and after I've beaten you bloody, I'll kick you out."

Errol nodded.

This seemed to satisfy the first somewhat. "Good. You know when to keep your mouth shut. The second thing is this: You'll take one watch out of three every day. Every fifth day your watch will rotate. Since you're taking Eck's place, you'll take his spot in the rotation. We get paid when we make destination and Ru sells his goods." Skorik grimaced and his nose wrinkled. "Right now he thinks there's money to be made in animal hides. Anything else you need to know, ask Rokha." He nodded at the Merakhi woman. "She's not only the sixth, she's the assistant factor and more useful than most of the refuse we've got around here."

He glanced up at the sun, his scar pulling with his grimace as if that golden fire constituted a personal affront. "You have watch in two hours." The first snorted. "Try to look intimidating, boy. I never liked Eck, but at least he scared off the dregs."

Errol watched the first slip back the way he came. "When do we leave for Erinon?"

Rokha shrugged. "Whenever the caravan master says, but it should be soon. He doesn't like Longhollow, never has. The horses are rested and the cargo's been loaded, so there's nothing holding us here." She dug into the back of the wagon, pulled out a pack, and proceeded to rummage through it.

"Bend down," she said. "This will sting, but if you make a fuss the other guards will make you regret it."

Fire blossomed on his head as she poured a thick, yellow-ish liquid on it. The smell reminded Errol of lemonleaf. Rokha waited a moment, then poked his cut with a finger. His head moved back, but he didn't feel anything except pressure. She threaded a needle, squeezed the skin around his cut together, and proceeded to sew him up with no more apparent concern than she would spare a cloak.

Errol tried not to think about what was happening on top of his head. "What else do I need to know?"

Rokha shrugged. "There's little left to tell. When we leave you'll ride where Skorik tells you, and when we camp you'll be assigned camp duties when you're not on guard. Aside from his taste for fights, Ru's not a bad employer. You'll want to challenge for fourteenth as quickly as you can."

"Why's that?" He hadn't planned on fighting again unless forced to.

"Because anyone who wants to join up as a guard will have to challenge the fifteenth to do it."

His mouth went dry as he pictured a long line of men with punja sticks, all of whom looked like Loman Eck, eager to beat him. "Who's fourteenth?"

"Norad Endilion." She shrugged. "He's a passable swordsman, but you won't have any trouble with him." She tied off the last knot and returned her implements to the pack. The sixth made to leave.

"What makes you think that? I had a hard enough time keeping Eck from killing me."

Rokha turned, her glossy black hair lifting slightly in the breeze. It struck Errol then. With her curved nose and tilted eyes, she was beautiful, like a hawk.

Her smile came at him, wide and teasing. "Eck was fifth before Ru busted him to fifteenth for sleeping on duty."

As he watched her leave, Errol shook himself like a dog coming up out of the water. His stomach growled and he went in search of food. Toward the end of the train of wagons that made up Ru's caravan he found a large flatbed cart piled with foodstuffs and cooking utensils. Next to it stood one of the fattest men he'd ever seen, almost certainly the cook. He turned at the sound of Errol's approach, his florid face and light blond hair marking him as a Soede.

Errol nodded a polite greeting. "Um, hello. Can I get some food? I haven't eaten anything since this morning, and I'm hungry."

The man's brows came together like a thunderhead. "You think I'm the cook, boy? You're lucky I'm too busy eating to fight. I'm not afraid of you or your little stick."

Errol backed away, his hands up. "I-I'm sorry. I figured since you were standing here by the cart . . ."

The man nodded, his extra chin flapping. "You thought somebody as fat as me must be the cook. I should sit on you. We'd see how well you twirl a staff after I broke all your ribs." Like every Soede Errol had heard, he shaped his words at the front of his mouth so that every word sounded as though it had an R in it.

A man stepped around the side of the wagon, stooped with age. "Everyone thinks you're the cook, Sven. Why shouldn't they? You're as big as a house, and you're never more than four feet away from the supply wagon. Now, move so the kid can get something to eat—that is, unless you've already wolfed down Ru's supplies for the next trip."

The big man redirected his anger at the newcomer. Errol breathed a sigh of relief.

"One of these days, Grub, I'm going to shut that mouth of yours."

The old man snorted, the gray wisps of hair on his head fluttering. "Yep. And then you'll have to start doing your own cooking. Not too likely." He waved an impatient hand toward Errol. "Don't let Sven bother you. I don't think he's ever actually had to fight anybody. He's the second. The only reason he's here is because Ru is the only caravan master that will feed him all he can eat."

Sven's anger melted from his face, transforming it until the burly man wore a wounded look on his blond features. "I don't eat that much, Grub." He turned to Errol. "Really, I don't, and it's not my fault nobody challenges me. I haven't had to defend my rank since I first took it."

Grub nodded in agreement. "Yep, but you've never tried for first, either, have you, Sven?"

Sven's eyebrows rose until his fleshy forehead bunched into rolls. "I'm fat, not stupid. Only an idiot would challenge Skorik."

Despite his resolve not to fight unless forced to it, Errol found himself intrigued. In the last three months, he'd witnessed some of the best fighters in the entire kingdom and had been fortunate enough to be trained by one of them. How did Skorik measure up to that? "Is there anyone in the guard besides me who uses the staff?"

"Jhade," Sven and Grub answered at the same time. Grub shook his head and went on. "Strange, that one is. She came from somewhere on the other side of the steppes. Hardly ever says a word. Eats by herself. Sleeps by herself. And makes anyone with enough sense to buckle a belt nervous just looking at her."

"Oh." Errol's shoulders sagged a fraction in disappointment. "I was hoping to find someone to spar with me."

Grub's eyes widened in surprise. "You've never been a guard before, have you?" When Errol shook his head, he went on. "I didn't think so. Most of the guards go out of their way to avoid exercise." He smirked and shot a look at Sven.

The blond man shrugged shoulders the size of hams. "I'll fight when I have to," he said around a mouthful of bread.

Grub laughed before he turned back to Errol. "She'll spar with you, Stone. If she's not working, sleeping, or eating, she's practicing with the sword or staff. Here." He handed Errol a large chunk of bread and cheese. Then he pulled the lid off a barrel and dipped a tankard. When he withdrew his arm, Errol smelled the malty fragrance of ale.

Errol took a step back. "Water, please, if you've got it. Else, I'll go find a place to fill my skin."

The cook shrugged and poured the ale back in the barrel, the picture of indifference. "Got water in another barrel over here."

He stepped up onto the cart and threaded his way toward the back. A moment later Errol held the same tankard. The ale smell still clung to it. He wanted to drink and puke all at the same time.

He looked up from the tankard to find Grub looking at him, his watery old-man's eyes filled with understanding. The cook nodded. "If there's anything else you need before we break camp, come and find me. On the road we'll eat three times a day, at camp in the evening and the morning and once while we ride. Caravans travel fast. 'Leagues are money' as they say."

Over the course of the next few hours, Errol met the majority of Ru's guards. Without question he'd never encountered a stranger assortment of individuals in his life. It was as if the caravan master went out of his way to hire the oddest people he could find. In addition to Skorik and Sven, there was Jhade, the woman Grub had spoken of. She was of indeterminate age and resembled no one he'd ever seen before. From the yellow tinge of her skin to the tilt of her almond-brown eyes, she was unique. She spoke in a heavy accent impossible to identify, and when he asked her birth village, she acted as if he hadn't spoken.

The sword strapped to her back proved to be as different as its owner. It curved where other steel ran straight, bore only one edge, and the hilt looked big enough for both hands. Her manner of speaking made Errol acutely uncomfortable. The closest she came to a smile was when Errol asked if she would be willing to spar with him using the staff.

The oddest member of the guard was Garret Conger, whose common name only accentuated his eccentricity. Short, even shorter than Errol, with a dark grizzled beard, he wore a tattered cassock and steadfastly maintained he used to be a priest, though he refused to answer any questions on how he came to change stations in life. A man more unlike Antil, or even Martin, would have been hard to imagine. Conger boasted a prodigious collection of swear words, many of which Errol didn't recognize, drank to excess, and demonstrated a broad variety of disgusting personal habits.

In time, Errol's turn at guard came, and he stood along the line of wagons loaded with animal hides, breathing through his mouth. Conger, the eighth, stood next to him reading out loud from a book on church doctrine and periodically scratching an armpit. Whenever he chanced across a section that he thought required comment, he latched onto Errol.

"That's it, boy! Look at this." He shoved the book into Errol's face just long enough for him to read the first word before taking it back again. "What do you think of that?"

Errol shrugged. "I don't know. I can't really read."

The scruff of Conger's beard quivered with his outrage. "That's ridiculous. How can you discern the majesty of the church's history if you can't read, boy? Humph. That must be corrected—I'll teach you." His gaze fell back to the text. "I tell you, Deas will wipe us out if we don't repent of our evildoings."

Errol gave him a sidelong glance. He tried to keep the smirk from his face, but couldn't quite. "You mean like swearing and drinking?"

It was the first time anyone had responded to Conger that morning, and his face lit with pleasure. "Yes!" He paused, nonplussed, and then went on in a softer tone. "I mean, yes, well, those are certainly habits to be avoided if possible, but there are much more important issues, like love for your fellow man, taking care of the unfortunate—that sort of thing." He looked away, scratching his throat just above his cassock. "I don't think Deas would begrudge a man a drink every now and then, and as for language . . . well, we all say things in the flare of the moment that we shouldn't."

Someone snorted a few feet away, and Errol spied a mop of curly brown hair that belonged to Onan. "Droppings, that's what it is. All the church's talk of Deas and lots and the barrier is just a ploy to keep people in line so those fat priests can line their pockets."

"The barrier is weakening." The words came out of Errol's mouth before he thought, as though Onan's rant had pulled the statement from him.

"Deas forbid," Conger said, scratching with one hand even as he genuflected.

Onan curled his forefinger and thumb into a ball and extended the other three fingers in the ancient sign meant to ward off evil. He glared at Errol. "Do you want to bring trouble on us, Stone?"

Errol tilted his head and smiled. "I didn't think you believed, Onan."

The guard hunched his shoulders as if trying to ward off an expected blow. "I . . . I don't, but there's no sense in taking chances. What would you know about it?"

Errol's smirk slid from his face. "I heard a couple of merchants talking a few months back. They said things were bad at the edge of the kingdom." He shrugged. "I've heard people mention it, but truth be told, I'm not even sure what the barrier is."

Onan swore, borrowing from Conger's extensive vocabulary. "Then you're a fool, boy, giving mention to things. Who knows what could be listening?"

Conger pulled at his jaw muscles as if coming out of a deep sleep. "The barrier?" He paused to interject a few swear words—Errol recognized most of them. "The first king bought the barrier by blood, boy, but that came later. Thousands of years ago, after Deas created the worlds and cast them among the stars, some of the malus, the ones who served him, rebelled out of jealousy. They took form and enslaved this world. Men and women were chattel, playthings. Then Deas's son, Eleison, came down. He took human form and fought, sacrificing himself to lock the malus away from his creation. But the memory of them remained, and through design and worship of the vile creatures, men opened a doorway for the malus to return, not in body, but in spirit. Eventually, war came that lasted for nearly a hundred years."

That didn't make any sense to Errol. "How could a war last that long? Everybody would be dead."

"The evil ones weren't trying to kill, boy. They wanted to corrupt. The corruption moved slowly. People didn't recognize it for what it was. Some said the weather was just changing. Others claimed nothing was wrong at all. By the time the truth became too obvious to ignore, everything in the steppes to the east and Merakh to the south had been lost."

A shadow passed in front of the sun, and chills like the skittering of rodents ran across his skin. "But there are men there," he said, trying not to believe. "I've heard the merchants talk about them."

Conger nodded. "Oh, there are men there. There are even merchants and caravans fool enough to trade into those lands for spices or stones, but the memory of demon worship lingers in those lands, and the taint lingers. Men and women willingly become conduits for the malus, the fallen."

"How did the first king create the barrier?" Errol asked.

"Don't talk nonsense, boy," Onan answered. "No man could do such a thing."

Errol looked at him in surprise at his sudden reversal. Onan blushed and waved for Conger to continue. "Go ahead, Garret. Tell the boy."

Conger smiled, pulled his shoulders back. "A hundred years after it started, the corruption spilled across the Sprata Mountains from the steppes and flooded up from the south. Men fought shapes and shadows that shunned daylight and came at them in the darkness. There was no kingdom of Illustra then, and no king, just a collection of provinces, each with their own ruler. They met at Erinon, the place farthest from the corruption, to choose a leader. The histories say they didn't know the consequences of their choice." Conger stopped to spit and swear.

Errol started at the interruption. The cadence of the man's words, rough though they were, had held him.

"What happened then?" Onan asked.

The would-be priest smiled. "They forced the kingship on Magis by lot. History says he fought from taking it, either through humility or premonition."

The hair on Errol's arms lifted. "Premonition of what?"

Conger didn't answer right away. He smiled in obvious enjoyment at the attention. "Magis finally accepted the crown and the fate they'd fashioned for him. He bade good-bye to his wife, Lora. Left his youngest son, Magnus, at Erinon, he did. Said a boy of fifteen had no place in a war, but he took the twins, who were barely a year older. Magis was said to be wise. Leaving Magnus may have been the wisest thing he ever did. Mayhap he just wanted one of his sons to survive him.

"They met the hordes close to the Forbidden Strait. People have wondered if the outcome would have been any different if he'd chosen to fight at the steppes." Conger shrugged. "We'll never know. He split his army and took his half south toward the bigger threat, met the enemy just past the plains of stone. Then he did something no one expected."

Onan, his eyes bright, pointed. "He went out alone."

Conger grimaced at the interruption. "Don't be ridiculous. They weren't even sure what they were fighting." He turned his gaze back to Errol. "They say he prayed all night before the battle."

"Of course the churchmen would say that." Onan's tone left little doubt about what he thought.

"Question some of it and question it all." Conger spit, left off the curse, and made a point of turning his back on Onan, who edged around to listen to the rest of the story anyway.

Conger shrugged. "Just before dawn, Magis had a vision. Some say Aurae came to him, others say he saw Deas or Eleison. But the message was unmistakable. He was supposed to challenge the leader of the horde to single combat."

Errol had heard enough tales to guess the ending. "And he vanquished the enemy and the rest of the horde fled."

The look Conger gave him made him blush with embarrassment. "Don't be stupid, boy. Magis was brave and by all accounts skilled with a sword, but he and his army fought something less, and more, than human. The leader of the horde accepted his offer. The next morning Magis woke to find the horde gone. How was he supposed to fight an enemy that disappeared?

"They stayed there on the edge of the plain waiting for word back from their scouts. But no word came. None of the scouts returned. When dusk fell, the horde returned. Magis and his army were surrounded. The enemy mowed them down until only Magis and his guard remained. Magis watched his sons die, hacked to pieces by men grown monstrous. Then the leader of the horde came forward and laughed at Magis's challenge and honor.

"But he called Magis from his guard to take revenge if he could."

"And then Magis killed him," Errol said. The hero always emerged victorious in these stories.

Conger shook his head. "This isn't a tale, boy. It's history. Magis was no match for the thing he faced, and he knew it. He drew his sword and advanced. The fight lasted less than a minute. The horde captain, the man-thing filled with the strength of a malus, toyed with Magis before it finished him, cutting him across the throat like a butcher. It held him upside down, shaking him and laughing as his blood sprayed the ground.

"And then Magis died."

Errol shook his head in denial. That didn't make sense. "If Magis died, the horde would have overrun everything. The story's wrong. And if the horde killed everyone, who would have brought the tale of what happened?"

Conger smiled. "You didn't listen. His guard still lived. The horde captain thought it would be amusing to make them watch their new king slaughtered like a pig. He tossed Magis's still-bleeding body aside and started for the guard, but when the last of the king's blood left his body to soak the ground, the horde fell dead. Thousands upon thousands of the accursed ones dropped in their tracks on the plains of stone and near the steppes. The guard stayed, paralyzed, thinking it a trick of some kind to give the demons sport. They huddled there through the night. When dawn broke and the dead remained, they were convinced. They fashioned a litter and carried Magis over the piles of dead and back to Erinon. The journey back proved to be nearly as hazardous as the battle. Too few men remained in the kingdom to uphold the law. But each night, shamed that their king died while they lived, the guard stood watch over his body, fighting any that came at them out of the darkness. Always they kept watch. When they reached Erinon, they refused the recognition of friends or kin. Forsaking their names, they called themselves the watch and traded in the marks and banners of their houses for mourning black. They swore an oath never to outlive their king in battle again.

"Magis purchased the barrier with his blood, boy. That was the deal he made. And as long as one of his descendants sits the throne, no one in the kingdom may call on the malus."

A memory clicked into place. Errol's stomach turned, trying to flee through his legs. "Rodran doesn't have any children, and he's dying."

Conger didn't speak as he nodded.

16

THE SHAPING OF WOOD

ERROL SQUINTED against the afternoon sun as he rode with his staff across his saddle and worked a piece of dried beef with his teeth. Grub made it on the salty side, but it gave his stomach enough to keep it from complaining. He ripped off a piece and stuck the rest in a pocket before turning his attention back to his staff. Splinters jutted from the formerly smooth ends, and small cracks fissured the end grain.

Soon or late he would have to make a new one, but he didn't know how. When Ru called a halt and directed the caravan to a clearing beside the road for the evening, Errol decided to seek out Rokha. The woman made him nervous. Her resemblance to Karma, the woman possessed by the malus in Windridge, still filled him with the desire to flee at times, but her storehouse of knowledge impressed him.

Jhade would have seemed a more logical choice for him to ask for help, but the strange woman didn't engage in extended conversation for any reason. She did, however, spar with an indefatigable enthusiasm that bordered on obsession. When she discovered Errol to be a willing staff partner, his every free moment became spoken for. His first lesson had proven to be quite educational. He rubbed a shoulder at the recollection. From the outset it was obvious she'd learned an entirely different way of fighting with the staff than he had. While Errol concentrated on attacking and defending with the staff, Jhade had attacked with wood, hands, and feet. He wore numerous bruises from her heels and hands.

So he decided it would be best to ask Rokha for assistance. Whether the topic was weapons or weather, she either knew the answer or knew where to find it. As he approached her, he shifted, rolling his shoulders under his tunic. "Rokha." He held his staff out for her inspection. "Do you know anything about making a staff?"

She cocked her head and looked at him with her dark eyes that always held a hint of fire. Every now and then she would flash him a smile that pulled the breath from his lungs. Now she just shrugged.

"Shouldn't you ask Jhade? She's the one who fights with the staff." Rokha patted the slim blade that never left her side. "I prefer steel myself."

Errol shrugged. "Jhade is a great sparring partner, but she doesn't talk much, and I need someone to teach me how to use a knife."

Her delicately curved eyebrows rose a fraction. "You don't know how to use a knife?"

He sighed in frustration. "Of course I know how to use a knife." He moved his hand. "You thrust and twist to keep the wound from closing." He let his hand fall to his side. "But I don't know how to carve."

"Everyone knows how to carve. What did you do with yourself growing up?"

"I drank mostly." The admission didn't bother him the way it once would have, and he thanked Rale in the vaults of his mind. "When I wasn't drinking, I was hunting plants for the herbwomen around my village. They paid me and I bought ale."

To her credit, she nodded as she gave him a look of simple acknowledgment without a trace of pity. "I wondered why you were so careful to avoid Grub's ale barrel."

He shrugged. "Can you teach me?"

Rokha nodded. "But I'm not going to teach you in ash or oak. It would take too long. Take an axe and find a piece of fir, or better yet, pine. I can teach you on that and then you can make a staff out of whatever you want."

Errol's search took him farther into the wood than he expected, and before he realized it the clamor of Ru's caravan faded and disappeared. Cedars populated this part of the forest, with an oak or maple thrown in here and there, but he found no pine or fir. He turned from the path he'd chosen, climbing a hillock that might offer him a better vantage point.

When he crested the hill, a small stand of pines presented itself at the bottom of a nearby hollow. He crisscrossed his way down the slope, lugging Grub's hatchet with him. Minutes later, with the tang of pine heavy in the air, he held a straight length of wood about two spans long. Green, it would be far too heavy to wield as a staff, but he only intended to practice carving on it anyway.

A few well-placed chops pruned the branch. He sighted along its length and congratulated himself on his choice. Already, he could imagine the outcome, smooth and white, whirling in his hands as he moved. Practicing with the pine might not be such a bad idea after all. The greater weight of the unseasoned wood would help him build the strength he needed to wield an oak staff someday. Errol hummed a tune to himself as he started the trek back to Ru's caravan.

He tried to retrace his steps, but each stand of cedar trees looked much like the others. By the time he heard the distant sounds of Sven arguing with Grub, only a sliver of sun showed above the horizon. He approached the camp with his branch tucked under one arm.

And stopped.

Errol held his breath and slid behind the bole of a large maple. The raised bark scratched him through his tunic, but he ignored it, used a breathing technique Rale had taught him to quiet the pounding of his heart.

He listened, taking slow, shallow breaths, but only Sven's insistence came to him through the trees. Errol cursed himself for leaving the camp without his real staff. What kind of caravan guard walks through a strange forest without his weapon? The whole reason Ru had guards was because people tried to rob caravans. He looked at the pine branch with disgust. He might as well try swinging a bar of iron. The hatchet made a handier weapon if he could catch his enemy unaware, but one twig snap and he'd find himself facing the point of a sword. With a long, slow breath, he leaned his pruned branch against the tree and edged around the trunk to look again.

They were gone. The two men he'd seen crouched behind a thick growth of laurel were nowhere to be seen. Had he imagined them? Possibly, but he didn't believe it. He held his position as the forest darkened, but nothing moved. Errol left his hiding place, forced by the encroaching darkness to make his way back to camp in the last of the dusk's light.

He skirted the fire, ignored the food Grub had laid out, and made for Rokha, who stood at the edge talking to Skorik. The first didn't look pleased at the interruption.

"It's about time," Rokha said. "I thought you'd decided to grow the tree first." She looked at the branch he held. "That's not too bad. It looks—" She broke off at the look on his face. "What is it, boy?"

Errol stammered under the first's glare. Had he really seen them or just imagined it? What if he was wrong? The sunlight played tricks with the shadows. In the end he shook his head. "Nothing. I just got a little spooked in the woods."

Rokha leaned forward, her eyes boring into his as if she meant to pry his concerns from him by strength of will, but at last she leaned back with a shrug. "You're one of the most nervous people

I've ever met. Whatever it is can't be as bad as you think. It's not like you've got the watch hunting you."

Errol's laughter sounded shrill in his ears, and a couple of the guards seated by the fire looked up. He dug out a knife Grub had loaned him and offered it hilt first to Rokha. She took it, frowned, and handed it back. From within her cloak she proceeded to bring forth an astonishing assortment of knives. Seeing the look on his face, she gave him a smile that made it difficult to breathe.

"I like knives," she said. Her husky tone brought heat to his ears. She selected the largest blade from the pile at her feet. "We'll start with this one. It's heavy enough to pull the bark and cut through the small knots."

One of the knives on the ground caught his attention. It looked just like the one Luis used. The flat, triangular blade was no longer than his shortest finger. He pointed. "Shouldn't we use that one?"

Rokha shook her head. "That's a carving knife. It's for detail work. What we need here is something a little heavier." Seating herself on the ground with one end of Errol's branch resting in her lap, she wrapped a cloth around the blade end and drew the knife toward her in a smooth motion. A long curl of bark slid off the blade showing the pale wood underneath. She repeated the motion a couple more times, then stood and gestured.

"Now you do it. Don't angle the knife too deeply or you'll splinter the wood." She gathered her cutlery. It disappeared into the pockets lining her cloak and she left.

He sat and tried to imitate her, but despite her warning, he buried the blade into the wood half a dozen times before he schooled himself to patience. It took him the better part of an hour to reach the point where he could draw a curl of wood from the pine as she had. When he saw her next, a pile of shavings, some fine and curled, others embarrassingly thick, littered the ground.

Rokha knelt with a smile, fingering one of the jagged chunks of pine. "It may take you a while to learn. Fortunately, there's a lot of pine between here and Erinon." She took the heavy blade from his hands and stashed it into her cloak. "You have first watch tonight."

An impulse bordering on need drove him. "Can I use your carving knife while I stand watch?" He tried but didn't quite succeed in keeping the pleading from his voice. Why was he acting this way?

Rokha considered the question before reaching into her cloak and pulling out the small-bladed knife. "Don't use it on that wet pine. Find something dry or you'll hurt the blade."

He nodded, having no idea where he would find seasoned wood. After pestering Grub and half the guards in the camp, he finally found a source of dried blanks. Norad, the fourteenth guard, carved as a hobby. He surrendered two fist-sized cubes of wood to Errol with a wry look.

"You never challenged me for my spot, Errol."

Not knowing what to say, he shrugged at Norad's observation.

"Someone must have told you that Eck was fifth. I think you could have challenged up to eighth without breaking a sweat. Most of us have never fought a staff bearer." The fourteenth gestured toward the lead wagon, where Naaman Ru stood discussing the next day's route with Skorik. "You know Ru pays his guards according to their rank. You'd make a lot more money."

Errol shrugged, hefting his staff. "I love working the staff."

Norad nodded and smiled.

"But I haven't fought very much," Errol went on. "I think there's more to fighting than just knowing the staff. Fights seem to be pretty unpredictable. I'd like to avoid them if I can. Grub gives me as much to eat as I want, so I don't really need a lot of money."

The fourteenth added another block of wood to the two already in Errol's hand. "You're uncommonly wise for someone so young, Errol." He chuckled. "I think you just made friends with at least seven of the guards."

Errol retreated to his post at the back of the caravan and considered the cubes he'd received. He lifted the first one and took an exploratory whiff. Pine. No mistaking it. The second one also proved to be pine. The third block appeared altogether different. Dark and strongly scented, it weighed more while possessing a rougher texture. Hardwood. He'd save it for later, after he acquired some measure of skill.

He pulled Rokha's knife from his pocket to work on the first block. There had never been any question about what he would carve, not since he'd watched Luis that day next to the river. So he would try to craft a sphere, but how did a reader put the essence of his thoughts into the lot?

Errol didn't have the least glimmer of an idea. Luis had never told him.

He gripped the knife in his right hand and shaved a curlicue from one of the sharp edges of the cube. Maybe if he tried to envision a sphere hidden within it would go better. He turned the cube and stroked the knife against the blond grain again, repeated the process until he'd broken each of the twelve edges. The cube didn't look much different. It would be more difficult to get a splinter now, but it was still undeniably a cube, not a sphere. The urge to attack the block with quick, savage cuts nearly overpowered him. He had never done anything so mind-numbingly boring in his life. How did Luis stand it?

Almost, he threw the block away. Frustrated at his lack of knowledge, Errol took a deep breath and let his attention wander back to his experience in the woods. One of those men resembled Eck. What would he be up to, skulking after the caravan? Did he mean to confront Ru? Or perhaps the former guard intended a more personal revenge. Revenge or attack? Errol turned the question over in his head, the knife and wood forgotten. Why else would the former guard follow the caravan?

"I thought you didn't know how to carve, boy."

He jerked at the warmth of Rokha's voice.

"Better not let Skorik catch you daydreaming on guard duty,

boy," she said. "His methods of encouraging attentiveness are painfully direct."

"Sorry." Errol tucked the knife away and noticed for the first time the small mound of shavings at his feet. He stared at his other hand.

There, resting in his left palm, lay a sphere of pine. He tilted his hand, felt tiny splinters of grain tickle his skin as he rolled it back and forth.

Rokha sniffed. "What game are you playing at? If you can carve that well, why go to the trouble of asking me how to make a new staff?"

Errol shook his head. "I don't know how I did this. I've never really carved before."

He left Rokha and edged around the wagon of skins to a deserted spot. When the campfire came into view, he stopped and held the sphere so that the light bathed one side. Slowly, he rotated his carving and searched the grain. His hand trembled and he held his breath.

There.

Yes glimmered in the flickers of firelight. What did that mean? Errol continued his search for another moment, but nothing more appeared. He returned to his place of watch.

Rokha was gone.

Luis had said his thoughts would create the lot. The question framed the answer. He cast back, trying to recall what he'd been thinking as he carved. Attack. That was it. He'd been thinking Eck would attack the caravan.

Errol dug the other cube of pine from his pocket. He needed the other side of the question, needed to somehow carve a lot that said *No.* Air filled his lungs as he breathed deeply. What had he been thinking about before?

He let his eyes relax to a near close and moved the knife along the grain. *No,* he repeated to himself, *Eck will not attack the caravan.*

The awareness of time slipped from him.

A distant rustle of sound brought him back to himself, and he looked down. There in his hand lay a wooden sphere, twin to the one that rested in his pocket. He walked back to the fire without a sound, unsure of what instinct drove him to secrecy. When he held the lot up to the light, *No* flickered with the dance of the flames.

Could it really be that easy?

He retreated back to the shadow of the carts but still within sight of the fire. Luis had used a simple canvas bag to choose lots, but Errol had never heard him attach any importance to how they were chosen. The only requirement seemed to be a choice made at random. An oversized pocket had been stitched to the inside of his cloak. He emptied it of the food he'd gotten from Grub and placed the two pine lots inside.

The balls rattled softly as he shook the cloth. He reached inside, his fingers tingling.

He held the ball to the light of the fire.

Yes.

Air whispered as he exhaled. He replaced the lot, shook his cloak, and drew again.

Yes.

Again.

Yes.

On the fifth draw the lot said *No.* But then he drew *Yes* twice more before drawing *No.*

And then *Yes* three more times.

Would that be enough to satisfy Ru? Luis had only begun to teach him how to read. During those lessons on the way to Windridge, the reader had hinted at the study of chance, but Errol didn't have the slightest idea what that entailed.

Rokha would know.

Errol held the lots so tightly his fingers ached as he went in search of her. The sixth stood next to Ru. The caravan master leaned toward her, the smile in his expression a mixture of affection and pride. Errol stood three paces away and waited for one of them to notice him. At last Ru's gaze broke from his contemplation of the Merakhi. His smile slipped away to be replaced by annoyance.

"What do you want, boy?"

Errol cleared his throat and stepped closer, bowing from the neck. "I'm sorry to interrupt you, caravan master, but I need to report to the sixth."

Ru's expression softened a degree. "Go ahead."

Errol hesitated, not wanting to reveal his ability in front of Ru. He scolded himself. She would just tell Ru later anyway.

The caravan master smirked and turned back to Rokha. "It seems the boy is smitten with you. I have the feeling his report is nothing more than an excuse to enjoy your company." He turned back to Errol. "Well, you will find I have little patience for distractions among my guards. Whatever you have to report to the sixth can be said in front of me. Out with it."

He inched closer and dug the lots out of his pocket, shielding them from the view of anyone who might be watching. "Eck is going to attack the caravan."

Ru's laughter caught him by surprise. "Oh ho. Not only have I found a new guard but a prophet as well. Rokha, the lad is inventive. In addition to being a fighter, he'd have us believe he's a reader as well. Tell me, boy, are all orphans so talented?" He turned to Rokha. "Of course, since there's nothing on his little balls of pine, there's no way to check his story."

Errol held out a lot for Ru's inspection. "Look. It's written right there."

Ru slapped his hand away. "Don't play stupid, boy. No one can read a lot except the person who created it. Him, or an omne. Now get back to work."

Errol gaped, clenched his jaws against anything he might say. Of course, not being readers, they couldn't read the lots, but how had he read Luis's cast? Putting that question aside, he considered the best way to convince Ru.

"Wait here," he said. He ran back to the fire, fetched a twig that lay on the edge, its tip burnt to charcoal.

"There is a way to prove the caravan is in danger." He brandished the twig like a churchman holding a crosier. "I'll mark the lot that says Eck is going to attack the caravan and either of you can draw."

The smile dropped from Naaman Ru's face as if it had never been. Rokha's expression became a mask. Errol ignored them and dropped the lots in the oversized pocket of his cloak. A couple of shakes later, he gestured to Ru.

The caravan master reached in and pulled out a lot. There on its side, plainly visible even in the soft light, a charcoal smear marred the pale yellow surface. Rokha and Ru stilled. *Good.* He had their attention.

He replaced the lot and shook his cloak. "Now you draw, Rokha."

She shook her head slowly, her expression unreadable. "You play at dangerous games, boy." Disapproval showed in every line of her stance, but she reached into his cloak and withdrew a lot just the same.

And showed the smear to Ru.

"Once more," Ru said, his voice tight. He nodded to Rokha, who circled around Errol, peering over his shoulder.

Ru hesitated, the muscles of his jaw bunching before he thrust in his hand and pulled out the same lot.

Errol had just enough time to sense Rokha's sudden explosive movement.

Then everything went black.

He woke, seated on a well-cushioned chair in Ru's tent. His hands were tied and the back of his head throbbed like a long-forgotten hangover. The lamplight made his eyes hurt. Naaman Ru and Rokha stood in front of him, their expressions hard. No one else was in the tent.

"Why did you hit me?"

Ru growled in the back of his throat. "Don't play the fool with me, boy. If you know enough to cast lots, you know I could go to the headsman for harboring you."

"What? Harboring me? You're not harboring me. I signed on to be a guard until we reach Erinon."

The caravan master gave short, jerky shakes of his head as Errol answered. "You're going to have to do better than that, boy. No escaped reader would dare show his face back in Erinon."

Rokha shifted behind Ru. "He's young. Perhaps he hopes to get back to Erinon and plead for mercy."

Ru snarled, turned on her. "I don't care if he's a babe at his mother's breast. You know the penalty for hiding a reader. The church will have my head and that of anyone who knows the boy's *talent*." He spat like a man tasting poison.

"The church doesn't know I'm a reader."

Ru and Rokha turned to stare at him as if he'd lost his mind.

Errol panicked. His tongue tripped as he tried to make it keep up with his thoughts. "A man named Luis, they called him Tremus, tested me in my village. Said I'd have to go to Erinon. He showed me how to make lots."

"We have to kill him," Ru said. "I won't count on the church's forbearance. Not where a reader is concerned."

Rokha nodded, but Errol couldn't tell if it was in agreement or simple acknowledgment. "That's pretty harsh, Ru—even for you."

Errol felt the deep *thrum* of fear in his ears. "I've never been to Erinon. Everyone thinks I'm dead. I fell off the bridge at Windridge and got washed downstream. None of my friends ever came looking for me." He clamped his teeth on the half truth.

"What if the boy is telling the truth?" Rokha asked.

"Don't tell me you believe him."

The sixth shrugged. "Think, Ru. Have you heard news of the church looking for a missing reader? Have you seen or heard a writ describing the boy?"

Ru shook his head. His color receded from purple to red.

Rokha pressed her advantage. "There's no law against having a guard who's going to *become* a reader."

"You're splitting hairs, Rokha."

She shrugged. "Have you considered the possibilities if you have your own reader?"

Naaman Ru gaped at his sixth. Then his eyes narrowed with unconcealed greed.

And then Errol heard it.

The sounds of fighting in the camp.

17

NAAMAN'S TALE

ROKHA SLIPPED BEHIND HIM and drew her sword. Errol ducked his head and tensed, waiting for the blow against his neck. Instead a soft tug pulled at his wrists and his hands came free. Rokha darted to the front of the tent and in one smooth motion tossed him his staff before she rushed out into the night.

Errol found Ru looking at him with his sword drawn. He clenched the wood in his fists.

"Move, boy. What do you think I pay my guards for?"

The night air cooled the sweat on his face as he lunged from the tent. His palms caressed the ash grain. Outside Ru's tent chaos ruled. Two of the fifteen, Norad and Jesper, were down, arrows jutting from their chests. Every other guard fought, pressed by one or more attackers.

Sven swung a massive sword, keeping two men at bay despite the shaft sticking from his thigh.

Errol watched as the massive Soede clubbed one man in the head. The man collapsed to lie in the dirt and shadows. Sven parried the frantic rush of the remaining attacker as he stepped on the fallen man's neck.

A sharp crack of breaking bone rose above the din.

Without warning a man leapt at Errol out of the darkness. Eck.

The whine of steel cutting the air sounded. Eck's punja sticks ended in four-pronged blades.

"Miss me, boy? I said I'd be back."

Errol moved left and parried, lashing out with one foot as Jhade had taught him. His heel caught Eck's kneecap with a crunch. He ignored the cry of pain, turned off the parry to strike Eck in the head and kicked the other kneecap.

Eck fell face-forward, thrashing against the ground, screaming. Errol struck him behind the ear for good measure.

He wheeled, searching for his next opponent.

There were none.

The fight had ended as quickly as it began. Silence covered the camp, as if the attack had never happened. Except for Norad and Jesper. Rokha knelt by each man, feeling at the throat. She gave a shake of the head and aimed a savage kick at an attacker who lay facedown in front of the two dead guards.

Sven sat on a crate, his hand pressed against the flesh around the arrow embedded in his thigh. "Grub! Get your lazy bones over here."

The cook came running. Blood traced a rivulet down one side of his forehead, across his eyebrow, and down his jawline. "You want me to pull that arrow, Sven?"

The Soede put his hand on his sword. "I wouldn't trust you to lance a boil. Rokha will pull it. Bring me something to eat. I'm starving."

The cook laughed and turned for the supply wagon.

"And don't forget the ale," Sven yelled after him. "I'm thirsty."

Errol moved around the camp. Most of the guards bore only minor injuries, but a few were major. On the far side of the wagons, a line of bodies gave mute testimony to the path Skorik had taken during the fight.

Errol counted them. Six. The first had killed six men in the space of a minute. He reminded himself never to challenge the first.

Ever.

A hand on the back of his arm startled him, and he ducked and whirled. His staff struck Rokha's sword at the same moment he met her gaze.

"Easy," she said. Her eyes burned with their own light and Errol could hear the deep intake of her breath. "That's it, boy." Her smile, predatory and radiant, lit the night. "But let's save it for the right people."

Rokha looked like a hawk after the kill, brilliant and fierce.

She stepped close, so close he couldn't focus. His skin flushed with heat and a delicious mixture of excitement and fear.

"Don't tell anyone that you're a reader." Her breath caressed his ear like a kiss. A hint of her perfume came to him, and he inhaled deeply. He turned his head, brought his face even closer to hers. Fire pounded through him.

He lived.

Light-headed and burning, his pulse roaring in his ears, he leaned forward toward the sixth.

She smiled, threw her head back, and laughed. "You feel it, boy? Now you know what it means to live."

Her lips met his, soft and warm. Hands found the sides of his face.

Rokha laughed deep in her throat as she pulled away. Her eyes danced. "You would have made a fine Merakhi, Stone."

Not *boy* or *lad*.

Stone.

He swayed on his feet. "My name is Errol."

When his eyes at last obeyed his command to focus, Rokha was gone.

He found her in Ru's tent with the caravan master and the first. Eck, quieter now, sat bound in the chair. He wore a swelling over one eye that Errol hadn't given him.

Skorik stood over him. "How many are trailing us?"

Eck smiled and spat. "All of them." He added a curse so foul Errol winced.

Skorik pulled his fist back, but Ru raised one hand to stop him.

The caravan master regarded Eck for a moment with his lips pursed, then walked over to the brazier and retrieved a glowing coal with the tongs. "Since your tongue doesn't seem to be particularly useful, I don't imagine we'll miss it."

Eck paled. "Twenty. There were twenty. That's all I brought. I didn't think I would need more. I shouldn't have needed more. That's it, I swear." His words sounded as if they were fighting each other to see which could be first out of his mouth.

"Check the camp, Rokha," Skorik said. "Count the bodies." He nodded at Errol. "Take the boy with you."

"Hardly a boy." She laughed and her eyes danced with mischief.

Errol's face tried to compete with Ru's brazier.

Naaman Ru held up one hand. "He stays."

Skorik nodded. They waited in silence.

"Ten," Rokha announced upon her return. "There are horse tracks leading back to the west, but it's impossible to know how many in the dark. They may try us again." She paused to wet her bottom lip, looking uncertain. "There's something else."

Ru turned at the catch in her voice but stopped on the verge of asking, and his eyes tightened. "Show me."

Errol trailed behind, unnoticed. The sixth moved with abrupt strides to the attacker's body that lay next to Norad and Jesper. Extending one foot as if she feared getting too close, she flipped the body over.

Ru cursed.

Errol edged around the first to see. Red surrounded the thrust wound in the attacker's chest, but the stain faded from his awareness as his gaze traveled up to the dead man's face. No, not a man—something else. Very nearly it looked human, but the nose flattened against the cheekbones and the nose bridge hardly existed. The mouth, gaping in protest at death, revealed pointed, dagger-like teeth. The furred ears, close against the skull, belonged on a wolf, not a man.

The first drew his sword, turned as if searching, waiting for enemies to come at them from the shadows.

"What is that thing?" Errol asked.

Ru appeared on the verge of sending him away before he spoke. "Rokha, go get Conger. Only Conger."

They waited in silence. The light from the first's torch sent flickering shadows that made the thing on the ground look alive.

Rokha returned, followed by the eighth.

"Rokha said you had something you wanted me to look . . ." The words died on Conger's lips as he caught sight of the thing on the ground in front of Ru. He knelt, his eyes wide with wonder as his fingertips brushed the creature's ears. "I've never seen one, but the historian Florian describes these in his *Examination of Peoples*." He straightened. "It's a ferral." Conger caught his confused look and went on. "It's a remnant."

Errol pointed a finger in accusation at the eighth. "You said all the malus died."

Conger nodded. "They did. This isn't a malus, exactly. It's a ferral, offspring of one of the fallen ones and an animal, a remnant of the time before Eleison." He shook his head, wiped his nose on his sleeve. "It looks almost human."

The caravan master nodded. "Skorik, get rid of it. Don't let the other guards see it."

The first dragged the body deeper into the woods.

Ru turned on his heel back toward camp. "I think I'd like to continue the conversation with my former guard."

As he entered the tent Ru asked, "Well, Loman, are they coming back?"

Eck licked his lips and shook his head. "I don't know. If you let me go I'll . . . I'll try to find out or . . . or I'll trick them into going somewhere else."

Ru's cold laughter filled the tent. "No. I think you can be much more useful right where you are." The caravan master leaned toward Rokha, whispered instructions Errol couldn't hear.

Her eyes widened. Then she nodded and left the tent.

"I think we have things in hand here, Skorik," Ru said. "You can go attend to your duties. Tell the guards they'll get the bonus agreed upon for combat."

The first nodded and left the tent.

Ru retrieved a chair from the far side of the tent and set it in front of his prisoner. He sat and regarded Eck with a look of patient concern. "Now, Eck, I'm going to ask you some questions. I won't bother asking you to reply truthfully. I'm sure you see the necessity of convincing me of the veracity of your answers."

Sweat beaded on Eck's face, shining against the pallor of his skin.

The caravan master held up a finger. "First, whose idea was it to attack the caravan?"

"Mine."

Ru shook his head and sighed. "Please, Eck. Although I have the highest regard for your fighting skills, you've never impressed me with your intellect. Someone planned this attack and provided you with the men to carry it out. Let me make this easier for you. Was it another caravan?"

Eck nodded without speaking.

"Ah, now we're getting somewhere. Which one?"

The silence stretched as Ru waited for an answer. Rokha entered the tent, exchanged nods with her employer, and stood to one side.

"You're not answering, Eck."

The prisoner's mouth worked and he strained against his bonds. The cords of his neck stood out against his skin with his effort to speak.

"He can't answer you," Rokha said. "Someone's put a compulsion on him—prohibiting him from speaking of the attack's source."

The master's head jerked in surprise. "Why would the church want to attack my caravan?"

"It might not be the church, Ru," Rokha said.

Ru paled. "There aren't any Merakhi in the kingdom."

Rokha gave an exaggerated shrug. "I'm here."

"That's different, and you know it. And you're only half Merakhi."

"Do you think the ferral attacked us by accident?"

Errol struggled to follow the twists and turns in the conversation. His heart skipped with each jolt of news. In the pit of his stomach, he suspected the abbot of tracking him. If Morin could descend to using a malus, what would prevent him from sending demon spawn after him as well? Rale's admonition to hide among the caravans now seemed weak protection.

"There are Merakhi in the kingdom," he said. Ru and Rokha turned, eyeing him as though they'd forgotten his presence.

A smirk stretched his employer's face without quite reaching his eyes. Ru became very still. "You seem to be possessed of a remarkable cache of information for one so young." His right hand drifted toward his sword. "Suppose you share with us how you know this."

Errol wet his lips and looked at Eck. Ru's tone held threats. Only moments ago he had been the one tied to that chair.

His gaze darted to Rokha. He pulled in a shaky breath. "The abbot in Windridge had a Merakhi woman in his cells. She had . . . there was something . . ." The words stuck in his throat.

Rokha closed the distance between them, knotted her hands in his tunic, and pulled him close. She ground out something in a language he didn't understand. "Did she have a spirit, boy?"

Errol nodded. "The abbot and the priest called it a malus."

Rokha wheeled on Naaman. "They've found me. They've sent a ghost-walker to take me back."

Ru's facade of self-control dropped away, and he let forth a string of curses that would have impressed Conger. In four quick strides he crossed the tent and struck Eck so hard his head whipped to the side. "If I don't think you're telling me the truth, I'll kill you with more imagination than you can conceive. Since you can't tell us who paid you, simply nod or shake your head when I ask you a question. Was the man who paid you to attack us at Longhollow when we left?"

Eck's head bobbed like a cork.

Ru nodded. "Excellent. Is it a caravan known to me?"

Eck's head shook from side to side. Sweat dripped from his nose.

Rokha stepped in front of Ru. "Was it a caravan master?"

Eck shook his head.

The questions poured from Ru and Rokha, but thirty minutes later they were no closer to the identity of their ultimate attacker than before.

Ru swore in disgust. "Take him to Skorik. He'll know what to do."

Rokha pulled her sword and cut the rope that bound Eck to the chair, but left his hands tied. Whimpers faded into the darkness beyond the tent flap.

With Eck gone, Errol became the object of Ru's attention. He gripped his staff, unsure of the other's intentions. To his surprise Ru extended his hand. Errol took it.

"My thanks, Errol. Your warning proved timely."

Errol shook his employer's hand, dumbfounded.

"Perhaps I should explain. I had Rokha warn the first of an attack while you were unconscious."

Errol nodded. Of course. Eck's men had counted on surprising the caravan. Even a few moments' notice was all Skorik had needed to turn the odds.

"But I have more to thank you for," Ru continued. "You managed to capture Eck alive for me. Now I'm going to find out who ordered this attack."

"How?"

Ru smiled. "You're a reader. Cast lots."

The threat in his voice was subtle but unmistakable. If Errol refused to cast lots for Ru, there would be a confrontation, and at the end of it Skorik would be waiting. His stomach lurched. A drink. He wanted a drink.

"The lots about the attack were the first ones I've ever cast. I don't know if I can do it again. I'm not even sure how I managed to make those. It just kind of . . . happened."

Naaman Ru grew still, still enough to be made from stone, before he spoke again. "I need to know who's after us, Errol. I must know. Rokha is, as you have heard, half Merakhi. Have you ever heard of such a thing?"

Errol shook his head.

Ru sighed. His eyes misted and he gazed across the tent. "It's a rare thing for a Merakhi woman to consort with a man from the kingdom. I was young and stupid with the flush of youth. My father was a noble in Basquon." The caravan master gave a bitter laugh. "I say *was*, but he may yet live. I've had no contact with him in nearly twenty-five years. Well, no matter. I grew up hearing tales of the might of the Merakhi, fierce warriors of the river kingdom who lived across the strait." He tapped his sword. "None in Talia or Basquon could best me. Every waking hour I possessed, I spent fighting, perfecting my skill. On my twenty-fifth birthday I fought the three best men in the region at the same time, men good enough to join the watch.

"I bested them all. Not one of them touched me. I thought myself the greatest swordsman of the day, maybe ever." He sighed. "I bribed one of my father's captains to ferry me across the Forbidden Strait." Ru chuckled. "The sea proved to be a crafty opponent. The greatest swordsman of the age spent two days puking over the rail, but at last we made the shore of Merakh. I joined a spice caravan on its way to the interior.

"I challenged at each village. Their men moved like leaves on the wind, yet each time I prevailed. Each time I would ask after their best, and each time the answer came back Amun Bes of Andria.

"Andria. You've never seen such a place. The white spires shine in the sun like a gift of light. I left the caravan to seek out Amun Bes's home. His guards almost shot me before I had a chance to issue my challenge. Then they laughed and opened the gates for the foolish kingdom man. Their master made a wager; told me he'd give me his daughter if I defeated him. If I lost, my life would be forfeit. I said I wanted no part of a Merakhi woman. I only wanted to match myself against the greatest fighter the world knew. Surprisingly, this gained me some measure of respect. He took me into his home and made me his honored guest. We fought the next day."

Ru stopped, his eyes looking through the fabric of the tent, remembering.

Errol leaned forward, caught in the tale. "You won."

The caravan master's brows rose at the question. "Did I? Yes, I suppose I did. What words can I use? You fight with a different weapon. Imagine your staff moving faster than thought, striking as though it lived, yet fighting an opponent whose skill matched yours in every way. Amun Bes of Andria matched me in skill and speed. I could not strike him, nor he me."

"Then how did you win?"

Ru looked him full in the face. "I was younger. Back and forth we moved, like a man dueling his shadow, but I had been fighting every day for years proving myself. Amun Bes hadn't faced a serious challenge in a decade. He tired. At last, knowing that he would lose through fatigue, he dropped his sword.

"The greatest fighter in Merakh bowed to me. I won without ever landing a blow. That night I saw his daughter. Such beauty and fierceness I'd never seen. I took her to be my wife."

"He broke the law of both kingdoms."

Errol spun to find Rokha back in the tent.

Ru nodded, tears tracked down his cheeks. "It is unlawful for people of Merakh and Illustra to intermarry. It took time for their ruling council to find us—almost a year. They killed Amun Bes and my wife. I escaped back across the strait, changed my name, and became a merchant."

Errol turned to Rokha. "You're his daughter."

She nodded. "The council swore to get me back."

"Why?"

"A trace of Akhen blood flows in my veins. I can sense the presence of compulsion. The council uses those born with the talent to search out kingdom spies."

Ru drew his sword. Its point centered on Errol's heart without wavering. "I have spent twenty-five years making sure they never take her. Now, reader, cast your lots."

Rokha put her hand on Ru's blade, pushed down. "Lower your sword, Father. He fought with us, remember?"

"I'm sorry," the caravan master said, sheathing his weapon. "I've forgotten my manners. Will you help us?"

Errol nodded. "I'll try, but I told you the truth before. I've only cast lots once. Luis didn't have a chance to teach me much."

Rokha stepped forward, put her carving knife and two cubes of wood in his hand. Blood filled the wood grain of one block.

"Norad's," she said. "He won't miss it."

"What do you want me to cast?" Errol asked.

"Find out who's after us," Ru said. "Cast for the church or the Merakhi. Can you do that?"

He shrugged. "Luis said that casting works best if the reader is familiar with the things or people he's casting." A chuckle escaped him as he thought of Antil. "I'm all too familiar with the church, but I've only met two Merakhi—Rokha and the one you called a ghost-walker."

"Rokha carries noble blood in her veins. That should be enough," Ru said.

For a moment, Errol couldn't seem to clear his mind. The fight, Ru's tale, Rokha's kiss all fought for his attention, yammering at him from everywhere inside his head. He took a deep breath, the kind he would take before a leap into the waters of the Sprata, and let it out. He fixed a picture of the abbot of Windridge and his cathedral in his head along with Antil and Martin.

The knife moved.

Minutes later, he stopped. The first lot rested in his hand. Errol lifted it to the light, turning it until he saw the word *Church* on it. All the blood had been carved away. He picked up the next block, felt the rough texture of the grain beneath his fingers, smelled the wood scent.

Karma sprang to his mind, her face twisted by the malus. It required no effort to hold her image. He feared he wouldn't be able to release it. A shaving of wood curled away from the block. Moments later the second lot was done.

"Which one's which?" Ru asked. "They look the same."

"They have to look the same," Errol said. "Luis says they're supposed to be as identical as humanly possible." He looked at Rokha. After hearing Ru's tale he could make out the resemblance to her father. "I used my cloak last time, but I think it's better if we use a bag."

She nodded, left, and returned a moment later with a gray sack that smelled of potatoes.

Errol put his hand in the bag and opened it. The lots clacked and he backed away. "You're supposed to shake it up."

"Who draws?" Ru asked. He stood on the balls of his feet, as if he were about to fight.

Errol shrugged. "Luis said it doesn't really matter. Once the lots are made by a reader you just have to make sure to pick at random."

Rokha shook the bag and held it above her head. Ru thrust his hand into the sack and pulled out one of the spheres. He looked at it, turning it over and over in the light before handing it to Errol. "What does it say?"

In the warm glow of the brazier a word became visible on one side. A thrill of success coursed through him at what he'd done. His mind boggled at the possibilities open to a reader. He rubbed the wood with affection. Now he understood why Luis considered those white stone lots his crowning achievement.

"It says *Church*."

Ru's sigh of relief filled the tent. "Better that no one was hunting us, but at least it's not the Merakhi."

With a small twinge of regret, Errol placed the lot back in the bag. "We're supposed to keep drawing until we're sure about the choice."

"Have you ever seen a lot drawn wrong on the first try?" Rokha asked.

Errol shook his head. "No, but Luis said not to take anything for granted."

She shook the bag and held it up for Ru once more. From the moment the caravan master put the lot in Errol's hand, something felt different. The grain caressed the ridges of his fingers as before. The ball possessed the same heft. Yet some instinct or intuition warned him.

When he held it up to the light, *Merakhi* glittered into view before disappearing. He rotated the lot twice more just to make sure.

"It says *Merakhi*."

Ru's brows drew together, his eyes wide. "I thought we were supposed to pull the same lot."

"Not every time," Errol said. But at the back of his mind a seed of doubt began to grow. He put the lot back in the bag. The sphere smelled like pine and potato now. "We're going to have to keep trying until one of them comes up more often than the other."

"How much more often?" Rokha asked.

"I don't know," Errol said. "Luis didn't get a chance to teach me that much. I think we'll know when we see it." He said this with as much confidence as he could muster, but his throat tightened as he released the lot into the bag.

Ru's next choice was *Church*. He relaxed a fraction, only to tense once more when the lot after that came up *Merakhi*.

"Maybe it's me," Ru said. He chewed his lower lip, his anxiety plain. "Someone else should draw."

Errol shrugged. According to Luis, the person drawing made no difference, but Errol didn't say so aloud. He'd never seen lots so evenly split, but his experience consisted of exactly two sets of choosing and a few more observing. He just didn't know what was possible and what wasn't.

By mutual agreement, Ru held the bag, and Rokha selected the lots.

Ten draws later, they knew no more than before. Each lot had been selected the same number of times and never twice in a row.

Even without Luis there to tell him so, Errol knew the pattern meant something.

But what?

"What does it mean, boy?" Ru asked. Tension vibrated through the timbre of his voice. Errol couldn't tell if the question held threats or not. Ru looked like he needed to fight something. Errol hoped it wouldn't be him.

"I don't know." He cudgeled his brain for any scrap of information Luis had given him that might help. There wasn't any.

"Are they both after us?" Rokha asked. Her hand gripped her sword, but she paled at her own suggestion.

Errol could only shrug. How many ways were there to say he didn't know? "That might explain it, but it also might mean that neither of them is after you."

Ru snorted. "That doesn't make sense. Someone put that compulsion on Eck, and only the church and the Akhen have the power." He leaned into his words, pushed them at Errol like a sword thrust. "Maybe you put a flaw into the lots, boy."

"What are you saying, Father?" Rokha asked.

"I'm saying our troubles started when this boy showed up." Ru's sword leapt into his hand.

Errol held up his hands. His staff fell to the ground.

"If you think killing an unarmed man will trouble me, boy, you're wrong."

Rokha stepped to her father's side but didn't touch his sword arm. "How close was Stone's fight against Eck?"

Ru's eyes narrowed.

Errol tried not to imagine that length of steel sliding between his ribs.

At last the caravan master nodded. "Too close to be a deception." Metal rasped as he slid his sword in its sheath. "We're not done with this, boy." He turned on one heel and left the tent. His yells for Skorik came back through the flap.

Rokha bent, then handed Errol his staff. "I didn't tell him Eck wasn't the only one in the camp under a compulsion. Father is unpredictable, especially when he's angry."

"Why didn't you tell him?"

She lifted her shoulders. "When you challenged Eck, I could see how scared you were, but you fought him anyway. I respect that. Besides, I told Father not to let you fight. Twice. He ignored me."

"Thank you." The feel of his staff back in his hands steadied him. "I don't know what went wrong with the lots I cast. Maybe we're asking the wrong question."

The sixth nodded. Her head tilted as she gave him a considering glance. "Who put the compulsion on you, Errol?"

"Luis, the reader who lived in my village. When he found out I had the talent, he told me I would have to go to Erinon. If I stay in one place too long, it takes over."

The tent flap fluttered, and Skorik appeared, filling the opening. "We're moving the caravan."

"At night?" Rokha asked.

The first nodded once, a quick jerk of his head. "Ru's orders." He pointed at Errol. "He says you're to take the point."

18

NIGHT MOVES

ERROL KNEW why Ru had positioned him as the vanguard—the master didn't trust him anywhere else. Not that he cared. If he ignored the sounds of the wagon wheels creaking behind him, he could almost believe he rode alone. That would have been nice. Trouble followed him and came to anyone around him.

He feared the attackers had come for him, not Rokha, and two men were dead, buried in unmarked graves along an anonymous stretch of road, because of him. Almost, he decided to turn Midnight around and tell Ru his suspicions.

The merchant would kill him before he could blink twice.

He had to get away from the caravan. Another attack would come—he knew it—and having been beaten once, the attackers would come in greater numbers the next time. Errol and everyone with him would be swarmed under.

Including Rokha.

He turned in his saddle, knowing he wouldn't be able to see her but searching anyway. Errol held no illusions about her feelings toward him. Her kiss had been more a victory celebration than anything personal, to be bestowed on the nearest ally.

He was glad it had been him.

Wood. He needed more wood. At the next opportunity he would cast lots to find out when the next attack would be. Rokha had gathered Norad's possessions. He would ask her for his blanks and carving knife. He would whittle until his hands bled to get an answer, even if it took all night.

And the moment he discovered an attack was coming, he would leave.

The caravan crept, feeling its way along the road, until the sun rose the next morning. When they stopped, Rokha gave Errol the knife and blocks without question. Ru eyed him with suspicion but only nodded when he volunteered to be on the first watch. The rest of the guards dropped to the ground where they stood, and soon soft snores came from the blanketed mounds that dotted their site.

His eyes burned with the need for rest, but he banished the thought of sleep as he held the first block of wood and concentrated on holding the answer to his question in his mind. *Yes,* he thought to himself, *they will attack in the next day.*

His strategy was simple. He would create lots to determine when the next assault on the caravan would arrive. If no attack was coming the next day, he would create lots to ask about the day after. And the day after that. As long as it took. His watch would last for six hours. If he worked steadily, he should be able to cast the entire week.

When Conger came to relieve him, the lots were tucked away in the large pocket inside his cloak. Roll after roll had given the same answer. No attack would be coming the next day or any day following for a week. He pulled the late-morning air into his lungs and staggered to his bedroll. Fatigue and relief pulled him into dreamless sleep, like a rock sinking into a pool.

The toe of Skorik's boot flipped him over and he started awake. The sun glowed red above the western horizon, bathing the trees with a ruddy glow. His heart pounded, and for the space of three breaths he struggled to place himself, fighting his disorientation. He looked up at the first.

"Your watch is in an hour," Skorik said. "You've slept through two meals and most of the day. Go see Grub."

Errol nodded and sat up. A single lot, of the same pine as the rest he'd fashioned, rolled from underneath him. He looked at the sphere and then turned to see Skorik watching the ball of wood as it came to rest against a clump of grass.

Their eyes locked, Errol held his breath as the pounding of his heart shook him.

"That almost looks like a lot," the first said at last. "But it can't be, because if it was I'd be required to turn you over to the nearest priest. The entire kingdom knows the law against any man, no matter his position, having a reader in his employ." Skorik grinned wolfishly and drew one finger across his throat. "The church guards keep their swords sharp just in case they come across anyone wishing to test their resolve on the matter." He bent and picked up the evidence of Errol's crime, and tossed it to him with a casual flip. "It's a good thing this isn't a lot. Of course, there's no crime against having a ball of wood that looks like a lot."

Errol tucked it out of sight as quickly as his hands could move. "I need to see Ru."

Skorik nodded. "Yes," he said as he turned away. "I imagine you do."

He found the caravan master conversing in hushed tones with Rokha by the lead wagon. At Errol's approach, they cut their conversation short. Ru's stare was hard and challenging while Rokha's eyebrows simply lifted to convey her curiosity. Errol moved his staff from his hands to the crook of his elbow, hoping Ru would take it as a sign of deference.

He reached into his cloak and pulled out a double handful of lots, held them where they could see them. "I still don't know who sent the attack, but they're not going to try again for at least a week."

The caravan master gave him a look made all of ice. "I trusted you the first time. I'm not in the habit of trusting anyone twice without proof."

"I'm not trying to mislead you." He grabbed the two lots that represented an attack coming the next day. "I'll prove it." The dust at his feet would serve his purpose. He bent to run one finger in the dirt, then straightened and smudged the lot for no attack. "Here." He thrust the lots toward them and took two steps back with his hands in the air. "Test it."

Rokha reached in front of Ru, taking the lots while her father kept his hands to his sides. "Did you not teach me to take advantage of any weapon that comes to hand, Father?"

Ru nodded. "This one may turn on its bearer, Rokha."

"All weapons are dangerous for the novice," she said.

The caravan master snorted. "You just described us."

She removed her cloak, pulled up the corners to make a crude sack, and dropped the lots inside.

With a sigh of resignation, her father reached inside and drew. The smudged lot lay in his hand.

Seven times Naaman Ru drew before the other lot came out. The muscles in his jaws finally relaxed and the look he now gave seemed more speculative. Errol sensed an opportunity to gain Ru's trust. He pulled the rest of the lots he'd made from his cloak. "We have at least a week before the next attack. I made a pair of lots for each of the next seven days."

Ru shook his head, his look disbelieving. "You did what?"

Rokha laughed. "Would a spy admit to anything like that, Father?"

Errol didn't know what to make of their sudden change in mood. He hadn't known what to expect when he'd come to Ru to tell him of the lots, but Rokha's laughter and Ru's unbelief took him off guard.

"Did no one in your village teach you the rudiments of logic, boy? A smith, perhaps? Or maybe a carpenter?" Ru asked with a smile.

Their amusement cut him. "In my village boys become apprenticed in their fourteenth year. By the time my fifteenth naming day came round I was already in the ale barrel. I don't even know if anyone asked to take me on. I'm pretty sure I was drunk at the time."

"Casting for every day took unnecessary effort and time," Rokha said. "After the first cast, you could have asked if we were going to be attacked in the next three days, then the next five, and so on."

Errol nodded in chagrin. He'd used at least twice as many lots as needed.

Ru's grin faded into thoughtfulness. "He's a little old to be an apprentice."

Rokha looked at Errol with a smile that turned his knees to water. "I think he'll prove to be a quick study, Father."

"Possibly," the caravan master said. "And of course he has . . . talent that any merchant would find useful. Since there doesn't seem to be any threat of an imminent attack on the wagons, we'll stay here and move out at first light. Errol, when we travel, you will ride with me."

"Why?"

"I'm going to teach you the basics of trade." Ru smiled, his eyes bright. "With my instruction and your ability, we'll make a fortune."

Errol gaped. "You want me to cast lots to make money?"

Ru's smile faded and he grew very still. "You object?"

He wanted to say yes, but the deaths of Norad and Jesper mocked him. The two guards died because he'd signed on with Ru. The right thing for him to do was to leave the caravan immediately, but the thought of the ferral unnerved him. Half-human things hunted him, and Errol desperately did not want to be alone. He swallowed.

"No. I don't object." Inside his head a small voice called him a coward.

⚜

The next day, as the caravan rolled west, Errol tied Midnight to the front wagon and climbed onto the seat to sit next to Ru. The man greeted him with a smile and a nod.

"Tell me, Errol. Why am I hauling animal skins?"

Errol shrugged. "To make money?"

"Correct," Ru said. "You see, we're off to a good start already. Of course the goal of any merchant or tradesman is to make a profit. Essentially, you have to be able to sell your goods for more than you paid for them, but along with that you have to pay your expenses as well."

For hours, Naaman Ru instructed Errol in the art of commerce, and he proved to be as stern a taskmaster in this subject as Rale had been with the staff. After each topic, he questioned Errol closely, changing the nature of his queries to ensure that his young apprentice fully understood. Any time Errol simply parroted back what Ru said, he forced him to say it in his own words and the questioning would begin again. By the time Errol's lessons finished, his head hurt with the effort of trying to remember everything the caravan master had taught him.

They repeated the process the next day and the day after. Errol proved to be a quick study. The considerable time he'd spent in taverns became an unexpected asset. The countless conversations he'd overheard in the last five years yielded insights against the backdrop of Ru's knowledge. As the caravan approached Dronfeld—a trade city built on nine hills and surrounded by some of the richest farmland in the kingdom—Ru wore the confident look of a man who knew he couldn't lose.

"Now, Errol, I think you understand the ideas of trade fairly well. When we get into the city, I'm going to take you with me as one of my bodyguards. It's expected, since we'll be carrying a substantial amount of money once we sell our skins. As part of my protection you'll meet the representatives of the five houses that control the business interests in Dronfeld. Later you'll help me choose which house to sell to."

The accusation in Errol's head refused to go away. He sighed. "What is it you want me to do?"

Ru chuckled and rubbed his hands together. "I want you to attend me and commit the representative of each house to memory. I'll tell each one we need to consider their offer. Then you'll cast lots and tell me which one will give me the highest price for my cargo."

Errol frowned. Ru had earlier said the price of a cargo would vary little from house to house, often only by a few pennies per skin. He mentioned this to the caravan master.

"Very good, my boy. You have been paying attention. But consider this—a few pennies per skin on every trip will compound over time. With enough transactions, I'll be one of the richest caravans inside of a year."

"From just a few pennies?" Errol asked.

Ru nodded. "I think we need to include a study of quantities in your education, Errol. You'd be amazed at what a few pennies per skin compounded over time will do."

Ru brought his caravan to a halt at the staging point east of the city—the only spot within a league that resembled level ground—and with Rokha and Errol in tow, went forth to do battle. The merchant quarters and their attached warehouses stood like monoliths on the river, blocky and intimidating. Each was run by a mix of outlanders and natives. Ru smiled and his eyes glittered as they dismounted their horses in front of the warehouse belonging to the Stelton enterprise.

As they entered the stone edifice, Ru schooled his features to solemnity and leaned over to whisper his instructions. "Pay close attention, Errol. When I meet with their factor, you and Rokha will be responsible for committing every detail to memory." He moved closer until Errol could see the master's excited pulse in his neck. Ru's voice became stern. "Above all, say nothing."

Ru turned and led the way into the offices of his first opponent. Before Errol's eyes could adjust to the change in light, a thin man not much older than Errol presented himself to Ru with a slight bow.

"Greetings, caravan master. My name is Ambra. How may I assist you?"

Ru gave a polite smile and turned to survey the rich ornamentations that decorated the office. He bowed in turn, deeper than Ambra. "My name is Naaman Ru. I've just come from Longhollow loaded with skins. I'm looking for the best price so that I can purchase some of your fabled grain for the next leg of my route."

"Skins?" Ambra asked. His face twisted as though Ru had somehow earned his sympathy. "I will tell the factor you are here." He turned and left, his face locked in that same expression.

Ru shifted until only Rokha and Errol could see his face. His expression never changed but he chortled under his breath. "Perfect. Absolutely perfect. Oh, it's going to be a good day."

Errol inhaled to ask him any of a dozen questions that sprang to mind, but before he could open his mouth a large pot-bellied man with the florid coloring and the harsh accent of an Einlander approached them. "Greetings." His voice boomed and echoed from the white stone interior. "I am Kedar Willam, the factor for Stelton House. How may I serve you?"

Ru bowed again, even more deeply this time, and spread his hands. "I have skins to sell, worthy Kedar, of the finest quality."

"Ah," Kedar said. "So my assistant, Ambra, told me. I had hoped he was mistaken. Such a cargo is usually in great demand in the northern provinces." He shrugged his shoulders. "But the winter this past year was milder than expected. The market is somewhat depressed, I'm afraid."

Errol blinked. *Milder?* He'd heard the merchants in Callowford say spring had been late in coming to the north—very late. He inhaled. Ru needed to know Kedar was either misinformed or trying to cheat him.

A weight on his foot turned his words into a gasp of pain. When Ru and the factor looked in his direction, Rokha slapped him across the face.

"I told you never to touch me again," she said. "Don't think you can get away with it just because there are others about."

Errol's face flushed. Kedar's roar of laughter filled the space until its echoes sounded as though a chorus of factors laughed at Errol's embarrassment.

Stelton's factor wiped tears from his eyes as he turned back to Ru. "Worthy master, I can see you have enough trouble without trying to negotiate a price for skins that won't sell. To help you out I will pay you last year's price for your cargo."

Ru donned a look of gratitude. "That is most kind, Kedar. I will take your offer under consideration." He gave Rokha and Errol a look made of daggers. "Right now I must return to my caravan. I'm afraid my choice in personnel this morning was misguided. I require a change of guards."

A brief spasm of desperation crossed Kedar's face. "I would hate for you to make a second trip, worthy master. Why not conclude our business before you attend to your guards."

The caravan master nodded. "You are most gracious, Kedar, but I'm afraid I have no choice in the matter." He stepped closer to the factor, and his voice dropped. "The girl is my daughter. Much as it pains me to put family before business, it must be done. She keeps the ledger."

Defeat wreathed itself across Kedar's features, and he bowed. "As you say. My offer will stand. Please allow Stelton House the honor of serving you tomorrow."

Ru nodded and then led them back into the daylight. Once their horses were well away from the enormous warehouse and its offices, he cackled with delight. "Oh, my daughter, that was very well done. In one stroke you gave me the perfect exit from Stelton House.

"And you," he said to Errol, "need to listen carefully to instruction."

"But Kedar's trying to cheat you," Errol said. "Spring came late to the north this last winter."

Ru nodded. "Yes, I know. I'd heard a rumor of such back in Longhollow—which is why I bought skins."

Errol shook his head, confused. "You don't care that Kedar is trying to cheat you?"

"Care? Of course I care," Ru said. "I did everything in my power to encourage it." He laughed at Errol's confusion. "Ah, my boy, you have so much to learn. The easiest way to get the best price out of someone is to let them think they can take advantage of you. Take two men, pit their greed and desire to win against one another, and you'll see them pay more for an object than it's worth simply because they can't stand the thought of losing."

Ru leaned across his saddle to give Rokha a hug. "That was brilliant. In fact, I think we should use that at each of the houses. By the time I return tomorrow, the five of them will be ready to kill each other to buy our cargo."

He turned to Errol. "Do you think you can repeat your performance, Errol?"

He nodded, but inside he was still trying to make sense of Ru's strategy.

"It's got to be natural," Ru said. "If the factor suspects that he's being tricked, he won't bid on the skins. No man takes kindly to being manipulated."

"I'll try."

Ru nodded. Though he'd seemed happy before, now he seemed positively giddy.

They arrived at the next warehouse on the river. Its walls were constructed of stone as well, but where Stelton House gleamed a bright white, the walls of Harrida House were a light gray.

They dismounted, and Errol repeated every motion and gesture down to the intake of breath and the gasp. He found his part easy to play. Rokha seemed to be taking an inordinate amount of pleasure in stomping his foot. He considered standing on her other side to keep her from breaking his toes.

After Harrida House, they visited the warehouses belonging to Weir, Davila, and Corloni. Each house repeated some variation of Stelton's excuse as to why they could not give Ru the price his goods deserved, and each factor suffered the dismay of losing a merchant with much-needed cargo.

Naaman clapped Errol on the shoulder as they rode back east of the city to the staging ground. "Perfection, my boy, absolute perfection. It appeared you were in genuine pain every time."

Errol shot Rokha a hard look. "I was."

"Really?" Ru said with a lift of eyebrows. Then he smiled. "Well done, daughter. I'm glad you left nothing to chance. Now, here's how we're going to make the houses of Dronfeld pay. I want you to craft lots, my boy, that will tell us who is going to give us the best price for our cargo and—" he laughed, rubbing his hands together—"who is going to give us the second-best price."

Rokha tossed her dark hair with glee.

"I don't understand. Why do you want to know which house will give you the second-best price?" Errol asked.

Ru snickered. "I think it's only fair to let them have first shot at selling us the cargo for the outbound trip. They'll cut the price so deep after losing out on our skins, none of the other houses will come close."

Back at camp, Errol sat cross-legged in a secluded spot with a dozen blocks of pine and Norad's carving knife nestled in his lap. He cleared his mind and pictured the factor at Stelton House. Kedar's florid face rose in his mind's eye along with his expression of desperate greed. Errol let every detail of the man and his business wash over him. It didn't take long. His habit of cataloging faces in his search for his parents proved useful. He opened his eyes and drew the small knife toward him, watching as a fine curl dropped to his lap.

Two hours later ten wooden balls and a pile of fragrant pine shavings rested where the blocks of wood had lain. He smiled in satisfaction. A couple of weeks ago it would have taken him more than twice as long to carve that many. Luis was still faster by far, and Errol didn't have a clue how to work in stone, but the carving knife felt like a part of him now.

Ru's enthusiasm burned as bright as ever when Errol told him the lots were ready for drawing. The caravan master summoned his daughter, and the three of them crowded into the wagon that the caravan master used for traveling quarters. Rokha took the first five lots and mixed them together. Somewhere in the camp or during their visit to the city, she'd managed to procure a proper cloth bag. The royal blue matched her vest. Errol thought it set off her dark eyes and hair to good advantage. As she shook the bag, she glanced in his direction and, seeing him eyeing her, tilted her head back and smiled with a hint of challenge.

Ru turned away and thrust his hand into the bag. "Let's see who we'll be doing business with tomorrow." The sphere he withdrew looked no different than the rest. "Well, my boy, who's it to be?"

Errol took the lot and held it up to the light of the lantern, turning it until the name came into view. "Stelton House."

"I thought as much," Ru said, nodding. "Kedar looked almost desperate when we left. Stelton House probably has a contract for skins they need to fill." His grin became vicious. "I'm sure we can help them on that account."

Ru replaced the lot and drew another dozen times just to make sure. Stelton House came out all but twice. The next set of lots went into the bag. Rokha drew this time. Davila House would offer the second-best price.

Ru beamed at him. "My boy, if everything works out tomorrow the way I think it will, you've earned yourself a bonus. Now, if you'll excuse us, Rokha and I have plans to make."

As he left Ru's wagon, he saw the caravan master unrolling a map that showed the region around Erinon.

Not knowing what else to do, he visited Grub for an early supper and then went in search of Jhade. It had been days since they'd sparred. She still had moves he didn't completely understand, and Rale's admonition to continuously work the forms was always in the back of his mind.

But the real reason he wanted to spar lay elsewhere. The lots he'd cast for Ru troubled him. Giving the caravan master an unseen advantage in negotiating a price was wrong, but there was also the attack on the caravan to consider. The fault for that almost certainly lay with Errol in some way. In a sense, Errol was just trying to pay Ru back for his trouble. In that light his efforts to help Naaman Ru made perfect sense, but his logic failed to comfort him. Could he really make up for the attack by helping Ru cheat others? He doubted it.

There would surely be a price to pay.

The sparring session with Jhade lasted nearly an hour, and Errol felt a sense of accomplishment at its conclusion. The woman managed to touch him only twice, while Errol landed a dozen hits during their contest. At the end, she'd bowed, acknowledging her defeat.

Still troubled, he fastened the knobblocks onto the end of his staff. He worked the forms, losing himself in the rhythm of the dance. The weights on the end of his staff barely slowed him now. Rale had been right. Time and food served to correct the five years he'd spent drinking. Though he would never be a giant, he no longer had to look up at every man in the camp, and even if his arms didn't become as large as Cruk's or Liam's, they were still strong enough to move his staff until it blurred. He wiped the sweat from his face and pushed himself to move even faster.

One day, he vowed, he would be quick enough to knock the lightning from the sky.

19

A CHANGE OF PLANS

A T NOON the next day, Ru rode back into camp looking as if he'd been named heir to a fortune. The guards
mustered for their pay. Errol, as the thirteenth—a promotion
resulting from the deaths of Norad and Jesper—took his place
at the end of the queue. As he neared the table Ru set up, he noticed each man received his wages with a look of surprise. When
his turn came to collect his pay, Ru surprised him by dropping
a gold crown to go with the four silver of his allotted pay. The
caravan master didn't smile but tapped his lips with his index
finger and nodded toward his wagon.

Inside, the caravan master pointed to a map spread on the small
table. Notations showed Erinon at the western edge of Green
Isle. On the coast of the mainland the city of Liester sat to the
south, Scarritt to the north, and Ambridge was positioned inland
to the east. "Never take anything for granted, my boy," Ru said.
"I expect Erinon will give us the best price for our grain, but
circumstances have a way of proving thoughts to be foolishness."
He put his arm around Errol's shoulders. "You've never been to
any of these cities, have you?"

Errol shook his head. Until the past few months, he had never left the area surrounding Callowford and Berea.

"I didn't think so. How necessary is it for you to know the cities before you cast lots?"

He shrugged. "Luis said I had to know it well in order to get an accurate draw, but Rale told me that if someone who knew the subject described it to me, it could be done, provided the lots are drawn often enough."

"Would you be willing to try, Errol?"

Ru's arm still rested in friendly fashion on his shoulders, but a warning of danger tingled up his spine at the thought of saying no.

"I'll try."

Ru clapped his hands. "Excellent, my boy. Stay here. I'll have Rokha join you. She knows the cities as well as I do. You like her, yes?"

He nodded, unsure of the direction Ru was taking.

"Excellent, excellent. I think she likes you too."

Ru departed, and moments later Rokha entered without smiling. For the next two hours she described Erinon and the cities on the mainland coast until Errol could see them in his mind. But she looked him in the eyes only once—and without the fire and challenge he'd come to expect.

For an hour after he finished carving the lots, the three of them drew, scrambled the spheres, and drew again.

Hundreds of times.

Finally, Rokha raised her hand, looking at the tally. "I think that's enough, Father."

The tedium appeared to have dampened Ru's enthusiasm. "Which one, daughter?"

"Erinon."

"Ah." Naaman Ru looked disappointed for the briefest moment before smiling in Errol's direction. "I see our purposes align, my boy. Your destination happens to be the most profitable port for our grain." He gave Rokha a long look before speaking again.

"I must speak with Skorik before we pick up our cargo in the morning. My thanks, Errol."

As soon as Ru exited the wagon, Rokha brushed past Errol and departed without a word. Left by himself, there was nothing for Errol to do except leave and rejoin the rest of the guards. Outside, ale and wine flowed among his fellows. Locks were placed on the wagon axles to keep them from being stolen, and the camp celebrated a successful sale.

In the midst of the celebration, Ru climbed past Grub atop the supply wagon and raised his hands for quiet. "My fellow adventurers, earlier I could see your surprise at the amount of your bonus. As it so happens, our hides were in more demand up north than even I realized. I think it only fair to tell you that I had help in negotiating top price for our cargo. Would you like to know who?"

A chorus of yells came from the assembled guards. Some of them struggled to stay upright.

Ru smiled like an actor playing his audience. "As it so happens, Rokha and our newest member, Errol, are skilled negotiators." He gestured to each of them in turn, offering them a small bow and flourish of his hand. "What say you all? Shall we keep them with us?"

The guards roared their approval. Rokha inclined her head briefly and favored them with a tight-lipped smile. Errol flushed at the applause and Ru's obvious manipulation. He could not stay with the caravan. Even now he could close his eyes and point without hesitation toward Erinon. The church's compulsion worked on him, though it did not trouble him yet. He left the wagons with the cheers of his fellow guards following him into the cool summer evening. The air here in the lowlands clung to him. He reached up and undid the laces at his throat.

Errol meandered, trying to work out Rokha's sudden change in attitude. Ru's daughter was five years his senior. He had no illusions that she would consider him a worthy suitor. . . .

But he'd thought they were friends.

Men drank and joked about the vagaries of women as a matter of course. Was Rokha's sudden change what they meant? He frowned. No, it didn't fit. Rokha, bold and alluring like a bird of prey, bore little resemblance to those pouty women who waved their fans and batted their eyes. Ru's daughter wouldn't ignore him without reason.

And the reason had something to do with Ru.

What was the man planning?

Frustrated, he sought a patch of open ground away from the noise and commotion of the caravans. He stood facing west and watched the sun cast its last feeble rays across the broad meadow and dip below the horizon. As dusk descended, he lost himself in his ritual of exercises, working them the way Rale had taught.

And stopped. He'd caught a glimpse of a figure ducking behind the edge of the last tent.

Skorik. Errol rested his staff in the crook of his elbow and walked toward the tent. By the time he got there the first had left.

⁕

The caravan pulled out of Dronfeld the next day. The wagons creaked under the mountain of grain Ru had negotiated. Days passed as they crept toward Erinon, lucky to make eight leagues a day. Errol ground his teeth at the delay. So near to Illustra's capital, he could almost feel the pull of the conclave ahead of him.

One evening, as the light faded and the rolling hills lost much of their color, the caravan crested a rise in the road and came to the village of Corwin. So close to the coast, villages occurred more frequently. They'd already passed through three that day. Each night the guards had looked forward to their reprieve from sleeping on the ground. Those who drew duty waited anxiously for their turn at the inns, eager to exchange their bonus for ale and beds.

As they parked the wagons, Errol unsaddled Midnight and led him to the picket line to place him with the rest of the horses. Rokha stood at the end rubbing the nose of Anoth, her stallion.

When Errol drew near, she gave the horse a firm pat on the shoulder and strode away, the tightness in her back radiating tension.

He curried and watered his horse, trying to devise some way to talk to the caravan master's daughter. Midnight nickered and nuzzled him on the ear, which brought a smile to his lips. He grabbed the horse's head and scratched the patch of white between his eyes. "At least you still like me. I wish I knew what I'd done to make Rokha look at me like slime on a pool."

"Women are hard to figure," a voice said just behind him. "Best not to try."

Errol took his time as he turned to face the speaker, not wanting to give Skorik the satisfaction of knowing he'd been startled. "Do you know why she's avoiding me?" He tried, but couldn't quite keep the challenge from his voice.

The first's eyes narrowed and his face hardened. "I know only what Ru tells me. And right now he tells me that he wants an extra guard on the caravan. You're last in line. That means you." His hand moved toward the sword on his hip, the motion slight but unmistakable.

As thirteenth, Errol didn't have any choice in the matter, so he contented himself with the knowledge that they would soon be at Erinon. He would probably never see Rokha after that. He nodded to Skorik. "I understand."

The first nodded and walked away in the direction of the inns, but after Skorik disappeared into the shadows Errol's skin prickled with the sensation of being watched. With a sigh, he grabbed his staff from his pile of gear near the picket line.

Besides himself, Conger, Sven, and Jhade had duty. Conger posted himself near the fire. He lifted his head each time he turned a page to check on the wagons nearest to him. Jhade stood as though she'd been carved from stone, her eyes unblinking and gazing out into the night. Sven kept close to the supply wagon. One fist held an oversized loaf of bread, while the other gripped a wedge of cheese large enough to feed three people.

"Pointless," the Soede muttered. And it was. The village of

Corwin probably didn't even boast a pickpocket, let alone a thief bold enough to try and make off with bags of grain that each weighed seven stone. For some reason, Ru wanted to keep him near the caravan tonight. But why?

Bored, and frustrated by his questions, he made a circuit of the camp. He moved away from Grub's supply wagon and smiled as the sounds of Sven's gorging faded. Twenty wagons later he came to the head of the caravan, Ru's quarters. The muted sound of voices came from within, and he slowed.

From where he stood he could make out the pitch and cadence of the conversation but not the words. Errol edged closer, stepping lightly to avoid noise. The voices belonged to Ru and his daughter.

"No," Rokha said. Her voice sounded defensive.

"No? Does a dutiful daughter say *no* to her father?" Ru's voice cut the air like a sword, sharp and pitiless.

"Does a father sell his daughter for a few bags of grain?" Rokha fired back.

"You're being emotional, child. This is our chance to make a fortune."

Errol's ears prickled. He dropped to one knee as though checking the sole of his boot. He suspected somewhere in the darkness Skorik watched him.

"What if the church finds out?" Rokha asked. Her voice now held the measured tone that Errol knew well.

"They're not going to find out. Only you and I know the boy is more than a simple caravan guard."

Silence fell over the interior of Ru's wagon, and Errol rose to move on. Then Rokha's voice came through the walls again.

"This is dishonorable, Father. I thought better of you."

The sharp retort of someone being slapped cracked through the air.

Errol gripped his staff and a roaring filled his ears. He'd hit her.

"I can see that I have been too lenient with you," Ru said, his voice cold as the wind in Soeden. "A daughter does not question her father's decision, and an employee does not gainsay her master. You will do as you are told. Now, I order you to find the boy and do as I have instructed."

Errol turned and retraced his steps back toward the supply wagon. He kept his pace as slow as he dared. Rokha would be approaching from the far side. To calm himself he counted the grain wagons again as he returned.

When he rounded the supply wagon he saw Ru's daughter there before him.

Sven looked in his direction as he entered the pool of light cast by the fire. "There he is, girl." He took another bite of cheese. "Probably been out swinging that stick of his in the dark again. Don't know why he's even here. It's not his turn for duty."

Rokha looked him full in the face for the first time in days. "I don't think anyone's going to steal father's grain tonight," she said. Her smile looked forced. One side of her face showed red in the firelight. "Why don't we go for a walk?"

His fury at Ru's handiwork made it difficult to think. With an effort he took a deep breath and unclenched his fists. He needed to keep from arousing her suspicion. What would he say if he hadn't overheard their conversation?

"How come you've been avoiding me?" The question came out before he realized he'd spoken.

Rokha shrugged and looked away. Then she took his hand and moved to lead him away from the supply wagon. "Let's check the picket line."

Errol didn't move. Ru's daughter tugged on his arm, but he resisted. Somewhere in the shadows near the horses, he felt sure, Skorik watched. They needed to find someplace where they couldn't be overheard.

"The moon's up," he said. "Why don't we get away from the smell of horses for a change?"

She looked as if she were on the edge of refusing but glanced once in the direction of Ru's wagon and, after a brief pause, nodded assent. As soon as they left the circle of light cast by the campfire, her fingers wiggled out from his and her hand dropped away.

The hair on his neck stiffened with the sensation of being followed, but when he turned as if to check their position, he could see no evidence of the first. Errol and Rokha walked side by side, their shoulders nearly touching, but Ru's daughter wrapped herself in chilly silence that left Errol floundering. He cast about for some topic that would distract her from her father's orders—whatever they might have been—but every idea seemed to lead inexorably back to her servitude and his unspoken bondage.

"Your father gave me a gold crown as a bonus," he said finally. He forced a chuckle. "The last time I saw that much money, I planned on using it to stay drunk on Cilla's ale for a week. Now I hardly know what to do with it."

"Who's Cilla?"

Errol sighed. A clear image of Cilla proved more difficult to recall by the day. Even now, as he tried, her features blurred, became a combination pulled from Myrrha and Rokha. "She's a girl who runs an inn back in the village I'm from."

"A girl . . . running an inn? Is she your age?"

"I suppose. Maybe a little older. Her father—"

"Do you love her?" Rokha asked.

No one had ever asked him the question before. *Love?* Most of the guards spoke of love as something men and women did rather than how they felt. The church talked about love, but that was usually about Deas's love for mankind or vice versa. He didn't have the faintest notion of what love between a man and a woman meant.

"I don't think so," he said. "Mostly, I just wanted to make sure she gave me enough ale to keep my thoughts and memories at bay."

Rokha gave a small, sad-sounding chuckle at this. "Typical man. Only out for what you can get from the poor girl. Now she's back there pining away for you."

Rokha made sport of him. Her tone wasn't unkind, yet her

words held currents and undertones that eluded him. "Not likely. I think she looked at me the way most people look at a stray cat or dog that's ended up on their doorstep. She gave me ale and let me sleep on the floor of the inn in exchange for pretty shoddy work on my part."

"I think she might be surprised at how much you've changed," Rokha said. "You don't sound like the person you describe. If you went back to your village, she'd notice you in a much different way." She sounded almost angry.

He shrugged, but the darkness swallowed the gesture. "I don't think I'll be going back, at least, not for a long time."

"What do you think about me, Errol?" Her words had barely the strength behind them to make it to his ears.

His mouth went dry. He licked his lips, trying to think of something to say. What did he think? "I didn't know a woman could be like you."

"Is that bad?" The challenge in her voice was unmistakable.

He rushed to answer. "No, not at all. I never knew a woman could be fierce and beautiful and smart before I met you. Every time I see you I think of a hawk, beautiful and deadly."

Her laugh, deep and throaty, sounded surprised. "I think I like that."

Errol took a quick breath. "Or my knees go weak thinking about the way you kissed me."

The laugh cut off as if it had never been. "I wish I hadn't."

He took a deep breath. This would probably be as good a time as any. "Because your father wants to use you to keep me with the caravan?"

A small quick intake of breath. "You know?"

"I overheard the two of you arguing tonight. When he struck you I wanted to go after him with my staff."

She laid a hand on his arm. "That would be a very bad idea, Errol. Father is deadly with a sword."

Ru had to be in his midforties. "Still?"

"I saw him spar with Skorik once," she said. "I'd never seen him lose or come close to losing before then. Father moved like something out of the stories."

He nodded, but in his heart he resolved to match Naaman Ru one day. He leaned toward Rokha, felt her stiffen in the darkness when he touched her shoulder. "I can't stay with the caravan once we reach Erinon. Would your father force me to stay?"

She sighed. "I think so. You've become the key to his wealth."

"Will you ask your father to let me go?"

He felt rather than saw the shake in Rokha's shoulders. "Daughters do not defy their fathers." Her voice broke, and she gave a small sniff.

So Ru planned to keep him against his will. How long would it be before the compulsion gripped him? What would happen if he couldn't obey? Errol shuddered. He didn't want to find out. A sudden gust of wind chilled him. The hair on the back of his neck rose in protest, and the sensation of being watched reasserted itself.

How well did Skorik see in the dark?

"I think we should go back," he said.

"What?" She sounded surprised.

"You can't help me without angering your father. I'm sorry. I was wrong to ask. I hadn't thought that out." He pitched his voice so that his next words wouldn't travel more than a couple of feet. "And the longer we stay here in the dark, the worse Skorik will think of you. He's out there hiding in the shadows, wondering what we're doing."

"You're serious, aren't you?" she asked. "You really mean to go back to camp now?"

"I said so, didn't I?"

She laughed, and a hand came up to touch his face. "You're a surprising man, Errol Stone. Here we are, alone in the dark where no one can see. You have it in your power to take liberties with me, with my father's blessing, and yet you refuse to take advantage of the opportunity." A hint of a growl crept into her voice. "I don't know whether to be insulted or complimented."

"So that's why you've been ignoring me?" he asked. "You

thought I was going to use you because your father wants to keep me with the caravan?" Laughter bubbled up inside of him. "If it makes you feel any better, I'm sure I'll regret the lost opportunity later."

She took his hand and pulled him to the ground. "Skorik will report back to my father everything he's heard and seen," she whispered. She put her mouth close to his ear. "I need you to help me prove I've been a dutiful daughter." Her breath fell on his skin like a caress, and he shivered.

Her hand slid up his back, knotted in his hair. With her other hand she pushed him back until he lay on the ground, then covered his face with her own. "Thank you, Errol."

"You're wel—" Her lips found his, and for a moment their kiss stretched interminably.

And ended all too soon.

When they parted, he rose and turned to go, but she caught his arm. "I will sow a seed of doubt in Father's mind if I can. If the trading houses discover he's used a reader against them, they'll have him killed."

"Thank you."

⚜

Two days later, under a lowering sky, the caravan moved west through Ambridge and approached Four Crossings. Too small to be considered one of the great cities, it sat on the crossroads that led to Port City to the east, Liester to the south, and Scarritt to the north.

The hint of salt hung in the air and at infrequent moments he heard the cry of gulls. Ten leagues remained to the coast, where ships waited to take them and their grain to the capital.

Where the conclave of readers waited.

Skorik led them along the highway that skirted Four Crossings, and when they reached the crossroads, the wagons turned south, to Leister.

Away from Erinon.

Ru intended to take a lesser price on the grain in order to keep Errol from reaching the capital. He pulled the reins, brought Midnight to a stop, and then heard a familiar growl behind him.

"Stay in formation, boy," Skorik said.

Errol jerked the reins, turning Midnight to face the first. "Why aren't we going to Erinon?" he demanded.

"The last guard doesn't ask questions of the caravan master, the first, or anyone else for that matter. Now get back in formation or I'll dock your pay."

It came to this moment. Errol would have to leave the protection of the caravan behind and journey on to Erinon alone. *So be it.* He inclined his head toward the first. "Please tell Master Ru that I thank him for the opportunity to work as his guard, but I must continue to Erinon. He can keep my pay."

He turned Midnight again and set the horse's head toward Four Crossings and away from Ru's caravan.

A weight concussed against the back of his head. The ground came up at him as he pitched forward from his saddle.

❧

Something hard bumped against his face. Again. He opened his eyes, tried to focus and found he couldn't because Ru's bunk was mere inches from his face. The wagon jounced, and his head bounced up once more. He stiffened and caught himself before smacking back into the floor. His skull throbbed in time to his heartbeat.

Errol sat up, probed beneath his hair with his free hand, and quickly pulled it away when his fingers grazed the spot Skorik had hit. No blood, but it was a wonder he could see straight. Ru's wagon lurched again.

The bunk offered convenient handholds, and he made use of them, pulling himself upright until he was able to take the three small steps to the door.

It was locked from the outside.

Naaman Ru meant to keep him with the caravan by force.

20

LOTMAKER

THE HOURS STRETCHED. Through the small window on one side of the wagon he could see the sun dipping toward the horizon, streaking wispy clouds with orange and red. The caravan would stop soon, if not at a village, then along the roadside. A village would be easier. Most of the small towns allotted ground for the merchants to use outside the local inns, gladly given in exchange for the coin the guards brought with them. A tug in his gut tracked the miles they'd moved away from Erinon.

The wagon took a series of sharp turns and then stopped with a creak of axles and the jingle of horse tack. Noises sounded without, and then the door opened. In the dim light of dusk, Errol saw Skorik and Ru waiting at the door.

"Come out, Errol," Ru smiled. "I want to plan our strategy for selling our grain at Leister."

Skorik's hand rested on his sword hilt. Behind them the rest of the guards busied themselves with the chores that went into making camp. Errol stepped from the wagon. A row of cottages with thatched roofs stretched away from the caravan. Camp would be easy to set up. The village would provide water and feed for the horses as well as ale and food for the guards.

He probably wouldn't be able to get anywhere near the inns. "I can't help you, Ru."

The faces of the two men darkened, but Ru's voice kept its cheerful tone. "Of course you can, my boy. Just keep doing what you did at Dronfeld."

"How long do you intend to keep me prisoner?"

A glint came into the caravan master's eye, and his smile hardened. "As long as it takes. With our combined abilities I can establish my own trading house in a matter of months. Skorik here will run my caravans, and in a few years I can build an organization that spans the whole of the kingdom. I'll have factors in every major city and more wealth than even the Weir family."

Errol shook his head. The caravan master's greed was making him insane. "Someone will notice you always end up on the right side of the trade. They'll come looking, and when they find you've been using a reader, they'll kill you. If they want to make you suffer, they'll let the other merchants have you first."

Ru cocked his head as if considering Errol's argument, but his eyes remained spellbound. "They won't do anything without proof. As long as we keep you out of sight, they won't have any."

It was irrational. Surely they suspected he would try to escape sometime, but Skorik never took his eyes from him and his right hand never strayed from his hilt. At that moment, Errol had no choice but to go along. He donned a calculating look, hoped it seemed sufficiently avaricious. "I think I should get paid more for my part in this than the wages of the thirteenth. What do I get?"

Now speaking the language of money, he had Ru's interest. "We all have unique talents that we bring to the group, Errol. If you want to be paid more, all you have to do is challenge the guards above you."

The extent of the man's greed surprised him. "What do I get paid for casting lots for you, Ru? What do I get for making you rich?"

Ru stepped close, the plastered smile gone, replaced by a sneer. "You get to live. And if you don't cast truly, I'll kill you myself." He turned to Skorik. "Put him back in the wagon."

Errol's stomach knotted. "When do I get to eat?"

The smile came back, fierce. "When you agree to my terms."

He shrugged. Nothing would be gained by fighting Ru now. Errol would only lose and make his eventual escape that much more difficult. "I agree. When do you want me to cast lots?"

Ru squinted with suspicion as he answered. "At Leister. Rokha and I will go to the warehouses to meet the factors. Then we'll come back and tell you everything you need to know."

"That will make casting the lots more difficult," Errol said. How long a rein was the caravan master willing to give? "It would be better if I went as well."

Ru barked a laugh. "Oh no, my boy. I think Skorik would get lonely here at camp without you to keep him company. If we have to draw the lots a few more times to find the best buyer, I'm more than willing. You'll be staying in my wagon from now on."

Errol nodded. Naaman Ru had no intention of giving him even an incidental opportunity to escape. The rein was short, very short.

He stepped forward, between the two men.

"Where do you think you're going?" Skorik said.

"I've agreed to his terms," Errol said. "I'm going to eat, and then I'm going to challenge Brelan Domiel for the twelfth."

The caravan master threw back his head and laughed. "That's the spirit, boy. Skorik, please make sure you accompany Errol wherever he goes."

⚜

Over the course of the three-day journey to Leister, Errol discovered a variety of activities Naaman Ru and Skorik permitted when he was not locked in Ru's wagon. He was forbidden to ride Midnight or any other horse but was permitted to walk—and while he walked they allowed him to work the forms with his staff. His working the forms seemed to please Skorik. The first would watch him with a smile twisting his face to one side and his hand resting on the pommel of his sword. To Errol it seemed as if Skorik wanted a challenge.

In truth that was Errol's plan. He'd beaten Brelan with ease and the following night had defeated Hiram Abiff, the eleventh, almost as quickly. But things stalled after that. Santosh Carmona, the tenth, guarded the caravan on the last watch, from midnight to dawn. When the wagons stopped each night, Carmona was already asleep.

It seemed Errol would have to wait until the shifts changed before he would get a chance to challenge for his spot.

The next day, with Errol confined to Ru's wagon, the caravan rolled into Leister.

Ru wasted no time putting him to work. The caravan master opened the door and entered holding a dozen pine blanks. Rokha followed in his footsteps. Skorik stood outside with his sword in hand. Ru's daughter assayed a tentative smile in his direction, which he returned. Since their conversation he'd resolved to keep her as an ally if at all possible. Perhaps she would change her mind and help him to escape.

"There'll be time for you to talk to Rokha later, my boy," Ru said, the greed in his eyes burning at a fever pitch. "Right now, there's money to be made. First we need to know which house will pay the highest price for our grain." He laid out five of the blanks.

"Then we'll need to know which cargo to buy for the trip to Scarritt." The caravan master put the remaining blanks aside.

Errol ignored the blanks. "You can't keep me here, Ru. Soon I'll be worthless, unable to cast lots for you even if I wanted."

Ru's smile hardened. "I doubt that, boy. Your skill and my cunning will make me the richest man in the kingdom. I won't have to settle for being a count. By the time I'm done, Rodran will make me a duke."

"You think so?" Errol made no effort to keep the scorn and

frustration from his voice. "You have no idea of the influence I am under. What do you think will happen when the church's compulsion takes me again? It's happened before. I won't even be able to hear you, much less cast. What will you do then, Ru?"

"Compulsion?" The caravan master's gaze snapped to his daughter. "Is this true?"

Rokha gave a curt nod, then stepped back.

Tension crackled between the three of them in the silence that followed. Then Ru looked at Errol as if seeing him for the first time. The caravan master raised an open hand. "Why didn't you tell me, daughter?"

"I tried, Father. On the day he challenged, I told you not to let him fight, that the caravan didn't want him."

Ru struck, the crack loud in the confined space of his wagon. "You foolish girl. Where are your brains? The ferral was never after you. It's him they want."

Rokha turned to Errol. "Is that true?"

He tried to swallow the lump in his throat. "Probably. I'm sorry. I should have told you. Do you know what it feels like to be hunted?"

Ru drew his sword. "You owe me, boy, and I intend to collect. You're going to cast for me." He stepped close, their noses almost touching. "You're going to cast right up to the day you go insane. Then I'm going to kill you." The smile returned. "Now, let's begin making my fortune."

After he'd completed the cast, Errol stretched as much as the low-ceilinged wagon would allow. "Is Skorik still outside?"

Ru nodded.

He brushed past him. "Excellent. I need to eat, and then I want to see if I can catch Santosh awake. Maybe after that I can challenge Vichay A'laras. I feel like swinging my staff tonight."

"Fight if you wish, boy. I hope you climb high enough to challenge Skorik. I trained him myself. The beating he'd give you would begin to pay the debt of your deception."

Errol caught up with Santosh at the wagon. The sleepy-eyed

Basqu nodded in acquiescence when Errol challenged him for his position.

From the start, Santosh fought as though he knew he couldn't win. Instead of attacking, he sought to keep Errol from getting close enough to land a winning blow. Each time the staff descended, he parried and circled, refusing to attack. Frustrated, Errol charged, feinted left, and then turned at the last instant. Santosh sought to parry a blow that no longer came from that direction.

With the sound of a fist striking a melon, Errol's staff hit Santosh on the head. The Basqu's eyes rolled up in his head and he collapsed.

Rokha, serving in her role as judge, bent and checked his throat for a pulse. Then she peeled back each eyelid. "He's fine." She gave Errol a speculative look as she stood.

Errol turned to Vichay A'laras. The Gascon, light-haired with the angular features common to his people, took a pull from his tankard and, with a pointed look at Santosh, pulled his sword and dropped it on the ground. Then he turned his back and drank again.

"What does that mean?" Errol asked.

A'laras faced him. "I will tell you what tha' means," he said. Like most Gascons he dropped the ends of many of his words. "Tha' means I have no intention of spendin' half the night unconscious on the ground. The ninth is yours."

Before Errol could enjoy the moment, Skorik stood at his elbow, breath hot on his neck. "Not that you have much chance of it, runt, but I hope you make it far enough to challenge me. I'll enjoy the beating I'll give you."

Errol only nodded, tried to put a fight with the first from his mind. His next step would be to challenge Onan and then Conger. The two men were the closest friends he had in the caravan, and if he managed to beat the two of them, he would challenge the sixth.

Rokha.

❦

Errol stared out the tiny window of Ru's wagon the next day and lamented the small section of landscape he saw. As they'd approached Four Crossings, Ru had decided he couldn't trust Errol traveling outside of the wagon. Until it had been denied to him, he hadn't realized how much he missed traveling on horseback.

Tugs deep within his chest, as if someone had grasped his heart, then pulled on it, told him the compulsion had strengthened. He stood in the center of the wagon with his eyes closed and turned a random number of circles. When he felt the pull in his chest at its strongest, he stopped to look out the window. The shadows of distant trees pointed to his right. He closed his eyes and repeated the process twice more with the same result each time.

With a sigh, he flopped on the small bunk. The pull wasn't his imagination at work. If he couldn't win his freedom, he had no doubt Ru would follow through on his threat. A wave of desperation like the cold winter waters of the Sprata washed over him. Frantic, he searched for some means of escape.

Bits of wood shavings lurked in the crevices between the bunk, cabinets, and desk. None of the lots Errol had carved remained. Ru burned them as they were cast. No pine blanks could be found anywhere within the wagon. He searched every drawer and cranny, peered under every cabinet. Nothing within the wagon could help him. After he died, nothing would testify that Ru had used a reader against church law to further his business. Errol's epitaph would be written with a few splinters of pine stuck in the cracks of the merchant's wagon.

They camped between villages that evening. By the time Ru unlocked Errol's prison, the sun's light cast long, feeble shadows on the ground. Onan waited for him by the supply wagon, a sparring sword held lightly in one hand.

"I haven't had a challenge in months," he said. "Not since Jhade came up through the ranks and passed me by. I figured you'd be seeking me out. Can't say as I like staff men so much. I'm better at fighting people who hold a sword." He stopped to give Errol a grin. "But I'll see what I can do to give you a decent bout."

After the first set of blows, it became obvious that Onan was not used to sparring against the unorthodox weapon. Each time Errol attacked his high lines Onan parried so quickly it seemed as if his sword moved of its own volition, but when Errol changed his assault to a low line just above the ankles, Onan floundered. His parries came at the last instant after a hesitation, and each time his face twisted in concentration.

Errol understood. Onan, older and more experienced, had fought so long with the sword and against the sword his responses no longer required thought, they sprang from his experience. He simply reacted. Once when Errol moved his hands to thrust the end of his staff toward the guard's midsection, Onan engaged in a double-circular parry, even though his sword engaged the staff at first contact.

Realization came to Errol then. Onan couldn't win. The eighth's responses were automatic and tuned to fighting another swordsman.

Errol stepped back and grounded the staff.

Onan stared at him in surprise. "What are you doing, boy? You're not conceding are you? This is your challenge, not mine."

He shook his head. To continue would be pointless. The matter had been decided. Further sparring would only result in Onan's needless defeat, and he might get injured in the process. Besides, he considered the man his friend.

"I'm offering you the chance to concede." Errol gestured with the wooden rod in his hands. "I can tell you haven't fought many people who use the staff."

Onan shrugged. "True enough, boy, but if this were a real fight I don't think I'd get the chance to surrender. Let's finish it." And he attacked.

For a moment the flurry of blows caught Errol off guard, and he backpedaled as he defended, but the momentum of the attack passed and Errol countered, launching blow after blow at Onan's low line. Forced into unaccustomed parries, sweat beaded on the eighth's brow.

In quick succession Errol struck his ankle, stomach, and sword hand.

The sword hit the ground. Wooden laths clacked softly. Errol's defeated opponent dropped to a sitting position on the ground with a curse. "Why do you all hit the same leg? That's the same ankle Jhade hit."

Errol offered his hand. "I'm sorry."

Onan took it, levering himself up on his good leg. "Humph. What for? Can't fault a man for wanting to earn a little extra. I'm just glad you're using ash instead of oak. Probably would have broken the bone if you'd landed a decent blow."

"Conger," Errol called.

The seventh lifted his head from his book and gave him a questioning look.

"I want to challenge you for the seventh."

Conger looked at Onan, watching Errol's previous opponent hobble across the ground. "Can I win?"

Onan looked first at Conger and then Errol. He gave a small shake of his head.

Conger scratched an armpit, then shrugged and went back to his book. "It's all yours, boy. See me after you get done fighting," he said without raising his head. "There's some amazing stuff in here."

Errol turned, found Rokha looking at him with the same measuring look as before. Without a word, she retrieved the practice sword where Onan dropped it. She dropped into ready position, gave a small salute with her weapon.

The smile she gave him made him sweat.

"I think I'm next, Errol."

21

CLIMBING THE LADDER

No!"

Errol turned to see Skorik standing by the supply wagon, his face livid.

Rokha rounded on him without frowning, but every line of her stance held challenge. "No? Doesn't he have the right to challenge me for my position?" Ru's daughter glared at the first. "More to the point, do you have the right to make my decisions for me?"

Skorik gaped. His mouth worked, but nothing intelligible came out.

Errol gaped at the realization. Of course. Skorik was in love with Rokha. No wonder the man despised him. He'd been forced to watch as Ru encouraged his daughter to show affection to someone else. Skorik had watched them kiss, had watched them lie together in the grass.

Despised him? The first probably wanted to kill him.

Errol lowered his staff, stepped toward his opponent, and whispered, "I think Skorik's in love with you."

She gave a throaty chuckle. "Are you just now figuring that out?" She patted him on the cheek. "Errol, you have so much to learn."

He snuck a glance over her shoulder. The first looked as if he would charge him any second. "Are you in love with him?"

She shrugged. Her eyes burned like embers beneath her lashes. "I haven't decided yet."

"Were you just using me to make him jealous?"

Rokha laughed and ran her hand along his cheek. "No, Errol. I wasn't 'just' using you. I meant every kiss, but you're not the one for me. That compulsion you're under will take you to the conclave at Erinon. Soon I think. A half-Merakhi has no business on the isle."

"Your father means to kill me. How will I make it to Erinon?"

Rokha stepped close. "I know my father. Wait for his anger to die down."

"And if it doesn't?"

She shrugged. "Then I will help you escape."

Errol nodded, gestured to Skorik. "He's afraid I'll hurt you."

Her eyes flared. She was the hawk once more. "You should look to yourself. I earned the sixth. Father had nothing to do with it. He didn't even want me as a guard."

"I don't want to fight a woman."

She shook her head. "Then you're a fool, Errol. Women won't hesitate to take your emotions and your noble intentions and use them against you. If you don't guard your heart, you'll end up dead."

Rokha stepped back, brought her sword back to ready. "Now, let's see how good you really are."

Skorik came over and stepped between them. "Since you mean to do this, I will judge." He shot a look at the pair of them and the watching guards, daring them to disagree. Then he looked at Errol, his eyes burning with hate. His lips twisted. "Have a care, boy. Winning could be the death of you."

From the beginning, Rokha made it plain she meant to defeat him if possible, and if she couldn't beat him, meant him to earn his victory. Ru's daughter flung herself at him, her sword flicking at his face, body, and arms.

Whereas Santosh had tried simply to defend, Rokha bet everything on her attack, even to the point of ignoring her defense. Time and again Errol hesitated, let opportunities to strike slip by, and the bout wore on in a frenzy of sword cuts and staff parries.

However hard she tried, Rokha couldn't penetrate Errol's defense, but she continued to expend her energy in extravagant attacks. Already, she panted and sweat, and her strikes began to slow.

Errol didn't need to hurt her; he could just wear her down.

Their battle raged back and forth across the campground. Her steps dragged across the sod. He feinted an attack toward her unprotected side, and she stumbled as she tried to parry.

Minutes later, exhausted, she tripped and fell to the grass. Errol stepped forward and pulled the sword from her grip, but when he held out his hand to help her up, she slapped it away. The look she gave him bore nothing but hatred.

Rokha ran from the circle.

Confused, Errol turned to see the guards looking at him in disgust.

Skorik appeared at his elbow, pulled him close to whisper in his ear. "I will make you pay for that, boy." He strode away, taking the same route as Rokha.

Conger edged up to him, his book closed around one finger to keep his place. "That was poorly done, Errol."

He shook his head. "What did I do? I was trying not to hurt her."

Conger shook his head. "It would have been better if you had. By beating her that way you said you had no respect for her as a warrior. You took her honor."

"But Skorik said he'd kill me if I hurt her."

"Hmmm, I doubt he would have followed through. The first growls a lot, but he knows the rules as well as any man. Most likely, he was trying to make you hesitate so Rokha could beat you."

How did I get into this? "What do I do now?"

Conger shrugged. "Don't rightly know, but I wouldn't sleep where Ru's daughter could get to me."

Errol laughed a bitter cough of a sound. Ru and Skorik would be locking him back in the wagon once he'd eaten. He wouldn't be in danger from anyone.

But if his plan to defeat Skorik didn't work, how would he escape without Rokha's help? The sixth position now belonged to him. He would have to fight and win five more times just to have a chance of escape. Jhade would be his next opponent. He felt confident of winning that bout, but after he fought her he would have to face Kajan Vujic, Diar Muen, and Sven before he could challenge Skorik.

And he didn't have the slightest idea of how to fight any of them. The only time those men had fought during his stay with the caravan was during Eck's attack—and Errol had been too busy trying to stay alive to notice their strengths and weaknesses.

Fishing the knobblocks from his pocket, he handed them to Conger. "I need help. Can you get these to Grub and see if he can find a way to make them twice as heavy?"

His friend looked at the hollow iron weights in his hand and shrugged. "I reckon, but you know you're not allowed to use those in a challenge."

Errol nodded. "They're for training. I'm not fast enough."

Conger snorted. "You're faster with a staff than anyone I've ever seen, boy. Just how fast do you want to be?"

The sky overhead was still clear, but off in the distance huge columns of white were building. Errol pointed to one flat-bottomed cloud that looked like an anvil. A bolt of lightning shot from beneath the billow, forked on its way to the ground. Rale's words rang in his mind. "Faster," he said.

He walked to the supply wagon, endured the other guards' frowns of disapproval as he ate, and went back to Ru's wagon even before Skorik came for him. Errol surveyed his prison. The tight quarters didn't afford him much room to move. He could stand between the bunk and the desk and take three, maybe four steps from one end to the other.

Four paces long and one pace wide. That's all he had. He seated himself on the floor, composed as Rale had taught him, and thought through the problem. In the end, he needed two things:

First, he needed to be faster, always faster with the staff.

Second, he needed information.

Access to that information would be cut off until morning, when they let him out for breakfast and a visit to the privy. With luck, he would be able to find Conger and learn what he needed to know in order to defeat the top four guards. *Luck.* He chuckled at the thought. He would need a lot of it, and it didn't seem to be an attribute he had in any quantity. And if Deas's hand was on him as Radere had said, he would need all the help the creator could give him.

He stood. How could he get faster in Ru's wagon? The enclosure made the abbot's cells seem large. Errol put his hand out in front of his body and curled his fingers in imitation of holding his staff. Casting back, he replayed each of the night's challenges in his mind.

Eyes closed, he moved his arms, concentrated on the tension he felt in his muscles, and made a mental list of the ones he used most. For over an hour, as the sky darkened and the sound of crickets built to a crescendo, he moved. Then he sat with his eyes open, surveying the cabin, devising exercises he could perform in the cramped space to strengthen the muscles that would make him faster. When he completed the list, he began and didn't stop until the sounds of the camp died away as one guard after another sought his bedroll.

❧

The next morning Grub stared at him in surprise as he heaped a plate to overflowing with eggs and cheese. As he went through the line, he stuffed his pockets with sausage.

When Skorik came to escort him to his makeshift cell, the first gave him an unpleasant smile. "I could almost thank you, boy. Ru's daughter despises you. In one bout you managed to turn all her affection for you to hatred." The first gave a raucous laugh.

Errol grimaced. Too late he understood he'd treated a wild bird of prey like a tamed pet. She'd never forgive him. "You're welcome."

Skorik grabbed his arm, hauled him close enough for Errol to smell the eggs on his breath. "Don't think this changes anything, boy. If you happen to climb the ladder high enough to challenge me, I'm going to beat you so hard you'll wish Eck had finished you."

Errol tried to jerk his arm away, but the first held him fast in a grip of iron. "And what will Ru do to you, Skorik, if you ruin his chance to be rich?"

The first snarled and pushed him away.

Errol spent the day in the wagon pushing his body through endless repetitions of exercises in the small space. He pushed, pulled, lifted, squatted, and stretched. Sweat rolled from his arms and legs to darken the wooden floor. When he became too tired to go on, he ate from the stash he'd filched from Grub, and then after resting or napping, he did it all again. The constant physical exertion kept him distracted from the pull of Luis's compulsion in his chest, but whenever he stopped he became aware of it. It didn't seem overpowering, yet. He needed time to get stronger.

When the wagon stopped at the next village, he almost sobbed with relief. He'd burned through his food hours ago, and his stomach squalled like a child throwing a tantrum.

Grub stared at the mountain of food hiding his plate. "You sure you want to eat all that before a challenge, boy?"

Errol shook his head. "I'm not challenging anyone tonight, Grub. I think I'll wait awhile. I'm just going to eat and then go through the forms."

"Good thing," the cook said. "If Sven sees you eat all that, he'll be jealous."

Errol looked around the camp. "Have you seen Conger?"

Grub nodded. "He went into the village to the smithy. Said you'd know what that would be about."

He gave a short nod. "Thanks, Grub."

By the time his plate became visible again, Conger walked back into camp, a new book tucked under one arm. "Here." He held out a new pair of knobblocks. "The supply wagon didn't have anything that would work, so I went to visit a smithy."

Conger gave him a lopsided smile "You owe me two silver crowns. Ordinarily, I wouldn't make a big deal out of it, but I just recently had a reduction in pay."

Errol laughed and gave him three. The new knobblocks felt twice as heavy as the old ones but looked almost identical, a slight increase in the wall thickness of the cylinder the only difference. *Perfect.* When he went through the forms, anyone watching would think he'd slowed.

He tugged Conger's sleeve, pulling his attention away from another book on church history. "Please don't tell anyone about the knobblocks."

The former seventh smiled. "Not to worry, Errol."

For a moment he debated what to do next—work the forms with his new staff weights or pepper Conger with questions about the men he would have to challenge. In the end, the weights won. His muscles ached with fatigue, but all his exercise would be for naught if he lost his feel for the staff.

Under the gaze of the first, who watched while he ate, Errol worked every move he'd learned from Rale and Jhade. The staff resisted him as though he were trying to swing the wood through water instead of air. He pushed on, swallowed thickly when his oversized dinner tried to come up on him. When Skorik called a halt to escort him back to the wagon and lock him in for the night, Errol almost thanked him.

❦

For the week it took to reach Scarritt, he followed the same routine. But distraction weighed on his mind, and he started at odd moments, found himself staring westward.

The morning they camped outside the city, while Ru and Rokha scouted the merchant houses in preparation for creating

274

the lots, Errol emerged from the wagon, passed the table of food Grub laid out for the guards, and sought Jhade.

The woman nodded and rose from her seat on an overturned crate and gave him a small bow. "You train well."

Errol bowed back. "Do you concede the fifth? I would prefer not to fight you for it. Hurting you seems a poor way to repay you for your instruction."

She gave another small bow. "I do not concede. I wish to see how much you have improved."

He'd suspected she would answer in this way. With a couple of twists of the staff, the knobblocks came loose in his hand. The weight of his staff, now unencumbered by iron, felt almost nonexistent. As he loosened up, the staff blurred in his hands and the buzz of displaced air caused the other guards to stare.

Jhade faced him, staff ready. At some unspoken signal, she attacked. Errol's only constraint now was the speed of his thoughts. His mind struggled to keep pace with the wood in his hands. When it caught up at last, Errol launched a flurry of blows that made it seem he handled two staffs at once. The fifth backpedaled, but Errol pressed his advantage.

He struck each shoulder. Numbed, she dropped her weapon.

With the same quiet dignity as before, she bowed, but more deeply this time.

He'd won.

Moments later Ru and his daughter returned from the merchant houses within the city of Scarritt. Errol knew the routine so well he didn't require Skorik's prodding to hurry back to the wagon. He listened to Rokha recount the details of each house and factor, then listened to Ru do the same.

It only took a few hours to determine where to sell their cargo and what cargo they should pick up for the trip south. It seemed they were supposed to haul hams to the city of Ambridge.

Throughout it all, Ru smiled so hard his face looked as if it would break. "It's too bad you can't find it in you to be more cooperative, boy. As the sixth you're going to be paid quite well for today's sale."

Errol gave a slight bow before he spoke. "Fifth. I defeated Jhade while you and Rokha were in the city. By the time we make Ambridge, you'll have to pay me even more."

The caravan master's smile slipped. "What game are you playing, boy?"

He gave an exaggerated lift of his shoulders. "No game, Ru. You said if I wanted to make more money, I had to challenge for it." He smiled. "You'll have to fill me in on the first's duties if I happen to make it that far. I don't know much about what Skorik does." He paused. "Oh, he sets the roster for the guards, doesn't he?"

Ru gave him a wolfish smile. "You think you're that good? Forget it. I trained Skorik myself."

"Yes, I've heard." Errol glanced at Rokha, trying to read her thoughts, but Ru's daughter refused to look his way. She stared at the door as though she couldn't wait to be through it and away from him.

Should he try to apologize? He held no illusions about whether or not she would accept. The insult to her pride ran too deep. Generations of warrior ancestors were probably screaming for his blood.

With a sigh he turned away.

He drilled for another two days, kept his desire to move up the ladder in check while he prepared. His appetite seemed to have a will of its own. Grub stared each morning and evening as he piled and pirated food.

The new knobblocks no longer slowed him as much. In fact, he moved the staff almost as quickly using either pair. One evening, as firebugs drifted in the summer air at their camp, Errol heard the sound he'd been waiting for: the buzzing of his staff as he whipped it through the air. He looked in satisfaction at the heavier knobblocks at each end.

He was ready.

❧

The next morning he sought Kajan Vujic and Diar Muen. The two men shared similar lanky builds, though Vujic's dark, bluff features bore little resemblance to Muen's bright red hair and blue eyes. Muen was the only man from the Green Isle in Ru's employ, and he spoke with the lilt common to those from there. In addition to their builds the two men also resembled each other when it came to their fighting style. According to Conger, the difference between the two was so slight they'd exchanged positions the first four times they fought. Then they hit upon the expedient of splitting the third's and fourth's portion in equal shares.

According to the roll, Vujic held the fourth. He peered at Errol through narrowed eyes. "I have seen you practicing where you think no one will notice. Is good." His deep voice carried approval. "My village is poor. Almenia, in Lugaria." He looked at Errol with a questioning look on his face.

Errol shook his head and shrugged. "I don't know anything about it."

"Ah, so. Is not important. Many of my countrymen cannot afford swords, so they use the staff." He smiled. "I have fought many who use the staff. Will be fun, yes?"

As Vujic described his homeland, Errol's stomach danced a jig against the rest of his organs. The Lugarian would know most of his tricks. Worse, his lanky build meant Errol would be open to counterattack.

When Errol took his position opposite Vujic, his heart beat as though he'd fought already. At the signal from Rokha, they approached each other, neither striking. The fourth's reach was even longer than he'd expected.

With a spinning move, Errol struck for the ankles. Vujic parried, and a swift flick of his wrist sent the tip of the practice sword racing toward Errol's unprotected head.

At the last instant, he brought the staff up to parry, just knocking the blade aside.

He counterattacked, but each strike clacked against the practice sword. There just didn't seem to be any way through the tall man's defenses. Vujic's reach kept Errol from getting close enough to use his greater speed.

Unless.

With a small nod, he committed to his plan. He would have to choose his moment with utmost care.

Errol slid his hands along the staff until two-thirds of its length extended in front of him, engaging Vujic's sword tip. With small beat attacks he knocked the blade aside, first toward the big man's inside line, then toward the outside. He watched, waiting to see which return was weaker.

There. When Vujic returned from the inside line, his movement lacked the strength of the other. With a deep breath, Errol forced the sword to the inside line again and stepped in to the return.

Vujic's eyes widened as he watched Errol step in and take the blow on his right cheek.

Weaker it may have been, but pain blossomed nonetheless, and his skin tore with a sound of ripping parchment.

But he stood inside Vujic's defense. The Lugarian stood wide open to counterattack. A split second later Errol stood alone. Vujic lay unconscious at his feet. He put a hand up to his cheek. It came away warm and sticky with his blood. Before he could ask Grub to tend the wound, Diar came forward to help Kajan Vujic to his feet.

"Most of the people in my village were more interested in the bow than the staff," Diar said. "If you can beat Kajan, I don't think I'd be able to give you much of a fight." He grinned, looking boyish. "Besides, I've never seen Sven spar. It'll be fun to see him move a sword around that belly of his. You're fast. If you can keep him from sitting on you, you might have a chance."

Errol nodded, then regretted the action. His face throbbed, and in his right eye, spots danced in time to his pulse. Pushing against his cheek to stem the flow, he sought Grub at the supply wagon. "Can you stitch me up?"

"I'll take care of it, Grub." Rokha stepped from behind the wagon. "Let's go to Ru's wagon. The light's better there. Maybe I can keep the scar from puckering."

She turned her back without waiting for a response. Errol followed her in silence.

Like the first time they met, she poured vile-smelling liquid on his cut. He tried not to wince at the sting and kept his gaze anywhere but on the needle she was threading.

Rokha pushed the skin around the cut together, her lips pursed in concentration. "That was a brave thing you did, stepping into Vujic's return stroke like that. And stupid. You're lucky he didn't catch you on the temple. In a real fight, you'd be dead now, instead of just bleeding. We spar in order to be ready, you fool boy."

He didn't know what to say to that and so settled for a small lift of his shoulders.

She pulled the needle through his skin, and he felt his flesh lift away from his cheekbone.

"You'll have to watch yourself against Sven," she said. "He's faster than he looks, and if you close with him the way you did Vujic, he'll take your first blow and then beat you senseless with his counter."

Rokha was helping him. He kept silent, afraid that saying anything, even thanking her, would break the spell and send her away in a fit of temper.

"Keep your attacks low, wear him down, and when he tires, work behind him," she said.

Errol nodded after it became plain she'd finished speaking. "I just didn't want to hurt you. I was stupid."

Her gaze shifted a fraction, moved from his cut to his eyes. The needle paused. "Yes. Sometimes I forget you're fresh out of your village." She resumed work on his cut. "I knew I couldn't beat you, but I wanted to see how far I could push you. You owe me a bout, Errol, and I intend to collect someday."

"When?"

She shrugged, but a hint of fire came into her eyes, and she wore a tight-lipped smile. "When it brings me the most attention and honor."

"What about Skorik?" he asked.

Doubt clouded her eyes. "I don't know. Maybe your speed will be enough. I've never seen anyone move a staff that fast." She moved to leave the wagon but turned at the door to look back at him. "Are you coming back out?"

He shook his head and laughed. "No. You can tell the first to lock me in for the night."

Errol sat on the bunk and waited for the sound of the lock. It didn't take long. As usual whenever Errol roamed free, Skorik had shadowed his steps and kept close.

Two more. Two more fights and he would be free to go to Erinon. Day by day the compulsion waxed and waned. Whenever the caravan journeyed in the general direction of the isle, Errol felt the tension in the back of his head easing, as though invisible hands soothed his muscles after a long day. It had happened when they had traveled north from Leister, but as they passed Ambridge, the tension returned, filling his head with a constant unease, like the buzzing of hornets. Under the influence of the compulsion, he often lost track of time, especially at night before he slept.

He only needed to find a way to defeat Sven and Skorik, but he needed to beat the first while Ru was away. With Ru's pupil unconscious, he could saddle Midnight and ride for Ambridge. His pockets jingled with more silver and gold than he'd seen in his life, certainly more than enough to buy his way to Erinon. Tomorrow he would challenge the second.

Skorik would have to wait until they sold their cargo at Ambridge.

22

THE INTERSECTION OF PROBABILITIES

THE POUNDING of his heart shook the bunk. Errol rolled to his side and unstoppered the waterskin Conger had snuck him the night before. Dawn broke cool and misty. Even so, sweat plastered his hair against his face and neck.

Today he would challenge the first.

He nodded to himself. Was he not second now? Had he not beaten Sven, wearing down the bigger man, staying out of reach until he could dart behind and beat him unconscious? Heaven's mercy, the man's skull must be thick. Or padded with so much fat it took a far stronger blow to knock him out.

He listened, waiting for Skorik to unlock his prison so that he could join the rest of the guards at breakfast. Minutes before, the sound of hooves thudding out of camp signaled Ru's departure. Rokha almost certainly had gone with him.

Today.

He could be free today.

The click of the key in the lock sent a thrill of excitement pounding through him, and he vaulted off the bunk. A tinge of orange-hued dawn fell across the planks of the wagon's floor. Skorik stood in the opening, casting a shadow that fell the length of the tiny room.

"Breakfast." He grunted the word and then turned.

Errol grasped his staff and stepped down, felt the springy sod give beneath his feet.

Now.

He could eat later.

"Skorik, I challenge you for the position of first."

The head of the guards turned, his eyes filled with mockery. "Ru said you would challenge me today. Said you'd wait until he was out of camp so you could try to escape." Skorik laughed. "I'm afraid I have to decline, boy."

No.

"You can't be any more disappointed than I am, runt," Skorik continued. "But it's only until the caravan master returns. Then I'll have the leisure to give you that lesson I promised."

No, it has to be now.

Skorik turned away. The first headed for the supply wagon, obviously expecting Errol to follow. Beyond the wagons lay the picket line for the horses. Close to the middle, Midnight nibbled at tufts of grass.

Errol would have to force the first to accept his challenge. When Skorik stopped to get his food, Errol continued past him, making for his horse.

Skorik's growl caught him before he'd gone five paces. "Get back here, runt."

Heads lifted as the rest of the guards caught the threat in his tone. Errol stopped and turned but didn't move to return.

"Hear this," he shouted. He paused to make eye contact with every guard in Ru's service. "I challenge Skorik, the first of the guards, to a bout, here and now, to determine who will lead." He let his gaze rest on the first for a moment. "What do you say, Skorik?"

Skorik's face flushed, and a vein throbbed in the middle of his forehead. "You'll pay for this, boy." He spewed a stream of curses. "You'll get your bout when Ru returns."

Now. Errol put as much scorn in his voice as he could muster. "When Ru returns? What does that have to do with us? Surely the first doesn't need the caravan master to watch over him in a simple challenge bout." He let his voice dip and saw the rest of the guards lean toward him to catch his words. "After all, I'm just a runt with a stick. Isn't that right, Skorik?"

A few of the guards laughed behind their hands or turned away, coughing.

"GRUB!" Skorik screamed. "Judge!"

It would be now.

Errol took a deep breath to collect his thoughts. Skorik would try to kill him. He felt for the ends of his staff, his gaze on the first, and removed the knobblocks. *Fast.* He must be faster than thought, faster than lightning. He faced Skorik across an empty space and waited.

The attack, when it came, was so sudden Errol wasn't sure he saw Skorik move. The first rushed him, trying to get inside the spin of his staff.

Errol backpedaled and willed his hands to move faster than ever before. The end of his staff disappeared, passed beyond human sight as he countered.

Skorik parried every blow.

The sword in the first's hand leapt at Errol like a thing alive, seeking, hunting him.

Only the greater length of Errol's weapon kept his opponent at bay.

Their battle hinged on a simple proposition. Would Skorik get inside the spin of his defense before Errol managed to land a blow?

He sensed, rather than saw, the flick of Skorik's wrist. Errol jerked back, and the sword grazed his forehead. Skorik pressed his advantage, and blows rained down like the staccato beats of a frantic drummer.

But Errol stopped them all.

Surprise grew on Skorik's face as his attack failed to penetrate.

Realization came to Errol in an instant between blows.

He could win. Defeat was not inevitable.

Joy welled up in him at the thought, and as he countered another furious attack, he smiled. For weeks he'd hoped for a miracle, waiting for chance to bring him his freedom, but the miracle could be of his own making. His body sang in time with the blows, and he laughed as he launched himself at his opponent. The air filled with the sound of his staff like a nest of hornets. Then his blows found something other than Skorik's sword.

The first stood like a rock in a storm, braving the torrent of Errol's attack, but his sword slowed as Errol's staff went ever faster.

A flurry of blows later, the first lay at his feet, bloody and unconscious.

He waited just long enough to assure himself that Skorik still breathed, and then he turned and strode without a backward glance toward Midnight.

Sven stepped into his path, and his grip on the staff tightened in reflex. If he had to fight every one of them to win his freedom, he would do it.

"What are your orders?" the big Soede asked.

Errol almost laughed. "Get out of my way. Make sure that somebody takes care of Skorik. I'm leaving."

The sound of a real sword being drawn split the air with a hiss. "I don't think so," Ru said. The caravan master stepped from behind the supply wagon. "I didn't think Skorik would be able to resist the chance to fight you, so I sent Rokha to collect the information on the merchant houses and their factors." He favored Errol with a smile that would have seemed benevolent in any other context. "I really would like for you to stay."

"I'm not staying. I am the first, and I am my own man."

Ru advanced on him, casually swinging his blade back and forth, snipping the tops off the weeds as he came.

Out of the corner of his eye he saw the rest of the guards back away. There would be no help. He turned on them. "Do you know why Ru wants to keep me here?" Leveling a finger at the caravan master, he shouted, "He's forcing me to cast lots to find the best buyer for his goods."

"Nonsense, boy," Onan said. "You're not a reader."

But Errol could see the rest of the guards knew the truth of his words. "Do you know what the church will do to you if they find out? You'll be lucky if you ever see the outside of a prison again."

"Pah! You're a fool, boy," Ru said. He waved his sword at the guards. "They have a chance to make more money in the next few months than they could make in a lifetime. Do you think they'll help you escape? The church is never going to find out."

Then Ru advanced on him.

Errol gripped his staff, trying desperately to decide whether or not to fight. Ru's blade glinted in the summer sun, keen and deadly. He backed away.

Then Naaman Ru rushed him, sword raised.

A wail like the cry of a wounded animal ripped the air, stopped the caravan master short. A line of purest black sped through the space between Errol and Ru. The moan dropped in pitch as the arrow passed.

Errol turned, saw gleaming blue eyes beneath a shock of white hair looking at him, eyes that held no hint of anger or compassion. His hands clenched. What were his chances of defeating both Ru and Merodach? He bit his lips—virtually none.

"Who might you be, friend?" Ru asked. "You're dressed like one of the watch. If you think that's going to scare me, you don't know who I am."

Every guard stood armed as Merodach sighted down a shaft that was trained on Ru's heart.

"I know exactly who you are. As for me, I might be the man who's going to kill you, Naaman Ru, but I hope that won't be necessary." Merodach glanced at the guards. "These arrows are poisoned. If one of them even grazes you, you'll die. Now, drop your sword and tell your men to do the same."

With a look of naked hatred burning in his eyes, Ru nodded once at Sven.

The clatter of arms falling to the ground sounded like freedom. Merodach eased the tension on his draw. "Wise choice, Ru. In fact, there are churchmen who already know you've been using a reader."

With indescribable satisfaction, Errol watched the blood drain from Ru's face. He wanted to savor this moment, wanted to bathe in it for as long as possible. Freedom was his.

"Boy," Merodach addressed him. "Get your horse. You're leaving now."

"Do you mean to kill me this time?"

Merodach's eyes narrowed as he continued to stare down the shaft of his arrow. "I could have killed you anytime I wanted, boy. Now get your horse."

Errol shook his head. He would gladly leave, but not like this. "I am the first in the caravan of Naaman Ru." He stood his ground, met Merodach's gaze. "And my name is Errol Stone, not *boy*. It will never be *boy* again."

A ghost of a smile touched his rescuer's lips. "Well spoken, Errol Stone. Now please get your horse."

Errol turned to Ru and bowed with as much irony as he could summon. "Master Ru, I regret that I must resign my position. I have pressing business elsewhere." He took a few steps toward where Midnight stood in the picket line before turning back. "And Ru . . ."

The caravan master looked at him, deflated now and wary.

"I joined your caravan under false pretenses and brought you some good . . . but even more trouble—for that you have my apology. You taught me many things in our travels. But you do not own me. In fact, I hold your life in my hands. If you come looking for me, I'll let every trading house from Stelton to Weir know how you cheated them."

Once out of the camp, they galloped their horses until they were out of sight of Ru's caravan, then switched to a canter. Errol had almost forgotten how good it felt to be on Midnight's back.

Merodach checked often over his shoulder for pursuit. After an hour, all of it spent in silence, he called for a halt.

"Why are we stopping?" Errol asked.

Merodach fixed him with a stare as sharp as Ru's sword. "Because I'm not going with you. Follow my instructions exactly. Ride west through Four Crossings until you get to Port City. Buy passage on the first boat headed for the isle and Erinon. I don't care if it's the leakiest tub in the harbor."

Errol shook his head. "If you weren't trying to kill me, why did you shoot at me?"

The watchman paused, his head tilted as if considering. "I learned the sacramental bread in your pack was poisoned. I tried to catch up to you, but you were faster across the river than I expected. I tried to separate you from your pack by herding you into the water. When you came up out of the river with the pack still on your back, I gambled on shooting for the pack." His mouth pulled to one side. "You're either extraordinarily brave or very stupid, Errol. Either way I failed."

Errol felt his mouth go dry, recalling how close he'd come to dying. "Why can't you come with me? Everyone thinks you were trying to kill me."

Merodach nodded. "And you need to go right on letting them think that. I wouldn't have put my nose into Ru's camp except at the utmost need."

"What will the church do to him?"

The watchman snorted. "The church doesn't care about some merchant's ambition, but if they ever find out you cast lots for money, no matter the reason, you'll wish you'd stayed back in that village you came from."

Errol shrugged. "Most times I wish that anyway."

Merodach nodded. "No one would gainsay you on that, but mind what I said and get to the conclave as quickly as you can. There'll be some protection there, but keep your eyes and ears about you. Danger treads the halls of the royal compound, and I won't be there to help you."

❧

Errol watched Merodach ride east. He didn't start for Erinon until the watchman disappeared over a distant hill. Since meeting the nuntius in Callowford he'd said more good-byes than he thought possible. As he kicked Midnight into a canter westward he tallied the friends he'd left, friends he'd probably never see again. The list started with Cilla and ended with Rokha, and in between, dozens of faces stuck in his memory.

The next morning he passed through Four Crossings with the smell of the sea calling him west, and he urged Midnight on. By midday he reached the coast and for a league rode a path along the edge of a cliff by the ocean's edge, marveling at the sight of so much water. Having lived so far inland all of his life, he'd never imagined anything to compare. Green waves struck the shore, cresting in their hunger, attacking limestone cliffs that remained oblivious. Farther out to sea, the water turned a deep blue, hinting at greater depth.

The road he traveled split Port City neatly in half. On his right lay the town proper. The din of a large open-air market drifted to him from inside the city wall. The smell of fish—fresh, salted, and pickled—hung in the air. Mindful of Merodach's admonition, Errol turned left and headed for the docks lining the shore of the enormous crescent-shaped harbor.

The compulsion that had thrummed in the back of his head for so long began to fade. Now he only felt eager and nervous. What would Luis and Martin think when they saw him? He fingered his staff. And Cruk and Liam? Reader or not he would challenge both men to a bout at the earliest opportunity. Let them see how he'd grown.

The breeze lifted the hair from his forehead. The sky glowed azure in the afternoon light.

Far across the strait his destination waited. Erinon.

I'm coming.

23

CHALLENGES

THE *REDOUBT* CAPTAIN surveyed the tide over Errol's shoulder as they began negotiations. No matter how Errol moved, ducked, or bobbed to force the captain to look him in the eye, Jonas Grim continued to survey the seascape over one of his shoulders.

The captain's jaws worked for a moment, and then he spat a brown stream of liquid onto the deck. "I hate horses. The strait scares them half to death and they mess up the hold."

Errol looked the length and breadth of the *Redoubt* and considered waiting until morning, despite Merodach's admonition. The watchman *had* said *ship*, and though Errol didn't know the difference between a ship and a boat, he guessed that if the captain's vessel was indeed a ship, it barely qualified.

He jingled his purse. "I'm willing to pay, as I said. I need to get to the isle as soon as possible."

Grim looked him over without managing to meet his eyes and spat again. "What for? It's not going anywhere." He put a hand on a curved dagger belted to his waist. "If you bring trouble to my ship, I'll gut you for fish bait."

Errol shook his head. "I have friends at Erinon I'm supposed to meet, and I'm months late."

The captain blinked several times in rapid succession. "Hmmm. Very well. Two gold crowns. Passage for you and the horse."

The price made Errol's eyes hurt. If he met the captain's price he would only have two gold and eight silver crowns left. "Five silver crowns," he said. "I'm buying passage, not the ship."

For the next fifteen minutes, Errol strove to keep the captain's piracy to a minimum. In the process Grim made use of an extensive vocabulary. The captain swore Errol's parsimony would endanger the health of his wife, who suffered from a mysterious ailment for which the doctors could find no cure. If a woman existed who could tolerate Jonas Grim, Errol wanted to meet her, and he very nearly said that aloud. He hoped Merodach was serious about needing to take the leakiest tub if necessary. Errol was sure he'd found it.

He took a deep breath. "Captain, before I arrived, you were getting ready to sail without any passengers. I'm offering nine silver crowns to get to the isle. That's nine crowns you won't get if I decide to wait until tomorrow morning." He pointed to a much larger vessel docked farther along the quay. "There seems to be a lot more people leaving Erinon than going to it, Captain. Empty ships don't make much money, do they?"

With a curse and a dark look for Errol and his horse, the captain waved them aboard.

Errol spent the next few minutes coaxing Midnight across the gangplank and into the hold. He rubbed his mount's nose often and made soothing noises until step by short step, Midnight came aboard.

His exultation at winning passage lasted until the boat cleared the breakwater. Then, open to churning waters that flowed through the Beron Strait, the ship bobbed like a cork in a barrel. Midnight's terrified whinnies came to Errol as interludes between bouts of seasickness. He clung to the railing and threw up in time to the ship's rising and falling with the swells.

"Ha," Grim said as he walked by. "That's what you get for taking advantage of a poor old sailor."

Errol fantasized about thumping the captain with his staff until Grim either passed out or made eye contact. He could do little else. The cramps in his stomach forbade movement in any normal sense. Ten leagues. He had to make it ten leagues across the strait, and according to Grim the passage would take three hours. He blinked. Even that hurt. If he ever saw Martin again, he would ask the priest what fate the condemned suffered after they died. There was surely a boat and an ocean involved.

An eternity later, slumped facedown on the deck, he felt a jarring bump as the *Redoubt* glided into dock. Strong hands gripped his arms and dragged him across the plank to deposit him on the wide pier. He lay there with his eyes closed. The clop of hooves announced the arrival of Midnight a few moments later. Someone—he had no idea who—bent down and looped the reins around one of his wrists. A wooden clatter to his left announced the arrival of his staff.

"Ya see, mate," Grim said. "The sea just don't care for some people."

Errol could hear the smile in the captain's voice.

"Aye, Cap'n. Truly spoken, that."

The sound of footsteps faded as Grim and his first mate left him to recover on his own. Midnight nuzzled his face, rocking his head from one side to the other. The movement made him throw up again.

Errol forced his aching stomach muscles to contract and sat up. He pulled himself hand over hand up the reins until he achieved a more-or-less standing position. A line of people waited to board a dozen ships headed for the mainland. Merchants in fine clothing jostled peasants in gray homespun, who kept their distance from noble families in their finery. Yet to a man their eyes were tight, and they leaned toward the nearest ship as if afraid of being denied passage.

A man wearing a long dark coat walked past him. He held a

small writing board in one hand and counted the crowd out loud, marking a tally at each score. At the end of the line, he spoke to the waiting captain, who gave a curt nod and began waving the press of people aboard.

"Sir," Errol called. His voice sounded distant to his own ears. He couldn't seem to get the sound of the sea out of them. "Sir?"

The man turned, noted his pallor and clothing, and gave a knowing nod. "First time on the sea, lad?"

Errol nodded, then wished he'd elected to speak instead. "And hopefully my last. Can you tell me how to get to Erinon?"

The dockmaster grunted at this and gave a fleeting smile. "It's not as if you could miss it. They say every road on Green Isle leads to the City of Kings, and they're not wrong." He pointed. "Once you get away from the docks, follow the main road. You can't miss it." Eyes the color of the sea looked him up and down. "What brings you to the city?"

Errol was too sick to even offer an evasion. He clambered onto Midnight's back. "I've come to be a reader."

The dockmaster's face closed, and his gaze grew cold. "You'll find the people of the city have little patience for such humor. I'd suggest you change it."

Errol blinked, not understanding what had raised the man's ire. He decided to change the subject. "How far is it?"

"Fifteen leagues."

The late afternoon sun made his decision for him. "Where's the nearest inn?"

❦

The King's Pleasure needed paint and repairs to the roof, but it offered food, which Errol declined, and a bed for one silver crown a night. After tending to Midnight, he climbed the rough-hewn oak stairs to his room and fell into a slumber. The floor seemed to buck and pitch like the deck of Grim's ship. He knotted his fists in the rough woolen blanket of his bed until sleep claimed him.

The next morning, true to the dockmaster's word, he found the road to Erinon. Broad and paved with close-fitting cobblestones, the route boasted more traffic in both directions than Errol believed possible. Supply caravans moved toward the city even as a relentless stream of families and individuals moved away from it.

As a caravan carrying salted fish passed by, he pulled his horse in line just behind. Only four men wearing blue livery guarded the thirty wagons, a fraction of what Ru would have used on the mainland. Errol rode close and hoped that any casual observer would consider him one of the guards. The closest guard spared him a brief glance and then ignored him for the rest of the trip.

The silence and the slow pace wore on him, but traveling in anonymity seemed safer than a headlong rush to the capital. He twitched the reins, and Midnight trotted up to the next guard, a portly man in his midthirties whose paunch stretched the fabric of his livery.

The man's bulbous nose and heavy eyebrows advertised his Einlander bloodlines. His gaze wandered over Errol, noting his weapon, but his countenance remained open.

Errol nodded in greeting. "I've never been to Erinon before."

The man nodded.

"Can you tell me something about the city?"

A shrug stretched the blue cloth almost to the breaking point. "What do you want to know?"

He'd decided to avoid the subject of readers if at all possible. "I have a friend in the city, a priest from my village. How would I find him?"

The man chuckled. "There are more priests in the city than rats. What order is he in?"

Order? Martin had never mentioned being in an order. "I don't know."

Another shrug. "Then be prepared to spend the next few years of your life searching for him. Erinon is the capital of the church as well as the kingdom. You'll find benefices by the score and priests without number. What's more, the church has scheduled a Judica. Any churchman entitled to wear more than burlap is coming to Erinon."

Errol digested the information in silence, holding his tongue against Martin's name. Prudence dictated he withhold everyone's identity until he knew whom to trust, and he would mention his connection to the conclave, however tenuous, only at the utmost need.

The clop of hooves on stone punctuated his next question. "Where would I go to join the watch?"

The guard pressed his lips together and smiled in a line of suppressed mirth. "The barracks of the watch are attached to the palace of the king." A breathy chuckle escaped him. "Do you mean to pick up the king's gauntlet, then, boy?"

The guard's attitude grated on him, but he needed information, not a fight. "What would happen if I did?"

The laughter faded, though the smile remained. "Ah, well. I never felt the desire to tie myself to the palace." He puffed out his chest. "Though I think the captains of the watch would find me worthy. I've handled a sword for more than a few years." His gaze drifted to the staff held against Midnight's saddle. "If you're serious, you'll want to trade that stick for a real weapon."

Now it was Errol's turn to laugh. "I've beaten more than a few swordsmen with this stick."

The guard stiffened. "No true swordsmen, I'll warrant."

Errol shrugged. "I have no idea how true they were. Most of them were caravan guards and they fought for money." Skorik's face flashed in his mind. "Some were truer than others, but they were among the most dangerous men I've met."

"Pah! Caravan guards. Drunkards that run at the first sign of danger." A blue-sleeved finger pointed at Errol's chest. "If that's all the experience you have, you'll want to save yourself the embarrassment of standing before the captains of the watch."

Errol forced a smile. This blue-clothed turtle of a man wouldn't last five seconds against Skorik. "I'll remember the advice." With another twitch of the reins he let Midnight drift back to his former spot at the end of the caravan. The first guard acknowledged him with a nod but still didn't speak.

That suited Errol—he preferred silence to idiocy.

⋯⋯

The next day, the villages came closer and closer together until the beginnings and endings could no longer be discerned. "Are we in Erinon, then?" he asked.

The guard on his left spoke, his voice conversational. "Not for some miles yet, though the people here would say different. The city proper is surrounded by Diran's Wall. It was intended to be the defense of the city in case of a siege when it was built five hundred years ago, but the area outside the wall holds more people now than the inside."

An hour later, Errol's senses were overwhelmed by the size of the city. How did so many people manage to live in one place? A year ago he would have laughed at the tale of it. Now he could only shake his head in wonder. Yet the bustle held a furtive undercurrent, and more than one merchant or goodwife cast nervous glances over their shoulder as they went about their business. At the sight of the guards a chorus of voices raised a clamor.

"The king can protect his fish," an old woman screeched. "Why can't he protect those of us in the poor quarter?"

A burly man snarled, showing broken and missing teeth. "Aye, there's that, there is. Even the king's city isn't safe anymore."

The guard next to Errol set his gaze ahead and refused to answer, his face carved from planes of stone. Errol had been in few cities, but the tension in the streets of the capital was unmistakable.

They passed a low building with a sign of the sheaf and pestle denoting it as a healer's. A handful of people waited out front, placid and calm, in stark contrast to the crowds he had just passed through. It was the first time he'd seen people in the city that weren't squawking or jostling for position. The healer, dressed in his white robes, came to the door accompanied by an older man, bent by age, and leaning heavily on a cane.

"You'll have to stay off that leg when the weather changes, Dane," the healer said. He called back into the shop. "Dorrie, bring Dane that bag of lamb's ear and soulsease tea."

A woman's voice answered. Errol had started to ride away when she appeared. He reined Midnight back to a stop. Her simple clothes and the smudges of dirt on her face belied the rich green of her eyes. A lock of sun-gold hair had worked its way free of her head covering. She pressed the bag into Dane's hands with a quick embrace and a smile that made the old man's eyes twinkle.

"There ye go, Dane," she said with a laugh. "Ye'll need to stop chasin' the lasses if ye want that knee to heal." Her laughter brought a blush to the old man's cheeks.

"Yer too good, Dorrie. Thank 'ee." He turned to the healer. "Thank 'ee Healer Norv."

Dane hobbled away, and the healer and his assistant escorted the next patient into the shop. Encouraged by the sign of kindness and generosity amidst the bleakness, Errol twitched the reins and continued on.

An hour later, at a shouted command from the front, the caravan turned aside. Errol watched them go, and then he approached the city wall from a low rise. Gates wide enough to accommodate twenty men abreast pierced the ancient gray stone every few hundred paces. Spires far higher than the one surmounting the cathedral at Windridge thrust skyward. People of unimaginable variety milled, bustled, ran, and did a hundred other things all at once in the streets. Each face he examined held some unique trait that Errol didn't share.

Errol gripped Midnight's reins as he passed through the imposing gate, until the ache in his fingers reminded him to relax. A forced grin met his request for directions to the watch's barracks and he resolved to avoid conversation if possible.

So slowly he wasn't certain when it started, the crowds of people began to thin and the sound of Midnight's hooves came to him more often. When he came to another wall—not as high as, but thicker than, the first—only soldiers and churchmen could be seen. He rode up to a smaller, guarded entrance.

A pair of bored-looking guards in red uniforms stood at attention with pikes crossed. "State your business," the left one said. His eyes never flickered.

Errol looked beyond the gate. Manicured grass stretched for a hundred spans before a monolithic building rose like a bulwark from the earth. To the right he saw what he guessed to be the king's palace, its towers soaring to stand watch over the city and the empire.

"I, uh, I'm here to see a friend. He's in the watch."

The guard, with the reddish hair and lilting speech of so many in Erinon, lifted an eyebrow. "No one's permitted entrance to the grounds without a pass."

Errol slumped a fraction in his saddle. "How do I get a pass?"

"The captain of the guard has to sign one for you."

That didn't sound so hard. "Where can I find the captain of the guard?"

The man beckoned Errol to the side, to a door that led into a guardroom where a dozen other guards lounged and threw dice. A man with two silver bars on his chest occupied a smaller room that lay beyond the first.

The guard opened the door and motioned Errol inside.

"State your name and business," the captain said without looking up from a stack of papers.

He cleared his throat. "Errol Stone. I'm here to see a friend who's in the watch."

The man at the desk lowered the quill and sat up in his chair with a smile. "Boy, the men in the watch don't have friends."

Errol shrugged. As far as descriptions of Cruk went, that was fairly accurate. "His name is Cruk."

The man nodded. "Aye, one of the captains. But how do you know him?"

"He lived in my village for the past five years."

"So you say." The captain nodded. "Can you describe him?"

Errol spread his hands. "He's about this wide, and a bit taller than me. He calls me *boy* all the time, and when I get too close to Cilla or do things he doesn't like, he throws me places."

A grin appeared in the captain's freckled face. "And this man is your friend?"

Errol shrugged. "He tried to teach me how to use a sword, but I wasn't very good at it. Cruk said the only thing I could do well was drink." Errol gripped his staff.

The captain's interest faded. "Be that as it may, I can't let you in unless it's official business."

Errol bit his lip in frustration. "Can you send someone to get him?"

A widening of the captain's eyes told Errol he'd just proposed something unthinkable. "Boy, unless you're the king, you do not summon one of the watch. They answer to him alone. You tell an interesting tale, but the only way you're going through that gate to the barracks is if you intend to challenge for a spot on the watch." He gave a contemptuous glance at Errol's staff. "Which, obviously, you're not about to do."

"All right, then. I hereby challenge for a position in the watch."

The captain shook his head in disbelief. "Are you that eager for a beating, or are you just ignorant?" He sighed. "Well, you're about to learn how the watch discourages people from wasting their time. Padrig," he yelled through the doorway, "conduct Errol Stone to the barracks of the watch and present him to the officer on duty." The captain shook his head again. "Good luck, boy, but I doubt if there's enough luck in the kingdom to keep you from the lesson you're about to get."

Errol shrugged. He'd been beaten before. If gaining access to Cruk, Martin, and Luis cost him a few bruises, then he'd just have to pay the price.

A large rectangular building housed the members of the watch. Five stories high and two hundred paces long, the building was constructed of the same gray stone he'd seen throughout the city, and it dwarfed every building he'd seen on his journey to Erinon. Yet it looked almost small compared to the king's palace.

"In here," Padrig said. He guided him through an archway that proved to be a tunnel leading to an immense courtyard. The reason for the immensity of the barracks became clear. The open area enclosed by the mammoth structure held the training ground for the members of the watch.

Stacks of weapons in racks lined the outer edges, and here and there, small knots of men trained. At the far end men practiced archery, some on horseback, some on foot. In the middle, men fought and wrestled without the benefit of weapons, their chests and backs gleaming with sweat. Closest to him, several men in black sparred well-dressed nobility, halting from moment to moment to give some word of instruction or to correct an error in stance or posture.

The men in black, men of the watch, didn't give their instruction in half measures. Mistakes apparently meant swift correction. Blood appeared commonplace. Errol watched an unconscious man being removed from the sparring area. He gripped his staff and held it close, as though the wood could give him some protection or comfort.

A man with a single red sword emblazoned on an armband noticed them and glided across the ground to them. "Another one, eh?" the watchman asked.

Padrig rolled his eyes and shrugged his shoulders.

"He's the third one this week." He turned to Errol. "I'm Lieutenant Garrigus." Deep brown eyes looked him over. "Hmmm. A staff man. We haven't had one of those in a while. Not a bad weapon, the staff, when it's properly used. Unfortunately, most men think it's a glorified club." He shook his head. "You won't be allowed to use the knobblocks. Take them off."

Errol slid his hands along the wood, twisted each weight loose, and stashed them in his cloak.

"What's your name?"

"Errol Stone."

The lieutenant nodded. "An orphan. Well, we've more than a couple of those in the watch. Why are you here, Errol Stone?"

He looked over at Padrig. "I have a friend here in the watch. This man's captain wouldn't send for him, told me the only way I might get to see him was to challenge. So I did."

Even before he'd finished, the lieutenant was shaking his head. "So you don't want to join the watch."

"No, not really."

The lieutenant's face darkened. "Soldier, escort this boy firmly out of the barracks."

Errol broke Padrig's grip and stepped away. "I came here to see my friend."

"I don't care why you're here," the lieutenant said. "I don't have time to spend on some peasant boy who wants to gad about the imperial grounds." He turned, pointing. "You see these men? They've taken the black as a pledge to give their lives to protect the king."

"I know the story of the watch," Errol said, "but I need to see my friend."

The lieutenant's eyes narrowed. "You want to see him? All you have to do is follow through on your challenge. You'll face five men of the watch. To join our ranks, you have to defeat three of them. If you manage to beat even one of them, boy, I'll go fetch your friend myself."

Errol's heart skipped a pair of beats. The best swordsmen in the kingdom came to the watch. How good were they, really? He took a deep breath. "All right, I challenge for the watch."

With a snort, the lieutenant led Errol over to an empty area of the courtyard and left him to loosen up with some of the simpler forms. Errol let his breath flow smoothly, calmed his mind, and thought of Rale, Jhade, and everything he'd been taught.

Minutes later the lieutenant stood before him, five men with practice swords behind him. He stepped aside to show a squat man ten years older than Errol, a silver sword on his breast. "Errol

Stone, this is Sergeant Olwen. He'll be administering your first beating. The four men with him are members of his squad." He turned, facing the sergeant. "This boy wants to see his friend. He seems to think members of the watch run messages. I would appreciate it if you could disabuse him of that notion, Sergeant."

The sergeant glowered. "Aye, Lieutenant. It'd be my pleasure."

The lieutenant smiled without humor at Errol. "Prepare yourself, boy."

As Errol removed his cloak, fire pumped through his veins. How would the sergeant compare to Skorik?

"Begin!" the lieutenant's voice cracked.

The sergeant charged, but Errol's staff, light and familiar after months of work with the heavier knobblocks, disappeared leaving only a high-pitched buzzing behind. He flowed and moved with the sergeant's charge. Almost before it began, the fight ended. The sergeant lay facedown on the ground, unconscious.

The men of the squad took a collective step back, and Errol heard a set of mutterings. "Never saw him move . . . nobody handles a staff that way . . . can't be a peasant boy . . . what's the lieutenant up to . . . better check the sergeant."

Errol grounded his staff and leaned on it. "I've had my fill of fighting, Lieutenant, and I really need to see my friend. I believe you said that if I beat even one of the five you'd get him yourself. How good is your word?"

Dark eyes flashed at him. "My word is good. But I also said you'd face five men of the watch, and five men you'll face." He turned to the man who'd been last in line. "Brascus, you can go. I'll be taking your spot."

His order drew looks from the squad, but no one spoke. Errol sighed and resigned himself to another four bouts.

Ten minutes later, angry but untouched, he faced the lieutenant. Three more men had been helped away, and it was likely that at least one of them had a broken ankle. Radere's words echoed in his mind. *"Deas's hand is on you, boy."* Is that how he was able to do this?

Errol met his last opponent's gaze. "Do we have to do this?"

The lieutenant licked bloodless lips and nodded. A crowd of watchmen had gathered, their stares intent, and mutters floated to Errol from the circle of men. Not all of them were unfriendly.

A new voice, crackling with authority, called the start in a clear tenor.

The lieutenant didn't charge but circled instead.

It wouldn't make any difference if Errol lost. He'd won the first bout and the lieutenant was honor-bound to follow through on his promise, but he wouldn't mind making the man pay for his name calling.

With his staff spinning, Errol flowed into an attack. The lieutenant tried to parry, but the blows came too quickly. His sword turned aside the first three strikes, but the fourth found his ankle, and the fifth found his ribs. The lieutenant doubled over.

Errol grounded the staff where the lieutenant could see it. "I could knock you out right now, Lieutenant, but I need you to go get my friend."

A man stepped from the crowd with two red swords stitched onto his armband. "If you wanted him to deliver your message, you shouldn't have hit him on the ankle. I'm Captain Reynald." He smiled. "Welcome to the watch."

"I'm not joining."

The smile faded. "Nonsense, lad. Do you know what you're turning down?"

Errol shook his head. "No, but it doesn't matter. I can't join." He turned back to the lieutenant, who'd managed to right himself. "Tell Cruk that Errol is here to see him."

The lieutenant left, limping, but he appeared to be trying not to.

Reynald approached him. "Captain Cruk is your friend, eh? Well, perhaps the lieutenant should have had the good sense to inquire before dismissing you, but Cruk doesn't use the staff."

Errol didn't feel like talking. "No, he does not."

The captain was undeterred. "Where did you learn it? I've seen more than a few staff wielders in my time. Your style is unique."

"Here and there." He pointed to a nearby bench. "May I sit?"

"Of course."

To his dismay the captain followed him to the bench, but no further efforts at conversation were made.

After ten minutes, the lieutenant returned with Cruk stomping at his side.

24

FAMILIAR FACES

I SEE YOU MADE IT ALIVE. BOY." Cruk growled at him, and then looked in disgust at the lieutenant. "This worthless excuse for an officer tells me you beat him in a challenge to get your message to me. I remember telling you before that a sense of humor wasn't allowed in the watch. Now, it seems they let any sort of jester in. Where'd you get that staff?"

Errol shrugged. "From a farmer near Windridge."

Captain Reynald stood. "Captain Cruk, Errol Stone has qualified to join the watch."

"Nonsense," Cruk said. "The only thing the boy does well is drink. He'll be the first to admit it."

Errol remembered a time when he would have either agreed with Cruk or hung his head in shame. Now the accusation might as well have been directed at someone else for all the impact it had. He met the captain's eyes, refused to look away. "Things change."

Cruk stilled, seemed to take notice of him for the first time. His eyes widened a fraction, and he turned toward his fellow officer. "Captain Reynald, Errol Stone is unable to join the watch. He has a prior commitment to the church that must be honored."

The captain refused to be put off. He gestured in Errol's direction. "Captain Cruk, this man issued a challenge and won. Not just a majority, Captain. All five bouts! And he beat a sergeant and a lieutenant in doing so." His voice had risen. With a glance to each side he stepped forward and spoke in lower tones. "You know we need men. Two thirds of the watch is gone, stripped from the king and assigned to the church of all things."

Errol had the impression that Reynald outranked Cruk in some fashion. But Cruk stood his ground, refused to be moved despite Reynald's argument.

"Captain, the boy's . . . Errol Stone's commitment is of the highest order. More than that I cannot say, but even if he defeated all ten captains of the watch, he still would not be allowed to join."

The sound of Reynald grinding his teeth sounded in the small space that separated the three men. "Don't you understand? He just might be able to do it. Even if he won't join, there are things we need to know. Where did he learn to fight like that? Who trained him? By the three, man, can you envision what a few squads of men with halberds could do on the field if they could fight like that?"

Errol felt a surge in his chest at Reynald's words, and he caressed the polished ash wood Rale had given him. The idea of losing himself on the stretch of green in the courtyard surrounding him held a certain appeal. Were readers allowed to train in arms? Luis had never said one way or the other.

He stepped in front of Cruk to address Reynald himself. "If my obligation allows it, Captain, I would be happy to visit the barracks and teach what I know." He grimaced. "I've never taught anybody before. I may not be very good at it."

Some of the tension eased in Reynald's forehead. "Don't worry about that. The officers can watch you and teach it to the men. We just need to see you fight."

Errol grinned. He knew what he wanted. Once released from

the compulsion, he wouldn't be staying long in Erinon—but having the chance to best Cruk would make a delay worth it. "Would I get to fight the captains?"

Reynald nodded.

Errol turned his smile on Cruk. "All of them?"

Another nod. Reynald gave a crooked smile. "For someone who doesn't want to join the watch, you're as ambitious as a noble's whelp. I see Cruk is known to you." He spread his hands. "Unfortunately, some of the captains are no longer assigned to the palace watch. They've been assigned to the benefices, and their whereabouts are unknown."

Cruk grunted over Errol's shoulder. "Is he that good?"

Reynald nodded. "Merodach should be able to beat him, perhaps Indurain. My sense is that the rest of us are too old."

Cruk's manner grew formal. "Captain Reynald." He bowed his departure. "Let's go, Errol. There are people that need to talk to you."

"What about my horse?" Errol said. "I left him at the gate."

"I'll send someone to take care of him," Reynald said.

Cruk didn't speak again until they'd passed out of earshot of the rest of the watch. "I suppose you'll want to stop for a drink on the way?"

He shook his head. "No, not unless it's water."

"How long have you been out of the barrel?" Surprise tinged the captain's voice.

Errol tried to count back and found that between running for his life and trying to escape from Naaman Ru, he'd lost track of the days. "I don't know. How long has it been since Windridge?"

"Five months."

"About that long, then."

Cruk's steps quickened and lengthened until Errol almost trotted to keep up. "Where are we going?"

"I'm going to drop you off at Martin's quarters. Then I'm going to get Luis."

Errol stopped, planted his feet on the stones of the hallway like a mule. "No, I want to go to the conclave. As soon as I present myself, Luis's compulsion is finished. I'm leaving." Having the opportunity to fight Cruk was not worth the wait.

A shake of the head greeted this. "You're not thinking, boy. We figured out long ago that someone's hunting you. If you really want to be free, you need to find out who, and this is the best place to start." Cruk checked the hallway and waited for a pair of king's guards to pass them before his voice dipped and he went on. "Something's not right here. Two-thirds of the watch is gone, and reinforcements from the mainland garrison are still two weeks away. I have the feeling someone is setting us up for an attack. It may not look like it on the surface, boy, but underneath, the city seethes like an anthill that's gotten kicked."

"What's happened?"

Cruk grunted and gave a crooked smile. "I think Martin and Luis should answer that. They'll want to pull every last scrap of information from you as they do."

Errol's stomach growled. "Will there be food there? I think my stomach is trying to eat itself."

They circled around the barracks and the palace on the walkway and Errol stopped, awestruck by his first view of the church at Erinon. A cathedral flanked by buildings that made the barracks look small dominated his field of view.

A low whistle escaped him. "How long did it take them to build that?"

Cruk's bark of laughter sounded harsh. "They've never really finished. It's the same way with the palace. It seems like no matter how big it gets, it's never big enough."

It seemed they approached a small mountain. Cruk led him to one of the huge arches on the left. As they passed under it, Errol looked up, and a sense of weight above him made him duck his head in spite of the height.

They headed deeper into the building, passed through innumerable hallways, each one smaller than the one before, until they walked a passage that was almost normal-sized. Fewer people filled the halls. Once, they passed a door just as a priest departed and Errol saw what appeared to be ornate living quarters.

He'd never seen the like, or even imagined it.

A few paces later they stopped before a thick walnut door. Cruk straightened his black uniform and knocked three times. A young man wearing a light-gray cassock answered and nodded greeting.

"Captain."

Cruk bowed, a slight curling of the neck. "Stewart, could you tell His Excellency that I've brought someone to see him?"

Errol stepped back. *His Excellency? Martin?*

Stewart stepped aside, beckoning them into a large sitting room. "Please have a seat. Whom shall I say you have brought?"

"An old friend with a taste for ale."

Errol made to protest, but a stern look and a small shake of Cruk's head stopped him.

Stewart's eyebrows expressed his surprise at the strange introduction, but he nodded with a smile and disappeared into the inner rooms.

A moment later, he reappeared. "His Excellency is just finishing his meal. He'll be with you in a few moments."

Stewart brought the smell of food with him from Martin's rooms. Errol stood, salivating. "Why don't we just go join Martin? I'm starving."

Martin's secretary looked shocked at the use of familiar address. Cruk growled. "Sit down, boy. The benefice will be with us when he's ready."

"The what?"

Cruk's hand clamped onto the upper part of Errol's arm. His voice dipped into an agitated whisper. "Martin has been restored to *benefice*. He'll be taking part in the Judica. Now be still."

The way he emphasized Martin's title left little doubt in Errol's mind where he stood in the apartment. He reclaimed his place and tried to ignore the noises that came from his midsection. A quarter of an hour slipped by before Martin emerged from his rooms. Errol stood and gawked at the change in his friend.

Martin glided into the room, resplendent in red robes with a wide gold belt and a large silver chain of office around his neck. With a serene nod, he bade them to stand. Errol gaped. The air of authority surrounding Martin appeared so natural. How had he ever thought him to be a simple priest?

"Stewart," Martin said, "I think that will be all for the day. Would you drop by the conclave and ask Luis Montari if he would be so kind as to join me for some conversation?"

He waited until the heavy door closed completely before unbuttoning the heavy scarlet robe and tossing it aside. "Praise the creator. I thought I was going to roast." He turned and smiled at Errol. "I apologize for keeping you waiting, but I didn't want to rouse my secretary's suspicion. Stewart means well, but he gets a little carried away with being adjunct to 'His Excellency.' He's very zealous on behalf of my position." Martin took a deep breath and exhaled with a shake of his head. "He's making me crazy."

Errol took advantage of Martin's pause. "Do you have anything to eat, Pater?"

The priest laughed and caught him in a bear hug. "Deas knows I've missed you, boy. It's a real pleasure to see you alive. And a surprise. Come." He led them into a sumptuous dining room. "Stewart brings me enough food at each meal to feed three men, just in case I've forgotten to inform him of a dinner appointment." He nodded toward a fluted bottle on the table. "There's a very nice bottle of wine to go with the duck, but if you need ale I can send for it."

"Just water for me, thanks." Errol said this as matter-of-factly as he could deliver it, but inside he exulted at Martin's surprise.

"Well, boy, I imagine there's quite a story there, but let's get you fed first. Your tale can wait until Luis gets here. That way you'll only have to tell it once."

Errol attacked the leftovers of Martin's repast like a wolf on a lamb. By the time a knock on the door signaled Luis's arrival, even Cruk's normally impassive face registered its surprise at Errol's appetite.

"What's happened, Martin?" Luis said as he entered the dining room. "Have we been found . . ." His voice died as he caught sight of Errol with the stripped bone of a drumstick protruding from his mouth. Shock and disbelief chased each other by turns across the reader's face.

"That's not possible," he said, his voice flat. "I cast lots. You were dead nine times out of ten."

Errol laughed. It felt good, cleansing, like a bath too long denied for his soul. "I'm glad I came up alive at least once. I think I can explain the other nine."

Luis's brows arched at this. Errol hoped it was at more than just his words, that the reader also recognized his calm assurance.

He pointed to the untouched bottle of wine in front of Errol as he helped himself to a seat at the table. "Would you be so kind as to pass me the wine, Errol? Surprises unnerve me, and it looks like we're going to be here awhile. Start at our separation in Windridge and don't leave anything out."

Martin and Cruk circled the table to take seats. Errol washed down his last bite of duck with water and began. He only spoke for a few minutes before Luis interrupted him.

"You had pneumonia?"

Errol nodded. "Anomar said I was as good as dead for two weeks."

The reader's face grew thoughtful. "That might explain it. There are writings in the conclave library that mention such outcomes, but I've never cast one."

"Well," Martin said with a smile, "it might be a good thing you haven't. Most of you readers think yourselves the closest thing to Deas. A little doubt will do you all some good."

Luis nodded toward Errol. "I think yon apprentice will take care of that for many of us."

Errol picked up the thread of his story, but a bare minute later Cruk waved his hand at him, bringing the tale to a halt again.

"You say the man's name is Rale?"

Errol nodded.

Martin turned toward the watchman. "You know the name?"

Cruk shook his head. "No. Never heard of it before. That's what bothers me. The watch makes it their business to know who the best are and where they are in case we ever have need of them." He cleared his throat. "Our network of informers isn't as well organized as the church's, but it's extensive in its own way. He's a staff man as well. We don't have many of those."

Errol leaned forward in his seat. Rale's story had been one of the things he'd wanted most to know, but pursuit had driven him away before the farmer could tell the tale.

Cruk shrugged his massive shoulders and leaned back in thought. A sudden smile split his face, and he laughed at the ceiling. "Oh my, that's too good." He looked at Martin. "I think Errol's teacher is none other than Elar Indomiel. Get it? Spell Rale backwards. It's Elar."

Martin laughed. "I always wondered what had happened to him."

"Who's Elar Indomiel?" Errol asked.

Cruk shook his head. "Later. We've already interrupted your tale twice. At this rate we'll be here all night." He waved an impatient hand toward Errol's half of the table. "Pick up where you left off."

Errol cast about for a moment before he picked up the thread of his story again. With some reluctance he related the tale of Warrel's death exactly as he'd told it to Rale. He closed his eyes as he did so, not wanting to shy away from the memory ever again. When he opened his eyes at the end, Martin, Luis, and Cruk regarded him in silence, but a tear tracked its way down Martin's cheek and Luis snuffled before blowing into a silk handkerchief. The frown lines of Cruk's face became deeper, making the captain appear grimmer. Errol didn't get interrupted again until he started talking about joining on as a caravan guard.

"You actually guarded for Naaman Ru?" Cruk asked. He breathed the name almost as if he considered it holy.

Errol grimaced and nodded. "I didn't know he was a swordsman himself until the night we were attacked by a man named Eck." He backtracked a bit to tell the story of his early days as a guard and then turned to Luis. "After we captured Eck, Rokha said there was a compulsion on him. I cast lots to see if the compulsion came from the church or a Merakhi. Now I think it might have been both."

"Why? I don't—" Luis began, but cut himself off with a shake of his head. "Never mind. Go on."

Errol told the rest of his tale with occasional interruptions. Toward the end, there were less and less. The only thing he omitted was Merodach's part in freeing him from Ru. He finished with his fights in the barracks courtyard. He looked up to find his friends smiling and shaking their heads.

Cruk spoke first. "I can scarce believe it. Meaning no offense, lad, but you're probably the worst swordsman I've ever seen."

"I'd like to try you sometime, now that I have a weapon I'm comfortable with," Errol said. Then he laughed at the surprise on the faces gathered around him.

Luis turned away from Errol with a look of reluctance to speak to Martin. "You know someone must be casting lots to hunt the boy, don't you?"

The reader spoke this slowly, and Errol sensed he'd tried to communicate something more to the priest.

Martin nodded but changed the subject. "What are you going to do about his casting for profit?"

Luis fidgeted in his seat, squirming from one side to the other between the arms of the chair. Then he waved a hand to brush the objection away. "As far as I'm concerned, it never happened. He did it under duress, and it's obvious he didn't profit from it. The conclave will never find out about it. I certainly have no intention of telling them."

Martin shook his head at this. "For some reason the boy has

enemies, Luis, and secrets have a way of coming out when it's most inconvenient."

Luis reddened. "We have to have him, Martin. Even more now than when we first learned of his talent." He sent Martin a pointed stare. "I did what should not have been done to bring him here."

Much of their conversation passed over Errol with only hints of meaning, but this last seemed plain enough. "Luis, how do we remove the compulsion? I can still feel it at the back of my head, like the buzzing of a hornet."

The reader looked embarrassed but held Errol's gaze. "Tomorrow, you'll present yourself to the conclave. Once you do that, you're free." His gaze became intent. "You're needed, Errol. More than you realize."

"Because the barrier will fall when Rodran dies?"

Martin growled deep in his throat. "Boy, don't ever say that aloud again. No one knows what will happen when the king dies and there are factions within the church that maintain the barrier is just a myth or a misinterpretation. Even if you prove to be right, they'll hate you for it."

Errol sighed. The church, the conclave, and the watch all held their own secrets. It seemed that events conspired to make him blind, groping for some way to understand what was happening. His questions led only to half answers and more questions. When would it end? "What do the prophecies of Strand say?"

Cruk looked confused, but Martin and Luis stared at him openmouthed, as though he'd changed into something unrecognizable.

Martin leaned back in his chair, staring at him. Errol refused to look away. Instead, he sat in his chair and kept his face impassive, as though he'd done nothing more than ask after the weather.

"Boy, you've come back to us with weapons on your tongue more dangerous than the staff you carry," Martin said. "Where did you hear about Strand?"

Errol sipped his water. He'd always believed Martin and Luis to be his friends, but how much did he know about them, really? What did they want and what did they want from him?

"There's a man in Ru's caravan," he said at last. "His name is Conger. He's a defrocked priest. I never saw him without a book in his hand. Usually it was something about church history. When we stood guard duty together he'd pull out one of his books and teach me to read using the interesting parts." Errol laughed at the memory of being bored for hours on end listening to Conger go on. "There weren't many of those, but the stuff from Strand caught my attention because, though I did not understand much, it sounded like some of the same things you and Luis used to talk around. I never got the chance to ask Conger about it. . . ." Errol leaned forward in his chair, willing Martin to answer him. "So now I am asking you."

Martin turned to look at Luis and laughed. "Your cub has teeth, my friend. I think Primus Sten will like our newest reader, if Errol doesn't drive him to distraction first."

Errol suspected the banter and the oblique compliments were the priest's attempt to divert him from his question. He folded his arms, leaned back in his chair without taking his gaze from Martin, and resolved to wait until the priest answered his question.

Martin turned serious. "Very well, I'll tell you as much as I think wise . . . and possibly a bit more. Strand prophesied about each and every king in the royal line, including Rodran." He waved a hand in the air. "Oh, he didn't call them by name, though that would have saved more than a little bloodshed over the years, but he numbered them all. Even the worst historian can count, and according to Strand, Rodran is the last of the royal line. In the prophecies, he's called 'Childless.' Appropriate, don't you think?"

"Who was Strand?" Errol asked.

Luis cleared his throat. "A prophet. His story is very nearly the equal of Magis, the first king."

Martin shifted his bulk in his chair. "Church historians say Strand saw a vision and for three days and nights he neither ate nor slept while he wrote what he saw." Martin shrugged. "Or was told. When he came back to his sense of self, he read the stack of parchment that bore his writing and, horrified, took it to the archbenefice of Erinon. Priorus impounded the prophecy on the spot. Such secrets are hard to keep. Over time the information worked its way into the writings of some of our more obscure benefices."

To Errol it seemed it all came down to one simple question, prophecy or not. "What does this prophecy say will happen when the king dies without an heir?"

"Your wits have gotten sharper since you stopped drinking, boy. That indeed is the question. The prophecy speaks of the land's savior, a . . . a new king," Martin stuttered. The priest looked away and busied himself with his goblet.

Errol waited for Martin to provide some explanation, but the priest merely traced a finger around the rim of his glass without expanding on his edited tale. By the look on Martin's face, there would be no explanations given.

"What does all this have to do with me?"

Luis cleared his throat but avoided Errol's gaze. "However the prophecy works out, the conclave will choose the next king."

"And someone is killing the readers," Cruk said. "They're trying to blind the kingdom and in the process have exposed more than a few cowards within the conclave."

This brought a grudging nod from Luis. "We were never meant to be warriors, and the bodies are often disfigured beyond recognition. I can hardly fault my brothers for running away when the faces of their friends and fellows . . . the faces were . . ." Luis blanched. "Excuse me. Many of those killed were my friends."

Cruk spoke into the silence Luis and Martin appeared unwilling to break. "Their faces were chewed off, boy," Cruk said.

An image of pointed teeth that filled an almost-human face came to him. Then he grew angry. He let rage burn in his gaze and regarded Luis in silence, waited until the reader fidgeted before he spoke. "When did you know that joining the conclave would put my life in danger? Windridge? Before we left Callowford?" His voice rose. "Is that why you used compulsion? Am I fresh meat?"

Luis blinked as though he wanted to look anywhere else but at Errol's accusation. "That wasn't my intention, Errol."

Errol barked a laugh in reply. "Intention? I thought you were all my friends. I've been shot at by assassins, hunted by a demon-possessed Merakhi, imprisoned and forced to cast lots against my will, and after all that you want me to sit here while you and Martin give each other knowing looks and talk around the things you don't want me to know. Were you ever going to tell me there are ferrals in the conclave?"

A pall covered the room. Only the sound of Errol's breathing, impassioned and labored, sounded within the space.

Cruk's hand rested on his sword. "How do you know they're ferrals, boy?"

Errol shook his head at the captain, turned back to the reader. "What have your intentions done except put me in danger? By the three, tell me what I want to know and what you want from me."

Cruk's hand spun him around. "How do you know they're ferrals?"

Errol met the captain's angry gaze, matched it with one of his own. "There was one with Eck!" He rounded on Martin. "Who's hunting me?"

Martin stood, pulled at his jaws. "I don't know, Errol." He held up a hand. "If I knew, I would tell you and use whatever influence I had to stop them."

Errol looked to Luis. The reader shook his head. "I've tried casting for our enemy, Errol, but other than Merakh, nothing comes up. I'm sorry. I am unable to frame the correct question."

Martin stared at him, and in the brown depths of the priest's eyes Errol beheld a vast sorrow and an even greater determination. "We need you, Errol, more than you know, but the fate of the kingdom rests on a precipice. How do we know we can trust you?"

"Trust *me*? How much more do I have to do?" Angry, Errol

stood and looked pointedly around the room as if searching. For months he'd puzzled over the priest's and the reader's every word and nuance. Each time he gleaned a piece of information that shed light on what the two men were about, he replayed every conversation all over again. Weeks ago, after listening to Conger on night duty, he thought he understood. Now he would put his theory to the test.

He met Martin's calm, assessing gaze with his own. "Does Liam know you plan to make him king?"

Martin and Luis didn't flinch, but Cruk's hand darted, and a foot of steel cleared the scabbard before he stopped, his face wreathed in a grimace.

Errol smiled without showing his teeth and nodded toward the watchman. "So it's true."

25

The Conclave

Luis bolted upright. His chair fell with a clatter against the polished floor. "We will not make anyone king. The lots will choose." Martin inhaled to speak, but the reader jerked toward him. "We will not. I told you before only a cast from durastone would suffice." He flung his hand toward Errol. "By now he's cast enough lots to know for himself."

Luis spoke the truth, but Martin's reaction gave the lie to the reader's words. When the answer came to him, he almost laughed. "If I were a reader," he said slowly, "and had to sculpt the stone to find the next king, I think I'd test it in wood first."

Luis paled.

"You've already done that, haven't you?"

Martin answered before the reader could speak. "Well, Errol, it seems we have no choice but to trust you." He looked toward Cruk. "That or kill you, and you're far too valuable for that. It is as you suspect. Liam will be king. That young man is the salvation of our kingdom."

"Who knows?" Errol asked.

Martin smiled. "Only those of us in this room, the primus, and the archbenefice. We controverted the power of the church and its Judica. If it became known, we would be excommunicated, including the archbenefice and the primus."

Cruk snorted. "At best."

After a moment, Martin nodded.

"But why?" Errol asked. "If Liam is to be the next king, then he's to be the next king. You could have waited for Rodran to die and the conclave would have selected him."

Martin nodded, but not in agreement. "Possibly. Forgive me if I speak obliquely, but our actions were deemed necessary to protect the future king. I cannot say more without putting him in danger."

Errol turned to Luis. "How close are you to the cast?"

"There are five lots left to craft," Luis said. "I have the stone, but it takes time, much more time, to sculpt stone than to carve wood, and for obvious reasons, we require a much higher degree of perfection."

White. Smooth as glass and as round as the sun. Errol remembered Luis's treasure, a crate full of stone lots that would determine the next king. Beyond doubt, it would be Liam. If there was ever a man born perfect, it was him.

"Does Liam know?"

Martin looked away. Luis and Cruk fidgeted.

Errol shook his head in disbelief. "You haven't told him. That's why he's not here."

Martin sighed. "For four years we've groomed him to take the kingship. Cruk, Luis, and I have taught him everything we know from sword craft to church history." He grimaced. "Liam will be a king for the ages precisely because he is uncorrupted by the power he will wield."

Errol nodded. "I doubt he'll thank you when the time comes."

"We are in your power now, Errol," Luis said. "If the Judica discovers that we've already cast for the king, there are men, powerful men, who will see us imprisoned for it."

"Or worse," Cruk said.

A sigh whispered through Errol's lips at the secrets within secrets. They tired him. "I won't tell anyone."

※

Guards patrolled the halls of the conclave in constant vigil. Men traveled the corridors in twos and threes, one man looking forward and one looking behind at all times. Everyone, reader or not, kept a ready hand on a sword, and the hiss of steel answered each unexpected sight or sound. Some, men who wore their struggle against fear in plain sight on their faces, went with naked weapons held at the ready.

Cruk growled at the sight as he escorted Luis and Errol. "A few more attacks and we'll be saving our enemies the trouble. We'll just carve each other up."

The only men who dared walk the halls alone without bared weapons were gray-clad monks. They shuffled through the corridors, their cowled heads bent toward the floor. One of them passed him just as Errol inhaled through his nose.

He gagged at the stench. When the man turned a corner, the air burst from his lungs. "Phew. Why don't they bathe?"

Luis exhaled with a heavy sigh. "They're monks from Carthus. Their vow of poverty constrains them from earthly indulgences."

Errol coughed. "I don't think heaven will let them in smelling like that. Even when I was a drunk, I let it rain on me every now and then. Someone should find something for the monks to do in the courtyard the next time a storm passes through."

Cruk inspected Luis's quarters while they waited in the hall. Satisfied, he waved them in and left. Immediately after his departure, Luis bolted the door. "Last week we found two readers dead outside their quarters."

"How many have been killed?"

Luis busied himself around his quarters. His hands drifted at the task, tentative and unsure. When he answered, his eyes were wide and haunted. "The conclave held a thousand readers once." He shook his head. "Some vitality was lost to us; perhaps it is connected to the weakened kingship somehow. With each year, fewer and fewer join our ranks. When I left for Erinon a little over five years ago, our numbers had dwindled to fewer than four hundred."

He turned away. "Now most of the rooms are empty. Apprentices who have no more than a year in the craft have their pick of journeyman's quarters."

The details drifted past Errol as if blown on a breeze. What he hadn't heard was what scared him. Luis hadn't answered his question.

"Curse it, how many are left?"

"Two hundred."

The air in Luis's room became stifling, difficult to breathe. "So two hundred have been killed since you left for Callowford?"

The reader shook his head. "No. At least, we don't think so. There are many factors. They've found about a hundred bodies over the last year. As for the rest"—he shrugged—"it is presumed they ran away. The primus and the king have sent guards to the mainland to try to bring them back."

"At least one was tracking me from Windridge," Errol said.

"After tomorrow," Luis said, "we'll have one more reader to help cast the lots when the king dies."

Errol strained against the implication. Could he stay? "How many readers will it take?"

Luis shrugged. "I don't know. It's never been done before. The lots will have to be perfect. Every benefice in the kingdom will insist on nothing less."

<hr />

Errol slept in Luis's quarters. Sometime close to dawn, the reader woke him. He wore the deep blue robes of his order, and his movements were slow, almost formal.

"Leave your staff here," Luis said. "Readers do not enter the conclave under arms."

At a prearranged knock from Cruk, they descended down

the broad stone staircase to the main hall of the conclave. Two watchmen stood guard at the huge double doors. As Luis approached, one of them opened the way with an effort. Inside, close to two hundred blue-robed men sat on benches arranged in half-circular terraces around a large dais.

Luis leaned to mutter into Errol's ear. "This is the meeting hall of the conclave. In this place the primus, first of the conclave, rules supreme." He nodded toward an ancient-looking man whose blue robes bore a single red stripe down each sleeve. "Not even the archbenefice can overrule the primus, unless at greatest need." Luis tugged on his sleeve. "Come, I'll introduce you to Enoch Sten. Address him as Primus. He holds more power than any in the kingdom except the archbenefice and the king himself."

They descended the steps, moving from the back of the hall toward the dais. Halfway there, the primus took notice of their arrival and smiled.

"Welcome," he said as they stepped toward the dais. "Secondus, you continue to surprise."

Secondus? Errol turned toward Luis, who held a look of regret, as if just then realizing he had forgotten to mention something. The news would have to wait; they turned their attention back to the primus.

Tall and spare, his green eyes piercing over his hooked nose, the man appraised Errol. Bits of wispy hair encircled the crown of his head like a halo. He put Errol in mind of an aging falcon.

"How old are you, boy?"

With a start, Errol realized he'd spent his naming day onboard ship. Small wonder considering he'd spent the crossing clutching the rail. "Nineteen, primus."

"He's old, Secondus, old to start the training, but strange times call for unorthodox decisions. You have tested him, yes?"

Luis bowed. "Of course. I think, Primus, that Errol's talent will justify the suspension of orthodoxy."

The old man nodded, then pushed himself from his seat. He grasped a dark staff held in a stand beside his seat and rapped its metal-shod end three times on the floor. The concussions echoed around the chamber, and all talk ceased.

"Hearken! One comes as a supplicant to our order," the primus intoned. "He has been tested by Secondus Luis Montari, and found worthy of admission to this body. So say you all?"

A chorus of "Aye" bounced back and forth between the walls.

The primus rapped his staff on the stone floor once. "Hearken! Does anyone have any objections as to why . . ." He paused to look at Errol. "I've forgotten your name, boy."

"Errol Stone."

Wispy eyebrows lifted in response. "Hmmm. Haven't had an orphan as a supplicant in some time. Interesting times, indeed." He turned back to the chamber. "Any objections to admitting Errol Stone to our order?"

Silence rested on the chamber. Errol's heart thudded his excitement against his chest.

For his part, the primus looked a little bored. Then he rapped his staff twice against the floor and called again in his clear tenor. "Hearken! If any have objections to why Errol Stone of . . ." He stopped with a look toward Luis this time.

"Callowford."

"Ah, yes. If any have reason why Errol Stone of Callowford may not be admitted to our order, let him speak."

Again silence fell over the chamber. This time Errol surveyed the audience and found the men occupying the benches wore the same bored expression as the primus.

"Once more," Luis whispered into Errol's ear.

"What's he going to forget this time?" Errol whispered back.

Before Luis could answer, three raps sounded on the floor as the primus straightened his weighted posture to ask the question for the third time. "Hearken! If anyone bears knowledge that would prevent Errol Stone of Callowford from becoming a supplicant to the most holy order of Urlock Auguro, let him speak now or bear the consequences of his silence hereafter."

Again silence filled the hall. Many of the men on the benches stood in preparation to leave. A few untied their scapula, and one had his robe half off.

"If it please, Primus, I have information that the conclave should consider," a voice called.

Errol knew that voice. He spun, searching. From behind one column, his eyes glinting with triumph, came the abbot of Windridge.

Morin.

Errol felt a savage grip on his arm. Luis's breath came warm against his ear.

"Say nothing," the reader whispered. "Absolutely nothing. Remember, the primus rules here."

The leader of the order of readers waved a fluttering hand at the abbot. "Come, sir. Let me hear your objection."

Morin took a deep breath as he surveyed the audience chamber. Every face turned toward the spot he occupied in the corner. He began in a booming voice, "This boy—"

And was interrupted by the sound of the primus's staff striking the stone. The sound, like a hammer against an anvil, filled the chamber.

The primus smiled at the abbot's confusion. "You misunderstand, good abbot." He pointed to a square of stone just in front of his feet. "Come here," he commanded, "and tell *me* your objection."

A glimmer of irritation flashed in the abbot's eyes, but he kept his smile and made his way to the dais accompanied by his guard. As he approached the primus, he bowed and gave an ingratiating smile before he shot Errol a withering look.

Bile filled Errol's throat, and he wished nothing more than to crush the abbot with his staff.

"Primus," Luis said. "There are things I must tell you. I need to speak with you . . . alone."

The leader of the order regarded Luis, his face grave. "I cannot stop in the middle of confirmation. You know this, Secondus. I must hear the abbot's objection."

Luis grabbed Errol by the shoulder and forced him back, interposed himself between him and the abbot.

The abbot of Windridge approached the primus, clearly eager to speak.

The primus held up one hand, and the abbot closed his mouth with a click. "You look familiar, good abbot," the primus said, speaking low, so only those gathered around him could hear. "But, alas, my memory for names and places seems to be lessened by the accumulation of years. Please introduce yourself."

The abbot bowed again. "Of course, Primus. Age is wisdom as we say in the cathedral of Windridge."

The primus's face wrinkled in disagreement. "I've met too many old fools to believe that. Your name, good abbot."

"Morin Caska," the abbot said, "of Windridge."

Primus Sten tilted his head to one side, looking thoughtful. "I think I've heard of you. Yes, I'm sure of it. It wasn't good. However, anyone can bring an objection and be heard." He held up an admonishing finger. "But be warned; this is the hall of the conclave. Any objection you bring can be quickly tested for its veracity. False accusations will not be tolerated."

Morin bowed obsequiously. "I assure you, Primus Sten, that the information I bring is true."

"Well then. Let's have it."

The abbot took a deep breath, as if to proclaim his accusation to all gathered. But at the primus's censorious glare his voice dropped, and he leveled his accusation in tones smooth as oil-covered water, even as he pointed at Errol. "This man has spent the last months in the employ of a merchant called Naaman Ru. Ostensibly, he was a guard. In reality, he cast lots to help Ru maximize his profits."

Primus's white-haired brows furrowed. "Is this true, Errol Stone?"

Luis interposed himself between Errol and his leader. "Primus, I can—"

An upraised finger halted him, and with a motion, the primus directed him to step to one side. "I think it would be best to let the supplicant speak for himself, Secondus. Well, boy?"

The primus's eyes lay among a network of wrinkles, like bird's eggs resting in a nest, but they held Errol with their authority. It would be futile to lie. With a crowd of readers at hand, no evasion would be subtle enough to hide what he'd done.

The abbot stared at him in gleeful triumph.

"Yes, Primus," he said looking down. "It's true."

The old man held up a hand at the cacophony that erupted from Luis and the abbot, stilling them. "Casting for profit is a serious charge, lad. Do you have anything to offer in your defense?"

Errol lifted his gaze to meet those green eyes. "Ru kept me imprisoned and under guard. It was either cast lots or die."

The primus nodded. "Not unheard of. There have always been men who desired the advantage a reader could bring to trade. How did you escape?"

Errol's heart quickened to a frantic pace inside his chest. "I challenged my way through the guard ranks to first and demanded he release me."

The abbot's face twisted. "Surely the merchant would not allow such a valuable asset to walk out of his camp. You against the celebrated Naaman Ru and all his guards?"

Errol's mouth dried. Some instinct that thrummed in time with his heartbeat screamed at him not to mention Merodach's role in winning his freedom. "I was helped by a friend. I can't say any more. I promised."

The primus's face clouded, even as the abbot's became savage with glee.

Morin bowed again, but not as low this time. "The boy is less than forthcoming. I'm sure you are aware, Primus, that his activity is against the laws of the kingdom. If it became general knowledge that readers of the conclave were influencing commerce for personal profit, the outcry against your order would be deafening."

"I am well-versed in the history of my order, good abbot," the primus said.

Errol was unused to the politics of the church, but he recognized the threat behind Morin's words. If the primus made him a reader, Caska would spread the tale of Errol's actions and stoke public anger against all readers.

His hands itched for his staff.

The primus's face clouded. "A serious matter," he said, his jaws working. "What would you suggest, good abbot?"

Surprise wreathed the abbot's features for the briefest of moments. Hunger flashed in the depths of his eyes before his deep bow hid it.

"The affairs of the order are your domain, Primus." He straightened. "But as the boy says, he cast lots under threat. I suggest you simply send him back to his village. I am returning to Windridge fairly soon. He can travel with my retinue."

As he said this last, the abbot's eyes grew wide with hunger until the whites shone all around.

The primus bowed. "You are wise, good abbot. And your suggestion has merit."

Luis made a strangled noise deep in his throat.

"But," the primus went on, "the boy's indiscretion is a threat to our order. As such it calls for something a bit, ah, more punitive than simple banishment." He turned toward the blue-robed men assembled before him, men whose attention had fled as the conversation they had no part in had proceeded. "Quinn, would you come forth?"

A stork-like man with a short, iron-gray beard separated himself from the crowd and came forward. "How may I assist you, Primus?" His eyes had a tendency to wander in and out of focus, as if he had trouble concentrating.

"I'm afraid my memory for the minutiae of conclave law isn't what it used to be, Master Quinn. What is the proscribed penalty for a reader of the conclave who casts lots for profit? Is it not true that penance of some sort is called for?"

Quinn didn't hesitate. "The proscription against casting for profit was first enacted during the reign of Belron, eight hundred years ago. Offenders were beheaded. A hundred years later, two readers were condemned and were drawn and quartered. Nasty business that. Then, five hundred years ago, five readers were caught casting for gain. They were thrown from the highest tower. Perhaps the most inventive manner of execution came about—"

The primus held up a hand. "Thank you, Quinn. I think we know the essentials."

They meant to kill him? Errol ached for the feel of ash wood in his hands. He took a step back in preparation to flee.

"Be still," Luis whispered in his ear. "The primus could tell you what he had for breakfast on this day twenty years ago. He tests the abbot."

Indeed, the abbot's face shone with naked desire as they waited for Errol's death sentence.

The leader of the conclave cleared his throat. "Yes, well, it would seem the way is clear. However, there is one small problem. The boy is not and never has been a reader of the conclave. Humph, not sure how we missed him. Everyone is supposed to be tested at the age of fourteen. If I remember correctly, cases where unattached readers are caught casting for profit are under the purview of the conclave." The primus smiled. "That would mean me, good abbot. Death seems a bit harsh, but certainly there is some penance called for."

Thwarted desire twisted the abbot's face. Then a smile split his visage like a cut of violence. "I would be happy to oversee the boy's penance, Primus. As an abbot, I have some experience in these matters."

The primus nodded.

Errol knew without doubt that, should the primus place him under the abbot's dominion, he would die.

He would fight first.

And live the rest of his life in hiding.

"You are generous," the primus said, "but I want to ensure

we make an example of the boy for those who think to test the seriousness of our order's charge."

The abbot opened his mouth to speak again, but the rap of the staff on the stone floor forbade any further discussion.

"Hearken," the primus called. "It has been found that the supplicant, Errol Stone, has used his talent for earthly profit."

The crowd of blue-robed readers gave a collective gasp. Gone were the half-bored looks and postures. They now regarded the men on the dais with pointed intensity.

"Further," the primus continued, "he is denied entry to our order and remanded to serve penance for his transgression until such time as the primus, the archbenefice, or the king shall determine. Such penance shall begin immediately and be carried out within the boundaries of the royal compound."

So they meant to hold him prisoner.

The abbot gnawed his lower lip, flecks of blood showing on his tongue. With a bow, he turned and strode from the chamber, almost running, bodyguard in lockstep two paces behind.

Two more raps from the staff signaled the end of the conclave's meeting.

The primus stood on the dais until the last of the readers exited the hall before turning his attention to Luis. "The boy brings powerful and desperate enemies, Secondus. I think we should retire to my quarters. There is much you have to tell me, yes?"

With that, he turned and exited through a narrow door hidden at the back of the dais. Errol and Luis followed him down a dimly lit hallway. Guttering torches threw ghastly shadows against the walls as they walked. The primus caught Errol's look and smiled.

"This hallway is rarely used anymore, and few know of it. In times past, the primus kept his quarters next to the hall of the conclave. I use them now for audiences instead of living space." He chuckled. "They're too dank for my old bones. I prefer the light of . . ."

His voice faded from Errol's consciousness as they rounded a corner.

The smell of filth drifted to him.

Three hooded monks approached, heads bent and feet shuffling.

At ten paces, clawed hands emerged from their sleeves to throw off their robes. Errol looked on faces from a nightmare. Ferrals. Pointed teeth gleamed wetly in the dim light. Red eyes shone with insane hunger. Dagger-like nails flexed in anticipation, eager for blood.

The spoor of corruption filled the cramped space. Luis and the primus gaped as the things charged, too stunned to fight or even flee. Errol darted in front of the primus, grabbed his staff of office, and swung.

The iron-shod end cracked across the head of the lead attacker. Blood gushed, spattering the gray stone with crimson.

Errol backed away, trying to find room to fight. Unable to move, the primus and Luis blocked him. "Get behind me!"

Teeth ripped into his arm even as he thrust the end of the staff into the face of another attacker.

With a howl, the thing sprang at him with its claws outstretched.

He ducked, tearing his arm from the mouth of its fellow. With a wild swing, he smashed the staff end against the ferral, but the blow missed its head and landed instead against the shoulder.

They closed on him.

He didn't have enough room. One or the other would take him. With a scream, Errol chose and aimed a crushing blow at the head of the ferral before him. The iron crunched through the creature's skull and the ferral dropped. Errol spun, even as a keening howl filled the hall. The creature behind him lay on the floor.

A long dagger protruded from its chest. Luis worked to push it deeper still.

The primus shook himself. His eyes blinked several times in rapid succession. "Quickly, we must get to my chambers. My guards are there. I'm a fool of an old man. This hallway is a death trap."

The head of the conclave hiked up his robes and ran, leading them onward. Errol gripped the heavy staff, darting glances behind every few seconds.

Their hallway merged with a larger one, where the primus slowed and strode toward a door flanked by two men in black. "We've been attacked." He pointed back the way they'd come. "The bodies are back there. Get them and place them in the old firing room." His face grew stern. "Let no one see them. No one."

The guards bowed in acknowledgment and the shorter one spoke. "Primus, let one of us run to the barracks to bring our relief."

The old man shook his head. "No. The boy here can defend me at need. Get those bodies now."

His tone brooked no disagreement. The guards left at a run.

"Inside," the primus ordered.

His quarters were richly appointed. Heavy tapestries in shades of blue hung on the walls, and thick carpets silenced the sound of their steps.

Errol found his way to a chair. The rush of battle drained out of him, and his arm began to throb. He ripped back his sleeve. Deep gashes and punctures filled the area between elbow and wrist. Blood dripped a steady beat on the carpet.

"Here, boy." The primus grabbed the hand of his wounded arm. In the other hand he held a decanter of a thin amber liquid. "This is likely to sting." With a flick of his thumb he uncorked it and doused Errol's wounds.

Fire raced up and down his arm. His arm felt as if it was being skinned. He ground his teeth. "What is that?"

"Skote," the primus said. "Boy, you've just had the kingdom's most expensive drink used on you to fight infection."

Errol sniffed. The scent of alcohol hit his nose with the force of a blow from a practice sword. A sudden craving for ale passed over him, but the pang of the wound seemed to be dying.

The primus rounded on Luis. "All right, Secondus, let's have it. What makes this boy so confounded important?"

Luis smiled. "Do you have a lot?"

The primus snorted. "Of course I do." He angled his steps to one of the cabinets that lined one wall and opened the doors. Inside, resting on stands lined with dark velvet, lay dozens of stone spheres.

To Errol, they looked identical to the ones he'd first seen back in Martin's cabin in Callowford, except the stone held a yellowish cast, as though the lots had aged. The primus reached out and picked one from the back row.

He brought it to Luis, his eyes wistful. "I haven't looked at these in a while. They were my first cast as a master." He regarded Errol. "That would have been about thirty years before you were born, boy."

Luis nodded. "Give it to Errol."

With an indulgent shrug, the primus put it in his hand.

"Read it, Errol," Luis commanded.

"Come, Luis," the primus said. "You know this is a waste of time."

Errol turned the stone against the light. "It says *Gallia*."

The blood drained from Enoch Sten's face, etching his wrinkles in shock. He snatched the lot from Errol's hands. "He's an omne." The primus backed toward a chair, felt behind him with one trembling arm for it as he sat. "By the three," he whispered. "The boy's an omne. And I just forbade him from the order and put him under penance." The old man's eyes glittered. "Why didn't you tell me, Luis? Am I that undeserving of trust?"

Luis bowed his head. "There was no time, Primus. Immediately upon his arrival, I brought Errol to the conclave."

The primus waved an imperious hand. "I think we can dispense with the titles, Luis. We're not in the hall anymore. But did you not think to mention his existence in all these months since your return?"

"The truth is I thought he was dead, Enoch. We became separated when we were attacked by the abbot's men in Windridge."

Lips pressed together in disapproval. "Didn't you cast lots to make sure?"

"Of course I did." Luis shrugged. "Nine times out of ten, they showed him dead."

Errol cleared his throat. "Anomar, the wife of the man who saved me, said I was more dead than alive for two weeks." The conversation disturbed him. The primus had called him an omne. He'd never heard anyone, not even Conger, mention the term.

Enoch grew thoughtful. "That would do it. The histories record a few such cases. By the three, Luis, you should have made sure."

"It was nine out of ten, Enoch." Luis spread his arms in defense. "And we had reason for haste."

The primus nodded. "Aye. Does Martin know about the boy's talent?"

Luis nodded. "He witnessed the boy's testing."

Errol had had enough. "What's an omne?"

Enoch looked surprised by the question. "You didn't tell him, Luis?"

Luis shrugged. "There were some compelling reasons not to." He gave Errol a brief apologetic smile. "I'm sorry, Errol." He turned back to the primus. "Errol was in the ale barrel when we discovered his talent. At the time I didn't want to burden him with more than the weight of his being a reader." He grimaced. "You may want to put me in penance with the lad as well. I put a compulsion on him."

The primus's eyes grew wide and his lips paled in anger. "You did what?"

Luis shrugged. "It ended as soon as he presented himself to the conclave. I thought it would help guarantee his arrival. He was less than willing to accompany me at first."

"Luis, you could have killed him!" Sten rubbed his temples. "With Johan Blik and Aurio Centez being killed months ago . . ."

Luis stared at the floor, shaking his head. "I didn't know they were dead until I came to the isle. I didn't consider that possibility when I put the compulsion on him."

Sten sighed. "You're the secondus now, Luis. It's your job

to consider every possibility. The conclave can't confirm a cast without an omne. We were blind, and you had the answer all along." He pointed to Errol. "You found the only omne we know of in Illustra, and you put him under a compulsion to drive him here. What if the compulsion had taken him while you were separated?"

"It did," Errol said.

The two men looked at him as if his presence in the room surprised them.

"I found myself walking away from the morning sun as if I were dreaming. Rale had to slap me awake. They sent me on my way shortly after. As long as I was headed mostly west, I was okay." He gave a lift of his shoulders.

"What's an omne?" he repeated.

The primus appeared to ignore his question. "Luis, I'm tempted to give you a penance to make the boy's look easy. An omne is one who can read lots cast by anyone," he said without looking in Errol's direction.

"Can't everybody do that?"

The question seemed to stoke the primus's anger. "By the three, Luis, didn't you teach the boy anything?"

Luis smiled, his dark eyebrows arching over his deep brown eyes as he spread his hands in apology. "I'm sorry, Enoch. When I discovered the boy was an omne, I began teaching him right away, but he didn't even know how to read. And I'm afraid that the most basic calculae of the order are still beyond him."

Enoch nodded, conceding the point. He paced the rug, each foot placed slowly in front of the other. "I'm too old for this, Luis. The kingdom is tearing itself apart. Benefices and dukes are jockeying for position in their attempts to be the next king, and half the conclave is dead or missing. The king's guard is down by half trying to find them. Two-thirds of the watch is across the strait. The southern provinces are screaming for help against the Merakhi invasion they think is coming, and someone is trying to blind the eyes of the kingdom by killing off our order." Enoch flopped in a chair. "The scope of the boy's talent must be kept hidden at all costs."

He looked exhausted, his skin paper-thin, stretched across his skull.

A knock at the door brought all of them to their feet. Errol gripped Enoch's staff of office, wishing he held the familiar ash of his own weapon. He vowed never to be separated from it again.

Luis admitted the guards.

Their usual stoic expressions seemed to be fraying at the edges. The shorter guard's eyes darted about the room as though he expected his nightmares to come for him at any moment. The taller stood with his jaw clenched. "The bodies have been stored, Primus," the tall one said. "But they seem to be decaying more quickly than a . . . um . . . human body. Already the smell is considerable."

Enoch nodded. "Thank you, Aden. Please send a messenger to the king. I request an audience at his earliest convenience."

The watchman nodded and closed the door.

That was it? Surprised by the brief conversation, Errol cleared his throat in an attempt to catch the primus's attention.

"Yes?"

He pointed at the closed door, beyond which the shorter watchman stood guard. "Aren't you going to have them go after the abbot?"

Enoch smiled as if indulging a child. "Why would I do that?"

Errol fought to keep himself from screaming. "Because he's the one who set the ferrals on us. He's been trying to kill me since Windridge."

The primus nodded. "Yes. No doubt the good abbot has much to account for, but without proof we can do little. And your suspicions, correct though they probably are, would be insufficient to convince the archbenefice and the king."

Errol waved his hands at his surroundings. "Then cast lots. I'll help make them."

Enoch shook his head. "That is not possible. You are new to our order, so there is much you have to learn. After Magis's war the provinces nearly descended into anarchy. The kingdom, welded together by desperation, fractured apart as provincial leaders fought for supremacy." His tone became almost mournful. "They were aided in this by readers who obeyed no law but their own desire for power. Magis's only surviving son, Magnus, decreed that all readers would henceforth be under the authority of the church, by compulsion if necessary." Enoch Sten sighed. "It was a dark time, but after twenty years it was done.

"Our order survives because we allow ourselves to be constrained. Whether to judge innocence or guilt by lot is for the archbenefice and the king to decide, not us. The archbenefice and king will never order a cast without proof. To do so would be to place the aristocracy and the church under the power of the conclave. Such power corrupts."

The primus took a deep breath. "At any rate the abbot has learned by now that the attack on us was unsuccessful. When no pursuit occurs, he may believe himself to be above suspicion. You have your penance to begin. Your exploits yesterday are on everyone's tongue. I understand Captain Reynald has requested your presence at the barracks courtyard. Have Lakken—he's the short one—escort you there. You'll stay with the watch until you're sent for." He smiled. "Once your staff is returned, please send mine back with Lakken, if you would. I can't wield it the way you can, but people expect me to have it."

26

ADORA

LAKKEN'S DEPARTURE left Errol at the edge of the yard clutching his staff. The wood, polished by his hands over the past months, comforted him like an old friend. He slowed as he noticed for the first time the variety of people. Knots of men sparred in the barracks courtyard as before. Besides watchmen dressed in black, young men wearing a broad range of finery littered the grassy expanse. With a grudging admission, Errol conceded that some sparred nearly as well as the men who instructed them.

On the balconies overlooking the courtyard, women watched the strutting nobles, giving appreciative or encouraging smiles as the occasion warranted. Though the summer air on Green Isle did not approach the sultry heat of the mainland, each woman fanned herself in complex motions. Something about the fans stirred a memory, and he dredged for it. After a moment, he gave up. It refused to surface, and he had other, more pressing matters.

The lieutenant he'd bested walked by, his attention on four pair of men who sparred with practice swords.

"Excuse me, Lieutenant Garrigus?" Errol called.

The watchman's face registered his recognition before the customary impassivity of the king's guard returned it to its neutral expression.

"I'm to report to Captain Reynald," Errol said. "Do you know where I might find him?"

The lieutenant pointed to the far end of the yard. "You'll find the captain instructing the sons of Duke Escarion over there."

Errol thought he'd heard a hint of disdain in the lieutenant's voice. He retreated to the walkway that bordered the large rectangle of the courtyard and made his way through the cacophony to the captain. As he neared the far end, more of the men who sparred wore the colors of the nobility and fought under the watchful eyes of watchmen of rank. It seemed the richest nobles commanded the highest-ranking members of the watch to be their instructors.

Curious, he tried to imagine how Duke Escarion, whoever he was, could merit the senior captain as his sons' teacher. Here at the far end of the field, spectators grew thick not only on the overlooking balcony but on the walkway as well. Tables and seats had been brought in order to accommodate them, and Errol had to pick his way among the press. As he moved, he became conscious of how plain the grays and browns of his clothes appeared next to the brilliant plumage of those who watched.

He threaded his way through the tight press of spectators, intent on working his way to Captain Reynald without bumping into any of the nobles present. He moved to step around a dark-haired noble whose indolent posture managed to fill not only his chair but most of the walkway as well. As Errol shifted, a glint of sun-gold hair and the flash of green eyes caught his attention. His feet stopped moving and he found himself before a woman about his age. Sensing his stare, she turned from the bout to meet his gaze.

Startled into motion, he turned away from the girl to hide his embarrassment and stepped on a foot extended well into the walkway. Errol bowed his head—"Your pardon, sir"—and shifted to move on.

Rough hands grabbed him from behind and spun him. The lord had vacated his seat, grabbing Errol by his tunic to pull him close to a face filled with disdain. "Watch where you're going, peasant." The man spat each word like a curse. Then he shoved Errol in the chest so hard he careened backward, tripped over unseen feet, and tumbled out into the courtyard to end up on his backside as the crowd laughed.

The two men sparring for Captain Reynald paused to share in the merriment.

"Derek. Darren," the captain yelled. "Do you think there'll be time to pause during battle for amusement?"

Neither of the young men appeared to notice or care that one of the best warriors in the kingdom found fault with them. As Errol scrambled to his feet, the older one, dark-haired and haughty, laughed. "But we're not in battle, good captain." He pointed at Errol with his sword. "And besides, it would be a shame to miss the antics of yon peasant." He turned a wicked grin to the other young man, blond but obviously his brother. "What say you, Darren? We could be witnessing the future king's fool."

Darren snorted, but otherwise said nothing to deepen Errol's shame or the hue of his face. "Go easy, Derek. It's a rare man who's never been embarrassed. Would you make it worse?"

The first man looked with affection on his brother at this. "If the peasant wants to keep himself from notice, he should perhaps watch his steps."

"He had eyes only for Adora," a voice behind Errol called out.

Derek's eyes widened, and he gave a mocking bow to Errol before approaching and putting a conspiratorial arm around his shoulder. "Your clumsiness is understandable, good man." He pointed his practice sword at the girl whose appearance had precipitated Errol's fall. "In truth, Adora has a reputation for causing the most graceful nobles to become awkward as boys."

Errol's blush deepened until he thought his hair would burst into flame.

"Enough!" Captain Reynald yelled. "You do yourself a disservice and dishonor your father, the duke. In battle, it matters not your birth. Your life will depend on the loyalty of those who serve with you—peasant or noble."

Darren looked down in shame, though he had done nothing wrong that Errol could discern, but Derek merely gave the captain that same impudent grin.

"Come now, Captain," the man who had pushed Errol said. "We're only having fun, and he is, after all, just one peasant."

"Just one peasant, eh?" The captain looked at the man with an arch of his eyebrows. "The fate of many can be bound to one such as him. Why don't we see what 'one peasant' can do?" Reynald crooked a finger at the man. "Come, Lord Weir, arm yourself."

The man's eyes grew wide. "What, you want me to fight the peasant?" His fingers flicked the air in Errol's direction as if he were banishing a fly.

"I don't *want* it," Reynald said, his voice soft, dangerous. "I insist upon it." He turned to the two brothers. "Go sit down and attend."

Weir rose and sauntered out into the sun of the courtyard. Derek tossed him his sword, and he swung it lazily back and forth. "Does he mean to fight me with that stick as if I was some sort of dog?" Lord Weir's face—women probably considered him well-featured—wore a self-indulgent look that appeared to be permanent. His chiseled features flowed into a sneer.

Errol gritted his teeth. "In truth, I'm not much good with a sword, but I have too much respect for dogs to use a staff on them."

Weir's face reddened at the insult and he spluttered.

Reynald winced at the jibe, then stepped over to whisper to Errol. "Weir thinks highly of himself, as do most of these." He gestured at the crowd. "But do no permanent harm to him. His father is a powerful and spiteful man."

He nodded, remembered his bout with Rokha. "I have more than my fill of enemies already. I think I can beat Weir without striking him, as long as permanent harm doesn't include his dignity."

The captain's face beamed. "No, I don't think it does. That sounds like an excellent idea, Errol Stone, most excellent."

Reynald stepped back, trying to suppress a grin as Errol and Weir faced each other. "Gentlemen, you will spar until one of you quits, is rendered unconscious, or I call a halt. Is that understood?"

Errol nodded.

Weir smiled. "You're having a really bad day, peasant. Perhaps a few blows to the head will relieve you of the memory of your embarrassment."

Reynald closed his eyes and shook his head. With a deep breath he raised one hand. "Begin."

Weir's first stroke made it obvious the man knew his way around the sword but also made it plain he'd never been in a real fight in his life. He jumped and pranced like a hero from the tales and seemed more interested in impressing the crowd than fighting.

His shock when Errol parried the blow aimed at his head was laughable.

Deprived of instant victory, his smile fled, and he riposted to strike at Errol's head from the opposite side.

Which was also parried.

Weir's legs lay exposed to the most rudimentary staff attack Rale had taught him, but Errol refused to take advantage of it.

Reynald must have noticed as well. The mirth in the captain's voice became plain as Errol moved, parrying each of Weir's attacks. "Come, Lord Weir. He's only a peasant after all. Surely one so skilled with the sword should be able to command, nay demand, the respect of one such as he."

Stung, Weir threw himself into an all-out attack that rained blows upon Errol's staff for ten minutes. At the end he stood, gasping, sweat streaming down his face, his sword arm so worn he could barely raise the weapon.

The nobleman hadn't even been as good as Norad Endilion,

the fourteenth. Errol stepped back, ground his staff, and leaned upon it. He would not shame himself by striking this fool. "Do you surrender?"

Weir sneered at him and rose to attack, but exhaustion tripped him and he fell.

"Halt!" Reynald called. He turned to regard the stunned audience. "With nothing more than a staff and without striking a blow, this peasant won." He turned to Weir. "If you are not man enough to apologize for your comments, Lord Weir, I wonder if you are man enough to lead."

Weir hawked and spat at Errol's feet. "I won't apologize to a dirty peasant."

Errol filled his voice with scorn. "I don't want your apology."

The noble pulled himself off the ground. "You will address me as 'my lord.'"

"You're not *my lord*. You're a strutting peacock who couldn't beat the least of the men I've fought."

Weir drew himself up and again spat at Errol's feet.

Reynald's face clouded, became a storm on the verge of breaking. "Does anyone else want to spar with the peasant?"

No one moved.

"I thought not." The captain pulled a dagger, bent to the hem of his black tunic, and cut a strip of cloth a handsbreadth wide. He moved to Errol's side. "Raise your arm, Errol."

Errol did so.

Reynald tied the cloth around his right arm before turning on the crowd. "This strip of cloth from my tunic signifies that Errol Stone is an honorary *captain* of the watch. He will undertake to teach those of you with the ability to learn"—he shot a look of contempt at Weir—"how to use the staff."

"I have no interest in the peasant's weapon," Weir said as he turned and strode away.

Errol watched him leave. Several of the onlookers left with him.

Derek came forward and offered Errol his hand. "I don't know that I want to learn the staff," he said. "But I think I'd better learn how to defend against it at the least."

His smile as he shook hands seemed genuine.

Darren leaned in from behind. "It's about time someone put that idiot in his place. And you did it without striking a blow. It's going to take years for Weir to live this one down."

Out of the corner of his eye, Errol watched Adora rise with a group of women and leave. He felt a curious pang at her departure.

As if Derek's and Darren's approval had broken a dam, a line of young noblemen came forward to shake Errol's hand, and he spent the rest of the afternoon sparring and instructing them on the use of the staff. After he had beaten most of them, pulling his blows to avoid injury, the nobles attempted to goad Reynald into a match with him.

The captain shook his head and deferred.

"Why not?" Darren asked.

"Fair question, lad," Reynald answered. "Attend." He held up a finger. "Never fight a battle that doesn't need to be fought." He raised a second. "Unless you have to, never fight a battle you know you're going to lose."

Those closest to Errol took a step back. More than one face looked at the captain in disbelief, searching, but Reynald's eyes wore no trace of mockery or jesting.

Twilight darkened the courtyard, yet the nobles were still watching and waiting for their turn with Errol when a nuntius strode through the press to hand him a rolled parchment. The seal of hardened wax left a warm spot on the palm of his hand.

"What's the message, nuntius?" Reynald asked.

The messenger looked at Errol, who nodded.

"Errol Stone," the nuntius declared in a clear tenor, "at noon tomorrow you are commanded to present yourself to the king in the royal throne room." He stopped.

Errol's heart decided to stop beating. Had the abbot somehow gotten to the king? Why would the king want to see him? What was he supposed to do or say or wear?

The nobles looked at him with renewed interest. Deep down, they probably didn't care if he was a villain or a saint, as long as he provided an interesting diversion.

"That's it?" he asked the nuntius.

The messenger nodded, adjusted the band of office on his arm, and retreated the way he came.

Reynald stepped in, pushed the nobles back to give Errol room. "That's it for today, my lords." He caught Errol by the arm. "I don't know what trouble you might be in, lad, but I'll stand for you if I can." With a wave of his arm, he beckoned to a grim-faced sergeant. "Gillis, accompany Errol Stone back to his quarters."

Errol nodded his thanks and started back to Luis's quarters, the watchman trailing him with his hand resting on his sword pommel.

"Right waste of time, this is," the man said once they were out of earshot of Captain Reynald. "As long as you've got that staff, with knobblocks on it no less, you should be protecting me." Short and broad-faced, the sergeant possessed the same dark sense of humor as Cruk.

Errol shrugged and pointed around the corridor. "The staff is a weapon that requires room to move. In tight spaces, a sword would be better. I'm just not much good with it."

"Aye, there's truth in that, there is." The man looked at Errol from the corner of his eyes. "You seem to have a little more sense than most of the nobles they bring here, if you don't mind my sayin' so, milord."

Surprised laughter burst from him and bounced back from the stone corridor as bubbles of sound. *Me? A nobleman?* His mirth threatened to run away with him. For a moment he teetered on the edge of hysterics. With a deep breath he took hold of himself.

"That might be because I'm a peasant," Errol said at last.

"Ah, well. That explains that, it does. But why were you ordered before the king?"

"I don't know?" He bit his lip. "Is there anything I should know?"

The sergeant grunted. "I've never been called before the king, and I'm not good enough to draw guard duty for His Majesty, at least not yet." They walked on. "But I'd keep that strip of cloth around my arm. It may not impress the king much, but it'll keep others from taking you lightly, it will. News will spread of what it means. It's not like a captain of the watch bestows his authority every day."

Errol started. "His authority? I thought I was just going to teach people how to use the staff."

The sergeant shook his head. "Aye, that's what it means, right enough, but only officers in the watch instruct. As long as you've got that armband on, anyone from a lieutenant on down is under your authority."

He finished the walk to Luis's quarters in a daze. Him? He could order the watch?

Luis opened the door to his knock, took one look at the armband, and sighed.

"Thank you, Sergeant," Errol said.

Gillis nodded and left.

Luis gestured toward the strip of cloth. "I see you made a new friend today."

"I didn't know, I swear. Captain Reynald . . ." Errol said. For some reason he couldn't identify, the strip of cloth made him feel suddenly disloyal, as if he'd chosen to associate with the watch instead of the conclave. But that was silly. The primus had ordered him to the watch as penance, after all. Only, having Captain Reynald tear the hem of his tunic and award it to him hadn't felt like penance. It felt like a reward.

"Never mind, Errol." Luis waved his concerns away with one hand. "The captain is a shrewd man and a skilled negotiator. He wants you for himself, but in this he is overmatched. He may be a captain of the watch, but he is outranked by the primus, and you are now the only surviving omne of the kingdom." The secondus smiled. "Ah, Errol, were we not in the middle of the greatest crisis our kingdom has seen in two millennia, we would have issued proclamations and held parades in your honor, and you would have been toasted throughout Illustra." Luis shook his head. "As it is now, we dare not let any know of your special ability, not even the king."

"Why does the king want to see me?"

"He keeps his own counsel, Errol. I don't know."

The idea of meeting the king both thrilled and frightened him. Rodran VI ruled an empire of provinces that spanned a continent. Millions of people owed their obeisance to him. For three generations, sixty years, he'd ruled from Erinon and enforced peace with the Merakhi and Morgols.

"What sort of king is he?"

Luis raised his hands, palms up. "The king is a man, Errol, forced by an accident of birth to assume the rule of the kingdom." He sighed. "By most accounts, he's been a good king. He's kept the empire strong so that the Merakhi and the nomads have kept their distance. He probably would have been considered one of the best kings ever."

"If he'd had a son?" Errol asked.

"Yes. If only he'd had a son."

"Why can't a male relative take the throne?"

"There isn't one," Luis said. "The royal line has never been overly large and in the last hundred years or so, it has shrunk. Rodran's younger brother, Jaclin, died ten years ago." His mouth thinned, leaving Errol to wonder what the reader wasn't saying.

"How did he die?"

Luis shrugged off the question. "Jac left behind a daughter, Adora. That's all there is."

Adora? What were the chances . . . ? The girl from the barracks courtyard was the king's niece? Errol's heart fell.

❧

The night passed in a series of waking moments interrupted by a restless doze. Errol often checked the window, only to find the moon still up. At last the sky pinked to the east and the stubborn sun rose to bathe Erinon in the orange light of early dawn. The grit of sleeplessness filled his eyes, and even the simple tasks of dressing and eating required concentration.

At ten o'clock a knock at the door announced the arrival of a tall, thin man Luis introduced as the king's chamberlain. Upon admittance to Luis's quarters with two servants, one male, one female, in tow, the chamberlain peered at Errol and began making impatient sounds as he circled him.

"No. No. No. This won't do at all. I see I should have gotten here earlier." The chamberlain stood so close Errol could have counted each hair of his eyelashes. He smelled of cloves and rose water.

The chamberlain raised his arm and snapped his fingers twice, and the male servant stepped forward, pen and paper at the ready.

"Will, I think a blue doublet and gray hose would be best. Hmmm. Also, bring a black belt and matching boots. I judge him to be nearly eight spans." The chamberlain peered at Errol's feet. "Make the boots a span and two. That should be close enough. And bring it all to the baths at the north end of the palace."

Will bowed. "Yes, Oliver." He turned and left, still making notes.

Oliver took Errol's chin in one hand and turned it first this way, then that. "Now for the hard part." He glanced over his shoulder at the girl. "What do you think, Charlotte?"

She held her lip between her teeth as she examined him from the neck up with the intensity of an herbwoman. "He's well-favored enough, but the hair is a loss, I think. It'll have to go."

"You're right," Oliver said, "but he has the facial structure to make a close crop work, if it's done well. What about the beard?"

Charlotte shook her head and touched a couple of spots on either side of his chin. "No. See the bare spots? Shaven is the only option. Still, I think he'll clean up well."

The chamberlain jerked his head in agreement. "Let's be about it, then. Follow us, boy."

Errol felt a little overwhelmed and vaguely insulted at their treatment. Was this normal preparation for an audience with the king? He needed help. "Luis?"

The reader looked at him with a twinkle in his eyes. "Oliver Turing is the only person in the palace who can tell the king what to do and get away with it. What chance do you think you have?"

"None," Oliver said. "Now, let's move, boy. I have to make you presentable before noon." He lofted an exaggerated sigh toward the ceiling. "This may be my biggest challenge yet."

Errol followed the pair of fussy servants to the baths, his mind conjuring frightening images of what would come. They passed through an oversized archway, and the chamberlain stopped before a doorway whose interior glowed from torches burning in thick steam. The air smelled of soap and rose petals. "Here." He pointed. "The hard soap on the table is for your body. The liquid in the pitcher is for your hair." His voice became stern. "Meet us in the antechamber in half an hour. Do a good job, or I will have Charlotte accompany you to do it over."

Oliver's female assistant neither smiled nor frowned but only took the statement as simple truth.

Eyes wide, Errol nodded, vowing that they would find no fault with his cleaning. A row of large copper tubs lined one wall. On the opposite side was the table. He disrobed and for the next twenty minutes, encased in steam, he bathed, scrubbed, and scoured. At the end he felt as if he'd taken off half his skin.

His garments, including his smallclothes, had been removed sometime during his bath and replaced by a thick blue robe. Belting it tightly around his waist, he found Charlotte and Will waiting for him in the antechamber to the baths.

She pointed to a chair. "The shave first, I think. Let's see what we have to work with before we cut the hair."

Will stepped forward, stropping a razor with practiced familiarity. Five minutes later, Errol was sure the servant had peeled his face like an overripe grape, but no matter how many times he raised a hand to his chin he could find no trace of blood.

Charlotte ran fingers across his cheeks with the trace of a smile. "Hmmm, there's more to work with than I thought." Her hand moved to his hair, ruffling, pulling, and combing. "Yes. Yes, I think that will do nicely," she said.

"What will do?" Errol asked.

She tapped him on the head with her comb. "Never mind, boy. I wasn't talking to you. Now, hold perfectly still unless you want to go before the king looking like a dog with the mange."

For what seemed an eternity, the only sound in the room was the snip of Charlotte's small shears. Cascades of dark, nearly black hair fell around Errol, and gooseflesh rose on his arms as unaccustomed whispers of air touched his neck. Just as Charlotte finished with a self-satisfied nod, Oliver strode through the door accompanied by Will, who held a pile of clothing.

The chamberlain stopped, his eyes wide. "Oh, Charlotte, you have worked a miracle."

She batted her eyes in response to the praise. "Don't I always?"

"Yes, dear. Now, lad, let's get you dressed. Hurry! It's almost time."

Errol took the proffered clothes and retreated to a dressing chamber, emerging moments later to find the chamberlain tapping one foot with impatience.

"Finally. Let's go."

"No," Errol said. "I need my armband."

"Ridiculous," Oliver said. "It will totally ruin the look."

Enough was enough. "I don't care. I'm not going before the king without the band Captain Reynald gave me." To show the strength of his intent, he sat down.

The chamberlain's mouth pursed in disapproval. "Will, get the armband and fasten it, tastefully mind you, on his arm."

⋆⟡⋆

The throne room of Rodran VI soared above Errol. Buttresses climbed skyward at even intervals along the walls. Tall, narrow windows filled the space between buttresses, and jeweled light streamed through stained-glass to fall gleaming like myriad precious stones. The polished granite floor echoed with the steps of his boots as he approached the carpeted stone platform at the far end.

Rodran sat on a heavy polished throne, backed by rich drapes of purple and scarlet. Marble statues of long-dead kings filled the embrasures on the walls. Errol walked with tentative steps toward the throne, the eyes of the statues and assembled nobles upon him. For a moment, he caught a glimpse of a shimmering wave of golden hair and he stumbled on nothing.

At the foot of the raised platform, a courtier with a ceremonial staff awaited him. King Rodran, old and bent with age, nodded as if asleep on his throne. Around him, four black-robed men of the watch stood guard, swords bared, ceaselessly scanning the hall for threats.

"Name?" The king's retainer tilted the staff to block Errol's way.

"Um . . . Errol, Errol Stone."

The staff lifted and fell with an echoing boom three times upon the floor, whereupon the retainer made his announcement in a high, clear tenor. "Errol Stone, so summoned, approaches the throne."

Rodran beckoned him forward. The staff moved back to its vertical position, and Errol mounted the steps and knelt.

27

WHAT TIDINGS COME

ERROL KEPT HIS GAZE on the floor, not daring to even lift his head to look Rodran in the eye. In spite of everything he had been told, fear of inadvertently giving offense to the king constricted his throat and he found it difficult to breathe. The floor wavered as if it were covered by rippling water.

Footsteps.

Another presence joined him on the platform.

"Primus," the king said. His voice trembled with effort and his words held a breathy quality, as though Erinon's monarch found the air too thick to breathe. "Is this the man?"

The first reader's face was grave as he nodded. "Yes, sire." He looked as though he wanted to say more, but his lips pressed into a line and he fell silent.

The king cleared his throat with an effort, a deep cough racking his frail body. "You cast lots for profit."

The announcement brought a gasp from the assembled.

The primus stepped forward, his mouth open to speak, but the king raised his hand. "More, I'm told you assaulted Lord Weir, a noble and the son of Duke Weir, one of my oldest friends."

Errol heard a satisfied grunt at this. He looked toward the leader of the conclave. The primus looked as if his hope was dying.

The king's scowl would have been terrifying had he not looked as though a breeze could knock him over. "Have you anything to say in your defense?"

Errol raised his head, suddenly furious. What had he done in the long months since the coming of the nuntius to Callowford that he had not been forced to do? Breath filled his lungs. *Curse them all.* If they intended to punish him for surviving, he'd let them know what he thought of them before they hauled him off to . . .

The king's eyes twinkled.

Rodran the VI sat on his throne, shivering despite the heavy robe he wore—his grand leonine head covered with the cloudy white of his long hair and beard, his eyes dimmed by time and fatigue. Yet what showed of those blue eyes twinkled. The scowl remained, his lips pressed together in a frown and his brows drawn together in regal disapproval, but light danced in the depths of the monarch's eyes as though he wanted Errol to share some private joke.

Errol released his anger and his breath, shaking his head. "No, sire. I have no defense." He bowed his head. "As you command, my liege."

A soft snort, and the sound of the king's lips flapping against each other sounded. "Your liege, did you say? We shall see." The king raised his voice to address the assembly. "Let no man think to test the crown." Under his breath he added so softly that only those on the platform could hear. "I am surrounded by vultures, courtiers pecking at my old bones."

Rodran looked over those assembled in the hall. He raised his tremulous voice. "Errol Stone, you are found guilty of violating the trust of the kingdom. You are herewith ordered to serve penance to the conclave in perpetuity until your crime has been expunged. Henceforth, let your deeds so shine before the people of the kingdom that they will laud your liege and lord." He coughed once. "Humph. This audience is concluded."

Errol's mind spun, trying to sort through the formalities of the king's language. Perpetuity? Did that mean he had to live out the rest of his life in penance? And what deeds would he have to do to expunge his guilt? He rose and looked at those assembled for some clue to the king's meaning. Weir and his father stood with disappointment etched on their faces. The rest of the nobles looked bored.

The king stood, and the crowd began moving away. The primus came to stand at his shoulder. "The king requires your attendance at a private audience. Come."

Errol trailed the primus, and together they followed the king and his bodyguards out the rear of the throne room. After a short distance down the hallway they came to a small chamber as richly appointed but more comfortable than the larger hall. The king seated himself with a sigh on a well-cushioned chair.

"Ah. That's better. Thrones are hard, boy. They're made for younger men." He waved a trembling finger at a nearby chair. "Sit down, gentlemen. I have no intention of looking up at you."

Errol sat along with the primus. His hands took turns gripping each other as they sought the familiar comfort of his staff. He felt naked without it. The door opened to admit Captain Reynald and another man the primus whispered was the archbenefice, Bertrand Cannon. Luis, Martin, and Cruk followed.

Errol didn't know what manner of greeting to give. The king had told him to sit down, but the instinct to bow his respects to the archbenefice overwhelmed him. He stood and did so.

"Ha." The archbenefice laughed. "He's got pretty good manners—obviously not a noble."

The king smiled. "I'm sure the boy expects a certain formal decorum in our language, Bertrand. Try not to disappoint him."

A catarrhal sound issued from deep in the archbenefice's throat as he tried to stifle his laughter. "We don't have time for that nonsense."

Rodran regarded Errol and the rest assembled there. For a brief moment, Errol saw the man the king had been before age and the weight of power had robbed him of his strength. "I'd like to know what's so important about this boy." His gaze swept the room.

"Me?" Errol asked.

"The enemy wants to kill you," the archbenefice said. "Which means"—he shot a look at the primus—"that they perceive some threat in you."

Enoch Sten, primus of the conclave, shrugged. "I can only surmise that Morin is attempting to eliminate those who can testify against him." He regarded Errol with utter calm.

A brief look of irritation, like a wisp of cloud passing in front of the sun, marred the archbenefice's face before he continued. "We must use their interest to try and bring them out into the open."

Errol didn't understand the archbenefice's meaning and looked to Martin for an explanation.

At a nod from the king, Martin spoke.

"They mean to use you as bait, boy," the priest said. Unconcealed scorn filled his voice. "Instead of the recognition you should have received for saving the primus's life, the king means to set you up as a target in hopes of luring our enemies out into the open."

"What do you think, Errol?" Luis asked. His voice sounded brittle, on the edge of breaking.

A sense of loneliness and betrayal stabbed Errol, kept stabbing him. In this room, not one of these men would come to his defense. To a man, they only wanted to use him to further their own ends. Jealously and envy of Liam so deep it threatened to drown him crashed upon him in wave after wave. He bowed his head, waiting for the flood to ebb.

At last the emotions receded, replaced by loneliness and longing for honest company: Rale, Anomar, Rokha, or Conger.

Even Ru had been straightforward in his greed and ambition.

What do I think? If he thought they would allow him to go, he would be off the island before nightfall. Errol stood before them, bound by the king, the primus, and the archbenefice, forced by the three most powerful men in the kingdom to bait their trap.

He took a deep breath and let them know what he thought. "I wish I'd never seen that nuntius in Callowford. Since I met that crow, I've left every friend to obey the church." He spat the words, throwing them with contempt at his puppet masters. Then he turned to look at the king, and stopped. Some sense of the king's nearly infinite sorrow struck him, and though Errol's anger still burned like a blacksmith's furnace within his chest, he could not bring himself to rail against this fragile old man. His voice softened. "More than anything, Your Majesty, I wish you had a son."

Quiet descended upon the room. Tears tracked down Rodran's cheeks, but he made no move to hide them or wipe them away.

"I'm sorry, Errol," the archbenefice spoke at last. "The kingdom is in our care."

Errol laced his voice with contempt. "And I'm a necessary sacrifice."

"If need be, we are all necessary sacrifices, boy," Cruk said. "We don't have time for you to feel sorry for yourself."

Stung, he rounded on the watchman. "Have I not done everything you've asked?" He thrust an angry finger toward the primus. "And more?"

"I don't think the demon spawn were after me," the primus said. "It was only after Morin failed in his attempt to gain control of you that they attacked. They could have killed Luis and me easily. The secondus and I stood, unarmed and defenseless. Yet all three of them went after you, Errol."

The king snorted his derision. "Five of the finest minds in the kingdom are gathered before me, and yet no one can tell me what makes this boy so important. What about you, boy? Do you know your part in this?"

Errol licked lips that had gone dry. "Sire, six months ago I was wandering the Sprata foothills looking for enough herbs to buy ale."

The king sat back, his face cold. "Secrets. I pray, gentlemen, that you know what you're about. Your plan carries risk, yet it is obvious the boy is crucial to it."

"And that is our chance, Errol," the archbenefice added. "By having the king forsake you in public yet keep you tied to your penance, we present our enemies with an opportunity to attack you again."

Errol shook his head. "Why not just take the abbot and question him?"

The archbenefice sighed. "The abbot is only the foot soldier of the enemy. We need to know who is pulling his strings. And for that . . ." He shrugged.

"You need bait for your trap," Errol said.

Awkward stillness filled the room. The men waited on him. They couldn't force him to be their bait, he saw. Luis's compulsion had been fulfilled and unless they put another one on him, he could tell them whatever they wanted to hear and then run for the mainland as soon as they turned their backs. The idea appealed to him. He could take his staff and find some corner of the kingdom where no one would think to question him and become a farmer. Why not? If it worked for Rale, it could work for him.

But he wouldn't leave. Absurdly, an image of sun-kissed hair filled his mind—an image of Adora, the king's niece. He shook his head at his folly. *Blind, stupid fool.*

The king must have misread his train of thought. "No? You mean to deny your kingdom this chance to unmask its enemies?"

Startled, Errol shook himself. "No, Your Majesty, I do not. What is your command?"

⌘

Footsteps sounded behind him on the path he walked from the barracks courtyard to the conclave, the same path he'd trod at the same hour of the morning for the past five days. High in the barracks and the conclave and the palace, men of the watch observed him, waiting for the enemy to make their move. The plan was simple—observe and wait for the enemy to attack, and then respond with enough force to drive them off without killing them.

Then follow.

Simple, they said. Somehow Errol didn't think so.

The steps came closer. He breathed through his nose, trying to catch a whiff of corruption, but the breeze, soft as it was, caressed his face and then blew past him. If someone snuck up on him, it wouldn't be smell that gave them away. He twitched his shoulders and clenched his staff. One hand slid up to check the knobblock fastened to the end. Plan or not, he would do his best to kill any of those things if they came near.

Two monks, their faces hidden, bumped him as they passed by. His heart stopped in his chest, but his nose registered only the usual smell of unwashed men, nothing more. He slumped in relief.

Late that afternoon, he would retrace his steps, ostensibly to continue his duties as staff master for the watch, but in reality to entice an attack. He straightened and quickened his pace.

Moments later, in the comfort of crowded hallways in the conclave, he made his way to the main workroom. An acolyte in a plain gray smock greeted him at the door and took him to a corner of the room filled with square blanks of wood and stone. Master Quinn gave him a welcoming smile and waved him to a seat in front of a table laid with a variety of tools.

"Now, Errol, we will continue where we left off yesterday," Quinn said. "Your aptitude with wood is considerable, but your knowledge of the properties of each variety needs work. Now, you are most familiar with pine." He paused.

Errol dutifully picked up the pine blank.

"Now"—he tapped another piece of wood—"this?"

"Poplar," Errol said. "Slightly denser than pine and of a finer grain, it allows the reader to make more casts with greater accuracy than pine." He completed the recitation and reflected he'd never been more bored in his life. For the next thirty minutes he parroted the previous day's lectures about each type of wood on the table. And every time he questioned the master on why he needed to know all the minutiae behind casting wood lots, Quinn gave the same answer.

"Tradition provides the bedrock of our craft."

Which sounded like an excuse not to answer.

Still, he persisted in asking even the most basic questions. "Why are lots round? Why not make it a different shape, or even put multiple answers on a single lot, like a cube?"

Master Quinn's beard quivered with affront at his queries, and his head trembled at the end of his long neck, as if Errol had uttered some sort of blasphemy.

"That's enough about wood," Quinn said. His voice took on the clipped tones of someone who wanted to change the subject. "Let us begin your education in stone." And the lessons in wood were repeated almost verbatim—except they talked about rocks instead.

After the second hour of hearing about the different properties of marble, granite, limestone, and a dozen other varieties of rock, Errol worked up the courage to ask a question that had nagged him since his time with the caravan.

"Why do we have to make different lots every time we want to cast?"

Quinn's eyebrow rose, and he looked on the verge of repeating his previous admonition on tradition, but at last he nodded. "You've stumbled on a question that has vexed the conclave since its founding. Many have sought the answer, both philosophically and practically. Their efforts are recorded in the scroll room, and they failed on both accounts.

"Fifteen hundred years ago, Finn Maccol theorized that if a reader could hold more than one image in his mind simultaneously, it would be possible to create a lot that held multiple answers." He shrugged his thin shoulders and turned to take in the entirety of the conclave with a wave. "A hundred years later, Dieter Klose postulated the existence of what he called the versis. It was a simple extrapolation, really, and utterly impossible, of course. But then . . ."

"Your pardon, Master," Errol interrupted. "What exactly is a versis?"

Quinn looked at Errol as if he'd forgotten he was there. "Hmmm? Oh yes, well, it's a universal lot, a single lot that can be used to cast the answer to any question. It's a ridiculous idea, of course. A reader would have to be able to hold an infinite number of images in his head at once. Sarin Valon—brilliant man—was a bit obsessed with the idea of making one. He had an incredible mind."

"Had?" Errol asked. "Who was Sarin Valon?"

Quinn looked surprised for a moment. "Ah, yes, you've only recently come to the isle. Sarin was secondus of the conclave and the most brilliant mind to come to us in generations. He died in an attack a few months ago."

After their first meeting with the primus, Luis explained he'd been elevated after the recent death of the former secondus, but he had refused to explain further. Errol leaned forward, eager for details Quinn might provide—both of Sarin and the versis.

The man shuddered. "Gruesome. His body was mauled beyond recognition. We had to identify him by the rings on his torn hands. He made the versis his life's pursuit. As I said, it's beyond human ability, and that's to say nothing of the impossibility of creating the physical lot itself."

Errol shook his head. "I don't understand. Why would that be impossible?"

Quinn sighed in irritation. "Haven't you been listening? The act of casting lots produces imperfections, nicks or dents, in the wood or stone. The broader the question, the longer it takes to cast a definitive answer, and the less reliable the results become."

"But, Master Quinn, if someone created a versis, the lot wouldn't degrade. There would be no other lots in the drawing for it to hit."

Quinn's eyes narrowed, then widened. "I never thought of that." He looked around, his birdlike head darting this way and that. He snatched up a block of limestone, the softest rock the conclave used for lots of any kind, and thrust it at Errol. "Here, sculpt a lot from this. It doesn't matter to what. I've got to get to the library. You've given me an idea." And the master flew from Errol's presence, leaving him holding the grayish lump.

Quinn had said the versis could answer any question. Could that be how his enemies were able to track him with such precision? He placed the limestone cube back on the table and sought out Luis.

He found him in one of the small private workrooms designated for use by the secondus, perched at a table by the window and sanding a piece of pure white durastone that shone with reflected light. Luis's hands hovered over the stone, and he paused at odd moments, whereupon he would take up a piece of emery cloth and brush the surface. Luis seemed unaware of his presence, and for a moment he was tempted to read the cast Luis had placed within the stone. He even leaned forward to search the gleam for the choice written there, but at the last instant, he backed off, clearing his throat.

Luis started and turned. Seeing him, he gave a nervous laugh, wrapped the unfinished lot in dark cloth, and placed it in a cabinet, which he locked. The set of his shoulders relaxed, and he regarded Errol with a friendly smile. "How go your lessons with Master Quinn?"

Errol gave a wry grin, not wanting to give offense. "Master Quinn sets a lot of store by conclave tradition. He doesn't always appreciate questions."

Luis chuckled. "He hasn't changed much since he was my teacher, then."

"I did manage to get him to answer a few," Errol said. "He told me about Sarin and the versis."

Luis betrayed no surprise but grew still, very still. "Really?"

Errol nodded. "Yes. You know what I think? I think Sarin was able to create a versis, someone killed him for it, and they've been using it to track me."

Luis darted a glance over his shoulder, but the doorway remained empty. "It's true the secondus pursued the versis. Ever since it became obvious the king wouldn't be able to sire an heir,

Sarin sought the universal lot. For years he pursued its creation until it became an obsession. In a way, Sarin's death was a release for him. He'd become . . . unstable." Luis shook his head. "The versis remains, and will always remain, a myth. It's better that way."

"Why?"

"The power to know everything is too much temptation for any man. In spite of what the people of the kingdom think, there are limitations to what is possible for the conclave—and that's a good thing. I disliked the ambition that drove Sarin to seek the versis. The primus suspected Sarin of seeking forbidden means to his ambition. He disappeared for months at a time, refusing to answer any questions about his whereabouts upon his return."

Luis turned away, ending the conversation, but the idea of the versis nagged at Errol. Somewhere in the jumble of everything that had occurred in the past few months, something nagged at him. Someone, or something, had tracked him across the entire kingdom no matter how fast he'd traveled.

What could do such a thing, if not a versis?

Errol returned to the arched workroom of the conclave. At the table set aside for his use, he considered the piece of limestone. Questions bounced around his mind like minnows darting through the depths of a pool. Something hunted him, but in the hunting, they'd left a clue to their power.

If only he could reason it out.

An hour later, the rock, uncarved and uncut, remained in his hand as his ignorance mocked him. His instincts told him he was on the right track. He knew it. Yet he lacked the background knowledge to make sense of what was happening. The gaps in his understanding frustrated him. With reluctance, he slid from his stool to remove the heavy blue canvas smock and exit the workroom. Errol took his staff and went in search of the conclave library and Master Quinn. He found the stork-like man submerged in a rack of scrolls, mumbling over a yellowed parchment. Errol sighed. The master was unlikely to appreciate an interruption.

"Master Quinn?"

No response.

"Master Quinn, I have a question."

The white-haired man raised his hand in a request for quiet. After a moment, he lifted his head. "Fascinating. Absolutely fascinating. I can't remember why I came in here, but I found the most amazing treatise on the implications of varying wood grain on lot accuracy."

Errol managed not to roll his eyes. Just.

"Can you show me where I can find all the scrolls on the versis, Master Quinn?"

The old man's attention had already returned to his study. He waved his hand toward a high bookcase on his right. "The scrolls and codex are arranged by date and name. Look for Dieter Klose. Year 1557, I think."

A half hour later, his eyes watery from the disturbed dust, Errol's fist closed in triumph around a large codex bound in brass and leather. With a soft clatter he deposited the book on an empty table as close to Master Quinn as he dared. He still lacked confidence in his reading and wanted to be near the master in case he needed to ask for help.

His fears were well-founded. From the very first page, it became obvious that Klose had enjoyed the finest education in the kingdom. His command of language and the technical terms he used to describe the minutiae of the casting process befuddled Errol. After he sought Quinn for the fifth time, his finger pressed on the codex under yet another indecipherable word, the master huffed his displeasure and led him to a large set of curved bookcases that formed the center of the library.

He pointed. "This is the core section. Here you will find reference tomes that will provide you with the definitions of the terms we use in our work." Quinn pulled out a well-worn volume and shoved it against Errol's chest. "As well as a general-purpose dictionary that was used during Klose's time." He plopped a dusty volume onto the first.

Errol sneezed.

"Now, please let me read," Quinn said.

Errol retreated with his books to the table to try to puzzle meaning from Dieter Klose's writings. For hours he slogged through it until his eyes blurred from the strain and his head hurt. Errol reached out and lifted the pages he'd read, pinching them together to see how far he'd come and how far he had to go.

He sighed. Over three-fourths of the volume remained and he wasn't even sure if Klose's book held the information he needed. Outside, the sun dipped toward the western horizon. Errol left the books on the table, marking his spot and signing his name on the sheet to notify the keeper not to return them to their shelves.

28

RIDDLES FROM THE PAST

FOR DAYS Errol followed the routine laid out for him by the king, the primus, and the archbenefice. He served in his capacity as staff instructor for the watch in the morning hours, walked as bait through the halls of the palace complex at the prescribed times, and spent the remainder of his time learning the craft of a reader.

This morning, like the others before it, he searched the crowd around the barracks courtyard for the shine of sun-blond hair that belonged to Adora. After a moment in which only less-inspiring shades were visible, he found it. As always, it framed a face of delicate features and deep green eyes. A sprinkling of freckles dotted her nose. She sat with her cousin Lady Edara, Lord Weir, and two other girls, fanning herself and watching the young nobles in their instruction. His heart leapt and fell at the instant of her sighting, thrilled to see her but filled as well with hopelessness.

Even had he not been a peasant, however temporarily elevated, he knew nothing about how to approach a young noblewoman. The rudiments of courtship remained unknown to him. Adora and her friends used their fans to communicate as often as they spoke, and their table had become an aviary of brightly colored visitors. For some reason he couldn't discern, the women surrounding the courtyard seemed particularly attentive this morning, eager. Even Weir, whose dislike for him intensified daily, looked with anticipation toward the sparring ground.

Captain Reynald strode from the depth of the barracks, his face wreathed in a smile of anticipation. "Errol, we have a treat this morning—a new sparring partner for you."

Errol turned to see Liam at Reynald's side, holding a practice sword and dressed in black. Liam had joined the watch. His fellow villager came forward, smiled in welcome, and held out his hand. "Errol, it's good to see you. They told me you'd survived Windridge, but seeing the news confirmed is a pleasure."

He shook hands. Over the expanse of Liam's shoulder, he could see women on the edge of the courtyard leaning forward—their gazes riveted to Liam, and their fans moving now to dissipate a momentary heat instead of communicating. Of course. Liam always had that effect on women. With chagrin, Errol noted that even Adora gazed at him.

"Liam bested me eight times out of ten yesterday," Reynald said. "I promised him a more suitable opponent today."

Liam gave him a warm, sincere smile. "I understand I wasn't the only one who bested the watch. Your exploits with the staff are on everyone's lips, Errol."

With a twinge of disappointment, Errol realized Liam meant every word. Human foibles such as jealously and envy were beneath and beyond him. A small voice told Errol that was only as it should be. The king should be the best. Errol started at the realization he would be sparring with the future king. Mistakes happened during bouts. Swords splintered and staffs broke, exposing dangerous, even deadly, points.

The kingdom couldn't afford such an accident. Not with Liam.

Captain Reynald's hand dropped. From the first, it became apparent to Errol that he would not be able to wear Liam down as he had Weir. The sword streaked toward him as if Liam had cast a lightning bolt. The future king's strength meant even the slightest twitch of his wrist sent the staves leaping at him.

The staff and the sword buzzed and hissed through the air as stroke met counterstroke. Errol's concern for Liam vanished as he moved. Glimmers of thought flashed through his mind, but one stood out from the others. Liam was better than Skorik.

Had they fought a month or even as recently as two weeks ago, Errol would have lost, but constant use with the staff had honed his abilities to a razor's edge. Another thought came to him: his skill matched Liam's. True, he could find no opening in the man's defenses, but neither had Liam been able to land a blow.

Back and forth they moved across the courtyard, blows moving faster than thought. Then, so slight that it might not have been there, Liam's foot slipped, and for the merest fraction of an instant his balance suffered.

An opening appeared. It would take a combination of blows to exploit, but it was there. Errol would win. For the first time in his life, he had the chance to be better at something than Liam.

And that was enough.

He stepped back, grounding his staff and sucking air into his burning lungs.

Liam stopped, a grin splitting his face under thick blond hair. He bowed. "I think I need to practice my footwork."

"Magnificent!" Reynald crowed, slapping them each on the back in turn. He looked over at the assembled nobles and laughed. "And totally useless from an instructional standpoint. Yon nobles doubtless were unable to follow your bout. I could barely follow it myself.

"Let that be a lesson to you both. Battles can turn on the smallest of incidents. The next time it may be you, Errol, whose footing is less than perfect." He nodded toward the onlookers. "Come. Let us see if any of them have the skill to understand what they've seen."

A score of gazes swept across him before settling on Liam as they approached.

A woman with olive-tinged skin and dark, limpid eyes, seemingly overwhelmed, pressed herself against Liam in admiration. "You were magnificent." She gushed with praise. "Tell me, are you yet betrothed?"

Liam's mouth worked, but no words came out. A slender girl with the reddish tint to her hair that proclaimed her Erinon heritage, pressed against him on the other side. She regarded the first girl with undisguised venom. "That was tactless, Liselle." She brushed Liam's hair back from his shoulder. Her hand returned to caress his cheek. "My name is Kyra. How can it be that you are not yet a captain of the watch, milord?"

Liam tried to back away. "Um, I . . . That is . . ." He cast a look of desperation Errol's way.

"You might have to use your weapon to clear a path," Errol said. The women clustered around Liam sniffed in disdain at Errol's laughter and renewed their intimate admiration of Liam.

Lord Weir shouldered a blond-haired beauty aside to approach. "Why did you stop?" Weir asked Liam. His voice sounded polite, almost deferential. "You seemed on the verge of giving the runt the beating he deserves."

Liam's expression never changed, but he shook his head in disagreement. "Errol had me beat, even if it wasn't obvious to all."

"Pah!" Weir said. "I saw the peasant back off in the middle of your bout, nothing more."

Reynald stepped forward. "Then you still have much to learn. Perhaps you'd care to come out to the courtyard and allow Errol to give you more instruction?"

Weir flushed. "I have no intention of giving some peasant with a grudge an excuse to attack his better." He turned, knocking over a chair, and left. A pair of men followed, but the women remained, clustering more tightly around Liam.

Errol moved away from the spectacle to retrieve his cloak and knobblocks. He turned to find Adora considering him, her green eyes intent and curious.

"Is it true that you're both from the same village?" she asked.

He nodded, not trusting himself to speak without his voice cracking like an adolescent. His heart should have begun slowing by then, but for some reason it continued to race. "We've known each other since we were children." He looked over to where Liam floundered, beset by the women who surrounded him. "He's always had that effect on women." Errol laughed and shrugged. "Can't say as I blame them. He's as near to perfect as a man can be."

"Really?" Adora asked. Her lips pressed together in a tight smile.

"Yes, my lady. Liam is good at everything, and not just good, the best. He's more of a god than a man."

She tilted her head to one side. "But you defeated him just now. Doesn't that make you the better fighter?" The lilt of her voice, an Erinon accent, gave her words an almost musical quality.

Errol laughed. Honesty compelled him to shake his head. "There's a lot of difference between a bout and a fight, my lady. Unfortunately, I've been in too many of both lately. Bouts are nice, clean, and they stop when a man is down. Battle is something else altogether—messy, bloody, unpredictable. You can't judge by a bout. Any man who thinks he can is a fool. Truthfully, if I were going into battle, I'd want Liam at my side."

"You're a strange man."

Adora's frank assessment left him speechless. He gaped.

The king's niece slipped her fan from one sleeve and tapped her right ear with it before snapping it open to fan herself in slow, measured strokes.

With a flush, he raised his hand to stop her. "Your Highness, Weir is right; I am just a peasant. I've heard of the fan language. I even saw it once on the way to Erinon, but I don't know what you're saying and I wouldn't want to embarrass either of us by pretending otherwise."

The fan disappeared back up her sleeve. "You may say whatever you wish, Errol Stone, but you're not *just* a peasant. My uncle taught me nobility comes from the heart, not the blood." She glanced over her shoulder at the press that still surrounded Liam before regarding him again with those impossibly green eyes. "Not every woman desires perfection."

She turned away, left him staring at her back.

⚜

Later that afternoon, he pored over his work in the conclave library, scanning his book for some clue to the creation of the versis. Time after time, his thoughts wandered from Klose's dry pronunciations to consider a cascade of golden hair and a pair of green eyes. He turned the page with a profound lack of motivation when a word in the middle of the second paragraph caught his attention.

Omne.

Bending forward, he dove into the text, reading and rereading until he felt confident in his conclusion. After the fourth time through, doubt and mistrust filled him. Was it possible that Luis had never read this particular text? Did the secondus not know the capabilities that Klose ascribed to an omne?

No, of course he knew.

Why had Luis concealed Errol's abilities? If Klose's speculation was true, if Errol could create a versis, they would be able to find their enemies. If they asked their questions carefully, they would even be able to determine exactly how to defeat them.

Why wouldn't the secondus want to find out if an omne, if Errol, could create the versis?

Errol gritted his teeth and, carrying the book with him, went in search of Luis.

He found him in his private workroom, black gloves on his hands, polishing a durastone lot. As soon as he saw Errol, he locked the lot in its cabinet and returned to his seat.

Without a word, Errol place the codex on the table and pointed to the passage.

Luis nodded, his face somber. "I had hoped you would never find it."

"Why did you lie to me?"

The secondus's eyebrows rose. "Lie? I didn't lie, Errol. I merely withheld information I thought to be harmful to you."

His surprise must have shown. Luis slipped off his stool, moved to one of the cabinets that lined the room, pulled a key from his pocket, and opened the thick mahogany door. He returned to the table cradling a book stuffed with loose pages in his arms. He flipped it open to a spot marked with a peacock feather and extracted a single page.

"As soon as I found out you'd survived, I came back to the library and removed every book I could find that mentioned the omne. I didn't count on Master Quinn's prodigious memory. This is a list of every omne that's ever served the conclave." He slid the sheet across the table toward Errol.

His eyes ran down the list, at first with interest, but skimming toward the end. Names comprised a column down the left-hand side with dates of birth and death noted out to the right. "I don't understand. What's the point?"

Luis's mouth compressed into a thin line, and his brows furrowed. He looked like a man who'd eaten something sour. "Look at the dates."

Errol did so. It took him a few minutes to realize the pattern, and a quick scan confirmed—not one omne in the last thousand years had lived past thirty-five.

"That's right," Luis said. "They all died early. Many died and left the kingdom without an omne." He shook his head. "The kingdom suffers in such times. Without an omne to verify the casts of the conclave, there is much opportunity for deception."

"How?" He suspected the answer already, but he wanted, needed, to hear Luis confirm it.

"Some died of natural causes or an enemy's attack, but the rest went insane trying to create the versis." He shook his head. "I think Deas reserves that power for himself."

He shook his head. That couldn't be right. "Someone has done it. They tracked me across the entire kingdom. Night or day, they knew where I was."

Luis nodded. "It does seem like a plausible explanation, but I don't think our enemies hold a versis. Their moves are at once too powerful and too weak to be explained by such. Consider . . . if they held such power, they could simply inquire as to the perfect time, place, and method to kill you, Liam, and the rest of us. No. If they'd managed to create a universal lot, the coming war would be lost already.

"Yet, you are right in that the precision and timing of their knowledge concerning your movements goes beyond what is currently possible in the conclave." His shoulders hunched as if he squirmed under the weight of his ignorance. "I can only conclude that they have made some discovery that surpasses the knowledge of the conclave."

"How come I've never heard of the Merakhi or the Morgols casting lots?"

Luis stood. "They do not. Those they find with the talent are turned toward a different craft." He spat the last word. "Ghost-walkers. The kingdom has enemies without and within."

Reticence marked the secondus's speech, his answers were uncharacteristically brief, and though he appeared relaxed, he seldom met Errol's gaze, finding, it seemed, one plausible reason or another to look elsewhere.

A sudden thought occurred to him. "If you and the primus don't want me to create a versis, what do you want?"

Luis eyes were intent, belying his relaxed pose at the table. "No more than what you've already proven you can do, Errol. Read others' lots."

"You think there's a traitor in the conclave."

The secondus turned away to fold his sanding cloth. "I acknowledge the probability, though I hope to be proven wrong."

"Why not cast for it?" Errol asked.

Luis laughed ruefully. "We have tried, and not only with the conclave. Remember that the question frames the answer. It is possible that we have not asked the correct question." He sighed. "Yet I think it more likely that those who are working to our downfall do not see themselves as traitors, but as saviors of the kingdom. The question, as of yet, cannot be cast. However, since you can read any lot, you might be able to discover those in our midst who seek to do us harm."

"When do you want me to start?"

"As soon as you complete your basic training with Quinn. Your movements will be easier to explain once you have done so." He rose. "I must see Martin on a matter. I will speak to Master Quinn and have him instruct you on what is possible and what is not for a reader." He gave a rueful smile. "I think his answer will be longer than you want, but Master Quinn is nothing if not thorough."

Before Errol could say or ask anything more, Luis was gone.

He stared at the place where Luis had been, turning the conversation with the reader over in his head. Nothing Luis said spoke of deceit or dissembling, but he sensed Luis and Martin still held something from him, and it gnawed at him. But what could it be? He had already surprised them into as much as admitting Liam would be king.

What was left to hide?

He took his staff, and strode through the dim halls of the conclave, heading for the barracks. His steps echoed strangely, and he walked another ten paces before it dawned on him that the watchmen who normally accompanied him in the passageways were absent. Perhaps Cruk and Reynald had given up on luring the demon spawn into attacking him. It had, after all, been over a week since the last attack and no sign of ferrals or the abbot of Windridge had been seen or heard.

What would they do now? King Rodran, the archbenefice, and the primus seemed content to bide their time and wait for their enemies to make their next move. To Errol it felt as if they waited for the headsman's axe to fall. With a twitch of his shoulders, he dismissed the matter from his mind. Nothing he could do would change events, and it seemed unlikely that the powers that ruled the kingdom would take him into their confidence.

He passed a group of monks, their shuffling gait barely intruding on his thoughts.

A whiff of corruption warned him.

He faced them, brought his staff up as clawed hands ripped off robes and charged. Mouths opened to reveal jagged teeth under eyes that looked too human to belong in those beast-like faces.

Eyes filled with bloodlust and madness.

The five demon spawn came flooding toward him without a sound. Errol watched as they spread along the hall, dropping to all fours. There were too many.

He filled his lungs. "Guards! Guards!"

They were on him.

The end of his staff took the first spawn in the throat, but as soon as the creature dropped, another took its place. Errol spun, caught another in the shoulder with the knobblock, but the thing shrugged off the blow and leapt at him.

Teeth sank into his right leg, and he howled in pain. He ducked one spawn and clubbed another. Then he thrust the end of his staff into the face of the creature on his leg.

It wouldn't let go.

Jaws clamped around his arm.

He couldn't fight.

Heavy paws hit him in the chest, and he fell backward. His head struck the granite stones of the floor. The last sound he heard before darkness took him was the ring of bared steel.

⁂

Errol swam toward consciousness, fighting to wake against a tide of pain that seemed to come from everywhere. He fought to push himself off the stone even as a weight against his chest forced him back down.

"Stop!" a voice thundered. "You'll bleed to death. Be still."

He lay back down, working to open his eyes. When at last he managed to force his lids open, the hall swam as though he peered through rushing water.

"Who?" he asked.

"Liam," a voice answered. A hint of blue eyes and blond hair swam in his vision. "Lie still," he commanded.

Pressure on his wounds made him cry out. Oblivion called to him, promising an end to the pain. He drifted to it.

"Stay with us, boy," a voice snarled. Cruk. Fingers pried his lids open and the watchman's lumpy face filled his vision.

Footsteps pounded down the hall, and men carried him while Liam and Cruk kept pressure on the worst of his wounds. They carted him, ignoring his moans and curses past the barracks to the castle infirmary where four men took him and laid him on a slab of stone. Someone forced a thick syrup of bitter-tasting potion down his throat.

Everything faded.

⟡

Consciousness returned so gradually that he found himself staring across the sheets at the people who surrounded him without realizing he'd awakened. Luis, Martin, and the primus occupied chairs at the foot of his bed, their faces wan in the fading light that suffused the room. Of Liam and Cruk there was no sign.

He wanted to speak, but the effort made his head swim.

Men he didn't recognize came to stand over him, their faces serious, grave. "You've lost a lot of blood. We've slowed the bleeding, but by the best of our art, we can only slow it." He looked Errol in the eye. "Do you understand what I'm saying?"

Errol nodded. "I'm dying," he whispered.

The healer nodded. "These wounds are beyond our ability to heal. We've never seen their like before. If only we could stop the bleeding . . ." He moved away.

Errol's eyelids closed, burdened by the weight of his blood

loss. His thoughts seemed slow to come to him, as if they kept time to the sluggish beat of his heart.

Bleeding. What did Adele and Radere give for bleeding? There had been a boy in his village, Corwin, who had bleeder's disease. At his birth, a midwife told his parents he wouldn't make it past his first year, but the herbwomen scoffed at the prediction.

Something. They had given him something to make his flesh and blood knit more quickly. It almost made him normal.

What was it?

So hard to think. He beckoned to Luis, the barest crook of a finger that felt as though he'd lifted the world. The reader stood by his bedside without apparent transition. Errol hadn't seen him move.

"Urticweed," he whispered.

Luis straightened. "Urticweed. Do you have any?"

"It's not an herb we use," the first healer said. "I don't know."

"Well, find out, man. We're losing him."

Boots pounded away.

The pain from his wounds faded from his awareness and he floated. Later, he coughed as warm liquid coursed down his throat. He tried turning his head. The fools were trying to drown him.

Hands held his head steady, and voices urged him to drink, to hang on. Hang on to what? He couldn't find an answer to the question. Darkness took him.

29

TRACKS

HE WOKE, light-headed and hungry. Darkness filled the room, relieved only by the flickering of candles placed at regular intervals in the sconces along the wall. Thick bandages covered one arm and both his legs, exerting pressure on his wounds.

The pain in his arms and legs had subsided, and the temptation to move his limbs beckoned to him. Errol lifted his head to see Luis slumped in a chair at the foot of his bed, head lolling to one side.

"Luis."

The secondus stirred and, seeing Errol awake, raised himself, rubbing the back of his neck with one hand. "How are you, boy?"

Errol shrugged. Nothing hurt overly much, which he took to be a good sign. "I don't seem to be dead."

Luis smiled. "You have keen powers of observation."

The wall of secrets between them still stood, but Luis seemed relieved. Errol took a deep breath. It would have to be enough. Perhaps in time he would be able to figure out what, exactly, Luis and Martin kept hidden from him. "How am I?"

"The urticweed saved your life. The healers have been dosing you with it at every opportunity. I think they'll want to talk to you as soon as you feel up to it. They have a newfound respect for herb lore, it seems. Your wounds finally stopped bleeding and your flesh seems to be knitting fairly well. They want to keep you here until you've recovered some of your strength."

"Why?"

Luis frowned, his dark eyebrows coming together, shadowing his eyes in the dim light. "They want to keep you from tearing your wounds open and bleeding to death. Healers hate that sort of thing."

"No, why do they keep attacking me, in spite of my fighting them off?" He watched Luis's face as the secondus pondered the question, searching for any sign of untruth or dissembling.

The reader leaned forward, resting his elbows on his knees. "It is as the archbenefice said, they sense some threat in you."

Errol laughed, his mirth sounding like a sigh of wind. "You give me thoughtful answers that don't tell me anything, Luis. Tell me, how many attacks have come against Liam since Windridge?"

Luis leaned back, his face impassive.

"If you don't answer, Luis, I will simply ask Liam the next time I see him. He'll tell me. He's incapable of lying."

The sound of a sigh ghosted to him. "You're right, of course. The truth is he has not been attacked—none of us has been. Only you and certain readers of the conclave have been targeted, and only you have survived. Yet, Liam has been surrounded by men, offering little opportunity for the enemy to strike."

The long familiar stab of jealousy struck Errol again at the mention of Liam's name, but time and circumstances had served to lessen its impact. Memory came to him then. "What did the Merakhi mean when she called him *soteregia*?"

Luis grew still. "It's an old word, so old that most people would no longer know its meaning, though the tongue is ours. It means savior and king. Since the time of Magis, every king of Illustra has borne the title of Soteregia. The word is engraved across the royal seal."

It made sense. Liam would be the savior and king of Illustra. He searched the ward. A healer's assistant, tall and clothed in white, stood by the entrance, too far away to hear their conversation.

"Is that the question you spent the last five years casting?"

Luis nodded. "It's practically all I've thought of for that time." He laughed, and a network of wrinkles made crow's-feet around his brown eyes. Light from candles danced from the smooth dome of his bald head. "I'm looking forward to the day when I can concentrate on something else."

"But if Liam is so important, why do they keep attacking me?"

"It is impossible to know what is behind their actions." The reader's face stretched in a rueful grimace. "We don't even know who our enemies are. More, we can't be certain how much knowledge of you and Liam they possess. They know you can defend yourself—else they would not have risked sending five ferrals to attack you. They know your village of birth, and by now they must know that you are attached to the conclave. I pray they do not know you are an omne, but the possibility cannot be discounted.

"Yet I think our enemy knows something about you that we do not, something beyond even your ability as an omne." He pulled at his jaw, and his eyes focused somewhere above Errol's head. "It may be that they cast against their greatest threat and determined it was you. If that is so, then they may not know exactly what makes you dangerous to them and they simply seek to kill you. In truth, their inability to see Liam as a threat is just as troubling. Either our craft has betrayed us or there is a power at work we do not understand.

"I must ask your pardon, Errol, and I think Martin seeks your forgiveness as well. We underestimated the determination of the enemy and so thought you would be safe with a pair of the watch to guard you. In that, we were wrong."

The mention of the watchmen who had trailed him for days

waiting for just such an attack prompted him. "What of the guards? They were not with me when I was attacked."

Luis shook his head. "Once you were moved to the infirmary, Cruk went in search of them. I have never seen him so angry. I think he meant to convey his displeasure at their failure with some physical demonstration.

"What he found shook him." He lowered his gaze until he looked Errol in the eyes. "Your guards are dead, taken by surprise. They raised no alarm. Their throats were torn out."

Errol's vision swam and he slept.

⚜

A bar of slowly moving sunlight moving across his face woke him. He thought of food first. His next thought was an awareness of Adora seated in a chair by his bed. As before, her presence fuddled him, and he felt an odd comfort in the knowledge that he couldn't trip over his own feet there in the infirmary.

"How . . ." he started and then thought better of it. "What's the hour?"

Her hair caught a shaft of sunlight and held it. "It's midmorning." She smiled, and her green eyes shone. "My uncle has forbidden disclosure of your attack. He doesn't want to alarm the people, but I overheard two of the watch talking and thought you might want something better to eat than the food the healers offer."

She lifted a cloth from the tray. The aroma of food flooded over him, and his stomach growled. Adora laughed. "I think I came just in time." Placing the tray on his lap, she handed him a fork and knife.

Errol looked at the utensils, his face burning. "Your Highness . . ."

"Adora," she corrected.

He nodded. "A-dora." His lips stumbled over her name as if he had never heard or thought it before. "I'm unfamiliar with the manners of court. I would ask your pardon if my ways seem offensive."

She straightened, and her posture and tone became formal. "Errol Stone, you will not offend me unless you continue to think that I would place so high a value on such things."

"Thank you, Your Highness . . . uh, Adora." Grabbing his fork and knife, he proceeded to attack the mountain of food on the tray.

"I thought that since you needed time to eat without the burden of questions, I could teach you the basics of the fan language." She smiled. "Would you like that?"

He nodded.

She pulled a blue-and-green fan out of her sleeve and, with a well-practiced flick of her wrist, snapped it open and began fanning herself. "If a woman fans herself slowly, it means she is at peace with herself and those around her." The fan moved more quickly. "This means she is agitated with her present company and desires them to leave."

Errol swallowed. "What about the signal you gave me at the courtyard."

Adora's cheeks pinked, but she gave no other sign that his question bothered her. "This . . ." She tapped the fan against her ear and ran it along her jaw. "I was telling you that I would like to talk with you sometime." She dropped her gaze. "It was an improper thing to say to someone I'd never met before. My mother always told me I spoke my mind too quickly." She moved to make another motion with the fan.

"I saw you in the city the day I arrived," Errol said.

Her fan stopped, obscuring half her face. "I often visit the shops." Adora's tone created distance between them.

Errol pressed on anyway. "Is a healer's shop among them? I passed one on the way in. I have heard that lemongrass makes soulsease tea a little easier to drink."

The princess dropped her fan, scanned the infirmary before speaking. "Please don't tell anyone, Errol. Uncle would be furious."

"I won't. Why do you do it?"

She shrugged. "Sometimes I do it to pick up information

that I think Uncle needs to know. Most courtiers never leave the palace. The only reports we get from the city are from the guard. Mostly I do it because the people of Erinon need help. Nobody in the palace really needs me, but they do."

A weight in his gut forced the next question from his lips. "Did you come to see me for the same reason you go to Healer Norv's?"

She gave a small shake of her head, her hair flaring in the light. "No."

"Then why are you here?" he asked.

"To bring you food and teach you the fan language."

He shook his head. "The infirmary would feed me, though not half so well, and though I appreciate your company, it is unlikely that I will ever need to know the fan language." At the risk of driving her away, he repeated his question. "Why are you here?"

Her eyes darkened from the shade of spring to that of storm-tossed seas. "I told you before that not all women seek perfection. I saw the mercy you gave Weir at our first meeting—mercy he didn't deserve—and recognized something rare in you. As for the fan language . . ." She snapped hers shut and rose to leave. "You may be surprised by what you may need to know in the future."

⚜

Errol passed the next two days in the infirmary, eating and drinking as much food and water as he could cram down. On the third day he woke to the sound of panic—clipped voices shouted instructions. Healers and guards swarmed into the infirmary.

One of the healers waved his arms. "Cots! And clear out the next ward. Get these men down and get as much water into them as you can." A flood of pale-faced guards, some being carried, others shambling, came into the ward.

Errol levered himself out of bed, did his best to ignore the way the room swam when he moved. Leaning on his staff, he tugged the sleeve of the nearest healer. "Put one of them here."

The man gave him a considering look, then called instructions. Two orderlies deposited a guard still wearing the red livery of his station into the bed. The man's eyes fluttered against flushed cheeks and he shook as if chilled.

"What happened?" Errol shouted to the healer who'd tended him, hunted for the man's name. "Healer Ian, what happened?"

Tall, with blond hair and a ruddy complexion, the healer snapped a quick instruction before answering. "Food poisoning. If we don't get water into these men, we're going to start losing them."

Errol shouted to be heard above the clamor. "Bad food or poison in the food?"

Ian Thorsund shook his head.

Alarm surged through him. The enemy's noose around the island tightened inexorably. What could he do that they wouldn't expect?

Errol staggered his way through the press of incoming healers and sick and stepped out of the infirmary. At the entrance, six watchmen stepped away from the wall and formed a protective ring around him. The polished wood of his staff burdened him even without the weight of the knobblocks, and he used it as a walking stick. Its clack as he worked his way back to the conclave echoed hollowly. None of the king's guard patrolled the halls.

The sounds of strident voices, the sound of panic, splintered the air. What could he do? Lieutenant Garrigus, the officer he'd fought when he first arrived, headed the detail charged with keeping him safe in the hallways.

The hallways.

A flash of insight jolted him where he stood. He grabbed the shoulder of the nearest guard to steady himself and turned to Garrigus. "Lieutenant, I mean to search the rooms of Sarin Valon, and I won't be asking permission. If you have any objection, you're welcome to safeguard anything I remove from there until we can get it to the primus. Is this acceptable?"

A moment passed as they walked together. The lieutenant's

lips pursed in thought. At last he nodded. "As far as the watch is concerned, you have the authority of a captain. How are you regarded in the conclave?"

He laughed. "To Master Quinn, I am the newest and lowliest apprentice, an ignorant boy who asks too many questions. I have no authority in the conclave to commandeer the belongings of Sarin Valon."

The lieutenant smiled, showing even, white teeth. "If trouble comes of it, I will simply say I was afraid of another beating if I disobeyed you."

Errol smiled in surprise. "Thank you, though if it comes to it, I think you'll be hard-pressed to convince anyone of that. Right now, I'm doing well to keep moving." As if to prove his point, sweat beaded on his forehead and his breathing became labored.

"Perhaps we should stop for a rest, Captain."

"No. I must look at Sarin's room now, before the turmoil dies down."

The trip from the infirmary to the second level of the conclave left him pale and shaking. He stumbled at the landing and only the lieutenant's quick grab of Errol's elbow kept him upright. Sarin's door was the third on the left, broad and carved of a deep red wood polished to almost mirror brightness. Errol's reflection looked back at him in lurid detail, giving him a deathly cast.

The door was locked.

"Force it," Errol said.

The lieutenant nodded to one of his men, a thick-bodied Bellian that reminded Errol of Sven. The sharp retort of wood splintering sounded through the hallway, but no one came to investigate.

Sarin's rooms were large and spacious with a broad fireplace in the sitting room and a bedroom and library on one side. The other side held a private workroom.

In the middle of the sitting room, a large, irregular black stain marred the floor. Errol pointed to it. "Is that where they found the body?"

"Yes."

Errol stared at the irregular discoloration on the floor as if it held the answer to his questions. "How many of the readers were killed in their rooms?"

The lieutenant squinted at him. "Only Sarin Valon."

Errol faced the watchmen and pointed. "I want four guards at the door, swords ready. The lieutenant will accompany me throughout Sarin's quarters. If we find anything of import, we will leave and go directly to the primus."

He forced his steps into the library. Books and scrolls filled the shelves. A thin layer of dust covered each volume. Errol examined a sampling of Valon's library, starting each at the beginning until he determined the subject matter. After half an hour he turned and led the way to the workroom.

Implements of every conceivable shape and size filled the space. Stone and wood blanks formed a neat stack against one wall. Errol took time to sort through some of them, curious. Wood and stone of types he had never before seen were mixed among more common types. A line of cabinets lined the opposite wall.

He tried one door after another. Without exception, they were all locked. "Lieutenant, would you open these cabinets? I doubt I have the strength for it at present."

The sounds of splintering wood filled the apartment as Lieutenant Garrigus systematically forced the paneled doors. Errol stepped forward, raising himself on tiptoes to peer into the first cabinet.

His breath caught.

Never in his life or dreams had he seen so many lots together in one place. Why, in the first cabinet alone there must have been hundreds, stacked to fill the space like so much cordwood. Polished wood of a dozen varieties gleamed, mixed with shining stone spheres that reflected the light in glittering hues. He moved to the next cabinet. It was the same, and the one after, and the one after that.

Whatever Sarin's killer had been after, it hadn't been these lots.

Errol moved back to the first cabinet and cautiously extended his hand to select a lot from the top. He gave a small chuckle, envisioning the chaos that would ensue if he took one from the bottom of the pile. Lots would cascade from the cabinet in a clatter that would last for several minutes and take an hour to clean up.

He held the sphere, an orange-hued polished maple lot, up to the light. The perfection of it made the pine lots he'd carved for Naaman Ru seem coarse in comparison. Conscious of Garrigus watching him, he assayed an attempt at conversation. "Amazing, aren't they?"

The lieutenant shrugged. "One looks much like another to me, a child's toy."

Errol laughed at that. "I used to play stones in my village, but we never had anything as perfect as these." He would have said more, but at that moment, the light caught on letters, and he stopped, his mouth open and his words dying on his tongue.

Sarin had sought the versis. Quinn had said so; old, eccentric Quinn, who looked upon Errol as just another apprentice; Quinn, who had no reason to lie.

Errol continued to turn the lot, looking for any other writing, testing his suspicions. *There.* He turned abruptly. "Lieutenant, find something we can use to transport lots. Something large. I have the feeling there will be others."

Garrigus's presence receded from Errol's awareness. Only the cabinets and their contents existed for him now. He took the next lot and held it to the light, his movements quick and precise. Two words gleamed, the same two words as before. He tossed the lot to the surprised lieutenant, who entered the room holding a large cloth square that looked to have been cut from Sarin's sheets. Before the lot landed in Garrigus's hand he'd already selected another, his heart racing and his mouth dry.

Again.

His hands shook as he pulled a fourth lot from the stack. The same two words gleamed on the polished surface as before.

Liam's name.

And his own.

His feet told him to run, find Martin, Luis, and Cruk and tell them of his find. Even now his unseen enemy might know Errol stood in Sarin's apartment. He hoped four guards would be enough to discourage attack.

He rushed to the second cabinet and grabbed a pair of lots. Turning them as fast as he dared, he searched for whatever words lay there.

When he saw them, a fist closed about his heart. *Callowford. Berea.* He thrust the lots at the lieutenant. "Here. We must hurry."

Garrigus's dark brows rose in surprise. "Why?"

"We're in danger. From the moment we entered this room." Sweat stung his eyes, and he cudgeled his mind for a decision. He longed, oh, how he longed, to remain and plumb the depth of Sarin's knowledge.

But to stay meant death.

They would have to leave, but should he take all the watchmen with him to keep safe or leave behind a guard to watch over the room and its contents? No, whoever he left behind would be dead in minutes.

Errol threw himself at the cabinets, his mind made up. He grabbed handfuls of lots from each of them and thrust them at the lieutenant. His hair stood on end, and he found himself sniffing the air, testing for the smell of filth and corruption.

He pointed toward the door. "Let's go, quickly."

As they crossed the threshold back into the hallway, Garrigus tapped him on the shoulder and nodded back toward Sarin's rooms. "Should I leave a man to guard the door?"

Errol shook his head. "Only if you mean for him to die. We're not safe here. What's the most direct route back to the barracks?"

Garrigus jerked his head to the left. "This way."

Errol turned to the four men accompanying them. "Which two of you are the fastest runners?"

The four exchanged glances and then two hands went up. "Soldiers Kernan and Torani," Garrigus said.

Errol pointed to the first man. "I want you to lead us back to the barracks. Stay fifty paces in front. If you see anyone in a cowl, yell a warning and run back to us. Don't fight; just run. Understand?"

The man's face went stiff at the mention of running, but he nodded.

Errol turned to the second man. "You'll trail us by the same amount. If anything comes up behind us, yell and join us. Six swords are better than four."

The two men moved out, and Errol tasted sweat as he waited for Kernan to take his position. A moment and a wave from the lead man later, they started. He knew it was crazy, but he couldn't seem to keep from smelling the air. Torani watched him, his face impassive as they opened up the distance behind.

Kernan rounded a distant corner, and Errol strained his ears listening for echoes of flight or conflict.

Nothing.

He found himself walking on the balls of his feet and wondering how long he would be able to run before he collapsed from exhaustion. They turned the corner to see Kernan ahead of them, walking with the calm assurance of one of the watch, checking each cross corridor as he came to the intersection, before moving on.

Errol exhaled and rolled his shoulders to ease the cramp between them. Perhaps he'd been worried about nothing.

"FLY!"

Torani's scream filled his ears. Footsteps pounding stone sounded behind him.

And the snarls of ferrals.

Errol forced his legs into motion. Fresh sweat burst from him, stinging his eyes. Abruptly, the sounds behind him grew louder and he turned to see Torani flying, his cloak billowing behind.

And then, twenty paces behind, came a wave of ferrals, low and running on all fours.

"How . . . far to the . . . exit?" Errol panted. He could barely breathe.

"Two more hallways," the lieutenant said.

A scream of defiance sounded from behind.

Errol stumbled as he looked over his shoulder. Torani had turned, swinging wildly with his sword, trying to slow the tide of ferrals, attempting to hold them at bay.

Selling his life dear.

The ferrals bayed and howled as they swarmed Torani under, but yips of pain mixed with the snarls, and the wave slowed.

The lieutenant tapped a man as they ran, and he slowed to take up a rearguard.

"No," Errol said. "We fight together. Do you hear me, Garrigus?"

The man paused, looked at Garrigus. The lieutenant jerked his thumb back behind them and with a curt nod, the soldier dropped back.

"Our orders come from Captain Reynald. Keep you safe at all cost," Garrigus said.

They ran on. Tears blurred his vision as the sound of whistling steel and snapping jaws came to him. Garrigus tapped another guard, and again, one of the watch drifted back to slow the attack.

They rounded a corner. There at the far end of the hall, a broad set of stairs led to the exit. Errol stumbled. Hands on either side of him held him up, propelled him forward.

Another watchman's defiant screams filled the hall until they cut off in a bubbling gasp.

He half fell, half ran down the stairs, making for the courtyard. Kernan waited for them at the bottom. As they passed through the door, Garrigus signaled the last two soldiers. They exited, then turned to hold the door closed, bracing it with their shoulders.

"Guards!" Garrigus screamed. "Guards!"

They ran on, the lieutenant screaming for the rest of the watch the whole way.

By ones and twos, black-garbed watchmen and red-liveried palace guards joined them, drawn by the alarm. With curt gestures, Garrigus dispatched the men to assist Kernan and posted a ring of steel a dozen strong around Errol.

Errol drew breath against the spots swimming in his vision. "Sarin's rooms," he said to the lieutenant. "We must have them." Then he passed out.

30

SECRETS

H E WOKE not in the infirmary but in Luis's rooms. A whiff of acrid smoke drifted through the window. Questions filled him. He swung out of bed and stumbled into the sitting room to find Martin, Luis, and Cruk looking at him.

"The lots?" he asked.

"Safe," Luis said, "so far as the ones you took." The planes of his face hardened until they could have been stone. "Someone or something fired Sarin's rooms during the attack."

A string of curses spilled from Errol. All that effort wasted. And three of the watch sacrificed so that he could escape. He filled a goblet with water and drained it. For some reason, he couldn't seem to get enough to drink these days. He regarded the men he set out with a few months ago, time in which he'd learned to be suspicious. Why were all three of them there? And where was Liam? Illustra's future king needed to be kept under lock and key until Rodran died. Martin should be with the Judica, and Cruk should be hunting the ferrals, finding their hiding place and their master.

Errol said nothing. He'd learned to hold his tongue as well. If he asked why they all happened to be together, he would doubtless receive a very long answer that would be totally unhelpful. They wanted something from him, something more than to simply serve as bait. They must.

He refilled the goblet, stalling, thinking. "They attacked us barely an hour after I left the infirmary for Sarin's rooms."

The three nodded but didn't speak. Oh, yes, they wanted something from him. He'd be lucky if he survived. He faced Luis. "Is it possible to cast someone's thoughts or ideas if they haven't had them yet?"

The secondus shook his head. "No. And it is forbidden to try. The church does not allow divination."

"That wouldn't trouble him. Sarin is somewhere close by," Errol said.

Luis shook his head. "Sarin is dead."

"No. I read his lots. Sarin is the one who tracked me, and I think he found a way to create a versis." He waved Luis's objection away. They could argue about it later. "I decided to search Sarin's room on impulse. If they can't cast my thoughts before I have them, then they're close, very close." He turned to Martin. "Where's Liam? He's in danger."

Martin adjusted his bulk in the large, high-backed chair. "Liam returned from the chase a few hours ago. He's safe, but he lost the trail of the ferrals."

"Where are the lots I took from Sarin's room?"

At a nod from Luis, Cruk went to a large oak cabinet and retrieved a thin-walled crate filled with the lots from Sarin's cabinets. He placed it on the table with a clunk in front of Errol.

Cruk, Martin, and Luis all looked at him with interest, but did they trust him? "What oath can I take to convince you that what I'm about to tell you of these lots is the simple truth?"

Luis hung his head, trying to hide a shamefaced look. Cruk pursed his lips, but whatever emotions lurked behind the expression, Errol couldn't tell. He sat with his arms folded, a weapon to be used or directed at its target.

Martin smiled; his mouth quirked to one side in a rueful grin. "You surpass us, Errol. I believe you will give us the truth, though we cannot reciprocate if you ask."

So, it was as he suspected. "What oath can you give me that I can trust?"

The priest-now-benefice nodded. "I swear that what we do is in the best interest of the kingdom and its people."

Errol snorted. "Am I included in those people, Martin? Are you doing what is in my best interest?"

Tension spiked in the room. Cruk's hand lay closer to his hilt now.

Martin sighed. "We all must make sacrifices, Errol."

Errol laughed, but the sound became harsh in an instant as something welled up from deep within him and hot, angry tears gathered at the corners of his eyes. "I thought you were my friends. Was I ever anything more than an expendable pawn for you to use to put Liam on the throne?"

Luis and Martin turned away. Only Cruk held his gaze. "No, boy, you weren't."

For some reason this honest blow sobered Errol's emotions.

Cruk stood. "Stop feeling sorry for yourself. Do you think you're the only one who's expendable?" He moved his hand in a circle taking them all in. "We are all expendable, all of us pawns against the enemy. If Martin tells me Liam must take the throne when Rodran dies or else the kingdom is lost, then everyone else becomes secondary." He moved forward, put his hand on his shoulder. "And I am your friend."

Errol turned away, found Luis gazing at him. "He's right," the secondus said. "We are your friends. You are like an unexpected jewel, Errol, an omne of the conclave and an honorary captain of the watch. Do not think less of yourself because the kingdom's interests must take priority over yours and ours. Brave men have sacrificed themselves so that you could live. You are a great weapon against the enemy."

He turned to Martin. The old priest's brown eyes were like

chips of dark slate under his sable eyebrows. He possessed steel enough in his backbone for a dozen of the watch. The hermit who had once lived along the Sprata had been left behind. "I can't give you what you most want, Errol. I wish to Deas I could."

"And what is it you think I most want?"

Martin pulled at the muscles of his jaw. "You are looking for family, Errol. I've seen the way you look at people, boy, the way you catalog their faces, recording the details of their countenance just before you lift a hand to touch your nose or your lips or any of the other features you possess." He turned his head slowly to look at Cruk. "Luis, Cruk, and I came too late to your village. You were already an orphan by the time we arrived. We never knew what Warrel said to you as he lay dying.

"We don't know who your father is, who your parents are."

The priest's observation struck too deep for response. Errol grabbed a lot from the box and thrust it against the light, knowing what he would see as he did so. He'd read this lot in Sarin's apartments. "This one has two names on it, Liam's and mine."

He put the wooden sphere to one side, grabbed another. In his peripheral vision he saw Luis and Martin go pale.

"That's not supposed to be possible," Luis said.

"This one says the same." He grabbed another. "And this." A dark stone, nearly black, came to his hand next and he rotated it slowly against the light. Luis had recovered enough self-possession to fetch pen and paper to record what Errol saw.

"This one says *Yes*," Errol said. "And this one, *No*."

A dozen more lots composed of different stone and wood reflected the same, either *Yes* or *No*.

Martin touched Luis on the shoulder. "What does it mean?"

Luis shook his head in doubt. "I don't know. Sarin was brilliant but erratic." He pulled a frown. "Enoch says Sarin changed. He became secretive, staying in his rooms constantly toward the end, coming out only once or twice a week for more blanks before going back in."

Errol saw a pair of lots he recognized toward the bottom of the pile and pulled them out. "This one says *Callowford*." He rolled it across the table toward Luis with a negligent flip of his wrist. "And this one, *Windridge*." A push and it joined the other one.

Luis looked at him, stricken. "Sarin," he whispered.

They went through the lots one at a time. Errol read the words written there and Luis wrote them down. By the time they'd finished, every city and village Errol and Liam had traveled through filled the list. Luis no longer doubted.

Sarin lived.

"How did you know, Errol?" Martin asked.

Errol shrugged. "I didn't. I thought Sarin had created a versis and been killed for it. Then we went inside his apartments and I saw the bloodstains on the floor, and I began to suspect."

"What did that have to do with anything?" Cruk asked.

"Lieutenant Garrigus told me Sarin was the only reader killed in his room. All the rest after him were taken unawares in the hallway. Even Sarin would have enough sense to lock his door. And his face was missing. They identified his body by the rings on his fingers. I think Sarin lured someone to his apartments where the ferrals were waiting. Then he slipped out of the city."

"But he has to be close. It makes sense now. Morin knew where to send the ferrals because Sarin knew about the primus's secret hallway."

Cruk breathed an oath. "They mean to attack the palace. Most of the guards are still in the infirmary."

Luis bolted from his chair. The legs rattled on the floor. "Come, Errol. We must get to the primus. We will marshal the resources of the conclave and track Sarin down, sector by sector, and building by building." He chewed his words, biting them off in staccato bursts. "We will find that traitor and his ferrals."

"He'll know we're coming," Errol said.

Luis stopped at the door. "The conclave is still two hundred strong. We will know where he is inside the hour. It's time to show your power, Errol."

Martin and Cruk turned to follow.

The conclave assembled in the expansive workroom. Primus Sten stood leaning on his staff before the blue-robed mass of readers, snapping out commands in crisp tones. A large map of the city covered one wall, showing each section and even each building in detail. Next to it an equally impressive drawing depicted the entire island. The primus took a stick of chalk and divided the city map into quarters and with whiplike precision assigned buildings to each of the readers.

One fellow, short and thick-bodied with dark hair and a beard, called for Enoch's attention from the second row. "Primus, it will take hours to cast Sarin's hiding place."

A smile wreathed Enoch's face and he nodded assent to the reader's concern. "Then we best be about it. Quickly, gentlemen, quickly."

The men attacked a small mountain of pine cubes with their knives, and the whispers of steel against wood filled the room.

In ten minutes, a blank for every building in the city had been carved and polished. The lots were deposited in a large barrel turned on its side and mounted on an axis. Slowly, so as not to damage the wooden spheres, a reader turned the barrel. The noise of hundreds of lots banging against the sides filled the hall with thunder.

The primus turned and beckoned him with one hand. "Errol, come make the draw."

Every eye watched him as he stepped to the now-still drum and unbolted the small door built into its side. He reached in and pulled the first lot to come against his hand.

In a clear voice that could be heard throughout the hall the primus commanded him, "Read it, Errol."

The bearded reader's voice cut in. "He didn't carve any of the lots; he can't possibly read it."

The head of the conclave surveyed the waiting readers, obviously savoring the moment. "Ah, but he can."

Excited whispers filled the hall as Errol turned the lot, searching for the words he knew to be there. "Watch barracks," he said.

A short, red-haired man jumped from his seat at the back of the room and ran forward to snatch the lot from Errol's hand. With a practiced twist he rotated the pine. He gasped, the intake of his breath audible in the silence.

"It's true." He pointed at Errol, his hand trembling. "He's an omne."

The hall erupted into bedlam, and Errol found himself mobbed by men who'd barely acknowledged his existence before. Only the pounding of the primus's staff against the floor restored order.

"Gentlemen, gentlemen, please. We have work to do."

At Enoch's direction he replaced the lot and the barrel spun again. An absolute stillness enveloped the hall as two hundred readers held their collective breath when Errol moved to select again.

"The Lot and Crown," Errol said. The lot he'd drawn was linked to the largest inn the imperial city boasted, and it was not the barracks. Again one of the readers came forward to confirm his draw, but disappointment etched the pale man's face. With a sigh, he nodded after taking a brief look at the surface of the lot.

They spun the barrel eight more times at Master Quinn's behest. The intricacies of conclave protocol were under his purview and he stood at the right hand of the primus, directing the number of turns of the barrel.

Each draw produced a different lot.

The primus nodded in resignation. "They are not in the city. We must cast our net wider."

The conclave reassembled at the map of the island, where Enoch wielded his piece of chalk like a weapon, dividing the island of Erinon first into circular sections akin to those on an archer's target and then with radial lines to yield a number of arced sectors. Then he numbered each of the sections. There were fewer of these than before, so only the fastest readers crafted lots.

Once again the primus directed Errol toward the casting barrel. The lots cascaded against the hollow steel, and the sound of drumming filled the hall.

Errol reached into the darkened interior of the barrel and selected the cast. He turned it against the light, read the inscription, and held the sphere aloft. "Section seventeen."

A tall, bald man, almost gaunt, with a neatly trimmed beard stepped forward and with a slow, serious nod confirmed Errol's draw. "Ayuh," he said, drawing the word out. "That's mine."

Errol replaced the lot, and Master Quinn stepped forward to spin the barrel himself.

His fingers trembled as he loosened the access panel on the barrel and selected a lot. Errol closed his eyes and grabbed the first sphere that fell against his suddenly clammy hand. When he saw the lettering, he thrust his arm into the air, jubilation pounding in his voice. "Seventeen!"

Two hundred blue-robed readers roared their approval until the hammering of the primus's staff restored order.

He addressed the tall reader with the beard. "Adept Gregoro, please confirm the draw."

Errol surrendered the lot to the same man as before.

The nod and the smile that blossomed in the midst of his beard caused another round of cheers. Master Quinn called for silence and directed Errol to replace the sphere.

Eight more times the barrel spun.

And seven more times, section seventeen was chosen.

Cruk spoke with Luis and the primus and then left at a run.

The conclave worked at a fever pitch, narrowing the search to smaller and smaller portions of the map. And then they had the building.

According to the readers that knew the island best, Sarin hid in a large mill on the river to the north of the city. Cruk, his face serious, reappeared at Enoch's shoulder, flanked by a full eight of the watch.

"Primus, the king sends his thanks. We are ordered to attack immediately. His Majesty directs Secondus Montari and Errol Stone to accompany us." He glanced once in Errol's direction. "We don't know what we'll find, and their skills may be needed."

The old man nodded, the wisps of his silver hair waving with the motion. "Have a care, Captain," he said to Cruk. "The lad is irreplaceable."

Cruk nodded. "I'm beginning to see that." He turned to lead the way out of the conclave.

Minutes later, Errol rode Midnight at the back of a contingent of guardsmen. Five score watchmen led the procession at a gallop, followed by half of the palace guard deemed healthy enough to fight. To Errol, their numbers looked pitifully small. The jangle of tack and weapons echoed in counterpoint to the thunder of hooves, and the populace of Erinon melted out of their way as they rode north.

The affluence of the environs close to the palace faded, and within minutes large buildings, some dilapidated, surrounded them. Rats ran through the gutters, searching and feeding on garbage. They crested a small rise in the road and descended toward a large mill that backed up to the river. A succession of waterwheels turned with the swiftly flowing current, their paddles dipping and spilling with small splashing sounds.

At the front, Cruk raised his hand, then signaled left and right. The mass of soldiers split to come at the mill from two sides. A moment later he raised a fist, and men with bows fanned out to cover the river. Fifty paces from the building, they stopped, cutting off the escape of whatever men or ferrals were inside.

Nothing stirred.

Cruk dismounted and approached with a dozen of the watch. The mill stood lifeless, its interior dark through the windows and its chimneys cold. Errol held his breath as the black-clad soldiers crept toward the door.

At a signal from Cruk, a squat, black-haired watchman kicked the door in and jumped back, sword at the ready.

Nothing happened.

Backs flat against the wall with swords bared, the rest of the watch waited in the stillness. At another signal, two watchmen rushed the door, and Errol winced in preparation for the inevitable sounds of slaughter.

Nothing came.

Wary still, more of the watch entered. Now the sound of footsteps, men's footsteps, came to Errol on his mount. No snarls or growls split the air. No sounds came to them of fighting or even of traps set by a retreating enemy being sprung.

Cruk disappeared inside the mill only to reappear a moment later to wave Errol and Luis forward into the building. Errol walked Midnight to the entrance, dismounted, and entered with Luis at his side. He stopped and blinked in the gloom, waiting for his eyes to adjust to the dim interior. When he could finally see, he fought to keep his stomach from emptying.

Food troughs, not tables, stretched through the center of the room. Before he could stop himself, he looked into the nearest one. It looked as though Grub had emptied his cook pot into it, spilling stew into the rough wood. That's what it looked like, stew. Errol bent and let his stomach empty.

When nothing remained of his breakfast, he straightened, turned away from the trough, and wiped his mouth. A rumpled line of rags ten paces wide, like an oversized dog's nest, ran the length of the far wall. He shuddered to think of the number of ferrals that slept there. Dizziness struck him at the realization they'd brought six hundred men and it wouldn't have been enough.

"Errol, Luis." Cruk beckoned to them from the top of a broad set of wooden stairs. "Come," he called. "This is something you need to see, I think."

Errol followed the secondus, glad for any excuse to leave the empty ferral den behind. Watchmen held torches to light their way, but what came to him first was the smell, almost overpowering as he descended the stairs.

Pine.

And then he saw it—row upon row of squared pine billets as thick around as his arm and a dozen feet long. Uneven piles of the wood lay stacked everywhere.

Errol tugged at Luis's cloak, pointed. "To what purpose? You could make thousands of lots with this. He couldn't use up this much wood in years."

Instead of answering, Luis pulled him around by the shoulder, forcing him to look toward the far wall, toward the river where the waterwheels turned. Small mountains of sawdust filled the space. Next to each pile an axle turned, linked to its waterwheel on the far side of the wall. Curiosity pulled his feet forward. He rubbed the sawdust between his fingers, feeling the sticky texture of the powder.

Luis stood a few paces away, staring around the room as if Sarin had spelled him.

"What do you see?" Errol asked.

"It's what I'm not seeing that bothers me. Everywhere I look, there are signs of casting—sawdust, pine blanks, wood shavings— yet there are no lots. Follow." The secondus led him across the room to a set of barred doors. "Here." He yelled for Cruk, and the captain reduced the doors to firewood.

Inside, thousands of lots sorted into small groups filled the space. Luis pulled one from a pile, handed it to Errol.

"What am I seeing?" Errol asked.

"Perhaps an old evil come new again," Luis said. "I think Sarin sorted his lots by cast. He's a very meticulous man." He reached into the same pile and retrieved four more lots. "Tell me, Errol, did you notice anything different in the lots you've read that were crafted by other readers?"

Errol lifted his shoulders. "They've all looked pretty much the same."

Disappointment twisted Luis's features. "I had hoped not. I've always wondered, but only an omne would be able to see the difference between one reader's lots and another's."

Understanding lit Errol from within. "Is that what you meant? Yes! Each lot's lettering looked different."

Luis glowed with relief. "Thank the three, Errol. Here." He thrust the lots toward him. "Tell me what you see."

Errol checked each sphere. "Someone different made each one."

Luis grabbed his shoulder, squeezed until Errol felt fingernails against his skin. "Are you sure, absolutely sure?"

He checked the lots again, but there was no mistaking the difference in the words' appearance. Each reader's word was as unique as his handwriting. He nodded.

Spots of color bloomed on Luis's face. "The secondus has figured out how to make it work." Luis clenched his fist and struck his forehead. "Of course. Stupid, blind fool that I am. I didn't see it."

"See what?"

"Sarin's given himself to a malus. That's where he disappeared to. He went to Merakh. He couldn't do it in Illustra. The barrier prevented him. He's made a circle with other readers."

Errol shook his head, perplexed. "I don't understand. What's a circle?"

Instead of answering, Luis gritted his teeth, cursed, and called to Cruk, who stood at the foot of the stairs. "Captain, we need to clear the building. Then it needs to be burned to the ground." He turned back to Errol. "Think of joining the minds of a score or more readers together, all working as one."

Now Errol understood. "He could cast any question almost instantly."

"Captain!" A voice yelled from the stairs. A watchman stood leaning over the rail, alarm writ in his posture.

"Yes, soldier?" Cruk answered.

"We found ferral tracks, sir, headed toward the water." The guard's words tumbled over each other.

Cruk nodded as if the soldier's information confirmed his suspicions. "Send men downstream on horseback. I want them found and stopped before they make open water."

The soldier's face paled and he shook his head. "Sir, there's a bridge a mile downstream. Lieutenant Stern dispatched a pair of the watch to check with the guards there. They've returned."

"And?" Cruk asked.

"Nothing has passed their way in the last two hours." The soldier licked lips gone dry. "The ferrals must have headed back into the city."

31

FLIGHT

THE MILL EXPLODED with motion as the watch and guardsmen poured out to remount their horses. Cruk led a mad dash of watchmen, guards, and two readers back to the palace grounds. No longer relegated to the back, Errol rode just behind the grim-faced captain.

Sarin had played them for fools. With knowledge of their coming, he'd pulled his circle from the mill and sent the ferrals back to the palace grounds, now stripped of half its forces.

Had that been his goal all along? To lure them out so he could kill the king and bring down the barrier? His throat tightened as a lump of fear settled in his stomach. Cruk's frantic shouts cleared the streets as they hurtled back to Rodran. Squawks of women and children filled the air as people fled the panic of their passing. When they arrived at the gates of the imperial compound, nothing moved, and for a moment Errol dared hope that the watchman had been mistaken.

But as they passed through, over the sound of the clatter of hooves came the screams of dying.

Errol rounded the barracks to terror. Ferrals swarmed over

fallen guards and watchmen as they poured through the door to the palace. Torn and ravaged bodies lay everywhere. Ferrals littered the ground as well, but too few. Far too few.

Cruk jumped from his mount in midgallop, rolled to his feet, and ran for the door, steel whistling through the air. He chopped like a butcher at the ferrals. Bits and pieces of the spawn flew from his blade and for a moment it looked as if he might force a way through the swirling pack.

Errol thrust the bladed knobblocks onto his staff and moved to Cruk's left, avoiding the rest of the guards. Rage and fatigue pounded in his blood as he struck, forcing himself to go ever faster. His guess back at the mill had been good. Too good. Ferrals filled the entrance, keeping them at bay, preventing them from reaching the king.

Jaws snapped at him from in front and behind. Without turning he thrust behind at the sound, felt the crunch of his staff striking deep, and then speared the thing in front of him through the throat.

Spinning, he cleared a space, moved around the edge of the broad doors that led inside. The press of ferrals was thinner there. If he could kill them quickly before they could react, he could force a way in.

Errol stabbed and sliced, aiming for eyes and lungs. With a surge, he forced himself past the last three ferrals guarding the left and pushed his way through the doorway. At once he found himself in the broad entrance hall of the palace with attackers swarming at him from the right and left and in front.

Errol retreated, tried to give himself space to move, but the press and tight quarters kept him from swinging his staff. He thrust and chopped, not daring to spin. A pair of jaws snapped at his legs. He launched a frantic kick.

"Errol!" Cruk's voice cut through the cacophony.

He stabbed at another muzzle, felt the crunch of blade hitting bone. "Over here!"

And then, like a wave that pulled sand from beneath the

feet, Cruk broke upon the ferrals from behind, hewing with his sword like a woodsman. A final attacker leapt for Errol's neck, fangs bared, but he had room to move now, and his staff took the demon spawn in the throat even as Cruk split the creature through the spine.

Cruk ran toward the king's hall, screamed for Errol and the rest of the guard to break away and follow. Errol pounded after him, accompanied by a score of watchmen and guardsmen. Isolated ferrals attacked out of the side hallways. Men peeled off to fight in ones and twos.

The hall lay just ahead, its doors battered, but still closed.

Errol breathed relief even as a boom of thunder filled his ears and the doors cracked and splintered.

A swarm of ferrals aided by a few men pushed forward, pounding at the doors with a heavy beam, forcing the opening. Screams of effort sounded from inside the hall as men worked to close the gap. Another blow like the boom of a drum sounded against the door, and a pair of ferrals squeezed through to attack the men inside.

Errol shouldered his way to Cruk's side and they fell on the pile from the rear, hacking desperately, trying to keep the spawn from reaching the king. Yelps and screams of surprise filled the air as the men and ferrals rounded to fight.

Now it was the spawn that had no room to move. Pinned between the king's men and the doors, they couldn't bring their greater numbers to bear.

Trapped, the attackers threw everything into breaching the doors. Another boom sounded and the doors sprang from their hinges. Ferrals and men poured inside, and at their center, bellowing in rage, stood the abbot of Windridge and his watchmen. Cruk threw himself at them, ducked under a panicked swipe, and took the first watchman through the chest. Before Errol could close the distance between them, Cruk parried a blow, spun, and caught the second man with an elbow to the face. With a snarl, he took him through the throat.

Spawn filled the space between the abbot and Errol. Side by side he and Cruk mowed down ferrals and men, clearing a path.

At the far end of the hall, behind the throne and surrounded by six guards, stood King Rodran, his arm trembling with the effort to raise his sword. In front of the throne stood Liam, sword bared and flanked by the sons of Escarion—Derek and Darren.

The attackers poured toward them.

Errol fought to close the distance. He no longer tried to kill the ferrals—simply aimed blows at their hamstrings, crippling them.

A melee formed in front of the king.

Errol chopped away a pair of ferrals and came face-to-face with the abbot. He flipped his wrists as he struck the abbot in the head so as not to hit him with the knobblock blade. The abbot dropped like a discarded puppet. Without pause, a trio of demon spawn leapt for the body, teeth bared.

Errol fought to keep them away, cutting, thrusting.

Then the space in front of him cleared.

Errol turned toward the throne and stopped, gaping at the sight of Liam with a sword.

Illustra's hope stood between Rodran and a knot of ferrals ten strong. He should have been swarmed under, but he flowed and moved like a dance of water. Ducking and spinning, Liam mowed the demon spawn down. Twice he thrust behind him, taking ferrals in the throat as if he had eyes in the back of his head.

Then only two ferrals remained. As one they launched themselves at Liam's throat, screaming for blood. Liam spun, his sword flashing, and cut through them both with the same stroke. The pair dropped to the floor.

"I've never seen anything like that in my life," Errol said. "Even in the stories, I've never heard of the like."

At his side, Cruk grunted. "Me neither."

Scattered knots of men filled the hall, hands on knees, gasping for breath. Cruk shouted orders, but Errol couldn't make them out. Fatigue hit him like a hammer. He'd never been so tired. Uncaring, he sat on the floor and watched as guardsmen moved from one body to the next, aiding wounded defenders or dispatching enemies.

Cruk came to him, spattered with blood. With a snarl that sounded eerily like the bark of a ferral, he nudged the abbot with his foot. "Is he dead?"

Errol shook his head. "No. Shouldn't be. I rapped him on the head. I don't think any of that blood on him is his."

"I wouldn't mind changing that." Cruk put fingers to his lips and whistled for a pair of guardsmen. "Search him for weapons and bind his hands behind his back. Take him to the king, then wake him with a good dose of water. Let's find out what he knows."

When the guards left, Cruk took a look around the hall, nodded once, and sat down on the polished granite floor next to Errol.

Errol panted for breath. "Is this what it was like when you fought the Morgols?"

Cruk nodded. "Every battle's different, but they all feel the same—hot and desperate. Six months ago I would never have guessed you'd be a fighter to make the watch proud."

Errol grimaced. The images of killing filled his mind, his eyes, and the coppery smell of blood came to him from everywhere. "I think I'd just as soon be back in Callowford trying to get Cilla to filch me a tankard of ale."

"I thought you'd given up ale."

He laughed. "I have, but if this keeps up I may take it up again." Errol thought about that and then shook his head. "Not really, but mercy, I sure am tired of fighting."

Cruk nodded. "Somebody's got to do it."

As word traveled through the city of the attack, people flooded into the king's hall until the press of bodies encroached upon the spot where Errol and Cruk rested. Cruk signaled to a guardsman who passed by with a flagon of water. He took a long pull from it and then handed it to Errol. "Let's go see what the abbot can tell us."

Errol moved to follow, then stopped to search the crowd.

He found her kneeling on the floor beside the king's steward, pressing her hands against a gaping wound in his side. The man wouldn't live, she had to know that, but no hint of it showed in her face or the glorious green of her eyes. Errol couldn't hear her words, but her face and posture carried assurance and comfort. Blood soaked her gown.

He followed in Cruk's wake. As he approached the throne he watched Lord Weir advance toward Rodran holding a sword bereft of nicks or blood and surveying the hall like a conqueror—his blue doublet as crisp and clean as ever.

Rodran, his legs trembling with the effort, lowered himself onto his throne. Six watchmen circled him, blades drawn. The primus and the archbenefice stood just outside the protective ring. Off to the left, Martin and Luis conferred, heads close and speaking in tones that didn't carry.

A palace guard poured water over the unconscious figure of the abbot, and two men of the watch hauled him to his feet. He hung in their grip, shaking his head.

Cruk knotted a fist in the abbot's hair and lifted his head. "Who ordered the attack?"

Morin spluttered, and at first Errol thought he must be coughing. Then the abbot's voice firmed and Errol stepped back in disbelief. The abbot of Windridge was laughing.

Rodran pushed himself up out of his chair and gave a curt nod to Cruk. "Bring him to my private audience chamber." The grand leonine head of the king surveyed his throne room. "And alert my chamberlain. Tell him to have the staff clean this mess."

Errol turned to make his way toward his quarters. If he slept for a week, it might be enough to wash away a fatigue so deep it made his bones ache.

Before he'd taken two steps, Luis touched him on the elbow. "I think you should be there, Errol. The king may need to know your part with the abbot."

He let his shoulders slump in surrender. With a sigh he turned and followed the group from the hall.

Compared to the throne room, the king's private audience chamber seemed cramped. The dais that held a more comfortable version of the throne rose three steps from the floor and the low-backed benches that lined the walls only accommodated scores, not thousands. Other than that, the two rooms were decorated in similar styles—rugs lined the floors, marble busts filled small alcoves along the wall, and the deep purple banners that signified royalty hung behind Rodran's seat.

In addition to the king and his six guards, the primus, the archbenefice of Erinon, Cruk, Captain Reynald, and Luis stood in attendance near the throne. At least a score of other people crowded toward the front, where a pair of watchmen kept a tight grip on the abbot.

Rodran settled himself in his chair, then pointed at the abbot of Windridge, his hand shaking with rage or age or both. "I will have the information I want, Abbot. Whether you give it to me willingly or unwillingly is of little concern. The conclave will test your words to see if they are true and if they are complete." He leaned forward, his rheumy old man's eyes boring into the despised churchman. "You will not be allowed to die until I am certain you have told us everything." His lips curled in an imitation of a smile. "It takes a lot to make me certain."

Errol sagged onto one of the benches, sweat soaking his tunic to leave patches of darkened cloth that clung to his skin. He hardly cared. Blood from a shallow ferral bite flowed down his leg, warm and ticklish. He'd have to see one of the healers. The wound would foul if he didn't.

In front of the king, the abbot continued to laugh, and he looked around the room with an imperious gaze, as though the audience had been assembled for his amusement. A crimson rivulet stained his chin. The light in the disgraced churchman's eyes danced as his deliberate gaze took in each face. More than one of those in attendance broke away from his insane stare. Morin only cackled in response.

When the abbot's dark, dark eyes came to rest on Errol, the

light danced and the smile changed into a rictus of insatiable hate. With a howl of rage, Morin smashed his elbow into one guard's nose and kneed the other in the groin, but before he could leap to attack, a half dozen watchmen weighed in and forced him to the floor through sheer numbers. Ropes were brought and one was tied to each arm and leg with a guardsman to hold it. The abbot returned to his scan as if nothing had happened, quietly searching each face in the room until he spied Liam standing to one side. He threw himself against the ropes, fighting to reach Liam until the guards pulled his feet out to send him sprawling across the floor.

Rodran leaned toward the archbenefice, his face troubled. "Mayhap, Bertrand, this is something you should deal with before we ask any questions."

With a nod the archbenefice descended the steps, his crosier held in front like a weapon, and approached the frothing abbot. "I adjure you by the three, speak your name."

The light of insanity faded from the abbot's eyes. For a moment they looked normal, dark brown and lucid. Morin threw himself to his knees attempting to kiss the ring of the archbenefice, who stepped back out of reach. "I'm Morin, Your Excellency. Don't you know me?" He looked around at the audience, scared and afraid. "How did I get here?"

Bertrand Cannon, archbenefice of Erinon, scowled at this and stepped closer, resting his staff of office on the abbot's forehead. "I adjure you by the three, speak your name!"

Tears poured down Morin's face in a constant stream, even as his mouth twisted and ragged laughter poured from his throat like a curse.

"Diabous."

The archbenefice's face hardened in determination and his voice rose and crackled with the power of command. "Come out of him, Diabous."

Morin bared his teeth like a ferral and spat. "You have not that power. I am here at his invitation."

Affronted, the archbenefice stepped forward and gripped the abbot's face in one hand. "Then, by the power given me, I command you to be silent."

The abbot flailed his arms, forcing the archbenefice back. Then he raised his head and howled. The hair on Errol's neck stood on end, called him a fool for being there. Morin, or whatever was left of him, fell to the floor panting.

Bertrand Cannon regarded him a moment, his head cocked in consideration, before turning to ascend the steps to stand by the king once more. "I think you can ask your questions now, Your Majesty."

Instead of speaking, the king nodded once toward the primus, and the first of the conclave approached Morin. He stopped short of the man's reach and cleared his throat. "Morin, can you hear me?"

Whimpers came from the floor. The abbot sat up, hugged his knees to his chest. "I want to go home," he said in a small voice.

"Mayhap in a while, Morin," the primus said. "First, I want you to tell me where Sarin Valon is."

Morin rocked back and forth like a child trying to shield himself from punishment. "When he found out you were coming, he fled to Port City."

Silence filled the chamber as the primus signaled Luis, who began whittling a pair of pine lots with furious strokes. After ten minutes of carving and sanding, the lots were deposited into a makeshift bag and Errol was commanded to come forward to draw.

He stood before the primus, his legs shaking like a newborn colt's.

Enoch looked at him, sympathy written in his eyes. "Just a little longer, Errol. I know you're tired."

He reached into the bag and drew. "It says *Yes*. Does that mean he's telling the truth?" Luis nodded, and Errol put the lot carefully back in the bag and waited for the secondus to shake before he drew again.

"No." He had enough experience now to know what would come next. After a series of draws during which Morin gurgled and sobbed from his position on the floor, no clear answer to the primus's question could be determined.

Luis turned to the primus and gave a small shake of his head. Enoch Sten sighed and came forward once more. "Morin, can you hear me?"

"Yes-yes-yes-yes-yes-yes-yesssssssssssssssss."

"Do you know where Sarin is?"

Morin buried his head between his knees, still rocking to some unheard rhythm. "No-no-noooooooooooooo." The word died in a soft wail.

Luis went aside and began work on another pair of lots. His motions were less urgent this time and a look of frustrated disgust wreathed his features as he carved. Minutes later, during which Errol could only listen to the mad raving of the abbot, he came forward with another pair of lots.

After a score of draws which failed to yield an answer, the primus sighed and approached Rodran. "I'm sorry, Your Majesty, our art is confounded."

The king's jaw worked back and forth before speaking. "How, Primus?"

"I know not, sire. It may be that the abbot's mind is broken by his possession so that he no longer knows truth from falsehood. Or it may be the malus that possesses him, though silent, works against us still."

"So we are left blind to our attackers?" the king asked, his voice laced with accusation. "Can none here suggest a way to force the truth from this wretch?"

Perhaps it was because he was so tired. Possibly he just wanted an excuse to leave the hall. Errol spoke out loud before he was fully conscious of it. "An herbwoman might be able to get the abbot to speak."

"What?" The king leaned forward. "Speak up, boy."

Martin gave his head a shake and the archbenefice of Erinon

looked as though someone had substituted vinegar for his communal wine.

Errol didn't care. "An herbwoman, sire. The ones I ran into all had veritmoss. It makes people tell the truth."

Bertrand Cannon's face darkened, but a raised hand from the king cut off any protest the clergyman or any other spectator might have voiced.

Rodran surveyed the crowd in the small chamber once more. "I want an herbwoman found." He looked on Morin with disgust. "And I want to know the depth of this man's treachery."

The archbenefice of Erinon cleared his throat. "Your Majesty, the church's proscription against consorting with evil spirits precludes us from using such a woman."

Errol had had enough—enough fighting, enough talking, and enough of churchmen who prattled on in their ignorance.

"The herbwomen I know never consorted with evil spirits," he said. Martin and Luis stood to one side, giving small but frantic signals to keep quiet. He didn't care.

"And you know this to be a fact, boy?" Archbenefice Cannon asked.

Errol shrugged. "No."

"As I expected. Your Majesty, these herb—"

"But I don't have to," Errol continued.

Rodran leaned forward, resting an elbow on one knee as he skewered Errol with his gaze. "Explain this, lad. I would have the truth."

Errol turned from the archbenefice and sketched a ragged, tired bow toward the throne. "Your Majesty, in my village there was an herbwoman. She was kind to me. She fed me when I was hungry and took care of me when I'd fallen in the ale barrel." To one side the archbenefice snorted in dismissal. "And," Errol continued, "when Luis discovered I had the gift to be a reader, she told me to come to Erinon, said that I was a good man, and that the kingdom had need of good men. That doesn't sound like someone evil to me.

"But if you want to make sure the herbwomen aren't evil, test them. Cast lots to see."

The archbenefice's face clouded, threatened to break into storm any moment, but the king looked thoughtful. He turned, addressed the primus. "Can this be done?"

Primus Enoch Sten licked his lips, eyeing the archbenefice. Then he nodded. "Yes, sire. The cast is a simple yes or no question."

Rodran leaned back, his breath coming in short gasps. "Then get an herbwoman in here, test her, and pry the information out of this wretch." He waved a tremulous hand at the crowd. "Now all of you go away. You make me tired."

With a grateful sigh, Errol sought his bed.

32

THE NEED OF THE KINGDOM

A WEEK LATER, Errol stood outside Rodran's throne room, scratching at the blue doublet that tickled his throat. His second encounter with Oliver Turing, the king's chamberlain, had gone even worse than the first. The chamberlain, given several days in which to make Errol acceptable for his presentation to the king, had embarked—in his own words—on a daring reclamation project.

Errol wasn't even sure what *reclamation* meant, but it didn't sound complimentary. However, there'd been little choice in the matter. The chamberlain, along with his minions, Charlotte and Will, had poked, prodded, plucked, and primped until they'd deemed him fit for viewing.

As they waited outside the throne room, Turing grabbed Errol's hand and pulled it away from his throat. "Good heavens, boy. Are you trying to undo three days' worth of work in a few minutes? Red scratch marks on your neck will distract everyone from your perfection. Now, be still."

Martin's chuckles drifted to him from across the antechamber. The priest sat at the end of a line that held Luis, Liam, and Cruk.

Errol caught Liam's gaze with a tentative wave. "What's it going to be like?" Liam's ceremony had occurred two days ago, and Errol had been honored to be a part of it. For the first time Errol could remember, Liam's perfection failed to rouse jealousy in him; he could only feel awe.

"You were there," Liam said. His blue eyes twinkled, and he gave a shrug of his beefy shoulders. "Hasn't the chamberlain told you what to do?" He gave a mock shudder. "Even I would be afraid to fight that man."

Errol snorted at the joke and shook his head. "Told me? He had me down here for hours last night, rehearsing the whole thing." Errol jabbed a finger in the air. "Stand here, boy. Walk this way, boy. Bow like this, boy." He rolled his eyes and pivoted to address the chamberlain. "You're in the wrong profession, sir. You need to sign up with the watch."

Turing smirked. "I am sure it would be easier than making rough young men presentable, but the king needs me where I am."

Out of a need to calm his nerves, Errol walked to the large double doors that opened to the entrance hall leading to the king's throne room. "What's taking them so long?"

Martin's face turned grave. "They're probably waiting for Rodran to arrive."

A stab of ice pierced him. If—no, when—Rodran died . . . "Is he okay? What's going to happen when he dies, Martin?"

The priest shrugged. "Rodran is old, Errol. All the power of the kingdom can't change the immutable reality that, soon or late, a man dies. We don't know what will come. There has always been an heir in the past."

Errol wiped a hand across his face, remembering the ferrals. "But if the barrier comes down . . ."

"Don't borrow trouble, boy," Cruk said.

A knock at the doors preceded the appearance of a king's guard, his red-and-gold uniform spotless and his brass buttons burnished to brilliance. "It's time," he announced.

Errol, his nerves stretched to breaking by the interminable wait, darted to the entrance. Martin, Liam, Cruk, and Luis formed a line behind him. Oliver Turing poked his head into the room. "Are we ready?"

A different guard opened the other door, and the little company proceeded into the entrance hall. In slow, measured steps, under Turing's guidance, they approached the throne room. At the broad opening they halted as the herald rapped his steel-shod staff upon the floor seven times.

"Hearken and hear! Hearken and hear!"

The buzz of thousands of voices faded to nothing in an instant. The herald rapped his staff upon the floor another seven times and repeated the call to attention, "Hearken and hear! Hearken and hear!" The bellow rebounded from the floor, embrasures, and ceiling until the throne room filled with the herald's exhortation.

Thousands of faces turned to regard Errol where he stood, flanked by king's guards, with his friends drawn up in a row behind. At the far end of the hall, Rodran sat his throne, his back bent by time and responsibility. Next to him, a second herald rapped his staff and called back.

"Who comes? Who approaches the throne?"

"Errol Stone, so summoned by His Majesty, Lord of the Watch, Keeper of the Faith, Master of the Lot, and Soteregia of Illustra, Rodran. Let all observe his unquestioning obedience and seek to do likewise."

The second herald stabbed the floor seven times. "Let him approach."

Oliver gave him a frantic wave, signaling him forward. Errol counted his steps. After twenty he stopped.

"Let the first witness of deeds step forward," the herald next to Errol said. "And let him recount the supplicant's exploits before the throne."

Liam moved around the group and knelt toward the dais at the end of the hall. After he rose, he described Errol's heroic deeds, his commanding voice daring any in the hall to question him. In the audience, Liselle, Kyra, and a dozen more ladies hung on Liam's every word and movement. Their eyes fierce, intent. Somehow, Errol didn't think it was because of the subject of his speech.

In truth, Errol didn't recognize the man Liam spoke of. His face reddened after the third or fourth minute. As time dragged by, the crimson flush above his neckline deepened, and he wondered absurdly if Turing would be mad at him for spoiling the look of the outfit with his embarrassment.

Finally, mercifully, Liam finished, but as he moved to take his place behind Errol, he gave him a clap on the shoulder that almost knocked him over.

At a signal from the herald by the throne, they measured another twenty paces, stopped, and repeated the process with Cruk.

Errol noticed the watchman's report was considerably less glowing than Liam's. Rodran smiled as Cruk recounted Errol's episode with Dirk outside the village of Berea. When the big man shared Errol's struggle to learn the sword, chuckles and chortles from those assembled filled the hall with whispers, and his face reddened again.

But when Cruk described Errol's deeds during the attack on the king in his plain soldier's language, not a soul stirred. The story held the hall in its spell. Errol looked at the floor, too self-conscious to meet anyone's gaze. Cruk finished, slapped him on the back, and retook his place.

Another twenty paces and Luis came forward. The secondus took his place in front of Errol and told of Errol's captivity in the caravan. A mutter of shock and disapproval rippled through the hall as the reader recounted Errol's imprisonment and how he cast for Naaman Ru's profit. Luis paused and turned, stilling the crowd with his quiet dignity.

Then he extolled Errol's resourcefulness and imagination in discovering Sarin's hand in the plot to kill the king, told how he'd crawled from his bed, weak with blood loss to uncover the foul plan by the former secondus. Then, in ringing tones that filled the hall, Luis announced Errol's status as an omne and proclaimed it as a sign of Deas's favor.

Errol wished with all his heart he were someplace else. He stared at a fixed spot of the carpet and tried to distract himself by counting his heartbeats. He'd almost reached five hundred when Luis squeezed his shoulder and resumed his place behind him.

After another twenty paces they stood directly before the throne. Rodran's rheumy blue eyes watched him, his expression thoughtful as Martin stepped around to stand in front of Errol and recount his deeds.

But the benefice didn't speak. He looked over the hall, his dark eyes fiery beneath his thatch of thick white hair, but minutes passed and Martin still kept his silence. Here and there, an isolated spectator stirred in their seat, and as the silence stretched, more and more of the assembled nobility and churchmen, robed in their finery, squirmed and gestured where they sat.

Rodran leaned forward. "What is the meaning of this, Benefice?"

Martin bowed. "Your Majesty, the deed I am about to recount is beyond all the others, both in scope and breadth of courage. Yet, I fear there are some in the hall who lack the depth to comprehend it. So, Your Majesty, I seek a boon."

The king smiled, obviously enjoying the drama of the moment. He leaned back in his chair and took a turn at letting his gaze sweep the hall. "Speak, Benefice. What is this boon you seek?"

"I would have Errol's deeds, including the one I am about to relate, entered into the record, that he might be an example to your subjects, both those living and those yet to come."

Errol jerked his head in surprise. The record was the official history of the kingdom kept by the royal historian. To be entered was considered an honor, or in the case of misdeeds, an infamy, greater than any other.

Rodran straightened on his throne, forcing his back from its weighted curve to address the hall. "The boon you seek is considerable. I would hear of this deed before I render such a decision. I pray you, speak in full, and let none think to abbreviate your words."

Martin pivoted and leaned close to Errol. "This may hurt, boy, but I would honor your courage."

Errol's throat tightened in fear, and spots swam before his eyes before he remembered to breathe.

Instead of standing and addressing the throne as the others had done, the priest walked a tight circle around Errol and the others, speaking directly to the assembly. His voice filled the hall with its bass resonance, echoing in the vast space with its warm, rumbling tones. As one, the assembled leaned forward, anticipating each word, hanging on each gesture.

Errol had never seen the man speak to a crowd before. Martin's oratorical skills surpassed anything he'd witnessed. The old priest held the crowd in his hand as he spoke of his move to the village of Callowford and how he and Errol had met.

And then he recounted the death of Warrel, his dying confession, and Errol's drunkenness.

Past embarrassment now, tears streamed down Errol's cheeks as Martin opened his past and strewed it across the throne room floor for the entire kingdom to see. The priest's memory and his gift of description cast Errol's life on a canvas for the entire hall to see in sordid detail. No account of drunkenness was too sensitive, no episode of sleeping in the gutters too embarrassing, and no occurrence of retching shakes too private to leave out. Errol cringed. He couldn't even remember some of the events described.

Then the pitch of Martin's voice changed. No longer subdued with the tenor of defeat, the timbre of triumph filled it as Martin told of how Errol overcame his drunkenness and came to serve the kingdom, though none helped or encouraged him.

Martin's voice rose. "I tell you, my king, my fellow churchmen, assembled lords and ladies all, though I watched him for years, I knew not the depth of courage that resided in Errol Stone. Stripped by fate of family, name, and dignity, he triumphed still. Can any deny Deas's favor? I am humbled by his perseverance and fortitude."

Martin fell silent.

Errol, his world laid bare, kept his head down, hiding his tears.

Through his shame, he saw the king shift his feet. "Errol Stone, look at me," the king commanded.

He lifted his head against the weight of Martin's testimony and met the king's gaze. Rodran grasped the arms of his throne and pushed himself, shaking and trembling on his old man's legs, to stand. Then he clapped.

The hall erupted in thunder as the assembly followed the king's example.

Errol collapsed, hiding his face.

"This is too much for him." A voice, Luis's he thought, spoke above him.

Strong hands grabbed his arms.

"Some men are more easily broken by kindness than censure," Martin said. "The kingdom has need of such men."

This made no sense to Errol. He wanted desperately to leave. Instead the king's guards hauled him to his feet, the hands gentle despite their strength.

"Errol Stone," Rodran said, "will have his story entered in the record. More, in accordance with his service to the crown, he is granted the Earldom of Breckinridge. Let our enemies tremble in the face of such courage. My lords and ladies, I present to you Earl Stone."

⛬

He walked the halls of the conclave the next day in a daze. Sleep had been hard to come by the previous night, and his introduction to the nobility this morning had consisted of attending the council of nobles in the palace. Much of the interminable discussion confused him. The nobles wanted to levy a tax to prepare for Illustra's defense. Yet many benefices in the church objected on grounds the tax would affect their income.

Released at last, he wandered, too tired to think straight but too keyed up to remain in his rooms. Not knowing where else to go, he meandered his way toward the courtyard by the barracks.

Maybe a few turns with the staff would tire him enough for sleep, or at least banish the fog from his mind.

With one hand he unbuttoned his rumpled blue doublet halfway down in an effort to dissipate some of the summer heat. The air hung thick over the island, like a sodden blanket that made sweating useless. He gave serious consideration to shucking the doublet and going about in just his under tunic.

Errol turned the corner to the courtyard to find Liam giving instruction to Derek and Darren. The usual gaggle of admirers watched. At his approach, the three paused and then bowed, bending deeply from the waist. Errol turned to see whom they bowed to, but the walkway stood empty.

When he turned back, the duke's sons stood smiling at him.

"Methinks it will take some time for the earl to become accustomed to his new status," Derek said.

Darren nodded but didn't speak.

Liam, looking as fresh as if he'd just bathed, stepped forward and shook his hand. His friend stood before him dressed all in black, a captain's insignia plain on his arm. Errol pointed to it. "When did that happen?"

"Right after the fight in the throne room. They'd offered the captaincy to me before, but Martin objected. Once we beat back the attack against Rodran, Reynald tore a strip from his cloak and put it on me in front of the king. Rodran made it official. There wasn't much Martin could do." Liam's smile broadened. "King Rodran has placed me in charge of his personal guard. Can you believe it?"

Errol nodded. "It fits you. You fight like a hero from the stories."

"Do you want to spar?" Liam asked.

Now that he thought about it, the idea lost its appeal. He eyed the shade where the assembled spectators watched with envy. "Maybe later. I don't think I'd be much of a challenge for you right now." He laughed. "Maybe not ever again."

He turned and faced the daunting array of nobles seated before him. Here and there among the finery he could see an empty chair, but the idea of seating himself among them made his feet itch to be elsewhere. Errol spied and made for an empty table at the edge where he could be part of the company but without presuming on anyone's acceptance.

As soon as he seated himself, Adora rose and came toward him with almost a dozen other ladies of the court trailing in her wake. They seated themselves, and a few of them pulled fans from their sleeves. One of them, a dark-haired beauty with olive skin, sat so close to him their knees touched. The look she directed at Errol was frank and her fan rested against her cheek.

"Hello, Earl Stone," she said. "Tell me, what do you think of your new station?" Her eyes danced as she spoke and her voice was filled with hints and suggestions that had nothing to do with her words.

"Stop it, Liselle," Adora said. "You're making him uncomfortable."

Liselle darted a look of irritation toward the king's niece. "Then he can tell me himself. I merely wanted to greet the newest member of the nobility. I'm the daughter of Baron Poulos. I'm not making you uncomfortable, am I?" She reached out, traced a line down his arm with her fingertips. "Am I, Earl Stone?"

Errol gaped at the woman, floundering for something to say.

Liselle laughed deep in her throat and leaned back, not so much sitting, as draping herself across the chair. With studied intensity, she lightly tapped her lips twice with her fan before letting it trace a seductive line down her chin and throat.

Errol had no idea what Lady Liselle's fan language said, but there was no mistaking her intent. Shocked gasps around the table only confirmed his suspicions. With his face flaming, he bolted out of his seat. His chair clattered behind him, and he turned to pick it up, trembling and awkward.

"Please excuse me," he said. "I need to see the secondus." He wanted nothing more than to flee, but the sight of Adora made him bold despite his heated face. Errol turned toward her. "Would you do me the honor of walking with me as far as the conclave?"

She nodded and with a last glare for Liselle moved around the table to join him.

When they were beyond earshot of the nobles, Errol cleared his throat. "What exactly did Lady Liselle say?"

Now Adora blushed, and she stared at the granite paving stones in front of her feet. "Never mind. I can't believe she said that in public. She's hardly better than a courtesan."

Errol's face heated again. "Oh."

The princess laughed. "If that's what the ladies of the court are going to be saying, maybe it's better that you don't know the fan language." She grabbed his arm, pulled him to a halt. "Have a care, Errol. There are rumblings in the palace about your elevation and support for the herbwomen. Palace politics can be dangerous, and with my uncle . . ." Adora dropped her eyes, not finishing.

"I understand. I'm sorry."

She gave a fluttery laugh and wiped away sudden tears. "Thank you. It seems like years since anyone thought of him as something besides the end of the royal line. He's almost alone now. Everyone is so busy maneuvering for the position they want when he dies, they've forgotten he's still alive."

She stopped; her golden hair swayed with the sudden change in motion. "What he really needs is a friend. The nobles are all trying to get something from him. The priests talk to him, but it's mostly stuff about his soul and dying well. The watch is loyal, but they serve the crown no matter whose head it's resting on." She grabbed his hand. "Would you be his friend?"

Errol nodded. He would never be able to deny those green eyes anything.

EPILOGUE

A Cast of Stones

A CRESCENT MOON showed above the roof of the palace opposite the conclave. Luis sat at his workbench, the last of the Callowford stones held in one hand and a polishing cloth held in the other. He let his eyelids drift lower until they were mere slits. Surrendering himself to his ability, he turned the stone, rubbing it in soft strokes here and there with the cloth as his instinct directed. At long last, he finished. One stroke more or less and the lot would be less than perfect.

"Is it done?" Martin asked.

Luis nodded. His heart couldn't seem to decide whether to hammer away in his chest or stop altogether. Years of effort lay before him in five score lots, one to represent each male in Callowford. And every year, with each stroke of the chisel or brush of the cloth, he had focused on the same question—who would be the next soteregia, Illustra's savior and king? At long last, he released the thought, felt the burden of that single-minded intensity lift from his soul.

He carried the first tray across the room to the drawing sphere, similar to the drum they'd used to find Sarin but more finely wrought. Supported by four rollers underneath, the container could spin in any direction, but was weighted so that a small opening at the top would descend toward the bottom as the sphere slowed. Then one of the lots, and only one, would fall from the hole. They'd moved the sphere from the main conclave workroom to his private one. No one must know.

With the care of a surgeon, he rotated the container until the hole faced up and then fed the lots in one by one. The soft clacking sound as they rolled in filled him with growing anticipation. By the time he let the last stone sphere roll from his fingers, his heartbeat rocked him back and forth where he stood.

"You'll probably want to close the door," he said. "The conclave is empty, but this will make a fair amount of noise even so, and it wouldn't do to have one of the palace guards interrupt us."

Martin pushed the door and after a moment's hesitation barred it. "I have no desire to be hauled in front of the Judica and forced to give an explanation."

That only made sense. What they were about to do would be considered tantamount to subverting the succession protocol. The members of the Judica were jealous of the readers' power. When Martin returned to stand by his side, he put his hands on the drawing sphere and pushed with all his might, spinning the container on its rollers.

The sound of over a hundred rocks tumbling against each other in the thick steel container deafened them, and Luis clapped his hands over his ears. With each rotation the hole drifted lower until it could no longer be seen. As it slowed, the noise subsided and Luis crouched beneath the sphere with his hands cupped underneath.

After six years and an eternity, a single lot dropped from the hole to smack against his hands. He held it up against the light of the window.

"Liam."

Martin breathed a sigh of relief and then whooped.

Luis found himself wrapped in the priest's hug. "You did it, Luis. By Deas in heaven, you did it!"

When he could breathe again, he rotated the sphere, dropped in the lot, and pushed against the steel until the drawing hole faced the ceiling. "We'll need to draw several times just to make sure."

Martin laughed and waved. "Of course. Of course." He put his hands behind his back and strolled around the room, his face wreathed in a look of contented accomplishment.

Luis spun the sphere.

"It's been quite a journey, hasn't it, Luis?" Martin faced the window, his eyes distant. "To think six years ago we started from right here, casting for the province and the city that would provide the next king."

The sphere stopped, and Luis caught the lot in his hands.

"Liam will be a king for the ages," Martin said behind him.

Some instinct warned him. Whether the lot felt cooler to the touch or just different, he couldn't say, but he knew even before he held it to the light.

"Errol."

Martin spun. "What? That's impossible. You must have done something wrong."

Luis spun in anger, thrust the stone at his old friend as though he could see something more than polished rock. "It's as perfect as I can make it. It says *Errol.*"

Martin licked his lips, and a sheen of sweat appeared on his forehead. "Draw again."

What else was there to do? He replaced the lot and pushed against the container with all his strength. Then he waited, standing next to his friend watching the glimmer of reflected light bounce back from the steel drawing tank. Gone was the thrill of moments ago. Now he eyed the sphere warily, as though it had the power to attack them.

"Liam."

He looked at the priest, but Martin knew better than to

celebrate now. His brows furrowed and he pointed a shaky index finger at the sphere. "Again."

Luis nodded, repeated the steps exactly as he'd done before, his reader's training taking over as doubt and disbelief banished rational thought from his mind.

"Errol."

They cast lots late into the night. After the first four, they'd started a tally sheet. At the end of the third hour, tired and fatigued by apprehension and lack of sleep, Luis shook his head and let the pen fall from his grasp.

"There's no trend, Martin."

His friend's face looked as if it might crumple any moment. "What does it mean, Luis?"

For a brief moment, the temptation to lie or pretend some knowledge overwhelmed him, but they'd been friends too long for him to try to salve feelings that way.

"I don't know."

Martin buried his face in his hands.

"Deas help us."

ACKNOWLEDGMENTS

There are so many people who helped bring this to fruition, but I would be remiss not to call attention to the Middle Tennessee Christian Writer's Group and especially Kaye Dacus, who teaches us all; to Dave Long and Karen Schurrer, my editors at Bethany House, who sweated the details and pushed me to be a better writer; to Lynn Rochon and Holly Smit, who taught me how to polish my work; and to you, the reader, because you love stories and tales as much as I do.

After graduating from Georgia Tech, **Patrick W. Carr** worked at a nuclear plant, did design work for the air force, worked for a printing company, and was an engineering consultant. Patrick's day gig for the last five years has been teaching high school math in Nashville, Tennessee. Patrick is a member of ACFW and MTCW and makes his home in Nashville with his incredible wife, Mary, and their four awesome sons, Patrick, Connor, Daniel, and Ethan. *A Cast of Stones* is his first novel.

If you enjoyed
A Cast of Stones, you may
also like…

No girl has ever become a prophet of the Infinite. Even though the elders warn that she will die young, Ela heeds the call of her beloved Creator and is sent to bring the Infinite's word to a nation torn asunder by war. There she meets a young ambassador determined to bring justice. Can she balance the leading of her heart with the leading of the Infinite?

Prophet by R. J. Larson
BOOKS OF THE INFINITE #1
rjlarsonbooks.com

"This tale captured me and held me hostage to the very last page. Breathlessly waiting for the next book."
—Donita K. Paul, author of THE DRAGONKEEPER CHRONICLES and THE CHIRIL CHRONICLES